Regina —
I am blessed to have
you in my life — you are
an upper! :")
Your sister-in-law,
Mary Ann Kerr
Heb 10:23
6-20-17
2

Cady's LEGACY

BY **Mary Ann Kerr**

THINK
WELL
BOOKS

thinkwellbooks.com

Cady's Legacy

All Scripture is taken verbatim from the King James Version (public domain)

Published in part by Thinkwell Books, Portland, Oregon
The views or opinions of the author are not necessarily those
of Thinkwell Books. Learn more at *thinkwellbooks.com.*

Design & Cover Illustration by Andrew Morgan Kerr
Learn more at *andrewmorgankerr.com*

Published and printed in the United States of America
ISBN: 978-0-9984894-0-7
Fiction, Historical, Christian

Books by Mary Ann Kerr

A WOMAN OF ENTITLEMENT SERIES:

Book One
Liberty's Inheritance

Book Two
Liberty's Land

Book Three
Liberty's Heritage

Caitlin's Fire

Tory's Father

Eden's Portion

Cady's Legacy

DEDICATION

I dedicate this book to David and Evelyn Kerr.
Your tireless work in promoting the pro-life agenda,
and your unswerving love for Jesus Christ blesses my heart.
I am grateful and thankful to be able
to call you sister-in-law and brother-in-law.
May God continue to direct your steps.

ACKNOWLEDGMENTS

CADY'S LEGACY, unlike Caitlin's Fire, was not an easy book to name. I had a couple titles picked out, and *Cady's Legacy* was not one of them. *Cady's Cache, Cady's Resolve,* and *The Song of Cadence* were all considerations. To fit in with the names of the other books, *The Song of Cadence* was eliminated first. The other two were strong contenders, but Andrew, my youngest son and book cover designer, didn't care for either one. He texted me and asked, "What about *Cady's Legacy?*" The name is perfect and fits the content of the story, perfectly. My editor and I were very happy with this new name. So…thank you very much, Andrew!

Cady's Legacy is an interesting read. Fran and Dual Eldridge are friends and avid fans of my books, as are their kids. I was talking to one of their sons, I've forgotten which one, and he was saying how wealthy my characters seem to be. I "reckon" I enjoy having my characters live in luxury. Perhaps the reason is that I was raised at a poverty level until I was fourteen.

When Phil and I were living in Denmark, I saw firsthand the glitz and glitter of wealth and influence. It was a fun experience, but I didn't lose track of the fact that millions of people, all over the world, live in poverty. Cady has been raised in abject poverty, and if some of you struggle with the fact that she had never seen the inside of a nice house, I taught students who could identify with her.

I'd like to first thank God for the stories He's given me. I have so many fans ask, "How do you come up with these stories?"

I have to answer as I've said before, that God is the author of creativity and from day by day these stories unfold. I may have an idea of what needs to be included in the story once it begins to develop. I finished book eight and in the prologue something happens that I know must be rectified by the ending of the story, but I don't know how it's going to happen until I am writing it. My editor said I write by 'the seat of my pants', and that is an actual style. Frankly, I feel God's hand on me and if you look, there is a salvation message in every one of my stories.

My desire is that my readers draw closer to God through the reading of an interesting novel. I give Him all the glory for giving me the ideas as I sit typing. Very rarely have I had to back track and change anything as the story unfolds. My editor caught one time lapse in *Tory's Father*. My timeline for what was happening in Boston extended over a longer period of time than what was happening at the abbey in Italy.

A novel begins at 60,000 words, less than that is a novella. My books are at 90,000 plus. I am writing book nine, which will be called *Maggie's Redemption*. I got to 22,000 words and realized my timeline was totally off. I had Mac McCaully and Ewen (from *Caitlin's Fire*) as young men and Maggie at 12 years old. She wouldn't have been born when they were young men! I'm glad I caught my mistake before I had gone any further. I had to cut out all the storyline of Mac and Ewen which put me back at 11,000 words.

My preface poem for *Cady's Legacy* is called Morning. I sent it to my eldest son and wife, and so the two of them gave a good critique. I switched a couple words and *voila*! Thanks for the help, you two!

We are also fast approaching Thanksgiving. There are so many things I am thankful for. Most of all I am grateful for God's hand on me. I never thought I'd be thankful for being an orphan, but as I look back, I know God protected me from a lot. He was my mother and father. His word says, He takes care of the widows and the orphans. I know this to be true. There were quite a few things about Cady with which I could identify. God is good, and I thank Him for blessing me beyond measure.

I am thankful for a Godly husband, children and their spouses, and grandchildren who love the Lord. I am blessed with wonderful relationships within the family and without. I have a brother, cousins, and in-laws who bless my heart with their goodness.

I am thankful for Andrew who makes the covers on my books, eye-catchers! I am thankful for Dori Harrell at Breakout Editing, who not only edits my books but has become a friend.

I am thankful for my fans who encourage me and sometimes make me laugh with their comments. Thank you for reading my stories

God is good, and I give Him all the glory.

List of Characters

MORNING

The morning stilled in hush and wonder
Awaiting light in all it's splendor.
Glorious creation with bated breath,
Waiting for dark to be put to death.

First the creeping with tentacled fingers,
Stretched across a deepened sky.
The streaks of dawn, the sun still hidden
The nightbird nesting, no more to fly.

The dusky hue of lightening shadows
Take form and shape before my eyes,
As fingers stretched turn into daylight,
And light pours forth from daylight skies.

A new day dawns in magnificent glory
God's creation—an ongoing story.
He who loves us and gave us his Son,
He abides in us and we are one.

MARY ANN KERR

PROLOGUE

Many will be purged, purified and refined,
but the wicked will act wickedly;
and none of the wicked will understand,
but those who have insight will understand.

DANIEL 12:10

RAIN BEAT HEAVILY ON THE TIN ROOF of the small cabin. It was little more than a shack. The wind cavorted, and the torrent slashed at every side of the one-room house. It poured off the eaves, making a rill of water surrounding the small structure. The noise inside was deafening as the deluge pounded at the tin.

It was bone-cold, and Cadence shivered under the thin, ragged quilt. When the wind suddenly abated, she heard drops of water hitting the buckets. The roof leaked, and the dampness seemed to cling to her. Her feet felt like blocks of ice.

What a misery, she thought as tears slipped in silent rivulets down her cheeks. She lay there in a ball, trying to get warm but knowing she wouldn't.

The cabin was cold and dank. Wood for the fire was soaked from days of unending rain. She'd tried again and again to get the fire started, but she couldn't get the wet logs to burn. Shivering uncontrollably, her teeth chattered, nervousness adding to the trembling.

Pa should be back anytime now, she thought as she huddled under the blanket, wondering if she should leave or wait until the rain stopped. *I've been beaten before. Reckon I can stand it again. I don't think it's going to stop raining. I may as well head out now while it's dark.* The cold seemed to crawl up her spine and into her heart.

Her younger brother, Timmy, had died a week and a half before while she lay tired and worn by the fever that raged within her own body. Her mother had cropped her hair short as a boy's in an effort to cool her down as the fever mounted. While she recovered, her mother had taken sick as well. Not able to fight off the hot fever, her ma had succumbed to it before a week was gone, her life snuffed out. Cadence sobbed as she thought of her mother. *Maybe she hadn't wanted to get better. I know how much she loved Timmy, always trying to protect him from Pa's fists.*

She uncurled her body and sat up, wiping her face on the tattered quilt. She said aloud, "My satchel's ready. Think I'd better get out now before Pa gets back."

No sooner had the idea been formulated and spoken, when she heard him outside the door. She shivered violently and lay back down. Curling up again, she tried to relax and act as though she were asleep.

Cadence peeked from under the thin quilt as he burst through the front door, kicking it shut behind him with a muddy boot. He stood there listing a bit, nearly dropping a satchel he held in his hand. She didn't recognize it, but the room was dimly lit.

Thoroughly soaked from his ride home from the tavern, Hannibal Cassidy looked toward the hearth. He stood swaying as he surveyed the one-room shanty. Cadence could smell him, reeking of alcohol, garlic, and some undefinable smell that was definitely unpleasant. She stopped peeking when she saw him stomp toward her bed in the corner.

He started to grab Cadence by her hair, but it was shorn too short. He dropped the satchel he carried and yanked her out of the small bed, dragging her onto the cold floor.

"Where's my fire, Cadence Cassidy? Why ha'ent you got a fire goin', huh?" he yelled as he looked down at her. "You lazy, worthless piece of trash!" He drew back his leg and kicked her hard, but she rolled as his boot hit—it wasn't as severe as it could have been. She grunted from pain and started to stand, but enraged, he kicked her again. She wasn't prepared for it. Her head snapped back, and she lay perfectly still, not wishing to incite him further.

Pulling her off the bed had removed the threadbare quilt that had covered her small satchel. He swayed as he opened it, and Cadence drew in a painful breath as he noted aloud her meager belongings. "Clothes, a couple rags, and a hairbrush." He threw the bag across the room.

"A-huh," he said, "gonna light out on me, hmm? I'll show you!" In a rage, he deliberately kicked the dropped satchel under the bed. He tromped unsteadily to the other side of the room and found a length of rope. After tying her ankle to the bed's leg, he fell onto the bed himself, leaving Cadence on the cold floor as he sank into a drunken stupor.

Cadence lay shivering and freezing. She felt carefully down her side, deciding no ribs were broken, although it hurt to breathe, and her side was painful to touch. *Maybe that one's cracked.* She was thankful she'd rolled with his kick. Her jaw was another matter. Stiff and swollen, it ached abominably. She sat up with a groan before recalling her pa had tied her to the bed. She knew in his state of drunkenness, he wouldn't awaken for hours.

I've been seventeen for two months. I've put up with this for seventeen long years, but no more. With Mama and Timmy gone, there's no reason to stay.

Sidling closer to the bed, she felt under it for her small keepsakes case. Her hand felt nothing, and a small panic ensued before she remembered she'd moved it up behind the leg of the bed so her pa wouldn't find it. As she slid her hand farther up, she connected with something else. *What's this?*

Cadence pulled out a beautifully tooled red leather satchel that was folded in half. Surprise filled her as she opened it and drew out a handful of banknotes and a thickly folded bunch of papers. She unfolded them but realized it was too dark to see what they were. She couldn't read very well anyway. Not having time to waste, she jammed the notes and papers back into the satchel. *That money will come in handy.* Breathing a sigh of relief, she felt her case right where she'd put it. She pulled it out from under the bed. Opening it, she drew out a small piece of broken mirror. With a diligence born of fear, she sawed at the rope that tied her fast to the bed.

CHAPTER I

My soul melteth for heaviness:
strengthen thou me according to thy word.

PSALM 119:28

HANNIBAL AWOKE WITH A RAGING HEADACHE. He opened
one eye, then squeezed it shut. His mouth felt full of cotton, and he could
feel dried spittle at the corners of his lips. He lay there a moment,
facedown on his daughter's bed, wondering if he was getting the fever.
The angle of his head pulled at his beard, and he started coughing,
suddenly aware he was freezing cold. *Reckon I'm not gettin' the fever. How come
that scrap of piffle hasn't made a fire? I'm sick of that girl.*

All at once realization flooded in, and he remembered tying her
ankle to the bed. *Ah, she can't be making it. Well, if I'm cold, she must be freezing.*
He rolled over and sat up, swinging his legs over the side of the bed. His
head throbbed with every little movement, and he shivered. Putting his
head in his hands, he thought of how miserable he was. *No wife ta cook for
me. Cady can cook, but she's not good at it. That girl's good fer nothing. I always
wondered if she's even mine. Callie swore she was, but she looks just like Callie, so
how is a body ta know?* He looked down, ready to aim another kick, but she
wasn't there. He heaved himself off the bed and got down on all fours to
look under the bed, but she wasn't there, and neither was the red leather
satchel. Cadence was gone, but what was more important, so were the

inheritance papers and the money. He cursed loud and long and started ranting as he picked up the end of the frayed rope. He got up, still ranting, and cursed some more.

She got them papers, but what's worse is that little wretch got the money! I know Callie taught her some. She knows how to read a bit, but she won't be knowin' how to read them there papers. But the money…it's hers, but I want that money! I never looked in that there satchel very close-like. When that banker opened the safety deposit box, the bee-utiful satchel was sittin' there, jist as pretty as anything I ever saw. Reckon there's enough money in that there satchel ta keep me till I die. I'm gonna have to find that viper. I want that money!

He stood, feeling a bit nauseated from too much drink. Listing a little, he stared down at the bed, suddenly realizing she'd taken her quilt too. He walked carefully over to his own bed and lay down on the mattress, his head still throbbing. He pulled the blanket over himself. *I'll find her… for sure I know I'll find her.* With that his last thought, he fell back asleep, hoping to ease the pain in his head.

Cadence Jean Cassidy was weary to the bone. Aching from head to toe, her unaccustomed all-night journey had taken its toll. She had barely recovered from a life-threatening fever. In addition to her face being swollen and bruised, she hurt like the dickens. She couldn't see it, but knew from past experience that the side of her face would be colored up an ugly shade of purple. Her mama used to make a paste she'd put on Cadence's face when her pa hit her. It helped to draw out some of the pain. She pushed the thought of her mother to the back of her mind. She didn't want to start crying.

She and her younger brother, Timmy, had been close. There were no neighbors near their place, and her pa hadn't allowed either of them to go to school or play with other children. Cadence could read a bit, but hadn't had much practice. There'd been no books, only bits of paper their mother had used to teach them the rudiments of reading and writing. Her ma had worked so hard just cooking, mending, knitting, making candles and soap and such that she didn't have much time to teach them anything.

Cadence walked along in the darkness, looking for all the world like a young boy. After severing the rope with her bit of mirror, Cady had bound her breasts with an old strip of material in an effort to flatten herself. She quickly donned her brother's clothes. Always small for her age, she fit quite well into her twelve-year-old brother's duds. His shoes and her shoes had always been high tops, so her feet were shod in boy shoes. She thought she might have the beginnings of a blister on her heel.

She'd put her meager belongings back into the satchel and stuffed that into the beautiful red leather one. With her hair shorn close to her head from having the fever, she knew she'd pass for a boy any day of the week. She had Timmy's battered hat on, pulled down low over her brow, and was glad for it, as it kept the rain off her head.

Their cabin was located on the east side of Sacramento, and she'd walked as far as Dixon, approximately twenty-two miles as the crow flies. She'd walked for miles and miles by her reckoning, and never having been out all night like this, it was spooky. Her side hurt badly, and she wondered if maybe one rib was broken or she'd gotten more than one cracked. It wouldn't be the first time. It was a minor annoyance compared to wondering what in the world she was going to do.

Rain poured down, making her even more miserable. She shivered in the cold, wet night air. Rain rolled off the brim of her hat onto her thin shoulders. The road was a sea of mud that sucked at her shoes with each step.

A couple of times, Cady felt the rumble of horses' hooves long before the riders were visible, and she hid behind the scrub oak or bushes that lined the muddy road.

When the first streaks of light appeared on the eastern horizon behind her, she found a barn set back a distance from the road, situated not too close to the main house. She drew near, making sure there were no dogs to give her away. Carefully, she opened the barn door a crack and slipped through, closing it softly behind her. It worried her a bit when she heard no squeaking...it meant the hinges on the door were oiled and well-used.

Climbing up a ladder into the loft, she crawled under some hay and pillowed her head on her satchel. She lay there quite some time, shivering, so she pulled out her tattered quilt and wrapped herself in it. She was overtired, and sleep seemed elusive. Thinking about her pa and how mean he was, she didn't think he'd come after her. He'd never loved her anyway. Her muscles tightened just thinking about him.

Her stomach rumbled. She'd had little to eat and hoped sleep would allay the gnawing hunger.

Cady thought back to the beatings and ugliness her father had heaped on her and Timmy. It seemed they could never do anything to please him. Life had been a misery, always walking on eggshells if he was around. She thought back to the one time her father had hit her mother. He'd come home one night drunker than he'd ever been. He'd punched her mama hard in the stomach. After reeling backward, she'd stood up straight and calmly spoke to him. "You ever hit me again, Hannibal, and it will be the last time. I promise you you'll find yourself at hell's door because I'll kill you. I swear I will, and the world will be a better place without you." She'd turned away as if nothing had happened. He'd never hit her again. Cadence had often wondered why her mother had stayed with her pa and why she hadn't protected them from his blows. Was it all right to have him not hit her but beat her children? Cadence shook her head, as if she could clear the bad thoughts.

She was beginning to warm up, but more importantly, she felt safe. Her pa would sleep off his drunken condition until late morning. Perhaps he'd be looking for her today, but he wouldn't look here. She decided she would stay put during daylight and travel again after dark. *If he looks for me at all, it will be during the day.* She shivered, sat up, and pulled some of the hay over her quilt. Lying back down on her good side, her ribs screamed with pain. The prickly hay scratched at her cheek, and she pushed it back. The other side of her face ached worse than any toothache she'd ever had. She wondered if her pa had loosened any of her teeth with that kick.

Tears of grief mixed with weariness trailed down her cheeks. Her stomach grumbled with hunger, and misery was her only companion.

She wondered why sleep seemed elusive when she was so incredibly tired. Instead of wondering why her mother had never protected her, she thought back to some of the things her mother had done to try to make life better. Her mind flitted to a conversation of when her mama had first told her about God and Jesus. Her pa had always told her it was a bunch of mumbo jumbo, and if there was a God, He didn't like Cadence—not one bit. She was a worthless piece of trash and just another mouth to feed. He'd said God made a huge mistake letting her be born. Her mama had told her later, when her pa wasn't around, that God never made mistakes. She'd said the bad things that happened were a result of mankind's doing, not God's. That the reason she lived in misery was her own fault.

Cadence asked her why she ever married her pa, since he was so mean, and she'd answered that Hannibal had charmed her right off her feet, that her own father hadn't liked him, so she'd run away to marry him...eloped, she'd called it. She hadn't known then, as she did now, how fond he was of whiskey, nor that he was so mean. It took her a while to figure it all out, and by then, her pride wouldn't allow her to return home. She'd said she was raised in a Christian home and she believed in God and believed He helped her live day by day. She said each day God was giving her grace. When the grace was gone, so would she be.

Cadence wasn't sure there was a God. He certainly didn't seem to care about her straitened circumstances.

"God, if you really do care about me the way Mama said, could you please help me? I don't know where to go or who to turn to for help." Cadence sobbed. She felt so alone and scared. She grieved for her mother and Timmy. All the sudden her eyes flew open as she realized by taking the red satchel, her pa was certain to hunt her down. She was sorry she'd taken it. There were banknotes in that satchel, and her pa would do anything for money, except work.

She finally fell into an exhausted slumber with tears still wet on her cheeks.

She awoke to the sound of voices. *Did I just fall asleep, or have I slept all day? It's barely light out.* She felt lightheaded and disoriented from the lack of food and water. She didn't dare stretch, as her sore muscles begged her to. The voices below continued to talk, and she stopped thinking of her own misery and listened.

Cady couldn't hear what was being said. All she heard was the sound of milk hitting an empty bucket. It was a soothing sound, and the muted conversation nearly lulled her off to sleep. It was some time later when the milking was finished that Cady became aware of the actual words.

"Son, you'll only do the evenin' milkin' and not the mornin' milkin' durin' the school year. I'll be doing the mornin' milkin' from now on 'stead of you. That a ways you kin get yerself off ta school. Tamorrow is th' first day of th' new school year, an' I don't want you ta be a missing a single day."

"Papa, yer the best father a boy could ever have. I love you so much!"

"Oh, Johnny, I love you, too. I couldn't have a better boy than you. Yer mama an' me, well, we think yer a gift from Almighty God. Yer a special present, and we're mighty grateful fer you, son. I never had much book learnin', but I want you ta have a chance ta be whatever you want ta be. A good education will get you there. Yer ma and me...well, we want th' best fer you, son."

Cady peered down through the boards of the loft and saw the boy, about the age of Timmy, throw his arms around his pa and hug him for all he was worth. She stared, seeing the love flow between the two of them, and was awed. She'd never, not in all her seventeen years, seen such a display of affection between a man and his son.

He wants his son to go to school, she thought, *and he's willing to work more so his boy can go. My, what love he has for him! I can't see why my pa couldn't have loved us. I never knew a man could be so tender.* She wiped furtively at her tears, careful not to rustle the hay. She suddenly realized it was just starting to get dark. *I must've slept the whole day through. I don't know where I'm going to go or what I'm going to do. All I do know is I need to get away from Pa. I can't live the way I've done...not a day more. He could cripple me the way he beats on me.*

She lay quietly and waited until the man and his son left. Peeking through the boards, she watched as the boy blew out the lantern. The cows were still in a large stall. She wondered why he'd lit the lantern. There was still some light out, but it was fading fast. She shook her head over the waste of kerosene.

Cadence lay quietly as she counted slowly to one hundred, making sure the boy and his father were far enough away. She gathered her few belongings and quietly descended the wooden ladder. She gasped with the pain of stiff, cracked ribs. They hurt with every movement, and she knew at least two were cracked or broken. She went over to the manger and saw oats still sitting in it. There was also a small, dirty bowl of cream, but she drank it gratefully, excusing herself to the cat it must belong to. She grabbed a couple handfuls of oats, filling her brother's pants pockets. Quietly, she listened at the door of the barn. Hearing nothing, she slipped out into the cool night air to continue her journey. She'd felt protected in the warmth of the barn with animals for company. Cady was hungry, sore, and bruised, but at least she now had something to eat. She trudged all night, again through the pouring rain. When the sky began to lighten, so did the rain. She climbed, with tired legs, up a fairly steep hill to a plateau and found a cave to sleep in. It wasn't very deep, but having walked in the heavy rain all night, she was grateful. She had a quick flashback, remembering her mother reading aloud about the Napa Valley and that it had many caves, some natural and some dug out specifically for aging wine. Her reverie was broken by the realization that the rain had turned to a light drizzle, but still Cady was glad for the cave's protection.

She wrapped herself in her ragged quilt. She was quite wet and shivered for the longest time trying to fall asleep.

She slept until late afternoon, feeling the warmth of the sun streaming into the entrance of the cave, warming her body. She lay there with her eyes closed. The sun felt wonderful on her face. She stopped midstretch, feeling the grab of her ribs. She was sore and exhausted but also hopeful.

The sun is a powerful thing. Here I've been so miserable, and my circumstances haven't changed any, but because the sun comes out, I feel things will get better. She started to smile, but her bruised face put a stop to that in a hurry. *Ooo, that hurts.* She put tentative fingers up to her face, carefully feeling along her jawline to see if her father's boot could have broken it. It was fat with bruising and blood, and she didn't know if it was broken or not. It was stiff and swollen to the touch.

She lay there trying to figure out what she should do, but she came up with no plan. She was sure, though, no one would be around the cave area. She just basked in the warm sunshine pouring into the shallow cave. She felt dry and sheltered and safe, until she heard the sound of a horse's hooves.

CHAPTER II

Casting all your care upon him;
for he careth for you.

I PETER 5:7

MATHEW BANNISTER HAD RIDDEN OVER, early in the day, to Sunrise Ranch. He was hoping to get some contacts to sell his wine. To date, all sales had been by word of mouth. Giovanni Coletti, the foreman of Chandler Olives, had promised Matthew when he was ready to start marketing his product, Gio would help. Rancho Bonito, Matthew's vineyard, was producing tasty grapes, and his Merlot was beginning to get noticed. He and his wife, Liberty, had sketched out a brand label and were having it professionally branded and printed. Now he was searching out possible marketing avenues, and Gio was a walking encyclopedia not only about nuts and olives, which were Sunrise Ranch's product, but also about marketing strategies.

Because of the heavy rain, harvest had been delayed, but Matthew was looking forward to a good crop. He'd hired on more men just for harvest and the crushing to follow.

Getting ready to start for home, his head was full of ideas, and his small notebook had several pages of names and addresses.

"I can't thank you enough, Gio. This gives me a whole list of possible clients—people I don't even know. I'm beginning to get orders by word of mouth, but to be able to market to businesses who will in turn market my product is a boon. I know this took most of your day, but again, I thank you for it."

"You are welcome. I wish you every success. When's that baby due?"

"Middle of October." Matthew grinned. "We think we're ready, but to my way of reckoning, a body can't be ready until they know what to expect. Liberty's beside herself with excitement. She never thought to have a baby, you understand. Doctor John said she could have a difficult delivery, this being her first baby and just turning thirty-two. We leave it in God's hands and try not to worry. He knows best."

Gio nodded sagely. "Yes, you are right. He knows best." He slapped Matthew on the back lightly and added, "Well, my friend, if there's anything more I can do for you, you just let me know. You have a good product, and I can only see it getting better."

"Thanks. I reckon I'll be on my way. It's getting close to dinnertime, and Liberty will be wondering where I've gotten myself to. Please give my regards to Adam and Eden. I'm sorry I missed them." He shook Gio's hand and stepped into the stirrup, swinging his long leg over his piebald mare's back. He nodded and tipped his hat to Gio. "Come on, Piggypie," he said. "It's time to go home." He squeezed his knees, and Piggypie, her black-and-white coat gleaming in the sun, headed out and down the long lane.

Liberty Bannister called out to Conchita Rodriguez, her cook and all-around help, as she exited the front door.

"I'm going for a ride—maybe up to the cave where my stepfather took me, if I can find it. It's time for me to lay a few ghosts to rest before I have my baby. Matthew tells me to forget about the past, and that's what I plan to do. I'm going to pray over that cave and not think about it anymore. Tell Matthew, if he comes home before I get back, that I'll be home in time for dinner…bye!" She closed the door soundly behind her and headed for the stable.

The weather had been dreadful for the past two weeks, with rain pouring down every day and night, keeping her virtually a prisoner inside. Today had started with a drizzle, but now a fresh wind blew, and the clouds had disappeared, leaving a beautiful blue sky with that pristine clearness that buoyed one's spirits. Liberty was quite pregnant. She was due in little more than a month. She counted on her fingers, as she'd done so many times before.

Let's see—today is September third, and I'm due the second week of October. I think October fifteenth, 1885, would be a perfect day to have a baby! She grinned to herself as she started counting. *A little more than six weeks! Wonder why, when you look forward to something special, time seems to drag by?*

Entering the dimness of the stable, she first went to the tack room. Matthew had built the stable with an eye for comfort, knowing that sometimes Rancho Bonito would overflow with company. There were two rooms along one side of the stable. One was fairly small and seemed to collect junk, but there was a bed in it for emergencies. The tack room was much larger, roomier, and homier. The walls were knotty pine, stained and varnished. It held a fireplace and a trundle bed with a thick mattress pushed up against one wall. A beautiful patchwork quilt Matthew's mother had made, covered the bed linens. There were some pegs on the wall for clothes, a small chest of drawers with a mirror over it, and a comfortable old easy chair with a side table. The other end of the long, narrow room was where the harnesses and saddles were kept. There was a skylight built into the ceiling, but there were no windows along the side, except at the end of the long room. The tack room smelled of leather but had been made into a spare bedroom, if needed. It was clean, private, and comfortable. Kirk, Matthew's brother, had often stayed in this overflow room when company filled the Rancho's bedrooms.

Liberty started to lug her saddle off the stand, but Donny Miller, a hired hand, strode up behind her.

"Let me get that, Miss Liberty. You shouldn't be lifting heavy saddles in your condition. Begging your pardon for saying so, miss."

Startled, Liberty turned quickly, and Donny reached out a hand to steady her. "Whoa there! Sorry if I scared you." His clear baby-blue eyes looked at her with concern. "Sure you want to go for a ride? It's downright muddy."

"Yes, I'm sure. I've been cooped up for far too long. I need to get out, and a good ride is just what I'm needing to clear my head." She smiled her best winsome smile, and Donny grinned back at her.

"Matthew told me how much he appreciates all your hard work, Donny. You've taken a big burden from him and Diego. We're grateful you fit in so well here. Remind me—how long have you been with us now?"

"Round about a half year. I like it here just fine, and glad the boss is happy with me. You take care, miss. I'll get you saddled up, and you come find me when you get back. I don't think you need to be lifting heavy things. You wouldn't want anything to go wrong, that's certain."

"That's true. I promise to be careful. I just feel so good and am glad to be over being sick. Five months of being sick was a long time. Look at me. I am getting as big as a house. Dr. John says I'm built for having babies, but I need to be careful because I'm not young."

"Well, miss, you look young."

Donny smiled at her as he threw a horse blanket onto her horse's back. He began to saddle her up as Liberty slid a bit into Pookie's mouth and looped the reins over her neck. Donny clasped his hands together, and Liberty stepped her right foot into them. He hoisted her up, and she slid her left foot into her stirrup, throwing her leg over Pookie's back.

"Thanks, Donny." She smiled down at him. "Mud or not, I'm going to enjoy a nice ride."

"Where d'ya think you'll go?" he asked. Concerned etched itself in his eyes. He was fully aware that Miss Liberty rode off many times, but being this far along, he didn't feel it wise.

"Oh, I've been thinking I'd like to ride up those hills." She nodded toward the hills where her stepfather had once taken her when he kidnapped her. She added, "I'd like to explore a bit. I've stayed away from there, but I think it's time to erase some bad memories. I'm going to try to find the cave where my stepfather took me."

Donny nodded his head, having heard the story from Diego. "Just be careful, miss. There's lots of rattlesnakes up there, as you well know."

"I promise to be careful." She walked Pookie, who was feeling quite frisky, out of the stable. It'd been two weeks since Pookie had been exercised, and she danced her way out, seemingly as eager as Liberty to be going for a run. Liberty walked her down the lane before she kicked her into a smooth canter.

Donny watched, his brow wrinkled with concern. Never without her gun, she wasn't packing, but he reckoned the belt didn't fit around her anymore.

Liberty had a good ride over small hills and vales, heading for the area Jacques had taken her when he'd kidnapped her. She was pretty sure she knew where it was. She'd never wanted to go there before. Her father, Alexander Liberty, had taken down the little shack where her stepfather had hidden before he tied her wrists together and took her up to the cave. She'd prayed over that shack with Matthew before they were even married. Alexander had planted flowers there and turned it into a lovely place. He'd told her it was a place of thanksgiving for God's protection over her. Now she'd make her peace at the cave before her baby was born.

She rode steadily up the last slope, fairly certain it was the one where the cave was located. Pookie's hooves clattered over the stones, and they finally arrived atop the little mesa. Liberty started across it, when suddenly Pookie got spooked and bucked. Liberty, an excellent horsewoman, would normally have been fine, but her attention was on the cave. She was taken totally off guard and thrown. She connected heavily with the ground, her head hitting a rock.

Cady, who started to come out of the cave, had startled the horse. She stood mesmerized by the scene before her. The woman was thrown off her horse and sailed through the air. It seemed to happen almost in slow motion, and yet almost in the blink of an eye. Cady ran to her, kneeling down on both knees. She felt quickly along the woman's legs and arms for broken bones but felt nothing out of place.

She suddenly realized the woman was expecting a baby. She wasn't a big woman, and Cady wondered how far along she was. She lifted the lady's head, and Cady's hand came away wet and sticky with blood. Her eyes widened with fear.

Aloud she said, "Maybe she's dead! Oh, what'll I do? I don't even know where to get help!" She stood up and looked frantically around her. The cave was well-screened by trees, but she could see over the top of them. She could hear a stream close by. She was at the very top of a hill and had a view of the valley to the west, over the tops of trees. In the far distance was an organized patch of green, and she decided it must be a farm of some kind.

"Maybe the woman came from there," she said.

She didn't know how to ride a horse. Her pa had one, but no one was allowed to ride it except him. The woman's horse stood above the woman as if sorry it had bucked her off. Cady knelt again and with gentle fingers felt a pulse at the base of the woman's neck. She needed to get help, and yet she didn't want to leave the woman by herself. It would take a long time to walk to the farm she could see in the distance.

She went into the cave and grabbed her ratty quilt and covered the woman with it. She lifted the woman's head and slid her cloth satchel under it. As she stood up, she gritted her teeth, grabbed at the horse's reins, and swallowing down her fear, decided the horse had to be tame, or the woman wouldn't have been riding him. She led the horse over to a large rock. Holding the reins, she climbed up the rock and pulled until the horse was closer. Her ribs hollered at her. Patting the horse's neck, she tried to reassure herself that the horse wouldn't buck her off. She quickly threw her leg over the saddle. The stirrups were too long, but she didn't know how to fix that. She kicked at the horse's sides.

The horse started down the hillside. Cady tried to pay attention to where she was and to keep the horse headed in the right direction. The ride down the hill was scary, and she held on to the pommel for dear life. She looked down and closed her eyes; it was a long way to the ground. Once she got onto the flat land, it was not so easy to see where she needed to go. But the horse stumbled a bit, the stirrups hit her sides, and she set off at an easy lope, with Cadence hanging on to the pommel, scared out of her wits but figuring the horse knew where to go.

Matthew was worried. He'd arrived home to find his wife had gone for a ride over two hours before. It was time to eat, and she hadn't returned.

"It's not like her, Diego," he said. He turned to Donny and asked again, "Where did she say she was going?"

"She said it was time to erase some bad memories and nodded toward those foothills. Said she was going to try to find the place where her stepfather took her when he kidnapped her."

Matthew felt a frisson of fear crawl along his spine. He'd never liked that area to start with, and to have Liberty go riding there without him didn't make him happy.

"Diego, saddle up and come with me, will you? Donny, you ride for Dr. John. Invite him and Sally to dinner, and tell him to bring his medical kit just in case. I don't like the feeling I'm having. It could be nothing, but with Liberty as far along as she is, I'd not like to be unprepared. Go, Donny, right now." He turned to Diego and added, "I'll run in and tell Conchita what we're doing, and I'm going to have Boston come with us."

Diego nodded his head. "*Sí, es* good plan. I go saddle up *mi caballo*." Diego often slipped words of Spanish into his speech when he was excited or worried.

Matthew strode to the house, praying as he went. "Lord, You are our buckler and shield, our protector. I pray Your protection on Liberty right now. Be with her, Father. I have a bad feeling, and I lift her up to You, knowing Your ways are higher than our ways. Thank You that You always know what's best. She's in Your hands."

He entered the house and found Conchita in the kitchen. She'd been his cook and housekeeper long before he married Liberty, and he loved her best in the world next to Liberty and his brother, Kirk. He didn't want to alarm her unduly, but she loved Liberty, and he wanted her to be prepared just in case there was trouble.

"Diego and I are riding out to find Liberty. Donny is inviting Dr. John and Sally for dinner just in case his expertise is needed. Could you please put water on to boil? I have a bad feeling—hope I'm wrong, but just in case, I'd like to be prepared."

"*Sí*, Meester Bannister, I weel do eet, an' I pray too." She patted him on the back. "Eet weel be all right, you weel see. Miss Libbee, she be een God's hands."

Matthew knew she was right, but accidents happened, and he wasn't taking any chances with the love of his life.

Going back outside, he saw Donny going lickety split down the lane, and Diego already in the saddle. Matthew set his lips in a straight line and knew his deep-set blue eyes were full of worry as he looked at Diego.

"Let's pray before we head out," he said.

Diego nodded in agreement, and both men removed their hats and bowed their heads.

"Lord, this may be a false alarm, and yet somehow, I don't think it is. Diego and I agree right now for Your protection over Liberty. May Your hand be upon her, and help us find her right away. Thank You, Father."

As Donny got to the end of the lane, he saw Pookie in the distance, but the rider wasn't Liberty, whose seat on a horse was perfect. It was a boy crouched low over Pookie's neck, hanging on for dear life.

"Hey, boy!" he yelled. "Hey there!" Donny galloped toward the boy.

Cadence, her eyes big as saucers, sawed on Pookie's reins, thinking it was the way to stop the horse. Poor Pookie came to a halt, most likely wanting to buck this rider off too.

"Hey, boy! What are you doin' on Miss Liberty's horse?" The man spoke gruffly without realizing it, anxiety about Liberty sharpening his voice.

CHAPTER III

But do thou for me, O GOD the LORD,
for thy name's sake:
because thy mercy is good, deliver thou me.

PSALM 109:21

CADY NEVER STUTTERED EXCEPT SOMETIMES around her pa, who would box her ears for it, or when she was extremely nervous or upset. "Oh, s-sir! Come quick! She-she's hit her head, an-and I didn't know what to d-do, and I can't ride a horse." Everything seemed too much. It felt as if everything came crashing in, and Cadence, who seldom cried, felt the tears start in her eyes yet again. Huge racking sobs enveloped her as the young man quickly got off his ride and plucked her off her horse.

Donny realized his tone must have frightened the dickens out of the lad. He pulled the young boy into his arms and patted him on his back.

"Sorry I yelled at you, but—" He was interrupted by Matthew and Diego, who came riding up at a hard gallop when they saw Liberty's horse.

At a glance, Matthew realized it wasn't Liberty in Donny's arms, but a young boy.

"Where'd you get the horse, son?" he asked sharply.

Cadence pulled away from Donny and gulped down her tears. "The horse got sp-spooked and bucked the woman off, and she hit her head, and it's all bloody, and I thought she was dead an'…an' I'm sc-scared of horses!" she said in a rush, her words all jumbled together.

"Donny, put the boy behind you so he can show us the way," Matthew said.

The man named Donny got back on his horse, and before she knew what was happening, he grabbed her by the arm and swung her up behind him. Cadence sat there stunned and stiff as a ridgepole, her ribs screaming pain where her pa had kicked her. She swallowed hard against crying out.

"Better hang on, boy! What's your name, anyway?" Donny asked.

"Cady," she muttered. "It's Cady Cassidy." She gulped down her pain and slipped her hands around his waist to clasp them. She felt terribly uncomfortable, but she figured since the man thought she was a boy, she could relax. They started off at a gallop, her ribs aching abominably. She felt she could faint with the pain.

Matthew smacked Pookie on her flank, sending her home. He had a question in his eyes as he looked over, galloping next to Donny's horse.

"That's the way, straight over those two hills and up the side of that high one there." She pointed ahead, and all three horsemen spurred their horses even faster.

Cady could only hope she was pointing in the right direction. Down on the flat ground, everything looked the same, even the hills.

She needn't have worried.

Matthew had, by now, taken the lead, as he reckoned Liberty had a pretty good sense of direction and probably had found the place where Jacques Corlay had taken her. Both he and Diego knew quite well where it was located and headed straight for it. Matthew prayed she wasn't hurt too badly and also that she wouldn't go into labor. It was too early.

"God's hands," he spoke softly to himself as he rode hard. "She's in God's loving hands."

They rode at a fast gallop, and Cady thrilled to it. It was like skimming across the earth. Her fear of the horse dissipated the more she rode. It was exhilarating. Cady's ribs seemed numbed from constant abuse. She thought of the woman who'd been bucked off her horse. The way she'd hit her head, she could be dead. What if she was leading the men to the wrong hill? What if they couldn't find her? She wondered how nice the worried man would be if she had pointed to the wrong hill. The three men had all mistaken her for a boy, and she didn't care to enlighten them. She was going to stay disguised as a boy until she felt it safe to do otherwise.

Donny felt the young boy's hands clasped in front of him and felt protective. He wondered about the bruised-up face. *Someone's been beating on 'em, that's certain. A bruise like that doesn't come from mere fisticuffs. Could've been a horrible accident, but given the fact he's alone, hiding out up in the hills?* Donny wondered what Cady's story was. If he'd run away from home, Donny was sure there was a good reason. *Being beaten all the time, most likely. Mayhap he's lost or something, but dollars to doughnuts, I'll bet he's run away from cruelty.* He smiled. He hadn't used that term in a long time. He'd read it as a boy in a Nevada newspaper. *Dollars to doughnuts, that's a funny saying.* His thoughts swung back to the boy. *I'm gonna take this boy under my wing and help him if I can.*

They started up the steep incline, and Matthew suddenly noticed broken twigs on bushes where most likely, Liberty had gone up. Soon they were at the top, and there lay Liberty, still unconscious.

"That's a bad sign," Matthew said. Dismounting, he knelt and felt for a pulse in her neck, and his breath whooshed out as he realized it beat steadily under his searching fingers.

Diego crossed himself and said a prayer. Donny swung his right leg over his horse's head and slid down and then turned to help Cady down.

Cady started to smile at him but stopped because of her stiff face.

Matthew threw the thin quilt off Liberty and felt down her arms, ribs, and legs for any broken bones.

"I already did that, sir. I don't think anything is broken, but her head is bloody. She flew right off her horse when he bucked," Cady said. "It's my fault, sir, that he bucked her off. I came out of that cave and startled him, I reckon, and that woman was looking at me and not paying attention. I'm s-sorry."

"She," Matthew said, "she bucked, not he. Pookie's a mare." He spoke softly as he felt for Liberty's pulse again—steady and strong. Gently lifting her head, he felt the back of it carefully. "She needs stitches, that's certain. Let's get her home, and Dr. John can see just what's the matter." He stroked her cheek and laid his hand on her forehead. "Lord, we lift Liberty up to Your mighty power. You love her even more than I do, and I ask…we ask, agreeing together, that You please bless her with a full recovery. I pray that our baby is all right and that You see fit to bring healing and wholeness of mind, body, and most of all spirit. We thank You in advance, placing her in Your loving hands. In the powerful name of Jesus we ask this. Amen."

Cadence looked on in wonder. "You believe in God?"

Matthew looked over at the boy in astonishment. "You don't?"

Cady shuffled her feet and answered, "I don't rightly know what I believe."

The man, Matthew, turned back and, with a tenderness Cady had never witnessed in all her entire life, lifted Liberty into his arms.

Liberty didn't weigh all that much. Matthew thought back to how he teased her about getting heavy with child.

He started toward Piggypie, but Diego got off his horse and said, "Eet ees a leetle déjà vu, Meester Bannister. Same place you hand her to me a couple years ago. Now, you hand her to me, an' I weel geeve her back to you when you up on Piggypie."

Matthew carefully shifted Liberty to Diego. He climbed back on his horse, and Diego, muscles straining, lifted Liberty up as gently as he could into Matthew's waiting arms. Matthew kissed her forehead and slowly started down the hill.

Donny turned to Cady.

"Well, boy, get your things together, if you want to come with me. I'll see you eat and have a place to sleep."

Cady stared at Donny, surprised he would even care. She picked up her quilt where Matthew had dropped it. One side of her satchel was covered with blood, but she picked it up and tried to wipe it off onto some grass. She went into the cave, hurriedly throwing her few things into the red satchel. She took a cursory glance around, making sure she hadn't dropped anything. She was ready to go, but felt lightheaded from a lack of food. Her stomach no longer rumbled. It was numb. The oatmeal she'd eaten the night before had helped some, but she'd eaten next to nothing for the past couple days.

Cadence went out to where Donny waited and put her hand trustingly into his. He swung her up behind him and started off after Matthew and Diego, who were going down slowly. When Donny caught up with them, Matthew spoke softly.

"Ride for Dr. John, Donny. Please hurry."

The day, starting out with a drizzling rain, had turned out to be fair and beautiful, but Hannibal Cassidy didn't notice. He lived on the outskirts of town and discouraged any visitors or company, keeping his family and lifestyle to himself. He didn't want anyone poking around in his business.

He spent the previous day cleaning up the cabin and arranging for a neighbor to feed the chickens and milk the cow. He figured he'd be gone for a spell and didn't want anyone saying he was slothful or didn't take care of things. His wife and children had always done the chores, and now he was stuck with all of them. It never crossed his mind that he should take a bath or cut his hair and shave.

Hannibal rode into Sacramento to pay the sheriff a visit. He didn't like the sheriff much. He'd spent more nights in his jail than he could count, but he swallowed down his little bit of pride and walked into the sheriff's office.

"Well, well, well, this is a surprise, whether pleasant or not, I can't rightly say." Sheriff Keegan looked at Hannibal Cassidy and tried his best to keep the distaste out of his tone and off his face. Hannibal Cassidy reeked of stale sweat, alcohol, and garlic.

Hannibal shuffled his feet and said, "I need to report a missin' person."

"Now just who would that be?" The sheriff felt sorrow for the man losing his wife and son, but knew, too, Hannibal was a drunk and grossly mistreated his family. Doc Adams had reported to him, saying he'd bound up both the Cassidy children's ribs more than once, and both had to have stitches several times.

"My girl, Cadence," Hannibal replied. "I'm thinking someone kidnapped 'er."

"How old is she?"

"Oh, round about thirteen. What does it matter?"

"Well," said the sheriff, "if she's ten, she could legally get married. I've known girls to get married at fourteen."

"I ain't talkin' 'bout her gettin' married." Hannibal's face reddened with anger. "I'm talkin' 'bout a kidnappin'. I got me a picture here, and I want it circulated, same way you circulate those pictures of men who need hangin'."

"Sorry, Hannibal, no can do," the sheriff replied in a calm voice. "For one thing, I don't think she was kidnapped. She most likely ran away from your cruel treatment. And second, you just lied to me about her age. You know quite well your daughter is seventeen."

Surprise mixed with consternation spread across Hannibal's face. "How the blazes would you be a knowin' that?"

"I happen to remember your missus coming in here to get you out of jail a couple months back. She had both children with her, and it was Cadence's birthday...her seventeenth birthday, as a matter of fact."

"Well, they grow so fast, a body can't keep up," Hannibal whined. He tried to think fast, but his mind grasped at straws. There wasn't anything more to be gained by talking to the sheriff, and he wished he hadn't even told him as much as he had. He turned to leave, but the sheriff forestalled him with his words.

"You can go look for her all you want, but I'm telling you, she is free to do as she pleases. You cannot make her come back to your shack and make a slave of her. If you go around looking for her, you might think about taking a bath and shave. You listening to me, Cassidy?"

"Yeah, I hear you, but I gots my reasons, and I'll be a lookin' fer 'er till I find 'er."

Donny rode at a fast pace into the town of Napa, only slowing as he entered the busy part of Main Street. He again got off his horse, right leg over his horse's head, and slid off, turning to help the boy down.

"You're a lightweight, son, that's certain," he said as he swung the child down.

Cady hung on to her satchel, which she'd placed between her front and his back to hold it in place. She didn't know how much money was inside the red one nor anything about the papers, but she was keeping it safe.

"All right, Cady, let's go find the doc," Donny said. "I just hope he's not out tending to someone else right now. Come on." He strode up the steps of the wood-planked sidewalk and down to Dr. John Meeks' office.

Cady had to take two steps to his one and hurried to follow right behind him. He didn't bother knocking on the curtained glassed door.

Dr. John was sitting behind a large desk, getting caught up on paperwork, and looked up in surprise as Donny strode in with a boy right behind him.

Dr. John looked at Donny and saw the worry etched in his eyes. "What's the problem, Donny? Somebody need help?"

"It's Miss Liberty, sir," he said as he removed his hat and closed the door. "She was bucked off Pookie and hit her head. She's unconscious, sir, and hasn't come to. It's been close to an hour, and we need you to come quick and look at her. Matthew and Diego are taking her to the Rancho as we speak."

"I told her to stay off horses!" John strode into the other room to gather up a few things, setting them on the examining table.

Donny and Cady could see him from the doorway as he hurried to the stairs and said, but not in a loud voice, "Sally, I'm going over to Bannisters'. Want to come?"

He hoped she didn't. It'd take too much time to hitch up the wagon.

"No, John," she answered in a quiet voice as she descended the stairs. "Both Hannah and Johnny are sleeping, and I don't wish them to wake up yet. Thanks for asking though. Will you stay for supper?"

Donny nodded in affirmation, so Dr. John nodded too.

"Liberty's taken a spill off Pookie and is unconscious," he related to Sally as he began stowing things into his medical kit.

"Oh my!" Sally said, her eyes widening with shock. "I'll pray everything will be all right." She looked at Cady. "What happened to you?"

Cady shuffled her feet, looked down, and mumbled, "I don't want to talk about it."

Dr. John had thought the boy's face an unfortunate birthmark at first glance, but saw Sally was right. It was swollen besides being bruised.

Sally looked shocked at the boy's reply and responded, "Where do you live?"

Cadence looked at the woman, knowing her misery showed in her gray eyes, but Donny interrupted and said, "He'll be living at Bannisters' and be my helper." He ruffled Cadence's shorn strawberry-blonde curls.

Sally continued to stare at the boy, feeling something about him didn't ring true, but she couldn't quite put her finger on what. Donny turned Sally's attention away from the boy by asking John, "When a body's unconscious for a length of time, can it leave lasting effects?"

"Well, we don't know rightly know that much about the brain yet," he replied. "I can't just answer your question with a yes or no." He finished packing by throwing some nightclothes into a satchel, kissed Sally, and added, "I may not be home tonight, so don't wait up."

Sally, pinked up by the public display of a kiss, replied, "Be safe."

Cadence stared at the two of them, but Donny grabbed her by the shoulders and steered her out the door ahead of himself.

Before Dr. John came out the door, he whispered to Cady, "You mustn't stare when people kiss other people like that. It's not polite."

"But I've never seen anyone kiss before," Cady replied without thinking.

Donny stared at the boy in surprise and wondered what kind of upbringing the lad had. He ruffled his hair again, trying to cover his consternation at the boy's reply. Donny had been raised in a loving Christian home, and it was beyond his ken that there were homes where love wasn't shown or felt. He squeezed Cady's thin shoulder as the feeling of protectiveness came over him again.

Dr. John came out of his office, and when Donny swung the boy up behind him, the doc saw the grimace of pain on his face. He clutched at his side, and the doc wondered about the face bruise. It looked painful.

Cady didn't notice his perusal. She was busy getting her satchel in place before they rode off to Rancho Bonito.

As soon as Donny felt her hands clasp in front of him, he kicked his ride into a gallop, hoping the doc was as good on a horse as he was driving his buggy.

CHAPTER IV

And when her days to be delivered were fulfilled,
behold, there were twins in her womb.

GENESIS 25:24

DONNY NEEDN'T HAVE WORRIED—the doctor was an accomplished rider. It was like a race to the Bannisters' Rancho.

Cady thrilled to the speed and the sense of freedom that riding a horse brought. She knew whatever it took, she was going to learn how to ride. It seemed like no time at all, and the three of them were at the Rancho.

Because of having to ride much slower, Matthew had just handed Liberty to Diego and was getting off Piggypie as Dr. John, Donny, and the boy rode up.

"She's still unconscious?" Dr. John asked as he got off his horse.

"Yes, she hasn't stirred at all," Matthew answered softly, worry shadowing his deep-blue eyes.

"Let's get her comfortable, and I'll see what's going on. Head injuries are always dicey, as you well know," Dr. John said. He asked Matthew, "How long was it before you recovered your memory after you got bashed over the head?"

"Almost a month I think, and if I hadn't hit my head again, I don't know how long it would have taken."

Donny lifted the boy down and stood waiting until the doctor and Matthew handed him their reins.

Matthew's arms were ready to receive Liberty back from Diego, and he carried her into the house.

The door was already open. Conchita crossed herself when she saw Liberty unconscious in Matthew's arms.

"I haf the hot water ready, Dr. John, an' I halp you eef you need me," she said. "Meanwhile, I pray." She left the men, knowing she'd done all she could for the time being. She'd heated the water and changed the bed linens so all was fresh and ready for the mistress of the house. She went outside to offer dinner to Diego and Donny, only to find a boy with a sorry-looking face.

"What happen to you, leetle one?" she asked.

"I...ah..." Cadence glanced at Donny, who looked back at her with understanding. Looking at Conchita, she spoke quickly. "I got kicked in the face, and it hurts to smile."

"Haf you put someteeng on eet? I haf the good cream, eef you don't haf anyteeng."

"No, I don't have anything for it and..." Her voice trailing off, Cadence was undone by the sympathy. Her mother had always been matter of fact when her pa hit her, and told her to keep a stiff upper lip. It was better not to let her pa know it hurt. But here was this sweet Mexican woman who didn't even know her but was willing to help. She started crying, and Conchita scooped Cady into her arms to hug her, but Cady flinched because the woman squeezed her ribs. Before Cady knew what was happening, the woman had pulled up her shirt to look at Cady's ribs.

Seeing the strips of cloth around her, Conchita assumed it was because her ribs were wrapped.

Cady had wrapped from her waist up to flatten herself out. She pulled the shirt out of Conchita's hands and pulled the tails down, smoothing the material with a look that said *don't touch*.

"You hurt your ribs too. I can see eet." Conchita clucked her tongue and added, "You come with me to eat, an' I haf cream for your face. We haf Dr. John to look at your ribs."

"No! I don't need anyone looking at my ribs." Cady's voice had risen a bit, and she added more softly, "They're just bruised, that's all. I know the difference when they're broken."

Donny, who stood behind Cady, shook his head at Conchita, who shrugged her shoulders.

"Okay, but you come eat now. We haf the good food to eat."

Donny said, "We'll come in as soon as we get these horses fed and brushed." He looked at the boy, who looked back with tired eyes. "On second thought, you go in and get some salve for your face. I'll do the horses, and then we can eat."

Diego had stood quietly by, watching all that had transpired, and said, "I weel take the horses. Donny, you go weeth the boy. What your name, *chico*?"

"Cady, it's Cady Cassidy, and I'm twelve years old," Cadence said. Her cheeks reddened with the lie, but she felt it couldn't be helped. She didn't trust anyone right now.

"Come, Cady Cassidy. You weel come weeth me an' eat. You too, Donny-boy." Conchita led the way into the house. "You call me Conchita. You muss know, Cady, you hired halp now. You no eat with Meester Bannister or Mees Libbee. They own thees Rancho and ees very good people, but we eat at different times. They's busy now, so we weel eat while we wait to see how Mees Libbee be. Most times we eat when they ees feenished eating."

Cady said, "You mean I'm hired? I can make some mon—" Her jaw dropped open at the sight of the front entry and great room. She looked around in absolute awe. In her entire life she'd never been in any buildings besides their shabby cabin; the doctor's office when he wrapped her ribs or stitched her up; the shed where they kept the horse, cow, and chickens; Sheriff Keegan's jailhouse; the saloon; and just recently, Dr. John's sterile office. She stood still, her eyes filling with the charm of it.

Donny and Conchita had headed for the kitchen, but Cady was still in the entryway, her head full of a warmth that hit her like a blast of fresh air. She walked slowly, swallowing down the impact the interior of this house was making on her. The great room on her right had enormous windows on the far wall, making her feel as if she were outside. The floor was a smooth red-brown tile with a huge colored braided rug. Two walls were of some kind of beautiful wood, and the fourth wall was painted a rusty red but was narrow where part of the room opened to the entryway. There were end tables, a large square coffee table made of varying shades of wood, and deep leather chairs, sofa, and love seat. A floor-to-ceiling bookshelf with staggered shelving held books, bibelots, and a few pictures. It was lovely. Cady was so engrossed in looking she didn't hear Donny telling her to come to the kitchen. He spoke again, and her head jerked up to look at him, as if mesmerized. She never knew a house could look like this.

"Come on, Cady. It's time to wash up so's we can eat."

Donny had no idea Cady felt as if she'd just walked into a dream.

"Sorry. I didn't mean to keep you waiting," she replied, but as she walked slowly into the huge kitchen, she almost cried from the loveliness of it. It was awash with light and smells and peace.

"You wash your hands there," Conchita said as she pointed toward the deep sink with a jug of water and soap next to it.

Cady started to wash. She picked up the peppermint-aloe soap and smelled it. Her mother had never put any scent into their soap. It smelled lovely, and Cady felt her chapped hands would heal if she got to use this soap very often. She soaped her hands and picked up the jug to rinse. "Where does the water go?" She'd never washed in anything but a metal washtub or basin.

"Eet go somewhere outside. I doan know where eet go. You ask Meester Bannister. He put een pipes to go somewhere underground. We eat now."

Conchita put four plates on the table and served Donny and Cady. She was going to wait to eat with Diego. Lupe and Luce, her nieces who also worked for the Bannisters, had gone to visit a cousin after helping prepare dinner.

Cady started to eat, but Donny forestalled her.

Putting a hand up, he said, "Whoa there, partner. Around here we pray first. We acknowledge the Almighty and remember that it is by His hand that we even have food."

Cady stared at Donny, embarrassed by her lack of manners. With the smells of food, she was ravenous.

Donny stared back, realizing this boy had no learning about God, or if he did, he didn't place any credence to it.

"Let's pray," he said. "Lord God, we are grateful You are a Father who cares about us. We thank You for loving us. We also thank You for this food. We thank You for Cady and for sending him our way. We pray right now for Miss Liberty. We pray for healing and nothing to be dreadfully wrong with her. We give You praise for Your watchfulness over us. Amen."

Dr. John folded up his stethoscope and looked over at Matthew, who sat on the bed, holding Liberty's hand.

"There doesn't seem to be anything serious other than needing stitches for that head wound. Her vitals are good, heartbeat strong, no thready pulse, no broken bones. The babies seem to be fine—"

"Babies? Did you said babies?" Matthew's face was a picture of startled surprise.

"Yes, Liberty's having twins. I heard two distinct heartbeats." Dr. John's eyes twinkled. "After all, Liberty is a twin. Congratulation, Matthew."

"I—we, ah, we didn't know! Twins! It makes perfect sense, but it certainly comes as a surprise. You really don't think anything else is wrong? Hasn't she been unconscious a considerable amount of time?" Matthew was feeling a bit overwhelmed with the fact of twins, but his first concern was Liberty.

"With head injuries, one never really knows. I think hitting the ground was a shock to Liberty's body, and it's taking time for it to recover. I don't believe she'll have any lasting effects from this. On the other hand, I don't wish to alarm you, but I don't know that much about head injuries. I need some hot water and some towels, please. I'll have to shave that area on her head and make sure it's clean. She sure has a lot of hair, doesn't she?" he asked as he examined her head wound again.

"Yes, she does. I'll get that water for you," Matthew said, still feeling befuddled by the knowledge that they were having two babies and not one. He went out the opened door and down the hall toward the kitchen.

When he entered the kitchen, the boy stood immediately up and stared straight ahead.

Donny dropped his fork in surprise.

"What are you doing, Cady?"

"The master of this house just entered…you're supposed to stand at attention," Cadence answered.

"Well," drawled Matthew, "I'm flattered that you show such respect. That may be the rule in your household, but here, we all have the same respect for each other. No one is considered better than another, son. We're all God's creation, and whether high born or low, it doesn't matter."

He turned to Conchita, who had covered her mouth with her hand to keep from laughing out loud at the boy's statement.

"We need some hot water," he said and saw the question in Conchita's eyes. "She should be fine barring any effects of the head wound. Dr. John doesn't seem worried, but then again, he doesn't know that much about head wounds. He just informed me that the babies' heartbeats are just fine." He saw the wonderment spread out over Conchita's face.

"Tweens! Mees Libbee haf the tweens? Praise the Lord she be all right, an' we haf the time to get ready for tweens."

The cook beamed and laughed a big belly laugh that made Cady giggle. She wasn't used to hearing laughter, and it caught at her heartstrings and made her feel joyful.

She'd already cleaned her plate and sat down politely at Matthew's words.

"Sorry," she said to Donny. "My pa made us stand whenever he came into the house, and we weren't to move until he said we could." She glanced at Matthew, who looked at her a bit closer.

"I want Dr. John to take a look at that face when he finishes with my wife." He saw the misery start in the youth's eyes and added, "He won't hurt you, and he'll have something to put on your jaw to take the swelling down. That must hurt like the dickens."

"Aw, I'm all right." Cady didn't want anyone looking at her too closely.

"Just the same, I want him to take a look at you." Matthew spoke in a serious tone. "I don't know why you were camped out by yourself in the mountains, and if you don't care to tell us, you don't have to, but if you're planning on working for me, you'll let Dr. John take a look at your face. I don't like my employees suffering for no good reason. You can bunk in the tack room in the barn, and Donny can let you know what needs done and how to do it. To my way of thinking, you've run away from home, and the good Lord led you to us." He smiled at Cady, who was sitting looking a bit dumbfounded.

Her mouth opened to speak, but she closed her lips on the words. She wasn't sure about the God part, but she was sure she wanted to stay here. She already felt safe, but knew too her pa would be looking for her because of the money in the satchel.

"I would like to work for you, sir, and I will let the doctor look at my face, but only my face." She glanced over at Conchita, whose lips tightened at her comment.

"I take thees into Dr. John," Conchita said as she started to lift the hot water from the stove.

"Let me do it," Matthew said.

Conchita took a couple towels out of a linen drawer and followed Matthew down the hall. When they entered the bedroom, she laid the towels on the nightstand to protect the wood from the hot water.

"Meester Bannister, I weel tell you that Cady, he haf his ribs bound up. I theenk besides hees face he maybe haf the broken ribs, but I doan know."

Dr. John, who was busy shaving a spot on Liberty's head, said softly, without turning his head, "I know the boy has something wrong with his ribs. I saw his pained face when Donny swung him up behind him on the horse. Someone has beat the boy with no compunction at all, poor child."

"I hope he'll tell us his story, but meanwhile, we'll pray and ask the Lord for guidance. I certainly won't go looking for where he's come from, if that's the treatment he gets at home. He can live here and work, and I'll pay him. I'd take him and not have him work, but I get the feeling he's not a boy who'll take handouts. He has to be fairly honest, or he wouldn't have told us he spooked Pookie. That's why she bucked."

"Aha, I wondered about that. Liberty's such a magnificent horsewoman I was surprised when I heard she'd been bucked off. I would assume her pregnancy has thrown her normal sense of balance off." Dr. John was carefully cleaning Liberty's wound as he spoke.

"What's that you're using to clean the wound?"

"Carbolic...we use it with gauze. Just a few short years ago, a doctor from England, a Sir Joseph Lister, discovered soaking the gauze in carbolic keeps the rate of infection down. It took a while before the medical profession accepted the relationship between infection and germs, but since using carbolic and iodine, the rate of infection has decreased dramatically."

He started sewing Liberty's head with catgut, taking small stitches. He finished up and placed a piece of the iodine gauze in place.

"There, that should do it," he said. "Look!"

Matthew and Conchita both watched along with Dr. John as Liberty stirred.

She lay quite still for a moment and opened her eyes. She closed
them quickly and then slowly opened them again, feeling nauseated.

CHAPTER V

He healeth the broken in heart, and
bindeth up their wounds.

PSALM 147:3

WHA...WHAT **HAPPENED? OH**...I'm going to be sick." Liberty tried to swallow down the feeling of nausea, but couldn't.

Matthew grabbed an enameled pan and set it in front of her. She rolled sideways, quietly sick into the pan. She felt wretched, her body sore from the shock of hitting the ground, but the nausea was overwhelming. She felt as if she had two heads, both thumping on a loud drum. She used the pan again and then fell back onto the pillow, shaken. She closed her eyes to stop the room from spinning.

"Is the baby all right? Am I all right?" Liberty thought she spoke aloud, but her words came out on a breath of whisper. No one heard her questions.

Matthew thought back to when he was attacked, robbed, and left for dead just a few months before. He remembered he'd been so nauseated for a time he'd wished he was dead.

Going into the bathing room, he filled a glass of water and wetted a cloth from the cold jug of water sitting beside it.

Liberty's eyes were still closed, but Matthew spoke to her softly, again remembering back to when he'd been bashed on the head. Noise had seemed to crawl through his head, wreaking havoc.

"Here, sweetheart," he said. He slipped his arm behind her shoulders to help her sit up a bit, handing her the glass of water. Her hand shook when she took it, and he helped her steady it to her lips. He sat gingerly on the side of the bed, waiting while she swished the water around, rinsing out her mouth. When she finished, he wiped her face tenderly with the cloth.

"That feels good. Is everything all right? Is the baby all right?" Her voice came out stronger, but her head was still spinning. She closed her eyes, but not before she saw Conchita and Dr. John observing her. She opened them again, waiting for Matthew's answer. She tried to focus on his face.

"Nice to have you back with us, sweetheart," Matthew replied with a smile in his eyes, not answering her questions right away. He kissed her forehead, and she leaned back against the pillows with a deep sigh.

"What happened? The last thing I remember was riding up the hill. Frankly, I don't remember much else. Something caught my eye and startled Pookie, I think."

"Yes, it was a boy. He was evidently staying in the cave and came out as you rode toward it. I'm pretty sure it scared Pookie, and most likely she shied away from him. The boy rode for help. I don't know any of the particulars yet and won't bother you with it now. You need to rest."

Liberty closed her eyes, "Yes, I feel so dizzy and nauseated. I was thrilled to be over being nauseated from the pregnancy, but here I am, at it again."

"Well"—Matthew winked at Conchita and nodded at Dr. John —"you do need your rest before those babies are born."

Liberty's eyes flew open. "Babies? What? What are you saying, Matthew...ohhh, I feel sick." She sat up, making a grab for the pan Conchita had rinsed out. When she was finished, she put a shaky hand up to feel where Dr. John had stitched her head. She felt it and lay back against her pillows.

Dr. John said, "Well, Liberty, perhaps you'll stay off horses until your babies are born. You definitely have a concussion.

Conchita took the pan and rinsed it again. "You rest, Mees Libbee. You rest and take care of those tweens."

"Twins, Matthew?" Her eyes connected with Matthew's, but she wasn't really registering what was being said. "Yes, I will take it easy. No more horseback riding." She looked over at the doctor, who stood looking smugly at her. "Dr. John, are you sure?" Liberty couldn't seem to keep a steady thought. She faced him, a question in her eyes.

"As sure as I know I'm standing here talking to you. Now, I'll leave you two alone and go check on the boy named Cady."

Both he and Conchita left the room, closing the door quietly behind them.

"Twins, Matthew! Wonder, will I have a boy and girl like my brother and me?"

"I don't know, but I am grateful no matter what you have. I had all kinds of scenarios running through my mind when we rode up to find you. Not one of them had as good an ending as what we have. I thank the Lord!" His deep-blue eyes misted with thanksgiving.

When Doctor John came into the kitchen, the boy and Donny had finished eating.

Conchita removed their plates and said, "You weel seet an' wait now. I haf made the best dessert for you."

Sopapillas were her favorite, and hers were better than anyone had ever tasted. She took some honey out of the large container to warm up, watching the thick syrup as she poured it into a pot on the stove. Later she would fill the deep-fried bread pockets with it.

Cady, in all her seventeen years, had never had dessert. She didn't think she even knew what it was but was embarrassed to ask.

She felt Dr. John's eyes on her, his careful perusal making her nervous. He walked over, gently taking her chin in his hand. He turned her face toward better light.

"You have very unusual gray eyes, Cady. I don't believe I've ever seen that color gray ringed by darker gray. I supposed I shouldn't tell a boy his eyes are beautiful, should I?" He smiled as he ran his fingers lightly but carefully down the child's jawline.

His subconscious took in the fact that the boy's bones were delicate.

Cady tried not to flinch, but she closed her gray eyes against his knowing ones.

"I don't think your jaw is broken, son. Conchita told me you got kicked in the face. Was it a horse?"

"No, sir, it wasn't." Cady's lips closed in a thin line to let him know she wasn't open for questions.

Dr. John, being who he was, didn't care.

"So who kicked you?" he asked.

"I don't care to talk about it," Cady replied.

"It doesn't matter whether you want to talk about it or not. If you've run away, and it's for a good reason, there is no one in this house who wouldn't protect you with their own life. Now again, I ask you—who kicked you?"

Cady's first reaction was of one of pure disbelief that anyone would protect her. Her gray eyes widened in surprise. *They don't know me or that I am worthless. They don't know my pa's told me that more times than I can count or remember.*

"I don't believe anyone would protect me with their life," she said flatly. "I am not worth anything to protect." Her eyes filled with sudden tears, the dam of silence shattered. She added brokenly, "My mama and brother died of the fever less than two weeks ago. The wood was so w-wet, and I couldn't get the fire st-started. My p-pa ca-came home and drug me out of bed and kicked me and then tied me to the bed because the house was c-cold." Cady took a big breath and continued. "Mama sometimes tried to protect me from him, but she's gone now, along with Timmy." She wiped her eyes on her sleeve and continued to talk. "I had a piece of—of broken glass under the bed, and I sawed the rope while he was sleeping off the whiskey. I had a few things in my satchel, and I ran away. I walked the rest of the night. When the sun started to come up, I found somebody's barn and slept all day the first day. When I woke up, I stole the cat's milk and some oats to eat from the manger and walked all night the second night. It was awful, and I was cold and wet. I found that cave to sleep in this morning when the sun came up. I woke up, thankful the rain had stopped, and I was just lazing in the sun, glad to be warm, when I heard someone riding up the hill. You know the rest."

Donny, Conchita, and Dr. John looked at Cady, shock and consternation clearly evident in their eyes.

Donny was the first to speak. "Do you think your pa will come looking for you?"

"Yes, he will. I know he will. He'll need someone to do the chores and wait on him. He'll want me to milk the cow and make food for him, now my ma's gone."

She didn't care to tell Donny about the money in the satchel...that Pa would come looking for her for sure, wanting that money back. She didn't know herself what else was in the satchel or how much money was in it. She hadn't looked yet, wondering if her pa had stolen it from someone. It scared her a bit, and she was superstitious, thinking if she looked in it again, it would conjure up her pa for sure. Cadence started to draw in a huge breath to sigh but stopped because of the pain in her side.

Dr. John said, "Son, you need to know that there is not one person on this earth that's worthless...not one! They may be shiftless, but that's their actions, not who they are. We are precious in God's sight. Every single one of us are God's creation, and we have value." His eyes showed compassion for her. "Now, let me have a look at those ribs."

"Thank you, but no. My ribs are fine," she said softly. "I've already checked them. I believe I've become an expert. One or two of them are cracked, but none are broken. I know that for sure. I've had broken ribs before."

"I could wrap them up so they won't bother you."

She shook her head, and her hands slid down to hold her shirttails in place.

"All right, but at least let me put some salve on that bruise. It stinks some, but it'll help make your face feel better. It won't feel so stiff or sore."

"Okay, some salve would be fine, but my ribs will heal—really, and they're not broken." Cady continued to hold on to her shirttails as she spoke. Neither the doctor nor Donny was going to pull them up.

Dr. John reached into his bag and pulled out a metal jar. As he unscrewed the lid, the ointment's pungent odor filled the room. He dipped his fingers into it, gingerly smoothing it over Cady's jaw and cheek. He was intent on what he was doing and became more mindful of the boy's delicate features.

"Your jaw is really swollen," he said. "You face is a rainbow of color. Bet you're thankful he didn't break your jaw. With a kick like that, he could have." He handed her the jar and added, "Put it on whenever you think of it. I guarantee that it will help heal your bruise quicker, and you'll find it feels better with it on. Sure your ribs are all right, son?"

"Sure, I'm sure. I don't wish to sound as if I don't appreciate your helping me, sir. I thank you very much, and my face feels better all ready."

"You're welcome, son. And now either I go home or I eat some of Conchita's wonderful cooking. I know what my vote is."

Donny stood up and said, "Come on, Cady. It's time for us to do a few chores afore we go to bed."

"No, you haf the dessert first," Conchita said. "I haf made the *sopapillas* to eat." She waved at them to sit back down. "And you, Dr. John, you wait for Meester Bannister, or you wanna to eat now?"

"I'll wait, thank you. It's always good to spend some time with Matthew. But more importantly, to eat some of your delicious food." He smiled at Conchita, who grinned back.

Hannibal Cassidy, after talking with Sheriff Keegan, went to the saloon to have a few drinks. He stood at the bar, a regular customer, and talked to the bartender named Jake.

"My girl's run off, an' the sheriff won't even look for 'er."

"Well, that's a fine kettle of fish. Isn't that part of his job? With all that's happened to you lately, you need all the help you can get."

"Don't I know it!" exclaimed Hannibal. "I sure as anything don't need ta be traipsin' around in the mud lookin' for my wayward daughter." Hannibal was hungry for approval, and the bartender had a good listening ear.

"Yep, she done took herself off." He dropped his voice to nearly a whisper. "Lessen somebody kidnapped 'er. Don't know why anyone would. She's a skinny little thing, not worth the food she eats."

"Why're you looking for her then? Why don't you just let 'er go?" Jake had heard stories but had never seen how mean Hannibal could be.

Hannibal looked across the bar at Jake, his lips in a thin, straight line. He wasn't about to tell anyone why he was after the girl. That was his business.

"Reckon it's 'cause I'm her pappy, and I just want to make sure she's all right."

Jake looked a Hannibal, a bit surprised by his reply. He wondered if the stories he'd heard about Hannibal's treatment of the children were true. He also wondered how much longer Hannibal would be coming into the bar, seeing as how his wife had died. Everyone in town knew Mrs. Cassidy had taken in laundry and ironed clothes. She'd also made clothes for people, to put food on the table for the Cassidy children. Unless Hannibal found work, he'd be out of money fast, to Jake's way of thinking.

Hannibal stood thinking for some time while he drank his whiskey. He wondered what course he should take. After a few drinks, he left the saloon, going in search of Cadence. Above all, he needed that satchel.

He went around town asking people if they'd seen his Cady. His heart was hardened, and he didn't care that folks looked at him in disgust. He didn't realize they considered him the town drunk. He hadn't bathed or shaved for months. At one time, he'd been a decent-looking man. Now, with his hair and beard filthy and matted, his body reeking and his clothes dirty, he looked exactly what he was, the town drunk.

He went into the mercantile store thinking perhaps Cady had needed to get some food or some sort of supplies before she set out. A bell overhead of the door tinkled when he opened it. He walked up to Mr. Freeman and asked if Cady had been in to buy anything.

"Nope. Why would you ask? You've never allowed your children in here. I heard tell you lost your wife and son to the fever. I'm right sorry, but I suspect they're in a better place."

"A hole in the ground ain't a better place, ta my way of thinkin'," Hannibal retorted, his tone angry. "They're rottin' away in the ground, and that's that."

"No, it's not *that's that*. There's a God who loves and cares for you, Hannibal Cassidy. Whether you recognize Him or not, He recognizes you. He created you to have a relationship with Him."

"Don't be a preachin' at me! I don't need it. You sound just like my dead wife."

"She was a good woman, and I'm sorry for your loss, Hannibal." Mr. Freeman didn't say anything more, and Hannibal went stomping out, slamming the door shut. Riding home fairly sober, he dropped by the neighbor's house to tell him he wouldn't be gone quite yet.

He went home, and the first thing he did was start a fire in the old stove and in the fireplace. The house felt cold and damp. He hauled water in from the pump, dumping it into a large pan on the stove, and heated some water for a bath. Boiling some water in a teapot, he made himself a cup of tea, which he sat and drank, eating a chunk of cold ham and a slice of bread that was going stale. Waiting for the water to heat up some, he went in search of his razor and strop. He found scissors and went outside to cut his beard off as short as he could before shaving the rest off.

He couldn't stop thinking about the money his wife had hidden in the bank all these years. *Over seventeen years she's been a hiding that money. Bet she planned ta save it for Timmy and Cady. Wonder 'bout those legal papers. I never did get a chance ta see exactly what they was. Wonder why she never lit out like Cady done? That makes me so angry, I could spit! When I get my hands on that girl, I'm thinking she'll be a joining her ma and brother! Wonder why I can't find no one who saw that girl. Wonder if someone around here is a hidin' her. I've hit a dead end, an' no mistake. Mayhap she'll turn up at Farrows'. I wonder…mayhap I should ride over to San Rafael an' see if she's gone ta her ma's people. I don't reckon Callie would've told her 'bout them, lessen she did when she was dying. If those papers Callie had hidden from me are a will, Cady stands to inherit a great deal of money.*

CHAPTER VI

Be not forgetful to entertain strangers:
for thereby some have entertained angels unawares.

HEBREWS 13:2

AFTER CONCHITA AND DR. JOHN LEFT the bedroom, Matthew continued to sit on the bed, a furrow marring his brows.

"You're sure you're all right, sweetheart?"

"Yes, just nauseated and a headache. I knew Donny didn't want me to ride out, but I felt so cooped up from all the rain, I needed a good ride. Once this room stops spinning, I can get up."

"Nope, you can't. Dr. John ordered some bed rest for you, at least for a couple days. He also said no real exertion until our babies come. You'll be busy making some extra clothes anyway, don't you think?"

"Yes...ohhh, my head is spinning. This is worse than pregnancy nausea. I didn't have the head spinning with it."

"I can say with all honesty, sweetheart, I know exactly how you feel, and I'm sorry. It's a horrible feeling. It almost makes you forget the pain of your wound, doesn't it?"

Liberty smiled wanly. "Do I have a wounded head?" she asked as she squeezed Matthew's hand. "I love you, Matthew Bannister. I love you so much it hurts."

"I know, Libby. I feel the same way. I reckon after Jess, I never thought to find happiness. God has blessed us so abundantly. You with your great green eyes that never gave away what you were thinking…all the hardship you endured living with Armand. Me with the bitterness of disappointed hopes in Jessica. God has granted and blessed both of us with a second chance. When I saw you lying there on the ground today, my heart felt as if it went into my throat. It was not only as Diego said, a little déjà vu, but frightening to think I could lose you. I trust God, but sometimes I wonder just how much. At that moment, I don't think I did. I know in my head His ways are perfect and just, but I could only think, what if I have to go on without you? I know I don't want to."

He leaned over and kissed her tenderly on the mouth. "How I do love you, my darling Liberty." He was still concerned about her and sometimes felt Dr. John a bit too casual about his patients. He kissed her eyes, which she closed willingly. There were dark smudges under them.

"I love you too, Matthew." She took a deep breath and slithered down the pillows a bit. "I think I'll go to sleep for a while. I feel so tired."

She mumbled something else, but it didn't make any sense to Matthew, who sat there a few more minutes praying. He thanked God Liberty was all right.

He got up and spoke softly. "C'mon, Boston." The dog, who was still a puppy, got up from his bed and went with Matthew, who headed for the kitchen but stopped at the great room when he saw his friend Dr. John waiting for him.

"What do you really think, John? What if Liberty were Sally? Would you have the same opinion?"

"What? Are you jesting with me, Matthew?" Dr. John's cheeks pinked up a little in indignation that his friend might think he'd not examined Liberty properly.

"No, not really. I reckon when it's close to home, one worries a bit more, that's all."

"Liberty's going to be fine. If anything untoward was going to happen from that fall, it'd already have presented itself. Those babies are cushioned in a lot of fluid that protects them. And Liberty, well, you saw for yourself. She's of sound mind. Her pupils aren't dilated, which is a good sign. I feel she will be just fine. She may have a slight concussion, but I firmly believe she's all right. Now, I'd like to relate a few things to you about the boy you discovered today." Dr. John filled Matthew in on the few things he'd found out about the child.

"He can stay here," Matthew said grimly. "It never ceases to amaze me when I hear of such depravity…kicking your own son in the ribs and face. Why, I wouldn't treat Boston that way!" He reached down and rubbed Boston's ears. Boston cocked his head to direct Matthew's knowing fingers to a particular spot behind his ear that he loved having scratched, and Matthew obliged him.

"I know what you mean. I've seen some pretty sad circumstances, being a doctor, but it never gets easier when you see someone mistreated. I'm glad the boy found you, Matthew. I believe God guided his path to cross yours. I know you'll take good care of him."

Matthew nodded his head and said, "Donny already seems to have taken him under his wing. He can sleep in the tack room and make himself useful. There are many things that need doing around here. I'm sure the boy will be grateful for a place to lay his head. You should have been in the kitchen when I went to get the hot water. Conchita had a difficult time not laughing. That poor boy stood at attention and said to Donny, 'The master of this house just entered. You're supposed to stand at attention.' He also told Donny he wasn't allowed to move after standing at attention until his pa said he could. Wonder what else his home life was like, poor child."

Elijah Humphries lay in bed. It was early morning, and he didn't wish to awaken Abigail, who still slept soundly beside him. He stretched, careful to not disturb her, and began to pray. He was a grateful man, an astute lawyer, and a dedicated Christian.

He began his prayer by asking God to forgive anything in his life he may have overlooked that wasn't pleasing to Him. Next, he spent a considerable time praising God for who He was and for what He had done, was doing, and would do. He also had a list of people he prayed for daily, and of course, Abigail was at the top of it. He prayed for Matthew and Liberty and Liberty's twin, Alex, and his wife, Emily, as well as their numerous children—especially Xander, who was Alex and Emily's seven-year-old boy and was Elijah's favorite of the brood. Liberty's father, Alexander, and her grandmother, Phoebe, were also in his daily prayers. He prayed for Adam, a young man who'd recently come into his life. He loved him like a son. His partners at the law firm and their families were not on the daily list, but he did pray for them on a regular basis. Next, he would spend time praying for specific needs that had come to his attention. He lay there and prayed for Moses Slocum, the telegraph operator who had pneumonia. He was quite ill, and it was touch and go whether he'd make it. He prayed for Mrs. Young, whose mother lived back east and was ill, and for Susannah Farrow, who'd lost her husband in a freak accident. Susannah wasn't well, and Elijah hoped the doctor could find what exactly was wrong with her. She was a lovely lady. He also prayed for the missing daughter she and her husband had told him about just a few short weeks ago. He wondered how he could go about finding where she had gone and whom she'd married some seventeen years ago. He prayed for God to give him direction and wisdom now that Oscar Farrow had died. It was imperative he do his best to find the daughter. He continued praying for some time before he quietly got up and went into the bathing room.

Elijah hated to shave and always felt a sense of accomplishment as soon as he was finished. He began to sharpen his razor on the strop. Once shaved, he heard Abigail stirring. He quietly left the room and descended the stairs.

Polka Dot, their nine-month-old dog, nearly wagged herself in two as Elijah came down the steps. She place her front paws on the first step, waiting for him to come all the way down. Abigail had forbidden the dog to go upstairs. Polka Dot had a nice cozy bed in the kitchen and another in Elijah's library.

He sat down on the second tread and loved on his dog. "Oh, Polka, you're such a good girl." He stroked her fur and rubbed her ears. She trailed after him, still wagging as he entered the kitchen.

"Good morning, Bessie. How are you this beautiful morning?"

"I'm grateful it's not raining, and I'm fine, Mr. Humphries. Fat as a cat and fit as a fiddle."

"Can I get a cup of coffee, please? Abigail is beginning to stir, and I'd like to take one up to her this morning."

Susannah Farrow lay in a huge, beautifully carved wooden bed. Tears seeped from her eyes. "Lord," she prayed, "I am so tired...so very, very tired. I don't think I'm strong enough to go on by myself. Thou knowest my heart. I would have been happy to go with Oscar. I don't understand Thy ways. I know, as Thy word says, Thy ways are higher than my ways, but, oh Lord, what am I going to do? I feel so alone... alone and tired. Wouldst Thou see fit, Lord, to take me home too?" She rolled over onto her back and stared at the ceiling as the tears trailed down the sides of her face. "If not that, couldst Thou somehow see fit to bring our Callie home? It's been a long time, Lord. Seventeen years, six months, and eleven days. I'd love to see her again. I cry out to Thee, Father, please bring my girl home."

She got up, feeling the pain in her stomach, and her head ached. "Mayhap I'll be joining Thee sooner than I thought. With this pain and tiredness, I do believe I'm dying." She spoke heavily but with no distress in her voice.

Tess knocked discreetly, and not waiting for an answer, entered the huge bedroom with a breakfast tray.

"Oh, madam, what're you doing up so early? You should be abed, resting up."

"I'm all right, Tess. I'm all right, really. There's nothing to be gained by moping around now, is there? I need to be up and about."

"Here's your breakfast, madam." Tess placed a large tray on the small round table beside the huge window giving a view of the back garden. A maze at the rear end of the garden, made of thick walls of tall hedges, wound its way around and around with dead-end paths. From this bedroom one could see the clear path to reach the huge gazebo located in the center of it.

Susannah sat down obediently, but she wasn't hungry at all. "Did Opal cut the rose for me?" she asked.

"Yes, madam. She said you were used to having a rose by your breakfast plate, and if Mr. Farrow couldn't place it there anymore, why, she would. We all love you, madam. You are beautiful inside and out and so very special to us."

"Thank you, Tess, and I know you care. Please tell Opal thanks for me, for such a lovely tray and being so thoughtful. I do appreciate it."

"Yes, madam, I'll do that. Enjoy your breakfast." She left, leaving the door slightly ajar.

Susannah took a huge breath and picked up her fork. *I must eat. If Callie does come home, I don't want to be in a weakened state and not be able to be up and about. I think I'm dying. Oh Lord, the pain in my stomach hurts badly.*

It wasn't ten minutes later that Tess tapped on the doorjamb. "Madam, Mr. Humphries is here to see you. Is it all right to bring him up?"

"Yes, of course," Susannah answered. She got up and donned a beautifully flowered peignoir over her nightdress, tying the belt snugly to her slender waist.

Tess went back down the stairs to the parlor and said, "Mrs. Farrow is delighted you are here. Please follow me."

"Before we do, Tess, please tell me—how is she really?"

"Not well, sir. Dr. Huffman can't find what's wrong with her, but he doesn't seem to think it's cancer, which is a relief to me. He said she's in a steady decline though. She seems weaker every day." She turned to lead him out of the room and added, "She's feeling very alone without Mr. Farrow here. Please come." She led him up the triple-wide staircase.

Halfway up the stairs was a huge landing. A baby grand piano, as well as huge Ming vases filled with plants whose foliage was beautiful, spoke of refinement and good taste. There were long windows across the back wall, looking out to a professionally tended garden. In one corner stood the piano and two wingback chairs, with a coffee table between them, faced so a body could view not only the gardens but the piano as well.

The stairs continued on the left, going opposite the way they'd come up to the landing. The impression was of beauty, elegance, and old-world charm.

Elijah sensed peace within the walls of this home, as well as tasteful sophistication. He knew the Farrows were very wealthy and philanthropists for the best causes. He'd handled their affairs for the past couple years and admired the no-nonsense way Oscar Farrow had dictated where his money was to go.

Tess stood at the doorway and waved him in. "Mr. Humphries, go right on in."

Susannah Farrow held out both hands to welcome Elijah. "Good morning, Elijah Humphries. Please forgive me for not rising. What a delightful surprise," she said.

He took both hands and squeezed them slightly before letting go. "It is my pleasure, madam." He saw the breakfast tray and added, "I hope I'm not visiting too early, but I need a little more information on your daughter, Callie."

"Please"—Susannah waved toward a couple cushioned chairs that faced each other with a view to the gardens below—"be seated. Would you like a cup of coffee or tea?"

"No, no thank you. I've just come from having my breakfast. Abigail said to give you her love. We're all so sorry about you losing Oscar under such tragic circumstances." He gave her a long look full of compassion and continued to speak.

"I looked at the will your husband made out. It looks as if your entire estate is to go first to you, and should you predecease your daughter, it then goes to your daughter and any progeny. There is a codicil that should Callie or any progeny not be found within a six-month period following your demise, the entire estate will go to the orphanage school that your husband founded. It's the San Rafael School of Primary Learning, run by Mr. Amos Kepler. Is this your understanding?"

"Yes, Mr. Humphries. Your mind is as sharp as ever. Everything you've said is correct."

"Well, I must admit Mr. Kepler's son, Edward Kepler, works as a clerk at my firm. He's quite a capable young man and probably inherited his work ethic from his father."

"I wouldn't doubt it. Mr. Kepler seems very dedicated to the school. He's been visiting me on a regular basis, twice and three times a week, since Oscar was killed. He feels terrible and told me he feels guilty that Oscar fell from the second floor of the school. Evidently Oscar leaned over the railing and somehow went right on over, falling to his death. Mr. Kepler said he tried to catch his coattails as he went over, but they slipped right through his fingers. He's tormented, poor man."

Elijah clucked his tongue. "I shouldn't wonder. I'd have nightmares. It's a tragedy, and no mistake." He hooked his thumbs into his suspenders and asked, "Does Mr. Kepler know he stands to inherit if you pass on and your daughter isn't found?"

Susannah looked startled by his question. "No, Oscar said telling people wasn't proper or needful. No one knows except you and me."

"Good. Let's keep it that way, shall we?" Elijah went to stand in front of the window, gazing out at the beautiful gardens and maze. A feeling of uneasiness came over him, and he was trying to figure what was bothering him, but Susannah broke into his reverie.

"I do hope you can find our Callie. I know she ran away from home, but we never knew who she ran off with or why. Oscar said we weren't to look for her because if she ran off, she didn't want to return anyway. She had just turned seventeen. I always worried that if she did come back, she wouldn't be able to find us, since we'd moved across town." Tears welled in her beautiful gray eyes.

Elijah turned to face her, and the light from the windows behind him lit her face. He knew she was forty-five, but she looked much younger. "Madam, I would like your permission to set the Pinkerton Agency on this case. It's been too many years, and the trail to find her would be quite obscured by now, but the Pinkerton Agency is renowned for finding their man, so to speak. Last year, Allan Pinkerton died, and his two sons have taken over the agency, but I believe we can trust them to be discreet as well as persistent."

"Whatever you think best, Mr. Humphries. I am willing to do anything to find my daughter."

Mr. Amos Kepler dressed carefully, making sure his cravat was elaborately tied. He'd polished his shoes the evening before with champagne, as recommended years before by Beau Brummell, who had set the dress code for the upper class of England.

Amos had a modest income as headmaster of the San Rafael School of Primary Learning. Meticulous in every aspect of his life, he dressed as befit his station, attended the Lutheran church every Sunday, and ran the school with precision, but he was a very lonely man.

This morning he planned to visit Mrs. Farrow, as he had done at least two days a week, and sometimes three, since Oscar died. She was about the same age as he, and a lovely woman.

He inspected himself closely in the mirrors and felt he passed muster. He was quite a handsome man, and he knew it. Amos' room was lined with mirrors, and he turned this way and that, making sure all was correct. His coattails were unwrinkled, his side chops tidily trimmed, and his full head of hair combed neatly straight back. He smiled at himself and left the room ready for the day ahead. He had a full schedule and planned to systematically tick off everything he'd set out to accomplish this day. First was breakfast. He made his way down the narrow stairs, whistling softly as he went.

CHAPTER VII

Therefore remove sorrow from thy heart,
and put away evil from thy flesh:
for childhood and youth are vanity.

ECCLESIASTES 11:10

AFTER VISITING SUSANNAH FARROW, Elijah rode home deep in thought. He decided to take a trip to San Francisco to visit his old friend George Baxter. He became acquainted with George before either of them had moved west. George had been the chief of detectives for Boston and had, two years previously, made the move to take over the San Francisco department. They had met in Boston over the affair of Liberty's first husband's murder.

As far as Elijah knew, he didn't have any clients coming in today. He tied up in front of his stately home and walked up the steps, thinking how blessed he was in so many different ways.

Thomas seemed to appear magically, opening the door before him.

"Thomas, how did you know I'd be coming home? Do you stand at the door all day and wait for me to appear?" he jested.

"No, suh. I was standing upstairs looking down at a family of quail a passin' by, an' you rode up. Is there anything I kin help you wif?"

"Yes, I decided to go to San Francisco, and I'll most likely spend the night at Liberty House."

Thomas knew that meant he'd be spending the night at Liberty's twin brother's house. He had a passel of children and a lovely wife. Elijah and Abigail had become surrogate grandparents for the children. Emily didn't have parents, and the Humphries, having no children, were a perfect match for stepping into that role.

"I'll pack a satchel for you, suh. The missus, she ain't gone down to the mission yet."

"Good, that saves time. Perhaps she'd like to go with me." He left the front entry in search of Abigail, and Thomas made his way up to Elijah's room to pack.

Elijah found Abby in the kitchen with Plechett, her maid, and Bessie having a late-morning cup of tea. He kissed Abby on the top of her head.

"Elijah, I didn't expect you back so early. Is anything wrong?" She got up swiftly and turned to peck him on the cheek.

"No, nothing wrong, my dear, but I've decided to go to San Francisco, and I'll probably stay the night. I'm glad you're not at the mission so I don't have to waste time going down there to see if you'd like to go with me."

"I'd love to go, and it won't take any time at all to pack. Plechett will help." She turned to the two women still at the table. "If there's anything you'd like to go do, you both have off until tomorrow afternoon once Elijah and I leave. I'll tell Thomas too. He might like to do something with Nelda." She winked at the two women. Nelda was the cook of one of Elijah's business partners, and Thomas was her beau. It looked as if marriage might be in the offing. Abigail loved nothing better than matchmaking. She was so in love with Elijah, she wanted everyone to be as happy.

Plechett stood up and took their teacups over to the sink. "I'll get you packed, madam," she said. She was a petit French woman with an accent. Abigail adored her, and the feeling was mutual.

"I hope you haven't started something for dinner tonight," Elijah said to Bessie. "If you have, I'm sorry to have ruined your plans."

"No, sir, I hadn't. I was planning to go on down to the mission, but now I believe I'll take the day off and do some shopping and relax. I'm reading an excellent book and have a hard time putting it down."

"What is the title?" he asked, knowing the book was from his library.

"Uncle Tom's Cabin," she replied.

"Did you know President Lincoln had the author, Harriet Beecher Stowe, to the White House? Many believed her book helped to declare war. I've read it. It's well-written and thought provoking. I read in the newspaper that it sold over three hundred thousand copies in little under a year. They say many women in Boston have named their baby girls Eva after the girl in the story—"

"Oh, I love that character. She's so upright and strong," Bessie interrupted.

"I'm glad you're enjoying it," Elijah said. "Well, I suppose I'd better get busy and pack. I need to tell Pippie to saddle up our horses. Perhaps I should shoot off a telegram to Alex and Emily to expect us tonight. Also, would you mind packing us a lunch? We'll stop either before the ferry or at the landing and have a bit to eat. Thanks, Bessie." He bussed her cheek, and she turned red as a beet. Smiling hugely, he headed out the kitchen's back door to tell Pippie to ready the horses, first recounting to himself what he needed to get done.

Liberty felt much better the next morning. She woke up feeling hungry but wanted a bath first. She opened the bathing room door to find the tub already full, the room steamy. *That Conchita knows me so well. What a blessing she is to me.* She stripped off the soft white nightgown and carefully stepped into the water, easing herself down into its silky warmth. *Better not get my head wet, with those stitches.* She reached up and felt the gauze taped into place. *At least it's not very big. I should cut my hair all off. That would be different. Except for my belly, I'd look like a boy.* She giggled. *Bet my hair would look just like Alex's. I don't think Matthew would like that. My, look at that tummy. I'm getting as big as a horse!*

She started to hum a song and then belted out "Ode to Joy." *I have never in my entire life been so happy. I don't remember ever singing much before I married Matthew.* "Lord," she prayed aloud, speaking softly, "I cannot begin to thank You enough for the change in my circumstances. I pray that my desires are aligned with Your will, that my attitudes are pleasing to You, and that I may be a blessing to others." She continued to sing while she finished bathing, delighting in the feeling of freedom, of being loved for who she was. She was a grateful woman.

Liberty donned a muslin dress with an empire waist and slipped on the *espadrilles* Conchita had given her. She brushed her hair carefully and pulled it back into a bun that covered the gauze. Fixing her hair in place with a couple combs, she hummed softly as she took a quick look in the mirror. She left the room, going down the hall to enter the kitchen, and saw Conchita's shocked face.

"You no supposed to geet up, Mees Libbee. Dr. John, he say you stay een the bed."

Liberty put a hand to her mouth, "Oh my goodness, Matthew told me that same thing yesterday, but it didn't really sink into my consciousness I guess, because I certainly forgot about it." She sat down at the kitchen table and added, "I'm really hungry. I didn't feel like eating last night, but I'm famished this morning." She started to get up to help herself, but Conchita forestalled her.

"You just seet, and I weel get you the breakfast," she said as she poured Liberty a cup of coffee first. "Perhaps you no need to stay een the bed, but you muss seet and relax for today an' tomorrow."

"All right, and thank you for having my bath all ready for me. I missed washing my hair, but that'll have to wait a few days, I suppose."

Both women heard the door open, but it was quiet, and they wondered who had come in.

Donny had sent Cady to ask Conchita if she wanted anything in Napa, as they were riding into town to get some bullets for target practice later.

Donny had said he was dumbfounded that Cady didn't know how to ride or shoot. He planned to rectify the situation as soon as he could. She'd cringed when he'd talked about rattlesnakes.

She walked softly into the kitchen, hesitant to enter the house without knocking, the way Donny had told her to do. She nodded her head at Liberty and spoke quietly to Conchita.

"Donny said to ask you if you need anything in Napa. We're riding in shortly."

"*Sí*, we haf used much honeys last night. I weel like to have some more honeys."

"All right. Anything else you can think of? Donny says you have an account, and we simply say the name Bannister, and it's written down on your account."

Conchita nodded. "*Sí*, we haf the account, but you muss be a part of Bannisters' Rancho to use eet. They muss know you at the stores."

Liberty sat with her eyes glued on the boy. Because she'd just been thinking about cutting her hair off like a boy's, she took a good look at him, struck by the thought that he looked very much like a girl. Liberty's green eyes widened.

"So you're the one who startled my horse?" she asked.

When he turned to reply, Liberty saw the bruised face and gasped.

"Yes, ma'am, and I'm sorry for it. I was lying in that cave, soaking up the sunshine, when I heard someone coming up the hill. I got up and started to come out to see who was coming, and I reckon I surprised your horse. I'm am sorry for it. It scared me when I saw you go flying through the air."

No one had spoken to Liberty about what had happened to the boy. She vaguely remembered Matthew saying something about it, but the trauma of her fall must have been worse than she thought. She couldn't remember much of the conversation from the day before, but knew she'd been sick. All of it seemed hazy. She didn't remember Dr. John being there at all, yet she had stitches. As Liberty stared at the boy, she wondered about the bruised face and how it happened, but Liberty was nothing if not circumspect when it came to relationships. If he wanted to share with her, he would.

"No one has told me about you yet. What's your name?"

"It's Cady Cassidy, ma'am. I reckon I need to get back and help Donny. He's teaching me how to saddle a horse." She felt uncomfortable under Liberty's continued perusal, and turned to Conchita. "Just the honey then?"

"*Sí*, I only need the honeys."

"Cady, how old are you?" Liberty asked abruptly.

"Uh, I'm twelve. I, uh, turned twelve a couple months back. Now, I really need to be going. Bye." Cadence turned to leave and tried to walk like Timmy would. He'd always bounced a little, but her mother had made her walk smoothly with her shoulders well back. Her eyes filled with tears as she thought of her mama. After she let herself out the door, she wiped her tears and nose on her sleeve the way Timmy did.

"Do you know what happened to his face?" Liberty asked. "He looks like a girl, don't you think?"

Conchita, startled, looked at Liberty. "*Sí*, that's what I am theenking. She no twelve-year-ole boy, no. She ees older."

"What happened to his face? I'll call him or her Cady, and for now, until we know for sure, we'll go along with *his* masquerade. I believe something is terribly wrong there. Do you know anything?"

"*Sí*, Mees Libbee. He spill the beans last night to Dr. John. He runned away from an evil father. Hees mother an' brother, they dies of the fever not two weeks gone. He was to make a fire, an' the wood was too wet, and he couldn't do eet. Hees pa, he comed home and keek heem ina ribs an' then ina face an' tie heem to the bed." Conchita wiped tears from her eyes with her apron. "I feel so bad about eet, and I keep theenking about eet today. Cady, he find he ees tied to the bed. He haf some broken glass under the bed, an' he cut the rope, an' he runned away. He one smart boy, eef he ees a boy. He look like a girl to me."

"That's horrible. It is beyond my understanding what people do to other people. So much evil—how it must sadden our Lord. You see how badly we feel about it, and we're only human with a limited perspective. Can you imagine how much worse God feels about it? It must hurt His heart to see broken relationships and hateful treatment."

"Miss Libbee, eet like your evil stepfather. He no theenk of good for anyones but heemself. Eet ees the same weeth Cady. We weel love heem so he can know what ees the right way to live." Conchita had dished up Liberty's breakfast while they were talking.

Liberty bowed her head and prayed over her food. When she finished, she said, "I agree, but I think we'll try to find out what town Cady is from. We could find out if his father is bothering to look for him so we can be prepared for whatever happens. Now, something has been niggling at my mind since I got up. Was it a dream, or did someone tell me yesterday that I'm having twins?" She smiled, pretty sure of Conchita's answer.

"Eet ees no dream, Mees Libbee. Meester Bannister, he telled you yesterday. We praise the good Lord for eet. Eet ees wonnerful. You making up for lost time, eh?"

Liberty laughed. "I suppose you could say that. I'm so thankful I wasn't hurt any worse than I was yesterday. Twins! Just think! Twins! I'd love to ride over to tell Papa and Granny. Maybe someone could ride over and invite them to dinner so we can share the good news with them."

"*Sí*, an' Meester Humphries and Mees Abby, they weel be happy for you too. Maybe you send telegram an' haf them come here. We can haf the beeg party!"

"That's a wonderful idea. Twins! It shouldn't be such a surprise, since I am one, but to me even having one baby is a miracle, and I cherish it."

"Every baby ees miracle, but tweens…eet ees special miracle."

The day was fair with a gentle breeze. Clouds puffed their way across the blue expanse at a seemingly fast pace. The sun felt warm and was a welcome change from the past couple weeks.

"I'm glad, my dear, you insisted I learn to ride," Abigail said. She was becoming quite proficient riding her gentle horse, Comet. "I should have learned to do this years ago, but even at my age it's become enjoyable. I can understand why Liberty enjoys it so much. I never knew how comfortable a split skirt is either." Her skirt was much longer than Liberty's, but her boots showed several inches, and Abigail felt quite liberated, showing so much boot.

They rode at a steady pace to the ferry in Sausalito. It ran five times a day and was nearly always on time.

"It'll be good to see Alex, Emily, and the children. I'm glad he had his middle name of Liberty become his last name, as it should have been at birth.

"A lot of men don't have a middle name, do they." Abby didn't ask a question but rather made a statement. She went on to say, "I do love that family, and it's exciting that Liberty's having a baby, as well as Emily. Too, I'm grateful for Alex and Emily asking us to be grandparents." Abigail added, with a grin, "I don't believe I've had so much fun in all my days."

"I haven't either," Elijah replied. "I thank God for the gift of Liberty, Alex, and now Adam in our lives. God has given us the children we never had and has blessed us with grandchildren we couldn't love any more than if they were blood relatives. My goodness, we're already here. That seemed like a short ride, didn't it?"

Seagulls swooped down on the freshening breeze, and terns rode the waves that slapped against the pilings, the smell of salt tangy in the air. There was a large wagon and a carriage ahead of them. Gazing out they could see the ferry was halfway back from San Francisco. Abby and Elijah dismounted and stood beside their mounts, continuing to talk as they waited.

"Why do you want to see George?" Abigail asked.

"Oh, I have a few things that I would like to run by him to see what he thinks. I hope he's not deeply involved in a case right now or too busy for me to take up his time. He's a good man, and I'm grateful to have such a resource to discuss ideas and get his opinion on some things."

"You visited Susannah today, didn't you? How is she doing?"

"She's not well, and Tess said Dr. Huffman can't seem to find what the problem is."

"Poor thing. She's had a lot to bear. I'll be sure to go visit her when we get back. She's a lovely lady, and losing Oscar in such a manner has to be a devastating shock to her. I do hope whatever is wrong physically isn't too very serious." Abigail looked at Elijah with a question mark in her blue eyes, sensing something but not knowing what it was.

"I believe it is serious," he answered. "Tess said she's not at all well, and of course coupled with the mourning of Oscar, she's depressed along with the illness. Not a good combination, I'm afraid."

"No, no it's not. I'll see what I can do about cheering her up when we get home." Abigail was thinking to maybe get Susannah down to the mission to meet some of the girls who were now there, but if she were too sick to get out, it wouldn't be a viable solution.

The ferry slid into its slip with expert precision. Elijah never tired of watching the pilot guide it in. He and Abigail watched as the horses in front of them balked at getting onto the ferry. Elijah, with a couple other men, helped the driver, but they had to put cloths over the pair of horses' eyes to get them onto the ferry. The driver thanked them profusely and left the blinds on until they disembarked on the San Francisco side.

Elijah and Abigail headed downtown for some needed shopping and then on to Liberty House, looking forward to their evening.

CHAPTER VIII

A merry heart doeth good like a medicine:
but a broken spirit drieth the bones.

PROVERBS 17:22

AMOS KEPLER FIRST WENT TO HIS SCHOOL to make sure everyone was doing their job properly. He always called it *his* school in his mind. He'd worked hard to make the school one that the townsfolk knew was of high repute. He took his job seriously. After reprimanding one of the staff for being late, he made his way to the Farrow mansion. Tess let him in, and as she went to tell Susannah that Mr. Kepler was calling, he looked at himself in the long, narrow mirror in the parlor, straightening his cravat. Smiling at himself, he whistled softly under his breath. *You're a fine specimen of a man, Amos Kepler. Yes siree, you are.*

Tess returned and announced, "Mrs. Farrow will be with you shortly, Mr. Kepler. She asked me to ask you if you would like to have some tea."

"Yes, that would be nice, Tess." He spread his coattails apart before he sat on the settee, to avoid wrinkling them. He checked his fingernails to be sure they were clean and tugged his shirt cuffs down slightly to make sure they showed just the right length below his frock coat sleeves.

Before Susannah came in, Tess entered the parlor with an intricately carved tea trolley. It rolled silently with barely a whisper of turning wheels, and so smoothly, not even the cups rattled. Tess had never liked

Mr. Kepler. She simply nodded at him as she took her leave. He sat there waiting, a bit impatiently, for his hostess, drumming his fingers on the arm of the settee. He looked around the elegant room with pleasure for the tasteful accouterments.

"Mr. Kepler, how nice of you to come see me." Susannah entered wearing a beautiful black silk dress. There were no furbelows to it, no noticeable buttons nor lace, but she looked elegant in its simplicity.

"Good morning, Mrs. Farrow." He stood up abruptly. "I do hope you're feeling better."

"I'm sure I'm quite fine, sir."

She proffered one hand, and he bent over it, his lips hovering close. She could feel his breath on the back of her hand and withdrew it quickly as he clicked his heels in the Prussian style and bobbed his head slightly.

Tess had followed her in and announced "Tea, madam" as she wheeled the trolley nearer to the coffee table. She laid out the two cups and saucers along with the tea service on the coffee table.

"I'll leave you now," she said.

"Please, be seated, Mr. Kepler. Two sugars, is that correct?"

"Yes, madam, but no milk."

Susannah sat and poured them both tea, adding scones to the small serving plates. She got up slowly, energy already expended by dressing, and went to the window to look at the sunshine.

"I know it sounds mundane, but the rain was better in keeping with my spirits. I feel totally adrift without my dear Oscar. The sunshine almost seems an affront to my mourning." She turned as Mr. Kepler took a sip of his tea.

He swallowed and said, "Madam, please join me. You need sustenance to keep up your strength. One cannot hope to get better nor to improve one's spirits without nourishment. Come," he said again and beckoned to her, patting the place next to him on the settee.

Susannah looked at him, a light coming on in her brain as she became aware of his intense perusal. The blood came up and into her cheeks. She realized for the first time his visits had a purpose, and it was not to improve her spirits. His visits were more than simply being friendly or attentive. Was he really looking to court her in the future? She looked at him steadily, meeting his hazel-green eyes with her beautiful gray ones.

"Mr. Kepler, perhaps I'm being presumptuous in stating to you that I don't ever plan to marry again, and I think it best if you leave off visiting me for some time. I, as you know, am deeply mourning my Oscar, and I'm not sure if I'll ever get over losing him." She picked up the servants' bell, giving it a healthy shake, to summon Tess.

Amos stood, the blood suffusing his cheeks. She couldn't tell if it was anger or embarrassment, but she didn't care either way.

"Good day, Mr. Kepler." She spoke softly but firmly.

"I'm sorry you feel this way, madam. I am sorry to have troubled you. I have no designs on your personage. Good day."

He left on his own, not waiting for Tess to come show him out. He collected his top hat in the front entry before closing the door after him with a decided click.

"He was quite angry," Susannah said aloud. "Now, why would that be?" She took a sip of tea, but it had cooled, and she didn't care to drink it. She sat for a time thinking about the visit, surprising herself with her thoughts. *I don't even care if I offended him. Perhaps it isn't nice of me, but I don't simply don't care right now. I am so weary.*

She called for Tess. "Mr. Kepler has left. If he returns in the near future, I am indisposed to him. I thought him to be kind, Tess, but I think he envisioned us to marry sometime in the future. Insane, isn't it?" She smiled up at Tess.

"Oh, madam, he's a cold one, and frankly speaking, it was audacious for him to come calling when you're still mourning your poor Mr. Farrow, begging your pardon for saying so."

"Yes, it took me unawares. He's been coming for nearly six weeks now, at least two times a week, if not more. Audacious is a good word, Tess. And now I believe I'm going back to bed." She went slowly up the stairs, and Tess helped to get her out of the beautiful black dress.

"Thank you, Tess. I am grateful you not only work for me, but that you're my friend. I can tell you anything. Yes, audacious is a good word for Mr. Kepler." She smiled wanly at her faithful servant, who helped her don her sleeping gown.

She got into bed, and Tess drew the covers up over her shoulders, worry for her mistress evident in her eyes.

Donny and Cady rode into Napa at a walk. It was very slow going, but Donny realized Cady was afraid of the horse. It surprised him a bit because most boys wanted nothing more than to ride and shoot. The boy hadn't seemed afraid riding behind him the other day, but now his eyes were enormous.

They tied up at the hitching post in front of the mercantile. Cady, watching how Donny slapped the reins on the post, tried it, and they wound sufficiently around, so she looked over at Donny and grinned at her success.

"Good job, Cady," he said, knowing the lad craved approval. He started to slap him on the back, but wondered how much of him was bruised, so didn't.

They went into the mercantile and bought bullets, but not on the Bannisters' account.

"How come you didn't charge it to the Bannisters' account?" Cady asked. She had been slowly walking around the store in wonder of all the items they could buy.

"I don't use their account for purchases that have nothing to do with the Rancho," Donny answered. "It's strictly to be used for items they ask me to get."

"Where do we buy the honey?"

"We'll go over to Diebel's General Store. The Diebels opened their store not long ago, and it's got almost any kind of food, as well as material and such that a body could want. It's amazing what a business can carry. I saw you lookin' in the mercantile store, but just you wait. Your eyes are going to pop out of your head when you see the merchandise in Diebel's."

The two of them walked companionably down the boarded walk. All the sudden, Cady saw a man coming out of the saloon. Her pa. He was shaved and cleaned up, but the walk was unmistakable, and she recognized his shirt. It was what caught her attention.

"Donny!" She took hold of his arm and swung him around in the direction they'd just come. "It's my pa, Donny!" she said, her voice low. "Don't turn around and look, but it's my pa who just came out of that saloon. He'll recognize my clothes if he looks this way!"

Donny shoved her toward the alleyway, into the dimness caused by the building's shadow. "You stay put!" he said. "I want to take a good look at him so I'll know what to look for if ever he comes around. Now, I mean it—don't move!" He casually went back around the building and leaned against its front as he watched the man who'd just come out of the saloon. He stared hard at him, memorizing his every feature. He knew he needed to pray for that man and love him with the love of Christ, but he didn't, and he knew it. He wanted to beat the man to a pulp for what he'd done to Cady.

He nonchalantly headed toward the saloon and watched as Cady's father climbed a bit unsteadily onto his horse and rode out of town. Donny hurried back to the alley.

"Your pa's gone, Cady. He rode out of town. Do you want me to go ask the bartender who he was looking for?"

"No!" She nearly shouted, loud to her own ears. Softly, she added, "Uh…no, no I don't. I know who he's looking for. He's looking for me."

She shuddered, and Donny pulled her to him and patted her back.

"It's all right, Cady. I won't let him touch you. Not ever again will he beat you. Are you listening to me, son? He's never going to touch you again. He's gone now. He's probably riding from town to town, asking about you."

"I know." Cady wanted to lay her head on his chest. The comfort she derived from this young man was something she'd never experienced. She pulled back and looked up into his clear blue eyes. "Do you think he's done asking around here?"

"I don't know, Cady. I have no idea what his plans are. C'mon," he said. "Let's forget about him and enjoy going to Diebel's." He pulled her by the arm and started for the general store.

Donny walked jauntily, wanting to impart a carefree attitude to Cady. He felt an overwhelming sense of protection for Cady, and it puzzled him that he felt so strongly about the boy.

They entered Diebel's General Store, and Cady saw why Donny had spoken so highly about it. It had all kinds of merchandise. In the front window, as they entered, was a mannequin dressed in a beautiful blue dress. Cady stopped dead and gazed at it in admiration. She'd never seen anything so beautiful. Her jaw dropped when she saw all the goods contained in the store. She hadn't told Donny she'd only been in a few buildings. Now she could add the Bannisters' beautiful house, the clean barn and tack room where she slept, the mercantile, and now this...this store that filled her with wonder.

Donny grinned. "Look around, Cady. We've got some time for you to just look and enjoy what they have to sell." He leaned back against the doorjamb and watched as the boy slowly went up and down the aisles, wonder and astonishment clearly evident on his face. Donny saw him look at the bolts of material stacked against the wall, and his hand went up to feel the different types of fabric. He thought it strange the boy would bother looking at fabric, but then Cady was a different kind of boy. He looked at the hats and feathers, shawls and frock coats too.

Cadence walked slowly through the store, awed. There wasn't just one of each thing either, but an abundance of some of the items, and different styles too. She stopped at the honey and went to the end of that aisle and beckoned Donny with her hand.

"Look at that. There are three different sizes of honey. Which one do you think Conchita wants, big, medium, or small?"

"She'll want the biggest one. She doesn't use it only for her *sopapillas* but for other things as well. She sure is a good cook. You'll like eating at the Bannisters. They'll fatten you up some."

She grinned. "I already like her cooking. Dinner was wonderful, and breakfast...I've never eaten such a delicious meal in all my born days. All right, I'm going to get this one then. It's heavy, isn't it?" she said as she took the big glass jar of honey down. Donny took it from her.

"It's a half gallon, and honey's heavy." Donny took it to the front counter, which had huge jars of all kinds of candy. He had a sweet tooth and asked, "What's your favorite kind of candy?"

She answered softly, not wanting the clerk, who had stepped up to help them, hear her. "I don't know, Donny. I've never had any before."

Donny looked at the boy, stupefied by his confession. "Well, let me introduce you to peppermints," he said. "You're going to love this." He turned importantly toward the counter and said, "This honey is to be charged to the Bannisters' account, but I'd also like ten peppermints not charged to their bill. I'll pay for them."

The clerk nodded his head and said, "How are you today, Donald Miller?"

"I'm fine, thank you. How are you, Abraham?"

"Fair ta middling, fair ta middling on this fine day. Grateful the rain has stopped, to be sure. Slows down customers, that's fer certain. Reckon now your grapes can be harvested."

"Yes, we're going to be very busy for the next few weeks at Bannisters'."

Abraham cut a piece of waxed paper and picked up a pair of large tongs. He took the glass lid off the peppermints and reached in to get them one at a time, counting out as he laid them on the paper.

Cady, who was standing right next to the jar, could smell the mint. Her mouth watered up in anticipation. Her eyes were large with excitement, and Donny smothered a laugh when he looked at her.

"Don't wrap the last two please. We'll have them now," he said.

Abraham dropped one into his hand and one into Cady's, who waited until they were out of the store to pop it into her mouth. Her eyes opened in amazement as the flavor exploded in her cheeks and tongue.

Pushing it over to one side, her cheek bulged out as she said, "Donny, this is a day I will never forget. Thank you!"

"You are welcome, Cady. You are very welcome."

Hannibal Cassidy went from town to town asking around if anyone had seen a strange girl. He told people she was of age but a bit demented and had wandered off. He said, pitifully, that his wife, who had taken care of the girl all these years, was very worried.

So far, he'd hit a total dead end. No one knew anything, and no one seemed to have seen her. He wondered if she were smart enough to travel only at night. It began to make sense, as people who lived near the main road had seen no girl traveling by herself.

Hannibal had cleaned himself up and realized that he felt better with his beard shaved off and a clean set of clothes. Callie had kept everything as clean as she could, and his children had always looked neatly dressed, even in old, patched clothing. He wondered again about the legal papers in the satchel and all that beautiful money. If he hadn't been so drunk, he'd still have it. He cursed himself under his breath, but the lure of alcohol was too much for him, and he continued to drink, loving the fog of unrealized dreams rather than his reality.

He realized he was headed in the direction of San Rafael, but if she knew nothing about her mother's side of the family, she might have gone south to Stockton. That town was booming, and she could lose herself there very easily. For some reason, he felt she'd headed west.

He rode out of Napa and said aloud, "I'll find her. I jist know I'm gonna find her."

CHAPTER IX

*For wisdom is better than rubies; and all the things
that may be desired are not to be compared to it.*

PROVERBS 8:11

ELIJAH AND ABIGAIL HAD a late lunch. The two had gone into the city
to do their shopping, which was limited because of being on horseback.

"There are definite advantages to having a carriage in the city," Abby
remarked drily, having seen some things she would have purchased. "But
I've enjoyed the ride on Comet."

"You can always get what you need and have them hold it. Then you
could come back with the carriage to collect it. We could do that
tomorrow, if you like."

"No, I don't want to do that. I purchased the few things I had on my
list, but I'll come down here and do a big shop some other day. You are
sweet, Elijah, to suggest it. I know how you hate to wait around in stores
for me. I'd rather shop when I don't feel like I'm making you wait while I
hem and haw about making decisions."

They headed slowly toward their destination, riding in a leisurely
fashion along the coast, enjoying the scenery. They would stop every so

often to watch the water break on the shore or watch the seagulls swoop down and scream out their delight. By the time they rode to Liberty House, the sun had hidden itself behind a bank of clouds, and a heavy fog had rolled in.

They rode to the back of the stately edifice because they were family, their horses' hooves clip-clopping on the cobbles. Renny came out of the stable, ready to take their horses.

"Good afternoon, Mr. Humphries, Mrs. Humphries. Nice to see you again. We received your telegram just a short while ago. Everyone in the house is excited to see you. Xander is hopping with excitement, and I officially welcome you to Liberty House." He grinned as he helped Abigail with her satchel.

"Thank you, Renny. We appreciate the warm welcome," Elijah said.

"Yes, we do, and thank you. We're looking forward to an evening of entertainment," Abigail said, her blue eyes sparkling with anticipation. "The children are so well behaved and a delight to be around."

They went over to the back door, which opened into a large, enclosed back porch and into the huge kitchen. They didn't have to open the door though.

Every few minutes Xander had been spying out the back porch, hoping to see Elijah and Abigail ride up. He missed them riding up but saw them starting across the cobbles. He opened the door with a flourish and bent over in a grand gesture, waving them into the enclosed porch.

"Oh, I'm so excited you're here. Oh, Abigran, welcome!" Xander gave her a big hug, but he was all eyes for Elijah. He knew Elijah loved him best, and the feeling was mutual.

"Granpajah, I love you," he said simply, and then he enveloped Elijah in a bear hug. Xander had named Elijah and Abigail a couple years back with the endearing names all the children used when addressing their surrogate grandparents.

"I love you, too, Xander Liberty—you are a special gift to me from God." Elijah hugged Xander to himself. "Goodness, you are growing young man. Look how tall you are now." He put his palm on Xander's head, and Xander ducked out of it to look up.

"Yes, I yam getting really big. I'm seven years old already, and I have chores and help Renny in the stable too."

Elijah ruffled his hair. "Well, you certainly are getting taller."

Arm and arm they entered the kitchen, which was overrun with children. Eleven-year-old Penelope Hope was trying to catch Jonathan Jay, who was almost three. He was giggling and running around to get away from her. Alexandra Anne, who was nine, was holding Phoebe, nearly two. Their nanny, Jane, was sick in bed, and Emily, their mother, was expecting her sixth baby. She looked exhausted but smiled a warm welcome.

She wrapped her arms around Abby and gave Elijah a kiss on the cheek. "I'm delighted you could break away from all your commitments and come visit us. Is this a short holiday or a needed business trip?" She was curious because generally they had over a week's warning before the Humphries made an appearance.

"I have a bit of business, but nothing dire. Abby is just along for the ride. She wanted to come and see you all. It's good to see you, my dear." Elijah kissed Emily on her cheek.

"Oh, I am so glad you're here. Alex isn't home yet, but he will be soon unless something delays him. He'll be pleased to spend the evening with you, as will I. Come. We can go to my sitting room and enjoy a little quiet."

Elijah and Abigail started to follow Emily, but Xander pulled on Elijah's sleeve.

"Wait, Granpajah. I want to show you my horse. Papa bought me my very own horse for my birthday! Can you come out to the stable with me, please, Granpajah? Oh, she's such a beautiful horse. You're gonna love her."

"I'd be pleased to go look at her." He made an apologetic face to the two women and said, "Excuse me. I won't be long, but it's getting dark, and I want to see Xander's horse without a lantern." He took Xander by the hand and said, "Let's go see her. What's her name?"

"I named her Minx cuz she's got a personality that makes you love her and cuz she lipped my hat right off my head!" He grinned at Elijah, his eyes shining his pleasure at having Granpajah to himself, a rarity in a houseful of children.

"That's a good name for a horse," Elijah responded as he stepped with alacrity down the back steps.

They strolled hand in hand across the cobbles to the stable, and Xander proudly opened Minx's stall.

"Oh my, she *is* a beauty. Look at her markings." Elijah was impressed. "What kind of horse is she?"

"She's an American Saddlebred. Papa told me that General Lee and General Grant and General Sherman all had Saddlebreds. He said Stonewall Jackson had one too, so it's gotta be a good horse, don't ya think?"

"Yes, of course I do, Xander. She sure is beautiful. Have you ridden her much?"

"Yes, I rides her every day. Papa said she's the kind of horse that can't stand around in her stable all day and that if she's my horse, I needs ta exercise her every day. I really yam getting better 'n' better, and I can even jump over little streams now. Oh! Here comes Papa. He'll be so glad you're here."

Alex came riding into the back courtyard, his horse's hooves clattering on the cobblestones.

Renny came running down stairs inside the stable. He had a loft apartment and loved the privateness of it, but also the ability to hear anyone coming into the back area. He grabbed the reins of Alex's horse and steadied him as his employer dismounted.

As Elijah and Xander exited the stable, Alex's face registered pleased surprise at Elijah's presence.

"Why, hello there, Elijah! It gladdens my heart you're here! Hello to you, Xander. Been showing Elijah your horse, eh?"

"Yes, sir, and I thank you again for her, Papa. I'll be thanking you forever! She's beautiful an' perfect, and you couldn't have gotten a better horse for me than Minx."

Elijah said, "She is a gorgeous horse. It's good to see you, Alex. I'm glad we can come barely announced and feel so welcome."

"You are welcome here anytime. I look forward to an evening of good fellowship," Alex responded. "I didn't get the message you were coming, but it is a pleasant surprise. Is Abigail with you?"

"Yes, I have a bit of business with George Baxter, but she wanted to come just to spend some time with you, Emily, and the children."

Alex clapped Elijah on the back and took Xander's hand in his as they mounted the back stairs.

The evening was warm, and after all the chores were finished, Cadence washed up. When she was finished, she went to Donny's room over the loft. He'd asked her to come up and play cards. He'd been showing her how to play rummy and double-deck solitaire. She thought it great fun and wondered how life could feel so wonderful and different than anything she'd ever experienced.

She felt relaxed and trouble-free about spending time with Donny. He was easy to be around and a very nice young man. He laughed a lot and made her laugh too. They'd played rummy, and she beat him for the first time. Instead of being upset, he'd praised her, slapping her on the back and telling her how smart she was. Next, they'd played double-deck solitaire, but she wasn't fast enough at it, and he beat her every time.

Later, he tousled her hair and told her it was time for bed, thanking her for the good time. She'd left and come down to the tack room, still amazed every time she entered it at how pretty it was. She didn't care that it smelled like leather. It was a clean smell, and she liked it.

She donned her brother's pajamas, patched and worn thin. Cadence could not remember when she'd been so relaxed or at ease. She sat on the edge of the bed. *For as long as I can remember, I've always been on edge, wondering what Pa would do next. I was never carefree. Oh, there'd be moments when he'd be gone and Mama would bring out snips of paper she'd saved and try to teach Timmy and me how to write or read our letters. This is the most wonderful time I can ever remember having. No one is angry with someone else, and everyone seems to be so considerate. I don't have to worry I've done something I'll get a beating for.*

That morning she'd accidentally kicked over the milk bucket. She'd milked the cow, her forehead leaning contentedly against the cow's side. When she got up, the three-legged stool somehow tipped, and stepping out of the way, she'd stumbled heavily into the milk bucket. She'd scrabbled to upright the bucket before it all drained out, only managing to save a little. With shaking hands she'd taken the bit of milk and showed Donny what she'd done. She hadn't cried, just bravely said, "I'm really sorry about this. I spilt the milk bucket."

Donny had seen her shaking hands as she handed him the little bit of milk that was saved.

"Yes, it happens," he'd said nonchalantly. "I did that same thing only last week." He grinned. "It's just as well. Conchita told me she didn't need much milk today. They keep it cold in the ice house, and she still has some leftover from yesterday. Don't worry about it, boy." He'd ruffled her hair.

She'd been amazed. As she fluffed her feather pillow, she realized all the people here had said they believed in God. She put elbows on her knees and her chin in her hands and thought and thought. *Does that make them so easy to get along with? Is that why there's a peaceful feeling around here?*

Her mind jumped back to what happened the day before, seeing her pa come out of the saloon.

That was frightening. What if he'd have seen me? Wonder if he'll come back around here? He must really want the money in that satchel, because he sure doesn't want me.

She decided to look into the red leather satchel. She took a deep breath, her side paining her, and got down on her knees, reaching under the bed for the bag. She knew it would be some time before her ribs didn't throb every time she moved. She pulled the tooled leather bag out and sat on the floor, staring at it with more than a little curiosity.

Cadence realized the floor was cold, so she crawled up to sit cross-legged on the bed, simply holding the tooled leather bag. It was shiny and glowed in the lamplight, and her fingers traced the tooling on the satchel. *Where in the world did Pa get this?* she wondered. *It's beautiful. Wonder, did he steal it? I've certainly never seen the likes of it in our house.* She dumped the entire contents out between her crossed legs and stared in total amazement. There was money and the thick sheaf of papers she'd seen before, but there were jewels too, some in settings and some loose. *He must have stolen it or robbed someone.* She picked up a beautiful purple ring set with diamonds all around it. She didn't know anything about diamonds or stones, but she could see it was beautiful and slipped it on her finger. It fit, a little loosely, but enough that if she wanted she could wear it and not lose it. She smiled thinking how grand it was and how ridiculous to think she could wear it posing as a boy. *Perhaps I should take the satchel to the sheriff in Napa. He would know how to find the real owner of it, I'll wager.* She picked up some other pieces of jewelry; the stones were gorgeous when she held them up to the light. She scooped up the stones and let them slide through her fingers, loving the play of light on the facets.

She unfolded the papers but didn't know enough about reading to figure out what they were. She did see her name, Cadence Jean Cassidy, and Timmy's name, Timothy John Cassidy. Her mother's name was there too. Callie Susannah Farrow. She sounded it out, speaking softly. In

Cady's mind, it should have read Callie Susannah Cassidy. *I didn't even know my mother's middle name. Wonder why it says Farrow and not Cassidy?*

So, I reckon Pa didn't steal this, but where did it come from? If he knew about it for very long, all the money would have been spent in the saloon. So where in the world did it come from? He must have just got it, because I know it wasn't under the bed the day before. Without his name on these papers, all this must have belonged to Mama.

She started to pile the money up and had no idea how much there was, but there was quite a stack of it. She sifted through the jewelry and saw two more rings, a brilliant-green one and a deep-red one, both surrounded by diamonds. She didn't know what kind of stones they were, but they had matching necklaces.

Cadence put everything back into the beautiful satchel and wondered if she should continue to hide it under the bed or if she should look for another spot. *I won't be taking it to the sheriff, 'cause it's not stolen. I'll wager Pa's looking for me...desperately looking for me.* She decided it would be best to leave the satchel under the bed. If she put it somewhere else, someone might come across it. No one seemed to come into this room unless they were saddling up a horse.

She got back onto her hands and knees and slid herself under the bed a bit, putting the satchel up near the head of the bed and back against the wall. Getting up, she brushed herself off and blew out the lantern. Quietly, she opened the door and slipped out into the main area of the stable and out a side door of the barn. It was a beautiful night, and she stood and looked at the stars and the moon and thought about her mama and Timmy. Tears slid silently down her cheeks. She was very grateful for Donny and the Bannisters taking her in, but oh, how she missed Mama and Timmy!

Elijah and Abby enjoyed their evening. Dinner had been a family affair, the children eating with the adults instead of in the nursery. It was a noisy but amusing meal. Elijah and Abby adored the children and were interested in listening to their conversation and watching their interactions. Finally, the children were all in bed, and Elijah, Abby, Alex, and Emily, along with Alex's nana, Penelope, sat in the parlor talking. Penelope was eighty-two, and although she had slowed down some, she was still a vibrant part of the family and sharp as a tack.

Emily said, "I hope you don't mind, but I need to elevate my feet." She started to rise, but Alex held out a hand to forestall her.

"I'll get it, darling," he said as he got up and pulled an ottoman over to the love seat they were sitting on. "Are you feeling all right?"

"Yes, just immensely tired. My ankles are swelling." She laughed as she glanced at the others, and added, "Indeed I'm swollen all over, aren't I?" Her violet blue eyes looked into Alex's, laughing away her discomfort. Her pregnancy was nearly over.

He picked up her legs, set her feet on the ottoman, and leaned over to kiss her forehead. "I love you," he whispered. He turned to Elijah and Abigail, asking, "Abigail, were you able to get much shopping done?"

"I certainly was, although I couldn't buy much because I'm on horseback, but it is amazing how much a saddlebag can hold," Abby said with a little smile curving her lips upward. She sipped her apple juice contentedly. With her legs stretched out before her, she leaned back comfortably against the cushy wingback chair.

"And you, Elijah? Just business, or pleasure too?" Alex asked.

"Both," he replied promptly. "I enjoy being with you and the children, but as I said earlier, I will be going to see George tomorrow on a small matter. He doesn't know I'm coming and may be too busy to see me. It's not anything dire—at least, I hope it's not." He smiled at Alex and continued, wanting to change the subject. "It's interesting that our new president has promised not to fire any Republican who is doing his job well. I believe President Cleveland will do a good job even though he's had no formal education. He's promised he won't hire anyone on the basis of party lines. It's refreshing, isn't it?" Elijah's ploy was successful, and the conversation veered toward politics.

Chapter X

The spirit of God hath made me,
and the breath of the Almighty hath given me life.

JOB 33:4

THE NEXT MORNING DAWNED BRIGHT AND FAIR. Matthew, lying on his side and facing the window, opened his eyes slowly. He stretched carefully so as not to awaken Liberty. Gazing out the window at the beautiful blueness of sky, he saw fluffy clouds scudding across the heavens. *The mud will be drying up*, he thought. *It's time to start harvesting the grapes.*

The evening before, he and Diego had gone through and checked the vines, tasting the fruit for sweetness and acidity. They knew there had to be a good balance between the sugar and the tannins. They would start harvesting where the grapes were ripest. A couple weeks before, they'd had workers strip some of the leaves from the vines to help the grapes ripen. He took a deep breath as he thought of all that needed done.

The next few weeks were going to be very busy, and he hoped they'd be finished before the babies came. The more he thought about it, the more he realized it wouldn't matter. He'd be here and available whenever Liberty went into labor.

He rolled over carefully, only to find Liberty was wide awake. He scooted closer and cuddled her, kissing her cheek and then her lips.

"I love you, Liberty Bannister. And why are you awake so early when you should be sound asleep?"

"Good morning to you, Matthew." She yawned. "I don't know, except I keep thinking about Cady. You know, Matthew, there's something about that boy that keeps niggling at the back of my mind."

"Don't you trust him?"

"Oh, it's nothing like that. Yes, I do trust him. It's just there's something that doesn't ring true. It keeps dancing around the fringes of my mind. Conchita and I talked about it, and both of us came to the same conclusion, yet neither one of us are sure."

"What conclusion did you two come up with?"

His eyes twinkled at her, and she could see he thought she and Conchita were imagining things.

"We think our Cady is not a twelve-year-old boy, but a girl, and older."

Matthew raised up on his elbow and stared at his wife with shocked eyes. "Why in the world would you think that?"

"Just look at him, *or her*." Liberty smiled because she didn't really know the answer herself. It was simply a feeling, and to her, Cady looked too delicate to be a boy.

"Well, let me see," Matthew replied. "You have an excuse, knocking your head the way you did, but Conchita has no excuse." He laughed down at Liberty.

"It's not a jest, Matthew. I'm serious. Take a good look at Cady today, and see what you think. I'm not imagining things, even if I did take a good bump on the head."

"I'm grateful you weren't hurt more than you were. It could have been a lot worse. I do love you so much." He traced her lips with his forefinger and, raising up on one elbow, kissed her long and deep.

She put her hands on both sides of his face and kissed him back. They both pulled back and stared at each other with flickers of warmth in their eyes, green meeting deep blue.

"I am so grateful God ordered our circumstances. I don't believe I'd ever have left Boston if it hadn't been for Elijah, and I would never have met you. I love you, Matthew. With all my heart, I love you."

"I don't believe I'd have ever let go of all my anger without your influence on my life. I love you back, Liberty Alexandra Bannister. With all my heart, I love you."

Matthew kissed Liberty's nose and announced, "Today, we begin harvest. I want you to relax and not do any of it this year. You're allowed to walk around and observe, but nothing else. No cutting grapes or trampling them this year for you, my dear! And if that niggling thought ends up being true, I think we should move Cady into a bedroom in the house. Did Donny tell you they saw Cady's father in Napa yesterday? Cady hid, and Donny watched the man ride out of Napa. He was going to talk to the bartender because Cady's father had come out of the saloon, but Cady said no, there was nothing to be gained from asking the bartender. Now I'm having problems thinking of Cady as a boy. It could be the reason *she* didn't want Donny to talk to the bartender."

His blue eyes were serious as he spoke, and then he added, "What cruelty for a man to kick a child like that in the face. Why, I wouldn't treat Boston that way."

Boston, who heard his name, jumped onto the bed, and that was the end of conversation. Liberty started giggling as Matthew tried to pull the big puppy off the bed. Boston dug in his feet for the fun game.

Matthew swung his legs over the side and stood up. "Are you hungry, Boston?"

The dog, ears perked, tipped his head from side to side, seeming to understand Matthew. He jumped off the bed and headed to the door, which was closed.

"In a few minutes, boy, in a few minutes." Matthew went around the bed, kissed Liberty again, and headed to the bathing room, closing the door firmly behind him. He didn't need Boston nosing at him while he shaved. He'd cut himself once when that happened. Once finished with shaving, he donned clean denims and a checkered shirt, and checking on Liberty, saw that she'd fallen back asleep.

Dog and master headed for the kitchen and the wonderful smells that wafted into the hall.

Conchita was frying bacon and making omelets. Lupe was busy chopping green peppers, onions, mushrooms, and tomatoes, while Luce was shredding cheese.

"Good morning, Meester Bannister. You ees up early. You starting the grapes today, noh? Diego, he out weeth the mens to geet them ready."

"Good morning. Sure smells good in here. Yes, we're starting today. I told the men yesterday that if the sun came up this morning, we were picking. We've a big day ahead of us, but it feels right to me. Looks like you're going to start me out right."

He found scraps, and going out into the covered part of the courtyard, fed Boston, who wagged his tail the whole time he ate. Matthew rinsed off his hands and poured himself some coffee. Taking his Bible off a shelf, he sat down to read while he waited for breakfast.

The sun was up streaking the sky with colorful brilliance over the foothills. The air, crisp and cool with a very slight breeze, made Cady not want to stand in one place very long. She kept moving and rubbing her arms to keep the chill off.

Donny and Cady were standing with the hired hands. Every one of the regular hires, as well as many itinerant workers, were milling around talking as they waited for instructions. Donny had taken Cady aside and explained to her a little about the grapes.

"Just like you, I've never been in a harvest before, but Mr. Bannister and Diego and even Mr. Liberty, Miss Liberty's father, have coached me on what to expect. When they start talking about the grapes, they get all excited about it." He smiled in remembrance and continued, "I was here when veraison took place, and Mr. Bannister showed me. It's when the ripening grapes begin to soften and the color changes from green to red. He told me that it's when the grape sugars start to accumulate in the grape berry. They have to wait to harvest until the grapes are fully ripe because grapes don't ripen any more once they're picked. Timing is crucial. They were worried about the rain, but it seems like it's going to be all right. I saw Mr. Bannister and Diego looking at the grapes yesterday, and they said the color, bunch size, berry size, and sugar content were perfect. They'll show us how to pick them. If these grapes weren't for wine but for table grapes, we'd have to pick them very carefully to not bruise the fruit. Diego said because these grapes are for wine, we can pick at a fast pace. They're all going to be crushed anyway."

When Matthew came out of the house, all the workers perked up, knowing he would get things rolling. Liberty, Conchita, Luce, and Lupe came out after him to witness the beginning of harvest.

"Thank you all for being here," Matthew said, looking around to assure himself he had enough workers. "Diego and I will show you how to cut the grapes using these billhooks." Matthew pointed to a basket full of what looked to be miniature sickles, but the blade was not curved as much. "Each of you take one, and we'll soon start."

Donny picked up the basket and said to Cady, "I picked these up last week from the blacksmith where Matthew had them made. Here, pass them around to all the workers so they can get one."

Cady picked up the heavy-duty basket and began walking around the circle of workers.

Once everyone had one, Matthew said, "I would like to dedicate this harvest to the Lord before we begin. Let's pray." He took off his hat, and so did all the workers. "Lord God," he prayed, "how we do thank You that You are Lord of the harvest. We are grateful You make things to grow and bear fruit. We pray that we can do that in our spiritual lives, but right now we want to dedicate this harvest of grapes to You. We pray You bless this harvest of 1885. May it be a good year. We also thank You for being with Liberty, and may she enjoy the harvest this year as a bystander. We pray this in Thy wondrous name. Amen."

Everyone started clapping and cheering. Matthew held up his hand and said, "Thank you. Those of you who've harvested before, pick one of these rows here and get started. The rest of you, circle there around Diego. He will show you how to cut the stems, as well as what a bunch looks like when they're not ready to be picked."

Diego had been translating for those who didn't understand English. He went to the end of a row and demonstrated slowly a couple times, cutting the stem of the bunch of grapes, and then he started cutting very fast, yet careful of the bunch he held in his hand. The work began.

Susannah Farrow awoke from a deep sleep. She lay quietly for a long time until she realized sleep had definitely eluded her. It was still dark, and the stillness was peaceful, yet she felt an overwhelming feeling of loss.

She lay for a while, thinking of happier times. "Oh Lord, I miss dear Oscar. If one more person says to me Thou needest him more than me, I think I shall punch them in the nose. It's not true, and Thou knowest it full well. How people can be so insensitive, I'll never know. Though Oscar and I never had a romantic love, I grew to love him in a manner outside of romance. For that, Father, I thank You. He was a gentle, kind soul. Thy word says in Ephesians that I must respect my husband, and I did. Oscar was wise."

She sat up, lit a taper, and touched it to the lamp beside her bed. It never ceased to amaze her how such a little light could dispel such a great amount of darkness. *It's like our lives. It only takes a spark of God's light in our lives to help us shine. Our lives are but a spark in the scheme of things, some too quickly snuffed out, like my Oscar.*

She picked up the beautiful timepiece Oscar had given her for her last birthday. It had come from the Boston Watch Company, and the cover was a gorgeous, intricately engraved piece of heavy silver. She ran her fingers over the lid, thinking of Oscar and how thoughtful he'd been.

She opened it and was not surprised to see it was only four thirty. She closed the lid with a decided click and picked up her Bible. Turning up the wick on the lamp, she grabbed a few more pillows from the other side of the bed, plumping them up. Slipping back underneath the feather-down duvet, she reached for her glasses on the nightstand and set them on the bridge of her nose.

Let's see, she thought. *Think I'll look at that Scripture again that the reverend told me about in Isaiah fifty-seven. Uhm, not more than verses one through three, if I remember aright.* She read aloud to herself, "'The righteous perisheth, and no man layeth it to heart: and merciful men are taken away, none considering that the righteous is taken away from the evil to come. He shall enter into peace: they shall rest in their beds, each one walking in his uprightness.'" She read it two more times and prayed about it. "So, Lord, didst Thou take Oscar out of this world so he wouldn't have to endure the wicked day? Oh Father, I pray for strength. Somehow, I do feel a bit stronger this morning. Not so befuddled and tired. I thank Thee for that. Help me be pleasing to Thee this day." She prayed for over an hour and then got up, tying the belt of her robe around her slim waist and slipping her feet into rabbit-fur-lined slippers.

"I'm hungry," she said with some surprise. She lit a taper, blew out the lamp, and made her way downstairs. The kitchen was beginning to lighten but was still dim. She lit a sconce near the opened doorway and went on to light several lamps.

CHAPTER XI

But the salvation of the righteous is of the LORD:
he is their strength in the time of trouble.

PSALM 37:39

SUSANNAH STUCK A FEW PIECES OF WOOD on the embers
still burning in the stove and poured water into the teakettle, setting it,
with some satisfaction, onto the stove. She hadn't really done much of
anything for over six weeks, not since a few days after Oscar had died.
She opened the cooler and saw a hunk of ham and sliced herself a piece,
along with a piece of cheese, setting it on a small serving plate. Her
mouth watered, and she decided not to wait for the water to boil.

I think I must be on the mend, she thought. *It's as if I've had a long illness
these past weeks. In truth, I thought I was going to die. I will mourn Oscar forever, but
I've felt so ill along with it, that I thought I was dying. I do feel better this morning.*

It was nearly time for Opal to get up, but hearing noises through the
wall from the kitchen, she rose and, still in her nightgown and cap,
wondered if Tess was already up. Opal's rooms were on the other side of
the back stairs. She peered into the kitchen.

"Miz Farrow," she said, "what are you doing up so early?"

"Oh, Opal, I couldn't sleep anymore, and I felt hungry, so I'm
rustling up something to eat. You don't have to get up yet. It's still early."

"Miz Farrow, it's time I was up. I'm usually out here in about ten more minutes anyhows. So I'll just go throw on some clothes and be back in two shakes of a lamb's tail. I'll get you something tasty to eat. Meanwhile, you just have a little snack."

Opal was thin as a stick, and all her clothes hung on her, but she always looked neat as a pin, and seeing her in her nightgown with her gray hair peeking out of her nightcap was something of a shock to Susannah, who grinned at her.

"I'll not eat much, just a bit with my tea. You get dressed, and I'll be right here, waiting for you."

Opal moved quickly back to her room. She could hardly credit that the missus was hungry. She hadn't eaten much for the past six weeks. It was a good sign to Opal, who'd been thinking of looking for other employment. She'd thought Miz Farrow was in a decline and not likely to recover.

Tess wasn't yet up but would be within the hour. Before Mr. Farrow had died, Opal, Tess, and Miz Farrow had one day a week where they breakfasted together and got caught up on the news from each other's lives. They hadn't met since before Mr. Farrow passed. Opal looked forward to the morning as she hadn't done for quite some time.

Elijah lay in bed, looking out the opened window. A gentle breeze blew in, ruffling the muslin curtains, which were drawn back. He could smell the tangy salt air and see the tops of trees, which he hadn't been able to see the night before. There were no streetlamps in this area, only the ones Penelope had put in, lining the long drive from the main road to the house, which was isolated—no other houses close and no need for streetlamps.

The evening before, Elijah had read his chapter in Proverbs, which he did every night, while Abigail had fallen asleep. Once he'd blown out the lamp, he'd gotten up and pulled back the curtains. He'd lain for quite some time gazing at the stars. Now, here he was awake quite early but able to see the sky and treetops. The days were beginning to get shorter.

The heavens declare Thy glory, he thought. *Last night the stars were so large and looked so close, I felt as if I could reach up and touch them. This morning the sun is already shining, and the heavens are as blue as Abby's eyes. Yes, the heavens declare Thy glory, Lord. I love Thee and am thankful for a restful night's sleep. I pray Thou wouldst grant a good meeting with George. I don't know why this thought keeps niggling in my brain. I need to talk to him and get some perspective on it. Help me this day to be pleasing to Thee. How I do praise Thy holy name. Bless the Lord, Oh my soul, and all that is within me, bless Thy holy name.* Elijah lay giving the Lord praise and glory and then went on with requests and petitions. He filled his heart and mind with the love of Christ, and as he lay there praying, he felt as if the Holy Spirit was filling up his cup, like the psalmist. He prayed for a long time, and when he finished, he lay listening for a bit for the Lord to speak to his heart.

Finally, he slid out of bed, careful not to disturb the covers on Abby, who still lay sound asleep. It was past the time she was normally up, and he figured the children had worn her out the evening before. He padded into the side room that had been updated with running water and flush toilets. He performed the dreaded task of shaving and once finished felt much better. He dressed quickly and efficiently, taking care not to make any noise. Letting himself out the bedroom door, he did not allow the door to make a click as he held on to the handle. He smiled at his accomplishment.

Descending the stairs, he whistled under his breath. Good smells assailed his nostrils, and he entered the kitchen to see Gussie and Penelope frying up bacon, eggs, and pancakes. His mouth watered, and he uttered a good morning to the room in general. Daffy, the family's dog, but really Xander's, came out of her bed to wag herself over to Elijah. She was Polka Dot's mother, and Elijah bent to pet her.

Penelope turned, giving him her wide smile. The apron was wrapped twice around her small frame and tied in a big bow in the front.

"Good morning to you, Elijah," she responded.

Gussie simply grunted out a good morning and turned back to her frying bacon.

Penelope asked, "Did you sleep all right?"

"I slept as if I'd been drugged. Must be all that fresh air when we crossed the bay. There's something about being out of doors for the majority of a day that seems to induce a good night's rest, don't you think?"

"I do. We see the ocean here, but it's not easy to get down to where it is. There's no beach right here. When I lived in Boston, my house was right on the strand, and I could comb the beach whenever I felt the urge.

The fresh breeze does seem to go hand in hand with a good night's rest. I agree with you. I reckon I need to get out more often. I do believe I'm slowing down a bit."

She poured Elijah a cup of coffee and set it on the kitchen table, knowing he preferred to sit and chat with her than to go into the dining room and sit by himself.

"I think that's God's plan as we grow older," Elijah responded. "We rush madly about for years and years, but when those years finally tell their tale on our bodies, well, we have to slow down. It is then that we start to enjoy the gift of life and the beauty around us at a deeper level. At least, that's what I've found."

Penelope made herself a cup of tea, letting it steep while Elijah talked. She pulled the tea ball out and opening it, tapped it out into the waste bin. Removing her apron, she smiled as she sat down across from Elijah at the huge kitchen table, looking forward to some time alone with him.

Elijah had no idea Penelope was as rich as Croesus and a philanthropist, but it wouldn't have surprised him. She used her money the way the Lord directed her and was careful to be a good steward. She never enlightened anyone as to just how much she was worth. Not even Alex had a clue. When she passed into glory, he'd find out soon enough, as he was sole heir to her millions.

"I agree with you, except I think there are other things that can crop up in your life to make you realize each day is a gift and one needs to grab that gift with both hands and make the most of it. When I lost my husband and children to a boating accident, I came, after a good deal of ranting and raving to the Almighty, to understand what you are saying. One needs to slow down and enjoy God's creation, to enjoy nature in all its fullness. Of course, I'm not talking about nature the way Henry David Thoreau did and all that nonsense of Transcendentalism. I don't believe at all in the innate goodness of man nor nature, but we should enjoy what God has given us with the full knowledge that His hand created it."

Elijah nodded. "Yes, and there's the rub, isn't it? So many people love the created rather than the Creator."

Penelope found Elijah a very astute person and loved his quick wit. She'd never had much patience with people who rattled on just to hear themselves talk.

The two of them started to eat their breakfast after Elijah prayed for God's blessing on the food. They sat immersed in conversation. The spark that fueled much of their talk was their incredible walks with Jesus, and they shared with each other some new insights they had recently learned.

It wasn't long before Alex joined them, followed by children. Nanny Jane was keeping the younger ones in the nursery this morning. Penny, Alley, and Xander were allowed to join the adults. They trailed after Alex into the warm kitchen.

"Good morning. Hope you had a good sleep, Elijah." Alex bent over and kissed Penelope on the cheek. "Good morning, Nana."

"Good morning," Elijah and Penelope said in unison; they looked at each other and grinned in pleased admiration of the other.

"Where's Emily?" Penelope asked. She didn't tell Alex, but she was worried about Emily and this pregnancy. It was taking its toll, and Penelope could see it.

"She's still sleeping," Alex said. "She didn't get much rest last night." He looked at Elijah as he added, "She's due anytime now and hoping for a boy, but I don't care what it is. I just wish she'd have it. She's worn out."

"Did you children wash your hands?" Penelope asked as she got up to dish up their breakfast, helped by Alex and Gussie.

"Yes, Nanna," Penny answered, "we all did." She went over and hugged her nana's waist. "Xander has dirty fingernails, and Papa made him take a brush to them."

"They're not dirty anymore. If you had to brush down a horse, your nails'd get dirty too."

"Would not."

"Would too."

"Wou—"

"All right, that's enough," Alex said. "Any more, and you can join your brother and sister in the nursery."

"I'm not arguing," Alley said. "*I* know better."

Penny stuck out her tongue at Alley but didn't say anything, as she didn't wish to get sent up to the nursery.

"Papa, Penny stuck out her tongue at me!" Alley said in a whiny voice.

"Hush, child. Do hush. No more tale bearing, and do keep your voice down," Penelope said.

"Is Abigran up yet?" Xander asked. "She wants ta see my new horse this morning."

"No, no, she's not up yet either, but it won't be long now. She was pretty tuckered out after playing checkers with you all last night," Elijah said.

"It was the first time I ever beat her." Xander grinned, but added, "But I think she let me win."

The children sat down to eat, and Penny prayed. When she finished, the chatter and noise level at the table rose to almost a din.

Alex said, "Please keep your voices down. It's much too early for loud noises."

There was much laughter throughout breakfast as the children shared anecdotes about their studies and activities.

Alley said, "I read an article in one of Papa's old *Youth Companion* magazines. It was about a Bengal tiger. Some people were down by a river, having a picnic lunch, and all the sudden they saw a tiger who was ready to leap on them. The men didn't have time to spring their guns, to take aim and fire, because the tiger was ready to jump. One of the ladies stuck out her umbrella at the tiger and opened it right in his face. The tiger turned tail and ran off into the woods!" Alley spoke importantly. "The article said it was a curious thing for the lady to do, but the reason she did it, they think, was so she didn't have to see the horrible tiger."

"I remember reading that!" Alex exclaimed. "You children are reading those old magazines? Why, I could get you the subscription. Your nana ordered those for me when I was growing up. There's some pretty good articles in them, wouldn't you say?"

The conversation veered toward some of the stories in the magazines, making breakfast an entertaining affair.

Alex got up and said, "As enjoyable as this has been, I really must be getting off to work."

"I plan to ride into town with you, if that's all right," Elijah said with a question in his eyes.

"Certainly. Would you like to meet for lunch?"

"Yes, I'm sure I'll be finished by then. How about the restaurant where we first met?" His eyes smiled in remembrance.

"Perfect," Alex replied. "I'll meet you there at noon, only this time, I'll know who I'll be looking for."

The two men went out to saddle up their horses, but Renny had Alex's horse already saddled.

"I'll have your Star ready in no time, Mr. Humphries," he said. "I didn't realize you were going out this morning."

"Thank you, Renny. I'll run back in and see if the missus is awake yet." He didn't like to leave her without talking with her first.

She was wide awake.

"I'll see you later, my dear," Elijah said. "Just wanted to check on you and make sure you're all right."

"I'm fit as a fiddle," she replied and planted a kiss on his mouth. "I was just being lazy, I suppose. I was too tired last night. I had a difficult time falling asleep, and I woke up in the middle of the night and couldn't go right back to sleep. It felt good to sleep in for a change. You run along now, and I'll see you later." With another kiss, she shooed him out of the bedroom.

He ran back down the stairs and said another good-bye to everyone in the kitchen as he made his way out the back door, where Alex was waiting for him.

As promised, Star was saddled and ready to go. Alex and Elijah headed toward the busy streets of San Francisco.

Hannibal Cassidy had no idea where to look for his daughter. He'd ridden from Napa to Vallejo searching, and spent the night in a hotel. He had some cash that he'd stuffed into his pocket when he'd peered into the red leather satchel at the bank.

He thought back to how surprised he'd been when he received a missive from the bank stating that they had notice of Callie Susannah Farrow Cassidy's death, and he was to present himself to the president of the bank. He hadn't bothered to clean up at the time. He'd been excited that the president of the bank wanted to see him and, extremely curious, had ridden straight away into town.

Hannibal arrived at the bank without having first made an appointment. The clerk looked at him in surprise and disdain when he announced who he was. He'd been made to wait for over forty-five minutes and hadn't liked it one bit. After the long wait, he'd met the president, who looked at him a bit askance but led him down a flight of stairs to a heavy door to the bank's vault, which he unlocked. It opened to a long, narrow hall full of metal safe deposit boxes on either side of the walls. After reading some paper to himself, the banker told him that Callie had made the initial deposit over seventeen years earlier but had upgraded it when she had Timothy. He took a ring of keys and unlocked a box that was over Hannibal's head, and pulling it out, he handed it to Hannibal.

Hannibal saw the red satchel and glanced inside. Not wanting to appear greedy, he closed it back up. The banker had him sign his name on a piece of parchment, which he didn't even bother to read before he left the bank.

He hadn't troubled himself to see what was in the bag. He'd simply stuffed a handful of the money into his pocket as he walked down the boardwalk. He'd felt in dire need of a drink and had gone straight to the saloon. *I only wanted to celebrate. I can't believe that my wife hid all that lovely money from me all these years. We could have lived in a lot nicer house than we do. Strange, I don't even remember getting home, but I do remember kicking that red satchel under the bed. I need to find Cady before she finds out who her grandparents are. If she goes there, I'll be out of all that lovely money. Maybe I should just start watching the Farrows' mansion an' see if Cady's already there or shows up there.*

CHAPTER XII

Only by pride cometh contention:
but with the well advised is wisdom.

PROVERBS 13:10

ALEX AND ELIJAH RODE SLOWLY into the city, talking as they went. The day was fair, and no fog hid the city from view. Wispy clouds stretch themselves out overhead, and the sun glistened on copper roofs.

"I know you haven't asked me directly why I need to see George," Elijah said. "I have no doubt you are curious. However, I have not spoken about it because I am not sure if what I am thinking is even valid. I may be grasping at straws. If there is validity to it, and George tells me there is, I'll share it with you this evening, but only you. I don't want to bandy about someone's reputation, especially if I am completely off on a tangent. I know you to be very discreet and also that you will pray about the matter if I tell you about it."

Alex grinned at him. "It all sounds quite mysterious."

"No, no, not mysterious at all, simply a matter I need to discuss with George." The two men rode companionably, each admiring the other for his integrity and relationship to Jesus Christ.

"Do you mind if I bring George along to lunch if he's free?" Elijah asked.

"I'd enjoy that. It's been several months since I've seen him. You know, I never did hear how he dealt with the A&B Construction Company."

Elijah, a bit chagrined, pulled up to a stop, as the two men had arrived at the street where they would part ways.

"I'm sorry. I never thought to enlighten you about what exactly was the outcome, and you were the one who discovered the discrepancies. Again, I'm sorry I forgot to tell you. George told me the politician who was getting the kickbacks from the A&B Construction Company was prosecuted and sent to prison." Elijah explained, "The company's managers, who'd been under Liberty's dead husband's direction, were also found guilty and are now residing in San Quentin. The company was shut down for a short time for the investigation and then sold off. Mrs. Jamison realized enough money from the sale to last her the rest of her life, if she's careful. Liberty's first husband, Armand Bouvier, and her stepfather, Jacques Corlay, who were business partners, would have been hung for their crimes if they'd ever been brought to light."

"I'm glad Mrs. Jamison finally got the money. What a tragedy for that family. Frankly, I don't believe suicide is ever an option."

"Nor do I. Mr. Jamison should have gone to the police and told them exactly what had occurred. He might have got his company back. No, I don't believe suicide is an option either. It was such a tragedy. I believe George told me there were seven men in all who either died from heart failure or committed suicide due to Corlay's and Bouvier's perfidious crimes. Twenty-seven companies, that we know of, were taken over by those two evil men. If you remember, Bouvier owed seventeen of them. We figure at least ten were owned by Corlay, but there could even have been more."

Alex shook his head. "The evilness of some men seems almost unbelievable, doesn't it?" He pulled out his watch, checked the time, and then replaced it into his fob pocket. "Thank you for telling me what happened. Every once in a while, I'd think about it and wonder how it all panned out, if Mrs. Jamison ever got her money." He smiled at Elijah and added, "Reckon I'd better get to work. I'll see you in about three hours." With a wave, the two men parted ways.

Elijah rode on thinking back on how he'd first met Liberty. Three years earlier, in Boston, her husband, Armand Bouvier, had been murdered. As it turned out, his business partner, Jacques Corlay, who was Liberty's stepfather, had orchestrated the murder. Bouvier had blabbed to Corlay that he was the beneficiary to his vast estate instead of Liberty. Corlay stood to gain much wealth by his partner's demise. Liberty had been cut almost entirely out of Armand's will. He'd left her a property in the Napa Valley. That was how Liberty had met Matthew.

"Interesting how it all turned out," Elijah said softly to himself as he rode toward the San Francisco Police Headquarters. "Lord, how I thank Thee for Thy wondrous provision in our lives. Liberty is free from the degradation of living with Armand or the fear of her stepfather. She is immeasurably happy with Matthew and now expecting this baby. I thank Thee for Thy provision. I pray you will bless this baby in her womb, whether girl or boy. I pray for good health and an easy delivery for her. I thank Thee that she is like a daughter to Abigail and me, and Alex like a son. And now, we also have Adam, who is like a son to us. How I praise Your name for all of them."

Adam had just recently come into Elijah and Abigail's lives. He lived near Liberty and was a wonderful Christian. Elijah continued to pray all the way to his destination.

He tied Star up to the hitching post, praying that George would be available. Entering the police station's double doors, an immense information desk sat facing him. On his right was a wide staircase leading up to the main offices, but Elijah knew better than to simply barge in on the head of the department. He walked up to the counter and stood for a few moments while a clerk finished a telephone call. He was busy scribbling on a piece of paper and once finished, tucked the stub of the pencil behind his ear.

"May I help you?" the young man asked as he hung up, his focus now centered on Elijah.

"Yes, yes, I believe you can. I would like to talk to Chief Inspector Baxter, if I may."

"Do you have an appointment?"

"No, no, I don't, but I do know that if the inspector isn't too busy, he'll see me. My name is Elijah Humphries."

"And I'm Billy," the clerk said. "Pleased to meet you, Mr. Humphries." He reached across the desk and shook Elijah's hand, something he did not normally do. "Let me see if the inspector is available." He telephoned upstairs.

"Yes, Inspector Baxter? This is Billy. There's a Mr. Humphries to see you. Yes, yes, of course, sir. I'll send him right up."

Billy seemed an affable young man.

"The chief's just now free. Please go right on up." He waved at the wide staircase.

"Thank you, Billy. You've been quite helpful." Elijah went up the steps with alacrity and down the hall. He paused to knock on the door, reading the printing on the frosted glass. *Chief Inspector George Baxter* was in black lettering, and below his name, *San Francisco Police Department* was printed just a bit smaller. Below that was *Detective Branch*. As Elijah started to knock, the door opened, and there stood his friend, George Baxter.

"Elijah! What a wonderful surprise. Come in. Please do come in." He didn't shake hands but gave Elijah a big hug. "So good to see you, my friend!" He waved Elijah to a comfortable settee by a large window. "Come. Sit down and make yourself comfortable." Two other chairs faced the settee, and as Elijah sat down, so did George.

Elijah perused his friend quickly, a warm smile in his eyes as he sat.

George had a deep groove in his left cheek and a little quirk at the top of it when he smiled. He was clean shaven except for a thin black mustache above his well-shaped mouth. Dressed as a gentleman, his cravat was impeccably done. Elijah wondered how he always looked as if he'd just left his tailor in a new suit. George never seemed to have a hair out of place or a wrinkle in his suit. He wasn't a man to spend time in front of a mirror, but he always looked as if he had. He was well turned out.

"I'm glad you came to visit me, my friend. I've been thinking of taking a couple weeks off and wondered if I might come spend the time with you?"

"There is nothing I'd like better," Elijah replied. The warmth in his eyes spread to a grin on his face. "As a matter of fact, it would be beneficial to me, just now, to have the pleasure of your company. When did you think you might come? Abigail will be delighted also."

Looking intently at Elijah, George said, "I was thinking to come at the end of the week. Cabot can take over for the time I'm away. He's quite capable, as you well know. Aha, beneficial to you, eh? So this is not just a quick-stop-to-chat visit, is it?"

"No, no, it isn't, George. I would like to run something by you and see if I'm off beam. I have had something rankling in my brain and need you to listen and see what you think."

George nodded. "Be glad to, Elijah. You're not one to look for trouble, but I can see this is bothering you. What is it?

"Frankly, I think what's been purported as a horrible accident having taken place is, instead, a murder."

George's eyes widened at the import of Elijah's statement. "Let's hear it, man!" he exclaimed, on tenterhooks to hear what his friend suspected.

"I came to see you because I'm not at all sure about the validity of my suspicions," Elijah said. "Let me give you a little background before I get to my story." He shifted his weight on the settee and crossed a leg over his knee, getting himself comfortable before he delved into the story. "There's a lady in San Rafael, a Mrs. Susannah Farrow, whose husband died a little over six weeks ago. Mr. Farrow was visiting the school he founded, the San Rafael School of Primary Learning. It is run by a Mr. Amos Kepler, a man of some prominence in San Rafael.

"Supposedly, Oscar Farrow leaned over the railing of the second story balcony too far and fell to his death on the cobblestones below. Mr. Kepler said he tried to catch his coattails as he went over, but they slipped through his hands. The death was not investigated because Mr. Kepler is known as an upright man of some significance. It is said he is tormented by the accident."

"How horrible, and quite unusual," murmured George, his eyes bright with curiosity.

"Yes," continued Elijah, "very horrible and quite strange. The problem is, there were no witnesses, absolutely none. Mr. Farrow was an incredibly wealthy man. He and his wife had only one daughter, who ran off years ago, when she was seventeen years old. There's been no contact with the daughter. If Mrs. Farrow should die, and the daughter not found nor any of her progeny within a period of six months, the entire estate goes to the school, and Amos Kepler, who couldn't seem to save Oscar, will distribute the monies as he sees fit.

And another moot point is that Mr. Amos Kepler has been visiting Mrs. Farrow two to three times a week for the past five weeks. Since he's been visiting her, Susannah Farrow has begun to decline in health. I think, somehow, he's poisoning her."

"Does Mr. Kepler know the particulars of the will?"

"Ah, right to the point, George. You don't miss a beat, do you? Mrs. Farrow says no. However, there is a problem with that fact. I have dealt with all their formal business and drew up Mr. Farrow's will. In my employ is a bright young man, Mr. Edward Kepler, Amos Kepler's son."

"Hmm." George's eyes were alight with conjectures. "So Mrs. Farrow does not believe that Kepler the elder knows anything about the contents of the will."

"That is correct."

George's mind was alive with anticipation. "Well, my friend, I can tell you, you're not off beam in your summation of things. I do believe I will have an interesting vacation." He smiled with good humor. "You say the younger Kepler works for you. So he's had access to the contents of the will—is that correct?"

"Yes, yes, he has," Elijah said heavily. "He's sworn never to divulge any information he comes across in the office, but I surmise this was just too much for him to keep and not tell his father. I can understand it. However, I will have to figure out what to do about him should it be true that he told his father about Oscar Farrow's will."

"Yes, I have to agree with you. I too believe a murder has taken place." George sat for a minute, staring out the window over Elijah's shoulder. His eyes swung back to connect with Elijah's.

"I wonder…would it be possible for me to come with you now?"

Elijah's eyes widened in welcome surprise. "I was hoping you could! I'm to meet Alex for lunch and wondered if you could come too. You can pack this evening and meet me tomorrow at the ferry. Would that suit you?"

"Instead, could we go today? I don't think this is something we care to wait on, especially if your Mrs. Farrow is being poisoned."

"Of course we can. I'll ride over to Alex's office to inform him of my change of plans and then on to his house to collect Abby. What say we meet at the three o'clock crossing?"

"Excellent! I will talk to Cabot first and head home to pack and get a bite to eat. I am always hesitant to take vacations, as I don't like to miss out on a good case. This vacation will be different and a lot more interesting. Thank you, Elijah, for coming to me. Had you gone to the authorities in San Rafael, there could have been talk that got back to Mr. Kepler. This way, we'll keep our investigation under wraps." George couldn't have been more pleased.

Leaving George's office, Elijah whistled as he made his way down the stairs. He waved a friendly good-bye to Billy and pushed his way out the heavy double doors. Star nodded her head up and down as Elijah headed her way. He gave her a loving pat, stepped into the stirrup, and started up the hill toward Alex's office.

Well, at least I'll have a professional to deal with the problem. I am grateful, Lord, I listened to Thy Holy Ghost impressing on my heart to see George. I thank Thee for Thy direction, and I pray Thou wouldst see fit to help us get to the truth of this matter and that justice be done. I know Thou art a just God and love truth, and right now, I pray that the truth will come out. I thank Thee, Lord.

Elijah arrived at Alex's office and tied Star to the short hitching post that doubled as a railing for the front porch. Going up the steps, he could see the slight stain in the boardwalk that Alex had showed him. Several years previously, Alex had lain there for some time before he'd been discovered. It had been dark and raining, and Alex had just locked his office door when a drunk man started shooting in the air. He'd caught a stray bullet in the chest. Alex had nearly died. His best friend, Danny, an excellent doctor, had patched him up.

Elijah stepped up to the door of the office and let himself in.

Alex looked up with surprise in his eyes. "Wasn't George available?"

"Yes, yes he was. I came by to tell you that he's coming up with me to San Rafael, but he would like to go today, not wait until tomorrow." He sat down in the chair across the desk from Alex, who looked even more surprised.

"I didn't want to say anything earlier, because sometimes a body can think things or dream things up, and that's exactly what it is, a figment of one's imagination based on no truth or very little fact. George believes I'm not off on some tangent, so I'll share with you the reason for my quick visit to San Francisco."

Elijah related what he knew about the Farrows and the circumstances of Oscar's death and the will's provision. As he spoke, Alex's eyebrows furrowed in thought.

"I think George is correct in his summation," he said when Elijah had finished his narrative. "I wouldn't wait on it either. Somehow, I have no doubt that your Mr. Kepler is poisoning Mrs. Farrow. I only have a bit of paperwork left, so let me ride home with you. Let's go. We may have time for a bit of lunch before you leave."

CHAPTER XIII

The LORD upholdeth all that fall,
and raiseth up all those that be bowed down.

PSALM 145:14

CADENCE FELT FAINT AND SICK to her stomach. She'd been working steadily for what seemed like hours. She'd awakened that morning with cramps and knew her monthly was due. She'd brought rags with her in her satchel but wondered how she was going to wash and dry them without being discovered. Her head ached, and she felt sore all over from muscles not used to the exercise of harvesting grapes. She stood up and put her hand on her aching back.

Liberty walked around checking on the workers who'd not harvested before. She would help them if they were still struggling with cutting the stems easily. Surreptitiously, she had been watching Cady, becoming more and more convinced that Cady was a girl. When Cady straightened up rubbing her back, Liberty made a spur-of-the-moment decision. Donny was not working far from Cady, and she walked over to him.

"I'd like Cady to do some cleaning in the house rather than harvest grapes, but I need to make sure you're all right with that. I know you've taken him under your wing, so to speak, and I don't care to interfere with that."

Donny, with surprise in his voice, said, "Certainly, Miss Liberty. You're the boss, not me. This seems a bit hard on him. He's white as a sheet this morning and looking peaked. You take him. It's fine with me."

"Thanks, Donny." She looked into his clear blue eyes and thought again how his eyes reflected a pure soul. She smiled and said, "You bless me, Donny."

Smiling back, he said, "I'm glad that's so. You bless me too, Miss Liberty. I'm grateful to have found such a wonderful Christian atmosphere in which to work."

"Well, we're thankful to have you. You're a good worker and a good man, Donald Miller. By the way, Conchita and I were talking and wondered about Cady. Matthew said you told him Cady's father was looking for him, that you saw him coming out of the saloon. Has Cady said anything to you about where he came from or anything more about his home life?"

"No, he's been fairly tight lipped about his upbringing. I do know it was rough. Cady spotted him coming out of the saloon, and I had him hide in an alley while I leaned against a storefront and watched to see what his pa was going to do. He got on his horse and rode out of town. Cady didn't want me to talk to the bartender. He said he knew his pa was looking for him. I took Cady into the store, and I never saw anyone look at the merchandise the way he did. Have you ever seen a boy finger material or look at feathers, hats, and frocks? He's a different kind of boy, but you're right when you say I've taken him under my wing. I love that little guy as if he were my own brother."

She nodded. "I'm glad you love him. He certainly hasn't had any male love from his father. I know what that feels like. You end up wondering what you did to incur their disdain, that the fault is somehow yours. I'm so thankful Jesus took that feeling away. I don't have to earn His love."

Liberty was smiling when she went to talk to Cady.

"Cady, I'd like you to come to the house with me. I have a few things that need doing and would like you to help me. I've talked to Donny, and he approves."

"Yes, ma'am. I'd be happy to help you in any way I can." Cady smiled, but she was in pain, and her smile felt stiff.

"Come along, then." Liberty looked anxiously at Cady. She wondered if her ribs were broken and if the bending over for cutting grapes had exacerbated the problem. *She looks like she's in pain*, she thought. *I'm confused. In my mind I think of him as her. Looking at frocks and hats? A twelve-year-old boy? Indeed!*

Cady followed Liberty into the Rancho. Liberty took her to the kitchen, had her wash her hands and sit at the table.

She washed her own hands and asked, "Conchita, could you please give us a couple cups of tea, no, make that three cups. I'd like you to take a break. Can we have some of that chocolate cake you made last night?"

"*Sí*, Mees Libbee, I do eet." She bustled around making the tea and cutting the cake while Liberty spoke to Cady.

"You don't look as if you feel very good this morning. You looked like you could faint out there. You're not used to working outside, are you?"

"Yes, ma'am, I am. I usually milked the cow, and sometimes I chopped wood. Yes, I'm used to working outside."

Conchita sat down, and the three of them looked at each other in silence for a minute.

Liberty said, "Cady, eat your cake. Have you ever had chocolate cake before?"

"No, ma'am, I haven't." She took a bite, and her eyes rounded in wonder. She licked the frosting on her lips and said, "I thought when Donny bought me the peppermint that I'd died and gone to heaven, but this—this is indescribable! I never knew food could taste so wonderful. My ma wasn't much of a cook."

"Cady, I'm going to say something to you, and I don't want you to be alarmed. Please know that we already care about you." Liberty looked at Cady with her green eyes full of love and reached over to squeeze Cady's arm.

"Conchita and I are quite certain that you are no more a boy than I am."

Cady's eyes opened wide in pure astonishment. Tears welled up and streamed down her face. She began to cry great racking sobs. Pushing the plate from in front of her, she laid her face on her arm as she sobbed.

Conchita beat Liberty to Cady's chair, and she pulled her into her arms. Cady felt as limp as a rag doll. She cried and cried.

"You won't tell…" She hiccuped. "Please promise me you won't tell anyone!" Her eyes were wild with fear. "If anyone says there's a runaway girl, he'll find me. I promise my pa'll find me, and he'll beat me all the way back home."

Conchita patted her back, but Cady pulled away to look closely into Liberty's eyes. For some reason, she knew Conchita would tell no one, but she wasn't sure about Liberty.

"Please, please promise me you won't tell anyone!" she begged.

Liberty spoke with authority in her voice. "Your pa will not drag you back home. That I can promise you. As far as telling anyone, I will tell my husband. He has a right to know that you are a female. He told me, only this morning, that if you were a girl, we should move you into the house. Although Donny is close, only a yell away, you are not protected where you are sleeping."

Cadence nodded. "I've thought about that too. If my pa scouted around here and saw me, even from a distance, he'd know it was me, especially dressed in Timmy's clothes." She drew in a deep, shuddering breath. "I'm s-sorry," she said. "It's my time of the month, and I...I'm emotional."

"Ah, that's why...I thought you didn't look well this morning," Liberty said. "I've never been bothered much by that. Now," she said briskly, "let's get your things moved into the house, and we'll decide whether to tell Donny or not. He's going to wonder why you've been moved inside. I do think I'll send him into town and have him purchase some new boy's clothing, or perhaps you and I could go. I can't ride anymore, but we have a carriage, and I don't think Matthew would mind me driving it." She had a sudden thought. "How old are you, Cady?"

"Just turned seventeen a few months ago. When I had the fever, ma cut my hair off, and that's what gave me the idea of dressing in Timmy's clothes and running away after she died. I miss her."

More tears threatened, so Liberty stood up and said, "Let's go get your things, and then we'll sit down and decide what to do. And by the way, you're considered an adult as far as the law is concerned. You need never live with your pa again."

"Is that really true?" she asked, then added, "He'll still be looking for me. I don't have much to gather up either. I only have a satchel, ma'am, and I can get it myself. And just so you know, my name is Cadence, Cadence Jean Cassidy. I can go by Cady or Cadence, but for now, hoping no one finds out about me, it's better that you call me Cady."

"Cadence is a beautiful name," Liberty replied. "How well do you like wearing boys' duds?" She grinned at Cady, who returned the grin in full measure.

"I like them a lot more than dresses. Gives a body a lot more freedom."

"I know. I have a sister-in-law who wears trousers every day, denims, and she works right alongside men repairing fencing and herding cattle."

Cady sputtered. "Surely you jest! I have never heard tell of such a thing."

"Neither had I until I met Caitlin McCaully, now Bannister. Matthew's brother married her this past February. She looks quite elegant in dresses, but working with barbed wire and with cows, she wears denims and looks striking in them." Liberty smiled and then went into her efficient mode. "All right, go get your satchel, and I'll get some fresh water for the bathing room. I'm going to have Lupe and Luce fill the tub, and you can take a bath and get cleaned up. I'll send Donny into town to purchase a couple pairs of boy's clothes for you. The outfit you have on should be burned. Is that all right with you? Then you won't have to worry your pa will recognize your clothes."

"Yes, of course it's all right with me. I also have this." She pulled up her shirt to show the material wrapped around her middle. "It's beginning to itch, and although my ribs *are* cracked, this material wasn't for my ribs." She smiled, her gray eyes sparkling at Conchita and Liberty.

All three laughed.

Cady got up and headed for the barn and the tack room. She got down on her knees and pulled the beautifully tooled leather satchel out, carefully dusting it off. She took out her grubby green one and folded the leather top down, stuffing the red bag into the bottom of her cloth one. She covered it with the few things she'd brought with her. She looked around to make sure she hadn't forgotten anything and went back to the house.

The kitchen was full of mouthwatering smells when Cady opened the front door.

Liberty went out to find Donny to ask him to ride into town. She felt cumbersome and knew it was why Pookie had succeeded in bucking her off. *That wounded my pride as well as my head,* she thought with a grin. She found Donny hard at work, his hat pulled down low over his brow.

"Donny, I'd like to ask you a favor. Would you please ride into town and buy a couple pairs of pants and checkered shirts for Cady? What he has isn't fit to wear, and I doubt it will survive many more washings.

Would you mind doing that?" She shaded her eyes to see his expression and added, "I'll tell Matthew I sent you into town. He seems to have plenty of workers this year."

"Sure, Miss Liberty, I'd be happy to go get some duds for the boy. Do you want me to get underthings and socks and shoes?"

Liberty pondered the question. "I hadn't thought of that, but yes, yes I do. I'll give you his old trousers and shoes so you have something to use as a measure. I'm having him take a bath, and I'll find something he can put on while we wait for your purchases. Thanks, Donny. I appreciate it." Liberty didn't tell Donny she was moving Cady into the house. It could wait.

"You're welcome," he said. "I'll go right now and have lunch when I get back." He'd been working the entire time they were talking, cutting clusters of grapes and dropping them into the wooden box next to him. He straightened up, and lifting his hat in a gesture of respect, he said, "I'll have those goods for you shortly, ma'am." He strode down the row of grapes he'd already harvested, heading for the barn.

Liberty went in search of Matthew. It took her a while, but she finally found him bent over, hard at work. She had the fleeting thought that Armand had never done an honest day's work in his entire life. As she walked down the row, she prayed, *Lord, help me get rid of all the negative thoughts. He's gone to his reward, his name blotted out of the Lamb's Book of Life, and I am sorry he never accepted you as Savior. I am, however, so grateful for You taking me out of that situation and giving me a joy I've never known in all my life. Lord, may it never become a gift taken for granted. Help me always to give thanks each day for Your wondrous provision.*

"Hello, you hard-working man!" she called out gaily. "I came to tell you lunch is almost ready, and I will be moving Cady into the house." Liberty looked around to make sure no one else was near.

"So your suspicions were correct. He's a she." Matthew smiled at his own comment. He stood up to talk to Liberty, wanting to look her in the eyes.

"Yes, Cady is Cadence Jean Cassidy. She didn't say where she was raised, but I'm sure we'll find out before long. She is seventeen, and I've sent Donny into town to get her some new boys' clothes, until we can figure out what is to be done about her. I was thinking, perhaps, she could stay here and help me with the babies, or we could send her to live at the mission, and Abby and Elijah could find her some work or teach her some skills. I suppose we can talk about that later. I just wanted you to know."

Matthew started walking with Liberty up the long row of grapes and realized most of the workers had stopped for lunch.

"I think it's important to find out a bit more about her father. The man should be locked up for the treatment he gave her. It sounds to me as if she's had a cheerless existence till now. We can make a home for her for as long as she wants."

Hannibal Cassidy talked to his neighbor about feeding the chickens and milking the cow.

"I don't reckon I know how long I'll be gone this time. I'm going to retrace my steps and see if anyone's seen Cady. I'll stop at the places I was afore and see iff'n they've seen the girl. Don't know why she lit out like that."

The neighbor did, but he didn't wish to incur Hannibal's anger, so he just nodded his head and said, "I'll have one of my boys over there mornin' and night a milking your cow. You don't have ta worry about a thing while you're a lookin' fer her. Godspeed, Hannibal."

"I don't believe in God, but thanks fer the thought." Hannibal left, going back to his house to collect his satchel and a few foodstuffs before he set off.

That first day he headed down to Stockton. He'd thought Cady may have lit out for San Rafael but had since realized she couldn't read and wouldn't know that was where her grandparents lived. He wondered why Callie had never tried to go home. She'd been raised in elegance, and when they were first married, things had looked pretty good. He'd thought she would come to him with all that lovely money with her but soon realized there was not a single bit of money coming his way from the Farrows. *Pride, I reckon,* he thought. *She wouldn't go home in her poor clothing. She had too much pride. Always did have her nose stuck up in the air with me. I miss her though, her quiet ways, her voice, but I ain't missing her cooking. She was a horrible cook.*

He continued reminiscing as he rode. He asked around at boarding houses, hotels and such, but he found no trace of Cady, so he headed north back up to Napa. He felt he'd depleted every source in Stockton and Sacramento.

CHAPTER XIV

For the ways of man are before the eyes of the LORD,
and he pondereth all his goings.

PROVERBS 5:21

GEORGE WAITED PATIENTLY at the ferry landing, arriving a little early. He was in no hurry, but he did look forward to this vacation away from the familiar. He'd had a good long talk with Cabot before he left the office.

"Not just a vacation, Cabot!" he'd said laughingly.

Cabot, his brown eyes twinkling, responded, "I've never known you to take a vacation, Boss. It's high time you did. I think you should go up to Elijah's and sit around drinking mint juleps." His smirk belied his words.

George smiled warmly at Cabot. "You did, did you? No, this is going to be my favorite kind of vacation. I've never taken one since Adeline passed away. It's a boring life to go sit in a restaurant or visit places of interest alone. I thought visiting Abigail and Elijah would be a pleasant way to take a vacation. Instead, I'm going to have fun proving or disproving a murder. We're already savvy to the suspect."

"Sounds a perfect vacation for you," Cabot said. "Don't worry about anything here, sir. I'll see to it we carry on just the way you like. We'll miss you here at the department. I must say I'm glad we're back to having men of integrity work here. You run a clean ship, Chief, and that's the way it should be. Harold Sawyers was as crooked as they come, and I'm glad he hung for his crimes. Head of a white female slave ring and head of this detective agency! Why, I'd have strung him up myself when I saw the misery of those girls in that warehouse."

"I know, Cabot. I know," George said heavily. "It never ceases to amaze me the lengths people will go to get some greenbacks into their pockets. It was by the good Lord's provision that Elijah and Abigail restored the San Rafael mission and were able to take all those girls from the warehouse. And I thank you, young man, that you're so dependable. I don't have to worry while I'm gone, knowing you are in charge." George stood up and added, "I need to get home and pack. I'll see you in a couple weeks." He shook hands with Cabot and walked out of the office.

Now, here he was at the ferry landing waiting for Elijah and Abby to show up. He thought about how he'd told Cabot that it wasn't a holiday to do things by himself. *I've never been really happy since Adeline died, except when I'm buried in work. I've never been one to enjoy being out unless I'm with someone else. I know it doesn't bother many other people to be on their own, but it does me. I feel a fifth wheel, and I've felt this way for years. I've been so busy at the department that I've not really made friends here in San Francisco. I suppose I need to do that. It takes time to build real friendships, a sort of sacrifice, to be sure, but I'm certain the end result is well worth it.* He smiled.

And that was how Abigail and Elijah saw him as they drew up on their mounts...George was smiling.

The wind was blowing hard as the ferry crossed the bay from San Francisco to Sausalito. Whitecaps bobbed, their foamy crests disappearing as quickly as they rose. Waves slapped hard at the sides of the flat vessel as mists blew their way into the open ferry. Abby had on a bonnet and was thankful for the ties. Both George and Elijah had removed their hats, or they would have lost them. Talk was drowned out as the wind snatched at their voices.

George's eyes gleamed with anticipation of good food, good company, and finding a murderer. He couldn't ask for more. He was content. Knowing Cabot was capable of handling any situation at the department took much pressure off George. He was grateful for the younger man, grateful too that Cabot and Maggie had asked Christ into their lives. They were a wonderful couple.

San Francisco's head detective had not taken any leave since moving west from Boston. He'd had a difficult time cleaning up the department after the last chief, who had himself been crooked.

George had gone one time over to visit his good friend Samuel Kerns, chief of Oakland's detective department. They'd gone to school together. When Adeline had been alive, she and Sam's wife, Kathryn, had enjoyed each other's company immensely.

Now here he was taking his first vacation, only it wasn't a vacation. It was a real case. He prayed he'd be able to clear things up for Elijah and for Mrs. Farrow. He prayed too that Mrs. Farrow would find her missing daughter. There were only four and a half months left, by his reckoning, before the estate, according to Elijah, went to the school, unless, of course, Mrs. Farrow should recover. George felt that if the elder Kepler had anything to say about it, Mrs. Farrow would not recover.

He looked interestedly around him. He saw Alcatraz closer than he'd ever viewed it before. He could see it on clear days from San Francisco. He thought back to his history lessons in school and remembered that it was a Spaniard who first called the island the Island of Pelicans. The island was abhorred by the Native Americans, who kept away from it, calling it Evil Island. George was a bit foggy on some of the history, but remembered that John C. Fremont, representing the US government, bought the island for five thousand dollars, and it was President Millard Fillmore who designated Alcatraz as a military reservation. George's attention swung the other way, and he thought of the vastness of the Pacific Ocean. George had traveled many times to Europe, crossing the Atlantic, but had never sailed on the Pacific.

They were nearing Sausalito, and the ferry slipped into its mooring with ease.

Donny rode into Napa, heading for Diebel's General Store. As he dismounted, he looked up in time to see Cady's father enter the only saloon Napa sported. He was pretty sure it was Cady's father, as he'd had a good long look at him the other day. Donny had been in the saloon a couple times when it was really hot, ordering a sarsaparilla. He decided he'd go over right now and see just exactly what Cady's pa was up to.

When Donny entered the swinging doors, he paused to look around. He tipped his hat to a couple men who looked up at him. He knew them from a couple barn dances he'd gone to. They both nodded in response. They were playing poker with a couple other men he didn't know. He walked up to the bar right next to Cady's pa and ordered a sarsaparilla. Cady's pa turned to look at him when he ordered. His eyes looked bland and were a bit of a shock to Donny. He'd thought he'd see evilness jumping out of him, the way Cady's face had been kicked. He looked down at the boots Cady's pa was wearing and realized those were most likely the ones that kicked his face, and a slow burn entered Donny's chest.

He said a quick prayer. *Lord, I know the offense against Cady is not my offense. You don't give me the grace to forgive because I haven't been wronged— Cady has. Help me not to take Cady's offense into my heart. I choose to act with Your righteousness guiding me.* His prayer stopped when he heard Cady's father's words.

"You live around here?" Hannibal asked him.

"Yes, I do," Donny answered shortly. "Why're you asking?"

"I'm askin' 'cause I got me a runaway girl. Name's Cady—Cady Cassidy—an' her ma is a crying her eyes out. The girl's a bit demented. She's seventeen and wandered off somehows, and we're a tryin' ta find 'er."

Donny had difficulty maintaining a disinterested air. He took a huge swallow of the sarsaparilla the bartender sat in front of him and said, "Well, that's a mournful story, to be sure." He turned the attention away from himself and spoke to the bartender. "Hey, Grady, have you seen any runaway girls around here? You'd be the one to know."

"Nope, ain't seen me nary a one. If she was a lookin' fer a room, she'd be a comin' here, and I ain't never seen her come in here. Sorry, man. I do hopes you find 'er," Grady said with some compassion in his voice. "She'd most likely go to San Francisco if she's that smart. Thet's whar most runaways go. You kin lose yerself in the city, and nobody's ever gonna find you. Mebe y'all should get the Pinkertons out lookin' fer her. Thet'd be yer best bet of findin' 'er." Grady spoke sagely. He'd seen enough runaways, and most of the time there was good reason for them to be running away. He looked closely at Hannibal's face. There was a closed, shut look to him, his eyes hiding his thoughts. Grady registered the fact that he wasn't a man to cross.

"I reckon that's a good thing to do, getting the Pinkertons an' all," Hannibal said, but he had no intention of doing that. Cady was considered an adult, only she didn't know it. He hoped he could find her. If he could only get his hands on that money, he would have enough to hire a housekeeper or a cook. He didn't need nor want Cady, but he did want that money. He buried his nose in his drink and said no more.

Donny finished off his sarsaparilla, laid a few coins on the counter, and said to Grady, "I'll be seeing you. We started harvest this week, but the missus, she wanted some things, so I was sent into town. Thanks for the drink." With that, he nodded to Hannibal and headed out the door, flummoxed by what he'd just heard. He hoped he'd maintained a presence of mind, but his head kept spinning. It made perfect sense, and he knew in his heart it was true. He blocked the information from his mind so he could concentrate on what needed done. Time enough later to chew on the fact that his new sidekick was a girl.

He strode over to his horse and extracted the newsprint with the trousers and shoes wrapped up in it. His horse was tied up in front of the General Store, and he could only hope Cady's pa didn't come in. He'd been going to ask the clerk for help, but he decided it'd be better to get the trousers himself. *I can't chance unwrapping this with that man in town. If he should come in here, it'd be disastrous.* Donny wandered around the store, but his eyes were looking out the window. He finally saw Hannibal Cassidy come out of the saloon, get on his horse, and ride out of town.

Donny wiped his brow on his sleeve and took his little package up to the counter, unwrapped it, and asked for help. He ended up getting a couple really nice checked shirts and two pairs of trousers and soft leather boots. He also picked up some socks and female underthings, his face red as a beet as he set them on the counter

"Want me to dispose of these old ones?" the clerk asked him.

"No, no thanks. I'll take them with me, and we'll find a bit of use for them, I'm sure." Donny answered with an aplomb he didn't feel. He didn't want to have to worry about where the items ended up. He agreed with Liberty's comment that they should burn up the old clothes.

Cady had never, in her entire life, enjoyed such luxury. She sat in the tub, the room full of steam, and relaxed. Liberty and Conchita had clucked their tongues when they saw the bruised, tender ribs.

"You're sure they aren't broken?" Liberty had asked, her voice kindhearted. "I've heard if you don't wrap broken ribs, they can end up poking some other organ in your chest. You want to be very careful."

"I know. I've had broken ribs before, and I know what they feel like. I have checked a couple times, and I assure you, they're not broken," Cadence had replied, "but they sure are bruised and cracked. It takes a long time for cracked ribs to heal."

The two women had left, quickly closing the door behind them to keep the warmth in the room.

Cadence shifted her body and watched the ripples in the tub. She had only bathed in a round metal washtub before. *This...this is heaven*, she thought as she stretched out her legs. She sat and wondered what exactly was going to happen now that Conchita and Liberty knew she was a girl. *Will they really want me to stay? Will they hide me if my pa comes looking? What will Donny think? Will he think I'm a big liar and despise me now? Oh, I do hope not. I don't feel I had any choice.*

She reached for the soap to shampoo her hair. It wasn't so difficult since her hair had been cropped short. She rather liked the feeling of freedom it gave her. She held her breath and scooted down into the water, letting it cover her head to rinse out her hair before she used the rinse water beside the tub. *I could get used to this*, she thought. *I never knew people lived like this. Why would Mama go from a home with money to an existence with pa? Were her parents cruel to her?* Cadence couldn't fathom why her mother would do such a thing.

She towel dried her hair and slipped on the robe Liberty had hung on a hook on the door, tying the belt around her slim waist. *I feel so clean*, she thought, *and I smell like the soap I used. I sure hope Donny isn't going to be angry with me. Oh, I do hope he'll still be my friend.* She padded back into the bedroom and slipped her feet into the slippers Liberty had given her to wear. She opened the door and headed for the kitchen, having no clue she looked so totally feminine.

Donny rode back to Rancho Bonito, his head whirling. He thought back to when he first saw Cady riding Pookie and her not knowing how, and him speaking to her gruffly, worry about Miss Liberty distorting his voice. He'd thought of Cady's delicate wrists and how anyone could kick a sweet boy in the ribs and face with no compunction. Now to find Cady a girl made it doubly evil, to his way of thinking. He thought of how protective he'd felt when Cady had first spied her pa coming out of the saloon. He pulled up his ride and sat for a moment, wondering how he'd never thought of Cady being a girl, not even when he'd watched her fingering material and looking at hats in Diebel's store.

"How could I ever have missed it?" he wondered aloud. "Cady looks, walks, and acts like a girl, and yet I've never come close to realizing it, not ever." He pushed back his hat and wiped at his brow with a big red-and-white neckerchief he kept in his hip pocket. He thought of how they'd played cards together, him showing her how to play rummy. He loved the way Cady's nose wrinkled up when she laughed and how her brows furrowed when she was concentrating. "Not in all my twenty-two years have I been so flummoxed as when I was in that saloon," he said aloud. "There was her pa acting like butter wouldn't melt in his mouth, talking as if he loved his daughter and how her ma was missing her, when I know her ma is dead. That man is a reprobate. He's unprincipled and thinks good is evil and evil is good."

He started up riding again, thinking about his feelings and Cady deceiving him into thinking she was a boy. *Reckon it doesn't matter that she did that*, he thought. *She probably hasn't trusted anyone much.* His eyes widened, and his heart beat harder as the realization hit him that he loved her.

"I love her!" he said aloud in a whisper of a voice. "I loved her like a brother, and now I love her like a woman!" Out of the blue, the sudden awareness washed over him. It consumed him. He was in love! He never knew it would be like this. His heart thrummed with it.

All at once Donny realized he'd been like a sleepwalker. He became aware of his surroundings and that he'd taken a lot longer than he should have for his foray into town. "Reckon my brain isn't functioning too well just now." He laughed for sheer joy as he kicked the sides of his horse and rode at a gallop. He wondered at the back of his mind how he could keep the knowledge of his love to himself. Cady had enough to deal with at the present time. *Wonder, does Miss Liberty know? Was that why she asked if Cady could go work in the house and then ends up having her take a bath? Bet she somehow figured it out. She's the smartest woman I've ever known. She could teach Cady a thing or two—that's certain.*

CHAPTER XV

The LORD will perfect that which concerneth me:
thy mercy, O LORD, endureth for ever:
forsake not the works of thine own hands.

PSALM 138:8

AMOS KEPLER WONDERED if Mrs. Farrow missed him. *Is she over her pique? I'd like to see her again. Perhaps I'll marry her. She's a beautiful woman and has much influence on the community of San Rafael. It is really too, too sad about Oscar. He was such a nice man, and I hated to see him die. I wonder if I'll ever get over the shock of it. It was horrible.*

He'd finished his morning ablutions and stood in front of his mirror, tying his cravat, which was the last touch of his morning's toilette. He looked at his trousers, reflected in the mirror, and made sure the cuffs were turned properly and his shoes shone with a new polish. A regular ritual, he jerked at his sleeve cuffs so they peeked out of his frock coat sleeves, and with another adjustment to his cravat, he left the room, whistling.

He had breakfast at Three Hawks Inn before strolling toward the school. He liked the prestige that came with running such a wonderfully equipped school, but he would prefer to be a man of leisure—to travel and study was his new goal.

The day was beautiful, the sky a seamless blue with a slight hint of breeze. San Rafael was gorgeous this time of year, the weather perfect, and several people were out cutting back shrubs and raking, getting their yards ready for the winter rains that were soon to come.

His next-door neighbors had given him some of their grapes, which were a delicious purple Concord. He knew they were first developed in Concord, Massachusetts, in 1849. That fact was something Amos looked up in the small reference library at the school. It was one of the benefits of running the school. He could take books home to read and order new tomes from the monies the Farrows set up for needed supplies. Amos loved learning for the sake of knowing new things. He studied avidly about birds and their habitats. He knew a variety of trees, shrubs, and an enormous amount of flowers, and he grew carefully chosen species in his yard. He was constantly studying mathematics and science, wanting to improve his mind. The city did not have a library, and he welcomed people to come in and read books at the school, but they were not allowed to check them out.

Amos had run out of ideas of how to make amends with Susannah. He wondered how he could talk to her without her maid running interference. He knew, with certainty, Tess would not allow him a visit.

Elijah, Abby, and George arrived in San Rafael. Abby didn't want George to enter by the back door for his first visit, so Elijah had them tie up in front of the stately house and would have Pippie take care of their mounts later.

George looked in appreciation at the large, two-story clapboard house. It was painted a suntan yellow with white trim. A porch spanned its front and wrapped itself around the right side. Above the porch roof, a balcony faced the street, with ornate, wrought iron railings. Located on the left of the front door, an imposing bay window was trimmed with white shutters. Rhododendrons in full bloom, their delicate blossoms splashing color, were situated on either side of the steps. The house was stately and beautiful.

"Looks like home," George said. "How you must love living here." They went together up the wide steps, and the door opened before they could knock.

"Welcome home, Mistah and Missus Humphries. Welcome home," Thomas said. He looked with pleasure at George. "Nice to meet you agin', Mistah Baxter. Long time no see!"

George held out his hand to shake Thomas' and replied, "Yes, it's been over two years. I remember the last I saw of you, was you guiding your entourage to board the train out of Boston. It's good to see you again too, Thomas."

George looked around himself in appreciation at the huge foyer. A wide hall stretched itself to the back of the house. To the left was a large parlor. A huge arch at least three doorways wide spanned the opening and seemed to beckon those in the foyer to enter its spaciousness. It was a grand room. He saw that the room on his right was a library. He was sure he'd be in there plenty of times in the next couple weeks. He took a deep breath of pure enjoyment of his new surroundings. He recognized the big oaken coat tree that looked well placed in its new home.

Suddenly he heard a couple yipping sounds, and a dog came into the foyer, wagging itself nearly in half at the presence of Elijah and Abby. She looked as if she were smiling, and George laughed as she started at his shoes and sniffed him up, still wagging.

"Goodness, I guess I didn't know you had a dog. She's gorgeous. What an unusual coat."

"Yes, yes," Elijah replied, "we got her this last spring from Alex's son, Xander. Liberty has one, Liberty's father has one, and Kirk, Matthew's brother, has one. As a matter of fact, your Cabot has one. Quite a litter of puppies, and Xander quite the persuader."

Abigail laughed. "I never thought to have a dog, and now I don't know why we never had one before. I love this puppy," she said. "Let me show you to your room, George. It smells as if we'll be enjoying dinner before long. I'm glad I took the time to send a wire to Bessie. We will most likely have a feast." She smiled at George and started up the stairs.

He followed her up the double-wide staircase, which allowed a view of the entry below, still looking around at his surroundings.

"It's a huge house, isn't it?" he asked.

"Yes, it's quite large, but when Alex, Emily, and the children are here, along with Liberty and Matthew, it doesn't seem so big."

"No." George smiled. "I don't suppose it does." He looked with astonishment when he got to the top of the stairs, which opened to an immense room, but what was such a surprise was the entire roof of the room was glassed. The light seemed as if he were outdoors. A beautiful, old chandelier hung over the center of the foyer, its sparkling crystals catching the light.

"What a wonderful idea," he said.

"Yes, it's one of my greatest pleasures. In the evenings, on clear nights, the stars seem to hang right above the glass. It's a wonderfully peaceful place to sit, but parties here are such fun.

"Here you are, George. I do hope your stay here will be as enjoyable to you as it will be for us," Abby said graciously.

She led him into a room that showed much thoughtfulness in decorating. The wall containing the fireplace was painted a slate gray. A fantastic picture of the ocean crashing on giant boulders, with sunlight diffused through the spray, made him feel as if he were standing on a cliff overlooking the sea. A lighthouse dominated the left portion of the oil painting and contained the colors of the room, which were gray and white with splashes of bright red in the pillows. The stark-white trim and a comfortable chair enhanced the beauty.

"What a beautiful room, Abby. I can see your taste is not all in your mouth," he said in jest.

Abby laughed. "Thank you. I'm sure Elijah will want to show you through the rest of the house, but you can freshen up a bit or rest, whatever your heart desires. You have a balcony here if you care to sit out here and read or simply enjoy the scenery. Dinner will be at six thirty."

George sat down in a slate-gray chair, pushing the red cushions aside. He leaned back in the chair and closed his eyes. He sat quietly, stilling his heart and thoughts, soaking up the peace that flowed around him.

"Lord," he prayed, "I ask for Thy guidance to help me find the solution to Oscar Farrow's death, whether it was an accident or murder. Please let me find the truth. I pray for Mrs. Farrow, that Thou wouldst comfort her heart. Also, Lord, I pray that her daughter can be found, and soon. Too, I pray that I may be a blessing to Elijah and Abigail while I'm here. May Thy hand guide me, and help me to always listen to Thee."

He sat for a few more minutes, simply resting. He got up and used the large bathing room and made his way downstairs, looking forward to some good conversation with Elijah.

George found him waiting in the parlor. When he entered, he looked around with pleasure. It was understated elegance, a grand room with a huge bay window that made the room appear even bigger. The far wall had a large fireplace with a beautifully carved oaken mantel above it. The accoutrements perfectly complemented the room. Two ornately carved wingback chairs, the upholstery a pale green, matched the pillows of the settee, which separated the wingbacks. A cheerful fire burned in the grate, warding off the chill.

Elijah stood, and a smile wreathed his face. "Come in, George. Please make yourself at home. I can't begin to tell you how grateful I am you came back with me." He gestured to the area around the hearth. The settee faced the fireplace, separated from it by a large square coffee table. To the right and left of the table were the wingbacks, and George selected one and sat easily, crossing one calf over his knee.

"You have a magnificent place here. I look forward to seeing the rest of the house, but for now I simply wish to relax before dinner and enjoy the comfort. I haven't taken any time off since I lost Adeline. We were the same as you, childless, but we were so in love, it was all right. When she became terminally ill, I felt so helpless. God didn't choose to heal her, and I thought I'd go insane with the sorrow and loneliness after she died. Now, the deep sorrow is gone, but the memories are good and a comfort. Time really is a healer when it comes to mourning. She'll always be a part of me and has left me a richer person for having had the years I enjoyed with her."

Elijah nodded. "I know how you felt when she was so ill. I felt desperately helpless when Abby was so ill. I cannot begin to tell you how I felt when she was healed. I still thank God every day for His healing touch. It's not something I will ever take for granted."

"No," George murmured, "no, I don't imagine you do."

Matthew had gone with Liberty into the house. He washed up and then headed back to the kitchen. Conchita was a bit late getting lunch finished up, but it was ready and waiting.

Cady was sitting at the table with Liberty and started to stand when he entered the room, but he waved her to be seated.

"I'm going to give you a little instruction, young lady," he said, his eyes smiling at her. "You don't stand when a man or woman enters the room. Men are supposed to stand when a woman enters the room, but not vice versa. You can stand if an older man or woman needs a place to be seated and everything is taken, but not when I enter the room, or my wife." He looked at her with Liberty's robe wrapped around her and wondered how any of them missed the fact that Cady was female. She was feminine and delicate.

"Liberty, you are a fantastically astute woman." He planted a kiss on her head. "Have you moved into the house, Cady?"

"Y-yes, sir, I have. I don't have that many things, just my satchel." She felt uncomfortable under his continued perusal. The only man she knew who was really kind was Donny. Nothing about him was a facade. He didn't act one way in private and another in public, the way her pa did.

"I'm glad. I'm not sure it's a good thing for you to be out in the barn with your father out looking for you. Frankly, I don't think he'd come here and snoop around, but it's better to be safe than sorry."

"Thank you, sir. Miss Liberty and I already talked about it, and she felt I should move into the house, so I have. It's a beautiful bedroom. It makes me feel happy, with all that yellow and the daisies and all."

"I said you should move into the house because Matthew suggested it this morning before we even got up. And as for not having much of anything except what is in your satchel, that should be rectified as soon as Donny gets back," Liberty said. "We're getting you some new boys' clothes. Also, Matthew and I were talking and wondered if you'd care to stay on and work for us. I'm having twins, and it's going to be a lot of work until I get into a routine. I'd really like you to stay on here and be a nanny when our babies come. Conchita agrees with me that it seems to be a perfect solution. We won't send you into town for anything, so you won't have to worry about your father finding you. What do you think about that?"

"I'd like that just fine. I don't care to be a burden on anyone. I had just planned to work at whatever Donny set me to, but to be able to stay in the house and help with babies, why, it's something I'm pretty sure I could do. I helped out with my younger brother when he was born. He was five years younger than m-me." Cady's voice faltered as she thought about her brother, and tears started, which she brushed away with an impatient hand.

"Cady, I don't know how much training you've had, or learning, but I'd like to help you and teach you a few things, same as Matthew just did. Do you know how to knit, crochet, or tat?"

"I know how to knit. I've turned many a sock in my few years, but I've never seen crochet. I have no idea what it is, and what is tat?" The blood crept up her face, and she looked at both Matthew and Liberty, her gray eyes enormous. "I would, more than anything in the world, like to learn to read and write. My ma tried to teach us, but we had no books and rarely any paper. My pa wouldn't let us go to school. My English is proper because my ma insisted on it. She was educated and even went to boarding school in Europe. I still don't know anything much about her background and have wondered and wondered why she ever married my pa."

Liberty's eyes misted up when Cady said she couldn't read or write. Indignation rose within her at the injustice of keeping a person ignorant and untaught.

"I will certainly help you learn how to read. That you talk as if you're educated will help you with learning. I have no doubt in a very short time you'll be reading books as if you were born to them. As far as tatting, it's making lace. My granny will come over here, and both of us will show you how to tat."

Donny's stomach growled. He was hungry and needed to eat lunch. He arrived at the Rancho, and instead of grooming his horse, he headed straight for the front door. He opened it. It had taken him quite some time and numerous admonitions before he'd opened that door without knocking.

He called out, "Hello, I'm back."

"We're in the kitchen, Donny," Matthew replied. "Come on in and have some lunch."

Donny headed for the kitchen and stopped dead in his tracks when he saw Cady sitting at the table.

"So, Miss Liberty," he said, "you figured out she is a *she* and not a *he*. I had a feeling you did, but wasn't sure."

"You already knew?" Liberty asked in some astonishment.

"No, no, I didn't. When I got into town, I was just getting off my ride when I saw Cady's pa go into the saloon. I had a good look at him the other day and was pretty sure it was him. I followed him into Grady's. I even talked to him——"

"You talked to my pa?" Cady interrupted as she started in her chair. She nearly tipped over her glass of water.

CHAPTER XVI

Remember ye not the former things, neither consider the things of old.
Behold, I will do a new thing; now it shall spring forth;
shall ye not know it? I will even make a way in the wilderness,
and rivers in the desert.

ISAIAH 43:18–19

"**Y**ES, I DID TALK TO HIM," DONNY SAID. "You could have knocked me over with a feather when he started talking about you." He glanced at Matthew and Liberty. "He talked as if butter wouldn't melt in his mouth. Said his daughter had run away, that she was demented, and her ma was crying buckets wanting her back. I had a difficult time not punching him in the nose, I was so angry. I diverted his attention to Grady." He looked at Cady to explain. "Grady's the bartender and owner. He told your pa that if you were at all smart, you'd make off to San Francisco and get lost there, that your pa would never be able to find you."

"That's what I planned to do. I decided that I could go there or to Stockton, but Stockton isn't as big as San Francisco. I thought I'd get some job at a telegraph office as a runner of messages or something. In truth, I hadn't thought about where I'd live, but I had to get away. I was afraid without my ma there, my pa could kill me, and no one would know, and worse, no one would care. He would come home so drunk, and he's a mean drunk."

"Oh, Cadence," Liberty said, "I am so sorry. I believe your mother did the best she could for you. You seem like a good girl, and you're smart too. It won't take any time at all to get you reading and writing. Half the battle is wanting to learn."

"Your name's Cadence?" Donny asked. He'd been wondering if Cady was her real name.

"Yes, it's Cadence Jean Cassidy. Did you say anything else to my pa?"

"No, Grady did all the talking after I asked him if he'd seen any runaway girls. He's the one who told your pa he's most likely lost you to the big city."

"Donny, sit down and eat with us," Matthew said. "We need to discuss a few things. We're going to need your help too. All things considered, Cadence, I don't want you going into town anymore. If you're outside, even here at the Rancho, I want you to stick close to Donny. He can help you learn to ride better, and he needs to teach you how to shoot. Once you get proficient, we're going to get you a gun and holster of your own. You can wear a sidearm the same as Liberty does when she's not expecting a baby."

Cadence, her eyes huge, looked at Liberty in awe. "You normally wear a gun?"

Liberty grinned. "I certainly do. I don't now I'm so big, but I will… after I have these babies and am able to get my holster belt back on."

"Well, if that don't beat all! I didn't know a woman can wear a gun."

"Remember my sister-in-law I was telling you about? The one who wears denims? She wears a gun too. Here in the West, I think it's important to know how to shoot and to wear one at all times when we are out and about."

Donny went over to the sink and poured water over his hands, washing with the soap made from Chandler Olives. It smelled of aloe and mint. He started to dish himself up, but Conchita slapped at his hands in a playful manner.

"You go seet, an' I geet eet for you. You ees one smart hombre, Donny, and I am proud of you."

"Yes," agreed Matthew, "I thank you for following Mr. Cassidy into the saloon. That was good thinking. You could find out exactly what he's up to. A second visit to Napa means he's pretty sure Cady came this way." He looked over at Cady, whose eyes were as large as saucers, listening to his every word, and added, "We'll protect you all we can, Miss Cady, but you also need to protect yourself."

"Thank you. I will do everything you tell me to. I don't want to ever go back. I feel so carefree here. It's as if I've come home. I can't really explain it…but it's a feeling of peace in my heart."

"Believe me when I say, I know exactly what you mean." Liberty did not elaborate, but Cady couldn't accept Liberty's statement as true. She remembered the continual fear and abuse of her father and decided Liberty didn't know what she was talking about.

Donny bowed his head to pray and then started eating hungrily. "Uhm, this is deeelicious, Conchita! What is it?"

"Eet ees the *chalupas*. Ees good, isn't eet?"

"Yes," said Cady, "it's very good. I can cook some, but my mother was horrible at it. She burned everything. I don't think she was taught to cook when she was growing up. I am self-taught, but I have never tasted food as delicious as yours, Conchita."

"Thank you, *señorita*. I start cooking when I am only five. My mother, she die when I am twelve, and I am cooking for all the family."

"I didn't know that, Conchita," Liberty said. "My mother died when I was seventeen, same as Cady, but I never did anything with food, except to eat it, until I came here." She looked over at Cady, knowing the girl didn't believe her about knowing how she felt. "I was married off at sixteen to a very evil man by a very evil father who turned out not to be my real father—for money. Matthew is my second husband. My first husband ended up murdered by my stepfather. Things have looked very bleak for you in the past, Cady, but I assure you, God loves you more than your mother ever did. I believe He has a purpose for bringing you to us. We will care for you as if you are part of this household—a part of our family."

Cady's jaw dropped at Liberty's words. "Please forgive me. It's true— I didn't believe you when you said you understand about feeling free. I reckon I can say I feel free, but I am also very afraid my father will find me."

Hannibal Cassidy was desperately looking for Cady. He decided his best bet was to go to San Rafael and begin keeping an eye on the

Farrows' house. There seemed to be no other option at this point. What the bartender said in Napa made sense. If he wanted to run away, he'd lose himself in the city too, but something kept niggling at him about the young man in that saloon. He'd acted too nonchalant. *Maybe I'm just imagining things because I want that satchel with the money in it. Iff'n Cady finds a job, she's not going to have time to learn to read better. Iff'n she can't read better, she's never going to know what's in those inheritance papers. Callie was smart to keep all that from me. Iff'n I'd a knowed her parents still wanted her, I'd a made sure she went home to collect all that money. She was their only child, and now all that's left is Cady.*

He rode at a leisurely pace heading for San Rafael. *I need a plan. Maybe I could kidnap Mr. Farrow. No, it'd be better to kidnap the old woman. She'd be easier to handle. I could hold her for ransom and make money that way. I'll have to think more on that.*

The windows in George's room faced east. When he awoke, he stretched and lay quietly, but his body wouldn't relax anymore. He swung his legs over the side of the bed and sat looking around with pleasure.

His wife, Adeline, had been an only child, born of wealthy parents. Not only did they have money, but the name Cunningham opened doors to the most prestigious homes. The Cunninghams were Boston Brahmin... the highest class of society in the city. He'd met Adeline at a special revival service. It had been a tent meeting. Adeline had been a devoted Christian.

He'd fallen in love with her at first sight, long before he'd known she was an only child of very rich parentage. It didn't bother him at all that she used her money to make their life much more comfortable. He worked hard but could never have afforded the house, lifestyle, nor entertainments they enjoyed because of her inheritance. He had been thankful and did not feel diminished by her private income.

George missed her, with an ache in his chest. *Life goes on*, he thought, *but it has lost much of its zest. I look at Elijah and Abigail and see such a closeness of thought, such a oneness—I miss that.*

He shook off his reverie and came back to his reality. *I think Abigail has the same good taste in decorating as my Addy did, and it's why I think of her. Ah well.* He got up and took care of his morning ablutions. Setting his new reading glasses on the bridge of his nose, he took his Bible and went out to sit in the morning sun on his balcony. He read Isaiah 55 and meditated on it for some time. He prayed, and when he finished dressing, he made his way down the double-wide stairs, still marveling at the glassed ceiling of the huge room he'd just traversed.

"Good morning, George." Elijah had been standing at the window watching Polka Dot, their half-Labrador, half-Australian shepherd running around the backyard smelling, her nose to the ground.

"Were you comfortable? Did you sleep or stay awake in a new bed?"

"Oh, I was quite comfortable, thank you, and I slept soundly. I had my door open to the balcony and awoke to birds singing. I feel rested and refreshed and ready for action." He smiled. "Guess that's the three Rs— rested, refreshed, and ready."

"Are you sure that's correct? I heard from Kirk Bannister that the three Rs are rope, ride, and repair fence."

They both laughed. "I don't believe I've ever met Kirk, although I've heard much about him. Just recently got married, didn't he?"

"Yes. You would have enjoyed that case, George. Murder for no apparent reason, but it seems to have straightened itself out without the help of the law, or perhaps I should say, in spite of the law. Are you hungry? I'm ready for some coffee and Bessie's amazing cooking." He turned and spoke so Bessie was included in his statement. "We are still very thankful this gal decided to come west." He turned back to George. "You had quite an entourage to see off on the train that day, didn't you?"

"Yes, I did, but I was happy to do it. How are you, Bessie?"

"I'm fine, sir. Thank you for asking."

She was getting some cinnamon rolls out of the oven, and Elijah's mouth watered with the smell.

"I have your coffee right here, and I'll be getting this icing on the cinnamon rolls. They'll be ready in a jiffy."

It was still fairly early, and Abigail was not yet up. The two men went out to sit at a table surrounded by huge pots of flowers overflowing their containers. Polka Dot ran around the table a couple times and then sat so that Elijah's hand would naturally drop right on her head. He stroked her soft fur a bit, seeming to fill her heart with contentment.

It was a tranquil morning; not a leaf seemed to stir. George, having already been out on the balcony, had noticed the sky with fluffy, puffy white clouds lying low on the horizon. The blue sky overhead was pure indigo. The heady scent of the flowers and the comfort of a good friend was a balm to George's soul.

"I don't believe I ever asked, but whatever happened to Mrs. Brown and her baby? She was one of the ones I saw off on the train that day."

"She ended up marrying the doctor in Napa," Elijah replied. "He fell head over heels the first time he saw her. She'd been experiencing some headaches and fainted. They have her Hannah and now another baby, I believe."

"The conditions I found her in were abominable," George said. He shook his head in remembrance, then asked, "When do you think we'll go see Mrs. Farrow?" He was starting on a new mystery, and it never ceased to give him joy to try to figure out the whodunits of a case.

"Soon as we finish eating, my friend," Elijah responded with good humor. He pulled out his watch from his fob pocket and glanced at it. "It's still a bit early to be visiting her. Round about nine o'clock should be about right."

George sipped the hot coffee and sat back. He closed his eyes momentarily and put his face up to catch the full sun. "I believe you have a piece of heaven here." He took another sip of his coffee and added, "I am so glad I came west. I haven't had much chance to enjoy myself, but I walk to work and enjoy the fresh air. The weather is astonishing after living in Boston, isn't it?"

"Yes, yes, it is. While you're here, I'd like us to go up to Napa and visit Matthew and Liberty. She's expecting a baby. That woman is so happy and content."

"She's a lovely woman, inside and out," George said. "I knew her mother, Violet. I believe I told you that. Violet Browning was married to Jacques Corlay. I remember being at Violet's father's funeral. I never could prove Corlay murdered him, but I know he did. Poor Violet. She was so bereaved. I felt sorry for her. One almost feels guilty when one enjoys such happiness and contentment and sees the desperate unhappiness of another."

Elijah looked at George, a little startled by the comment. "Yes, that is true, and yet most times it boils down to choices, does it not? Violet married Corlay, but she didn't have to. It was a choice."

"Yes, that too is true, but look at your Liberty. It wasn't her choice to marry Armand Bouvier. She was literally sold to him. Many times the unhappiness is not due to our own choices but someone else's." George decided to change the subject, "Wonderful coffee."

Elijah nodded but said, "I think when we finish here, we should walk down to the mission, and I'll give you a tour, and then we'll go to Susannah's house. The mission is on the way."

"Good plan."

Hannibal Cassidy scouted around San Rafael and finally found where the Farrows lived. He didn't want to ask many questions, as it was a small community. He didn't care to have his presence bandied about.

He stood outside the stately residence and stared. It was huge and imposing, and the thought crossed his mind that Callie must have loved him very much to give all this up for him. The house was off the main street and seemed to have acres of land with it. It was two storied, with a circular drive and lined with trees around the front.

He rode back to the main street where he'd seen a sign for an inn. Riding up to Three Hawks Inn, he thought it small compared to the inns in Sacramento. This one seemed to be the only place to stay in the small town. Tying his horse at a long railing, he walked up the one step onto the boardwalk. Pushing through the glassed front door, he strode to the reception desk.

"Afternoon," he said as he removed his hat. "What are your rates?"

"Good afternoon to you. My name is Eli, and the room rates are twenty-five cents a night. If you want breakfast and dinner, it'll be another fifteen cents."

Hannibal plopped three dollars on the counter and said, "I'll start with this. If I need more time, I'll pay up as I go."

"Right, sir," Eli said. "Bathhouses are down the street, twenty-five cents for a full tub." He nodded and added, "Please sign here, sir."

He turned the ledger around, and Hannibal was caught off guard. He did some quick thinking and taking the quill, wrote down his neighbor's name, Johnny Sears, with a flourish.

Eli said, "Right, everything seems to be in order. Now please follow me, sir."

He led Hannibal up the narrow stairs. Taking a set of keys, he opened the door and walked into the room. It was strictly utilitarian, no frills, but it was exactly what Hannibal wanted.

"Commode is a right turn down the end of the hall. Enjoy your stay, Mr. Sears."

Hannibal pulled aside the curtains, happy his room faced the main street. It would keep him from being bored to death. He could watch the happenings of the street when he wasn't out on it himself.

He sat down on the bed and bounced up and down, checking the mattress. It would suit him just fine.

CHAPTER XVII

Iron sharpeneth iron;
so a man sharpeneth the countenance of his friend.

PROVERBS 27:17

ABIGAIL MADE HER WAY DOWN THE STAIRS and into the kitchen, grabbing a cup of coffee on her way out the door to where Elijah was sitting with George.

"Slept in this morning," she announced unnecessarily. Her slender form was wrapped in a beautiful blue silk robe and matched the deep blue of her eyes.

Abby had never been a woman one could call beautiful, but somehow, being in her presence for a very few minutes made her beautiful. She exuded Christ's peace and love. It made her a radiant woman who everyone seemed attracted to.

Both men stood, and George pulled out her chair, but first Abby kissed Elijah on the mouth, surprising George but causing his lips to turn up in a smile.

"Good morning, Abigail," he said.

"Good morning, George. How are you this morning?" she asked.

"In the pink," he answered with a grin. "As I said to Elijah, I am rested, refreshed, and ready for the day, madam."

"I'm glad," she said simply. "Have you two been concocting plans?"

"Yes, yes, we have," Elijah said. "We're going down to the mission. I'll give George a quick tour, and then we'll go on over to Susannah's and have a chat. I wonder how she's doing." He said it as a statement, not a question, and added, "Well, my dear, we'd love to stay and enjoy your company, but we have an agenda and some work to do. We will plan to be here for lunch, or should we meet you for lunch at the mission?"

"I think the mission," she replied. "Bessie and I will head down there after I have breakfast and attend to a few things around here. I have some catching up to do. I'll see you at lunch." Elijah kissed her before they headed out the door.

Arriving at the mission, George was amazed by the size of it. The integrity of the building had been kept when the exterior had been remodeled. They entered the wrought iron gates and walked up to the front door.

Entering the foyer, George saw that from the windows far above their heads, light diffused throughout the front entry. It was bright and cheerful. Against the far wall was an oaken pew, flanked on one end by a huge plant and on the other by a large round end table topped with a picture book and vase of freshly cut flowers.

The mission exuded charm and modern comfort blended with age and culture. It looked to George, as Elijah led him through it, that every effort had been made to preserve the history of the structure and yet provide comfort within.

Elijah took him through the entire building, showing him how several rooms, now unoccupied, were decorated with different color schemes. He led him out back and showed off the vegetable garden the women tended, as well as the roses and flower gardens. There was a fountain, and benches were placed strategically for relaxing and conversation.

"It is very tastefully done, isn't it?"

"Yes, yes, it is," Elijah replied. "My Abigail likes nothing better than to decorate a room, unless it's matchmaking a couple." Elijah laughed fondly, and George joined him.

"Well, I must say, she's done a wonderful job here."

They peeked into the kitchen and saw Bessie and Abigail already there.

"You've done a magnificent job decorating and setting up the garden plots," George said to Abby. "It's really quite homey for such a large institution."

"Thank you. We try to keep it as homelike as we can possibly manage," Abby replied.

"Would you like anything more to eat?" Elijah asked George.

"You must be jesting, Elijah. I couldn't eat another bite after that huge breakfast. I am looking forward to meeting Mrs. Farrow. Shall we head that way?"

"Certainly. I do believe we have whiled away enough time." He pulled out his watch again and saw it was close to ten. "We certainly can visit her now.

"We'll see you later," Elijah said to Abigail as they headed out the door.

The mission was located on the corner of the main street. The two men made a right turn to go down a couple more streets, conversing as they walked.

"Oscar's death occurred a little over six weeks ago. I have been extremely worried about Susannah. It's one thing to suffer the loss of a loved one, but to go into a physical decline the way she has is simply not normal. Susannah Farrow is not a woman to mope around. Normally she is full of vitality and quick of wit."

"If she's being poisoned slowly, it would most likely resemble a malaise of some sort, I should think," George said, "a general all-over feeling of going downhill."

"Yes, yes, I believe that's what it's been. Tess, her personal servant, told me that Dr. Huffman couldn't find anything specifically wrong with her, that it was just a steady decline in health. Tess has been quite worried about her."

As they crossed the street toward the Farrow mansion, George, always one to sense things, felt the back of his neck prickle. He laid his hand on Elijah's arm, and the two men stopped midstreet, surprise clearly evident in Elijah's eyes.

George, with no explanation, slowly turned around and perused the other side of the street, letting his eyes drift slowly across the hedges and shrubs that lined the street. He saw a sudden movement, and although he continued to turn his head, his eyes were fixed on the spot where he'd seen movement. He saw it again and knew the two of them were being watched.

He turned and, with a nod of his head at Elijah, who'd been completely silent, began to walk again toward the long drive of Susannah Farrow's house.

Elijah wondered why George had stopped but didn't ask.

Once they were inside the confines of the huge opened gates of the mansion, George slowed his pace and spoke to Elijah.

"We are being watched, Elijah. Can you believe it? There is someone in that screen of bushes who's keeping watch over this house. I find that interesting. Would your Mr. Kepler be doing that?"

Elijah looked dumbfounded at George but shook his head.

"No, no, I don't believe he would. He's a bit of an oddity. I know this is criticizing, but he's not a man to ever walk where his shoes might get dirty, so to speak. You know the type. Are you're sure, George? I'm not questioning your wisdom, but surprised someone would sneak around and watch this house. I wonder, should you tell Mrs. Farrow?"

"That will depend on her state of mind and whether she's able to handle such information. If she's ill, I don't think it wise to add another concern. She will have enough simply dealing with her health. If, on the other hand, she is better, I will certainly tell her. She must watch her step. I don't suppose being in mourning the way she is, she gets out much."

Elijah sighed and said, "No, no, she doesn't. I don't believe she's been out since Oscar's funeral. It's customary to closet one's self, isn't it? Poor woman, to lose her husband like that, and I have no doubt Kepler pushed him over that balcony."

Elijah was glad George had not spoken to him when perusing the hedges. He would have turned around and stared. It was a natural reaction. Fortunately, he'd kept his eyes on his friend.

"George, I believe you were meant to be here at this time. I think this whole thing is turning into a mystery, and you're the man to figure it out, but I don't believe it's Amos spying on the house."

Elijah looked up to see a man descending the front steps of Susannah's home. He suddenly realized it was Amos Kepler. He was heading straight for them.

He turned and grinned at George. "I know it to be a verifiable fact that Amos Kepler's not spying on this house. That's him heading toward us."

That bit of information took George by surprise, and he watched closely as the other man drew near, assessing his walk and general appearance.

Elijah lifted his hat to Amos, speaking politely to him. "Good day, sir! And how are you this beautiful day?"

Amos lifted his hat in return, but his face was flushed a beet red, anger barely contained. "I'm quite well, Elijah, and you?" His voice was clipped, outrage evident in every word.

"I'm doing well, Amos, doing well. Please meet my friend George Baxter. George, this is Amos Kepler, who runs a private school here in San Rafael, the San Rafael School of Primary Learning. Amos' son, Edward, clerks in my office."

George lifted his hat and nodded to Mr. Kepler, his eyes searching him out without Amos realizing he was being taken apart—clothing, demeanor, and looks by an astute detective. George's eyes were bland as he replaced his hat and reached out to shake Amos' hand.

"Pleased to meet you, Mr. Kepler." George was glad Elijah hadn't revealed his profession.

Amos Kepler, looking apoplectic, shook George's hand but abruptly turned toward Elijah. "You have business with Mrs. Farrow?" he asked rudely, his voice still sounding curt. He looked as if it took every ounce of willpower to not to let his anger explode.

Amos looked George up and down, feeling diminished in his presence.

George always looked impeccable, as if he'd just walked out of an expensive tailor shop.

The man's attire and demeanor were something Amos had, for as long as he could remember, craved to achieve, and something this man seemed to take for granted—suave and debonair without trying.

"Yes, yes, I do have business here," Elijah answered. "I certainly do. Good day, Amos." Elijah tipped his hat one more time, politely, and without further ado started walking. He didn't wish to answer any more questions.

Amos wanted to know more but hesitated, which was his undoing, because Elijah moved away, and it was too late to ask what his business with Mrs. Farrow was.

George, walking by Elijah's side, ruminated on the information he'd just gathered.

"Amos Kepler is an exceedingly proud and exceedingly angry man," he said softly.

"Yes, yes, it does seem that way," Elijah answered. "I have never seen him so discombobulated. I've a feeling he wasn't allowed in to visit. Wonder if Susannah is worse. I pray not."

The two men walked up the wide cement steps to a long porch across the front of the house. Elijah took hold of the brass knocker and gave it a couple sharp raps, prepared to wait for a time before the door opened.

To his surprise, the door flew open.

Tess stood tall, ready to tell Mr. Kepler a thing or two. She looked at Elijah and George, batting her eyes in total surprise.

She seemed to deflate in front of them as a look of embarrassment replaced the look of umbrage on her face.

"Sorry," she said, "I thought it was that Mr. Kepler come back again to annoy us further. Please, do come in."

Elijah, a bit surprised at her comment, said, "Thank you, Tess. This is a very close friend of mine, George Baxter. Is Mrs. Farrow able to see us this morning?"

"Oh, I have no doubt she'll see you, but please come wait in the parlor, and I'll see if she's amenable to having visitors." She led them into a large parlor located off the huge front entry, her shoes clicking on the black-and-white marble floor. She pushed open farther an already opened door and ushered the two men in. "Please," she said, "wait here, and I'll notify Mrs. Farrow you're here." She gestured to a couple chairs.

Elijah, who had been to the Farrows many times, sat down, but George walked slowly around the room, which was tastefully but elegantly done.

Victorian in appearance, the settee and side chairs were a tufted pale apricot. The frames of the chairs were curved and carved dark mahogany. Splashes of cream and orange and pale green, as well as the apricot color of the settee, were blended into a pleasing pattern on the heavy drapes, which framed the windows that stretched across the outer wall. A gorgeous painting of George Washington kneeling in prayer hung over the fireplace, and brass candlesticks hugged one corner of the mantel. The walls were the palest of creamy apricot, and the accouterments suggested refinement at its best.

George finally sat down and looked over at Elijah. "What a beautiful room" was all he said.

Elijah nodded. "You should see the stair landing. I think it's my favorite place in this entire magnificent house."

Tess came back in with a small tap on the door before entering. "Mrs. Farrow is waiting to see you," she said. "Mr. Humphries, she's delighted you are here and has asked that you join her in her sitting room. Please, come this way."

She led the two men down the hall toward the back of the house to a circular room that was all windows for walls. It seemed more like a sunroom than a sitting room, because it was awash with light and flooded with a peaceful air.

Susannah stood up when the two men entered the room. She was dressed in unrelieved black, but the gown was a beautiful silk with tiny jet buttons traveling up the front. When she stood, the gown swept around her, the tight sleeves ending in points over the backs of her hands. Her strawberry-blonde hair was swept up into a loose bun from which a few tendrils escaped, softening the look of mourning.

Elijah strode over to her, taking both hands she held out to him.

"Good morning, Susannah, how are you?"

"I'm fine, Elijah," she said, "I'm feeling so much better."

"Susannah, this is a friend of mine, George Baxter. George, please meet Mrs. Susannah Farrow."

Susannah turned to proffer her hand to George. Looking up into his eyes, she felt a frisson of shock. *I feel I know him*, she thought. *It's as if I've known him for a long time. Goodness, how strange.*

George took Susannah's hand and looked down into a pair of the most beautiful gray eyes he'd ever seen. They were an unusual gray ringed by darker gray. The black dress enhanced the color.

"Madam, it is my pleasure to meet you."

"Any friend of Elijah's is welcome, sir. It is with a sense of joy that I welcome you to my home," she said with a gracious air. "Please be seated." She turned to Tess. "Tess, dear, please have Opal make up a tray." She turned back to her guests. "Tea or coffee?"

"Tea for me," George responded, and Elijah nodded in agreement.

Tess left, closing the heavy door behind her. Both men were still standing.

"Please," Susannah said again as she gestured to a couple chairs, "be seated."

George looked down at Susannah and smiled, the quirk in his cheek evident at the top of a crease that couldn't really be called a dimple.

Susannah felt flustered and was amazed by her own reaction to this man. She sat in her usual chair, her back ramrod straight. Elijah and George made themselves comfortable.

"We happened to meet Amos Kepler on your driveway, madam," Elijah said. "Was he here for one of his regular visits?"

"N-no." She glanced quickly at George, hoping he would not think her rude. "I told him the other day not to visit me anymore." She blushed and didn't realize how becoming it was. "He...oh, Elijah, I think he has every intention of courting me," she said in a rush of words. "I've never, ever cast my eyes in his direction nor let him think such a thing is possible, and between you and me, it is an affront to me, when my poor Oscar is hardly cold in his grave!" She took a deep breath and tried to still the rush of emotion that overcame her.

"Susannah"—Elijah cleared his throat and asked kindly—"how well do you know Amos?" He shifted his weight a bit in his chair, uncomfortable with the information he planned to share with her this day. "What I mean is, were Oscar and you friends with him, socially? Have you had him to dinner and such?"

"N-no. The only time we had him to dinner was when we invited the entire staff of the school here. Frankly, although his credentials were impeccable, neither Oscar nor I cared much for him. Oscar felt he was the right person for the job, and although it was years ago, had reservations about him personally." Susannah glanced over at George, whose eyes were fixed on hers. She blushed and looked down at her lap, asking herself, *What is the matter with me?*

CHAPTER XVIII

But whoso hearkeneth unto me shall dwell safely,
and shall be quiet from fear of evil.

PROVERBS 1:33

SUSANNAH LOOKED AT ELIJAH, CURIOSITY clearly stamped in her gray eyes. "Why, Elijah, why are you asking me this?"

There was a tap on the door, and Tess came in pushing the intricately carved wooden tea trolley into the sitting room. Tea, steeped in a rose-flowered teapot, and the smell of freshly baked croissants wafted into the room.

"Will that be all, madam?" Tess asked.

"Yes, thank you, Tess, and please tell Opal thank you. This is lovely."

George liked Susannah Farrow's manners. She was quite a striking woman, with a look of strength about her and yet a look of femininity. Her gray eyes were luminous. She was gracious yet totally unaware of her charm.

"I shall pour," she said as she picked up the teapot.

George had a quick flashback of Adeline showing him the proper way to pour tea. She had told him that it was an art form in the class of society in which she had been brought up. They had laughed together, but he saw before him a woman who excelled in gracious hospitality, and was thankful for the memory she had evoked.

Susannah handed them their tea and scooted a little side table closer to George's chair so he could put his saucer and scone on it. He smiled at her gratefully, noticing her blush and wondering about it. Elijah had the coffee table close at hand.

As Susannah sat back down, she said, "Before you answer my question, I will tell you something." She picked up her teacup and saucer, taking a little sip of her tea. "I am a bit frightened by the intensity of Mr. Kepler's persistence. I told him outright the other day I didn't wish him to come visit me anymore, that I had no plans to ever marry again. He left incensed that I would cut off his visits that way. He has since come to the door, but I have told Tess to tell him I am indisposed and will not be visiting with him. He came to visit me today, and Tess told me he was infuriated she would not let him in."

George nodded knowingly.

Elijah sat chewing on a scone as he digested the information she had shared. He took a sip of tea, setting his cup down as he leaned forward to speak earnestly to his hostess.

"Susannah, after visiting with you the other day, I felt uneasy. I went straight home, had my majordomo pack me a few things, and rode to San Francisco. Abigail came with me. We stayed with our surrogate son, and yesterday morning, I rode into the city to visit George, who is a wonderful friend. I met him when we both lived in Boston. Since then, he has moved to San Francisco and taken over as head of the detective branch of the police. I met him in the same capacity when we lived in Boston."

Elijah took another sip of tea as Susannah looked at George in wonderment. Her eyes swung back to Elijah, who cleared his throat, as he was wont to do when nervous.

"I talked to George about your situation because, madam, I was quite sure that you were slowly being poisoned."

"Poisoned!" Susannah exclaimed. "Why would anyone want to——" She stopped talking abruptly, her eyes widened, and she said, "Ah, that's why I've been feeling so poorly. How did he find out about the will? Amos, I mean. How did Amos find out about the will?"

Suddenly, her eyes brightened with tears. "Did he kill Oscar?" she whispered. "Did Amos Kepler push Oscar over that balcony?"

"You are very quick, madam," George said. "It is Elijah's and my belief that he did. I am so sorry for your loss. I lost my wife to cancer, and I cannot imagine your sorrow and shock at a death so sudden. It is like John Donne said in his poem, 'No man is an Island,' the part where it says, 'Any man's death diminishes me, Because I am involved in mankind.'"

"Exactly, so, sir," she responded. "But how can you be sure? How can you prove it?"

"We cannot prove yea or nay at this point, but it is in my estimation quite clear. He stands to inherit a great deal, does he not?"

"Yes, he does, but again, I ask you, Elijah, how did he know?" She dabbed at her eyes with a black lacy handkerchief tucked into the wrist of her sleeve.

"Madam, there is the conundrum. I'm not quite sure, but I have a strong feeling that a clerk in my office related the terms of the will to him," Elijah replied.

"But why? Why would he do that? Isn't he sworn not to disclose paperwork he comes across?"

"Yes, yes, he is," Elijah replied heavily, "but you see, the clerk is Edward Kepler."

"Oh my," Susannah responded. "Edward…I've known him since he was a little boy. Coming across that information would have been difficult knowledge for him to keep to himself, wouldn't it?"

"Yes, yes, it would have been very difficult, but he, in all fairness to integrity, should have done so," Elijah said.

"Yes," George interjected, "telling his father no doubt precipitated your husband's death, madam. In my line of business, I have found some men will do anything for money."

Elijah said, "What is now of great concern is your own person. George and I believe he began poisoning you. He may indeed have planned to marry you, but the outcome, you understand, is he wouldn't have to funnel the money through the school to gain access to it. It would be his by inheritance."

Susannah listened carefully. "I understand what you're saying, sir. He would marry me, and then I would conveniently die, and he'd have the money. Will you go ahead and hire the Pinkertons, Elijah? I want to find Callie or find what happened to her. Perhaps she has children."

"Yes, I do plan to hire the Pinkertons on this. Time is running out, and we need to find your daughter before the six months is up."

George spoke up. "Madam, do you know your house is being watched?"

"What!" Susannah cried. "What are you saying? My house is being watched? By whom, sir?" Susannah for the first time seemed moved by a bit of fear.

Elijah interjected. "When we were crossing the street...George, you tell her. You know what happened better than I do."

"Mrs. Farrow—"

"Susannah," she interrupted. "If you're a close friend of Elijah's, let's drop the formalities. Please call me Susannah." She turned a full smile on him for the first time, and George was bowled over. He smiled back, and the two sat looking at each other without a word until Elijah finally cleared his throat.

George recovered first. "Sorry. Where was I? Ah, yes, we were crossing the street, and right in the middle of it, I felt a prickling sensation on the back of my neck. You, I am sure, know it, that feeling someone is staring at you but don't know from whence it came. Elijah and I stopped, and I turned and perused the trees and bushes lining the opposite side of the street, and I saw movement. I kept turning my head, but my eyes were focused on a certain spot, and there is no doubt someone was hiding in those bushes. I thought at first it may be our Mr. Kepler, but Elijah assured me that Kepler was not one to dirty his shoes."

At the last comment, Susannah smiled at Elijah. "Exactly so, sir. Those few words describe Mr. Kepler perfectly." She turned to face George. "So what am I to do? We only have women here. If someone should care to break in, I do know how to use my derringer, but Oscar said my little gun wouldn't hurt a fly."

George responded, "John Wilkes Booth used a derringer to kill President Lincoln, madam. It can do damage, but it's a close-up and one-time-shot type of gun." He crossed one leg over the other comfortably and drummed his fingers on the arm of the chair, thinking of how this woman could be protected.

Elijah said, "Madam, I think you should come stay at our house until we can straighten all this out. I have a feeling we have two different things going on here. I could be wrong, but I believe whoever was in those bushes across the street is unrelated to Kepler. My desire, at this point, is to keep you safe. Abigail would be delighted. I could hire a few guards for you, to patrol the grounds and keep your belongings and your servants safe."

George stopped drumming, uncrossed his leg, and sat back. "Excellent, Elijah. That is an excellent plan. Are you amenable to it, Susannah?"

"Why, if you hire guards, I should be perfectly safe here, shouldn't I?" She looked over at George and glanced at Elijah. "I don't care to leave my servants if it's dangerous."

Elijah said, "You are on vacation, George. You can stay here with her, if you don't mind. I'll go back to our house and collect your things. I don't want Susannah left alone."

George looked over at Susannah, fully agreeing with Elijah, and she was smiling at him.

Elijah got up. "Thank you, madam, for the tea and scones. I shall go home and be back shortly."

"Perhaps," Susannah said, "you and Abigail could come to dinner. We could have a nice evening together. I've been too ill to be very lonely, but a game of whist would be amenable to me. Is that all right with you, Elijah?"

"Thank you. We'd love to come. I'll tell Abigail about this evening, collect George's things, and head back here. After that, I'll hire some guards, and then I have a bit of work to catch up on. I'm sure George will keep you entertained."

"First, Elijah, let me pray." She turned to look at George. "You are a believer, are you not?"

"Yes, madam, and not the Sunday-go-to-meeting kind. I love the Lord with all my heart, soul, mind, and strength." George was not at all ashamed of his personal relationship with Jesus.

Susannah beamed. "Let me pray then. Father God, how grateful we are that Thou didst love us before the foundation of the world. That Thou didst know us in our mothers' wombs, that Thou dost love us with an unfathomable love. We don't deserve such love, but Thou gives love and life itself. Protect us, Father, guide us, and help us to find Callie and a witness to prove Amos killed my Oscar. My comfort is that I know he's dancing for Thee, having the time of his eternal life. We thank Thee in advance for what Thou hast planned for us. In the peerless name of Jesus we pray. Amen."

Susannah got up and showed Elijah to the door. "I do hope whoever is spying on this house will be caught. It's not nice thinking someone is out to get you or to spy on the comings and goings of my home."

She gave a wave of her hand as Elijah bade her good-bye.

George was standing right behind her, and as she turned, she looked up and into his eyes and saw something there that caused the blush to rise up her neck and into her face, but at the same time, delighted her.

Hannibal had arisen a bit late. He had imbibed too much the night before and was in a terrible temper. He got up and donned a pair of dirty trousers. Scratching at his bare chest, he unlocked his door and went down the hall in his bare feet to the commode room. He stepped on something sharp and let out a yelp and a curse.

Once back in his room, he sat down on the only chair and saw he had cut his foot. He dabbed at the blood with a dirty sock and then pulled both socks on. He tugged his boots on, tying the short laces, which had knots in them to keep them useable. He stood up and kicked at the bedpost with a booted foot and then went over by the window to sit in the room's only chair. He drew the flimsy curtain aside and stared down into the street as he put on his shirt, doing the buttons up the front while he thought about what he must do.

I've got to find Cady, he thought. *I need that money.*

He grabbed his hat, locked his room, and went down to get some breakfast. He was hungry, but more, he was thirsty.

He ate slowly, trying to while away the time. When he was finished, he walked to the street where the Farrows lived and hid behind the bushes to keep a lookout on the house.

Cadence had never, in all her born days, been so carefree and happy. The grief she felt over her mother and brother were overshadowed by the newness of her life. There was always something happening, and evenings were her favorite time because many times, they played games.

Liberty sat with her each morning after breakfast, and she was slowly reading *The Adventures of Tom Sawyer*. She loved reading about his exploits and wondered if he'd win Becky Thatcher's heart.

Liberty had given her a spelling list, and every day she worked on learning how to spell. Many of the words were familiar, but sometimes there were words she didn't know, and Liberty made her look them up in Noah Webster's dictionary.

She was becoming proficient in writing her name. Liberty said she must copy the spelling list and write down the meanings of the words. At first she only printed, but Liberty had a copybook that had all the letters done in cursive, and Cadence was practicing.

She sat at the table, looking for all the world like the boy she had posed herself to be. Her strawberry-blonde curls gleamed in the light, and her brow was furrowed in concentration.

Conchita looked over at her and smiled.

"You ees steel looking like the boy, Cady. Do you like the clothes Donny, he peeck out for you?"

"Yes, they're a lot more comfortable than girls' clothes. Wonder why that is?" Cady was beginning to question everything and enjoyed listening to conversation. She realized when she had been at home, it was most of the time very quiet. No one talked because no one wanted to draw Pa's attention.

Cady looked over at Conchita. "Why did you come to the United States?"

"I didn't comed here. I be borned here. I was borned just below San Franceesco, but eet be Mehico then, not United States. When United States haf the war weeth Mehico and they ween, all Mehicans, they become United States citizens. I be borned four years after these lands are no longer Mehico, een eighteen forty-seex. It be automatic whether you want to be or not. Eef you no want to be US citizen, you muss move further south."

Conchita was making *enchiladas de pollo*, and Cady could smell it, her mouth watering.

"Did you start speaking English when you were little?"

"No, I be speaking Spaneesh unteel I am twenty-nine. I am speaking Engleesh for seex years now. Diego, he making me speak the Engleesh. My parents, God rest their souls"—she crossed herself—"they never learn the Engleesh."

"So, you are thirty-five?"

"*Sí*, but I am feeling much older." She smiled at the young woman and added, "An' I much smarter than thirty-five."

She laughed her contagious, explosive laughter, and Cady couldn't help but laugh.

"I'm going to get smarter too. I want to learn all I can about all kinds of things. Liberty is showing me how to sit and walk and—"

"Anyones know how to seet." Conchita looked at Cady, surprise filling her dark brown eyes.

"Not properly, they don't. A lady is supposed to stand by a chair and feel the seat with the back of her leg and without looking, sit with her back straight, not touching the back of the chair. She said she's only teaching me this in case I am in polite society. She doesn't expect me to sit like that all the time, but I'm learning proper manners. That's why she is setting so many utensils at my plate, so I will use the proper ones. I'm learning a lot. I just hope I can remember it all."

"Oh, you ees the smart one, Cady. You weel remember." Conchita nodded her head sagely. "*Sí*, you weel remember."

CHAPTER XIX

Then shall ye call upon me,
and ye shall go and pray unto me,
and I will hearken unto you.

JEREMIAH 29:12

DONNY WAS KEEPING HIS FEELINGS tightly in check. With all that Cady had to deal with right now, he didn't feel proclaiming his love for her was wise. He hugged his thoughts to himself, and the more he hid his thoughts, the stronger they became. He didn't want a strain to come into their relationship if she didn't feel the same way. He would wait and see how things progressed.

This afternoon, he was taking Cadence out for a ride. He whispered her name under his breath. "Cadence." He liked the sound of it, but he never called her anything but Cady. She was still hiding her identity to all except those inside the house.

He was surprised how fast she was becoming proficient at riding a horse. He decided proficiency had a lot to do with willingness. Once she'd lost her fear of horses, she was a natural, and he was proud of her.

Donny was working, cutting clusters of grapes quickly, his thoughts keeping the same pace. There was much to do during harvest, and he felt as if he were slacking a bit to take Cady out riding, but it was at Matthew's suggestion. He'd told Donny that Cady needed to learn how to ride and shoot as soon as possible, that it was a priority.

He grinned to himself. *How did I ever think she was a boy? She is so feminine, and pretty too.* He grinned again, and his inattention cost him.

"Oh, drat it all," he said. He stood up and looked at his finger. The cut was deep. *I'd better go in and have it tended to.* He walked a long way down the row and decided he'd better wrap his kerchief around it, as it was bleeding profusely.

He went into the Rancho, calling out as he entered, but stopped dead in his tracks when he saw Cady. She was dressed in one of Liberty's dresses, and it fit her just fine.

"I, uh, well, uh, you look nice!" he said. "I've never seen you in a dress, and you caught me by surprise."

"What'd you do to your finger?" she asked. She took him by the elbow and led him to the kitchen sink.

"What you do?" Conchita asked.

"I cut it on a billhook," he said. "Got to going too fast and not thinking about what I was doing, I reckon."

Conchita said, "Let me see eet."

Cady started unwrapping it before he could. She gasped when she saw it. "It looks really bad. Maybe I should ride into town for Dr. John."

Liberty entered the kitchen. "We will get someone else, but you're not to go off Bannister property unless you're accompanied. We have plenty of workers this year. Matthew will be fine."

"I can ride into town. It's just my finger that's cut."

"Let me see," Liberty asked. "Oh, Donny, you do need Dr. John for this. It needs carbolic and stitches. You'll want it cleaned out. An infection could easily set in there. Let me pray. Father, we know that You are the ultimate healer. We thank You for Your lovingkindness and goodness. We pray right now, in the name of Jesus, that healthy healing will occur and Donny's finger will be fine. Thank You, Father. Amen."

Cady was in awe of the prayer, and Liberty acting as if God was right there with them gave her the shivers.

Liberty said, "Cady, go find Matthew, but hurry and change your clothes first. You don't look much like a boy in that get-up!" She laughed.

"Nope, you sure don't," Donny agreed, his eyes glinting in appreciation. His finger had not really hurt before, numb from the shock, but now it was screaming with pain. He sat down at the table, with his elbow on it, holding his arm straight up, hoping to slow down the bleeding.

Cady ran to her room, changing quickly into denims and a checkered shirt. She slipped her arms into the leather vest and buttoned it up, not because she was cold but because Liberty said it aided in keeping her looking like a boy. She slipped on the fine leather boots Donny had purchased, loving the smell of the leather, and headed out the door.

It took her quite some time. She never could find Matthew, but she found Diego.

"Diego, Donny's cut his finger really bad with a billhook and he needs stitches." Cady gulped in air, breathless from running. "Liberty told me to find Matthew, but I can't seem to track him down. I've wasted time trying to find him. Liberty wants someone to ride into town to fetch Dr. John, but she won't let me do it."

"No." Diego stood up, stretching his back, and said, "I weel go. Right now, I weel go. You go back an' tell Miss Liberty I go geet heem." He smiled, his teeth showing very white under his mustache.

Cady raced back down the row, heading for the house. *Donny's finger looks awful*, she thought. *He's cut it clear to the bone. I'm sure glad blood doesn't make me woozy. Poor Timmy used to faint whenever he saw blood.*

She entered the front door, accidentally slamming it behind her. "Sorry!" she called out as she went directly to the kitchen. "I couldn't find Matthew, but Diego's going to ride into town right now. How are you feeling, Donny?"

"Oh, I'll survive, but it hurts like the dickens."

"I'm sorry," said Cady as she sat down next to him at the table.

Elijah left the Farrow mansion, and as he approached the gates, he thought maybe it'd be a good idea for the gardener or coachman to shut them. They were wrought iron and very heavy. The entire property was enclosed with tall fencing. Next to the gate was a gatehouse Susannah said was occupied by their coachman and his wife.

Elijah felt eyes on him as he left the grounds. He didn't know if he imagined it, but he didn't like the feeling. Now, he thought he knew what George felt, as the back of his neck prickled. He'd felt that prickling before when he'd entered a house where someone was full of evil. It was as though his spirit recognized the evil around him. Elijah didn't like it one bit.

He picked up his pace, walking swiftly across the street but at an angle to avoid heading in the direction where George had seen the snoop. He arrived at the mission in short order and went to the kitchen, wiping his brow on a beautifully embroidered white handkerchief. He wasn't out of shape physically. He'd walked and worked off the paunch he used to carry around in Boston, but whenever he was nervous, he seemed to sweat.

"What's the matter, Elijah? You look as if you've seen a ghost." Not waiting for a reply, Abby asked, "Where's George? What have you done with George?"

"George is fine, Abigail," he replied quickly. "I left him at Susannah's. She's invited us to dinner, and George will be staying with her instead of us."

He said the last bit in a rush, and Abigail turned to stare at him.

"But, Elijah, you've been tickled pink that he came home with us. Why would you have him stay with Susannah?"

"Sit down, Abby. Never mind. Let's go to your office. I need to talk to you with no interruptions and no listening ears."

His face was so serious, Abby became worried.

"What is it?" she asked as she closed the door behind them. "What is going on?"

He turned to face her. "Abby, the reason I went to see George was because I think Amos Kepler murdered Oscar. Geor—"

"What! What are you saying? You think Amos murdered Oscar? Oh my good heavens, that's horrible. Oh, Elijah! Are you sure? How could he have done such a thing?"

"Well, we haven't proved it yet, but it certainly looks to be true. I wanted to run the facts by George, and he agrees with me. He took vacation earlier than he'd planned because we also believe Amos has slowly been poisoning Susannah."

"Oh my goodness! Why, I can scarcely credit it. Oh, such evil! You know, Elijah, I never did like that man, but to murder and…but to what purpose? Why would he do such a thing?"

Elijah sat down and related to Abby the terms of the will.

"But did Oscar tell Amos he stood to inherit?"

"No, no, he didn't," Elijah responded heavily.

"Then how did Amos find out? Who else knows about the terms of the will?"

"Abby," Elijah said ponderously, "you forget that Edward Kepler is my clerk."

Abigail gasped, putting a hand to her mouth. "Oh—oh my. I see now. Oh, Elijah, and he's such a nice, personable young man."

Elijah responded, "I feel bewildered by it all. Someone I thought was an upstanding man in San Rafael to be a murderer and his son a blabbermouth. It is unthinkable, really."

Abby sat down at her desk chair as if her knees had buckled under her. "I almost feel as if I'm in shock."

"There's more, Abby. Someone else, and it's not Amos—we met him on Susannah's drive today—is spying on Susannah's house. That's why George is staying there. I'm to collect his things, but the snoop is across the street, lurking in those bushes. It makes my skin crawl to know someone is spying on her."

"I should think so. Do you think Amos hired someone to spy on her?"

"I don't know, but I should think not. It doesn't make sense. She's not going anywhere. He knows she's in mourning and won't be leaving or going out, so why hire someone to watch her or the house?" He looked across at her. "I think the two things are unrelated…the murder and spying. Frankly, we don't even know if it *was* murder, and according to Amos, no one else was around. It will be interesting to see how George goes about getting to the bottom of this. I do, however, have every confidence in him. It's why I went to San Francisco. The San Rafael police respect Amos—know him on a personal level, and that is one reason Oscar's death wasn't even investigated. They believed Amos' explanation of it. After all, everyone knows Oscar was Amos' boss."

"You know, Elijah," Abby suggested, "it might be more circumspect for me to go stay with Susannah than George."

"No, no, my dear girl. I'm not putting you there in harm's way. And besides, the whole reason for George to stay is so a man can be in the house as a protection. You know Geordie, Oscar's majordomo, asked to be released the week after Oscar was buried. He wanted to return to Scotland and find employment there. Tess and Opal are in the house, but a man should be there in the house too, for protection." He shifted his weight in his chair and sat thinking for a minute.

"Frankly, my dear girl, all things considered, I think it's a very good thing for both George and Susannah to be together. It is, of course, far too early for your matchmaking skills to come into play, but I believe there to be a real connection between the two already. They were staring at each other, and I had to interrupt them to finish the conversation. Yes, I'm quite sure George is smitten, but he will never say so. He's a man that keeps things pretty close to his chest."

Abigail was delighted. "Oh, Elijah, those two would make a wonderful couple. I never had a chance to meet Adeline, but George was so in love with her, he's never taken a second look at another woman. Oh, I can't wait to see them together this evening. Yes, he should definitely stay there to be a protection for her, poor thing. What a muddle it all is, murder and spying. We need to pray, Elijah. We need to pray that God's protection covers Susannah and even George, since he's staying there. Oh my."

Hannibal Cassidy stood behind a bush, watching as a man headed into the front gates of the Farrows' estate. He was neat looking with a tall top hat. He strode down the long drive as if he owned it, but staring at him, Hannibal saw him use the knocker on the front door. *Must not be Mr. Farrow*, he thought.

He'd never met Mr. or Mrs. Farrow and had no idea what either of them looked like. As he stood there, he saw two men crossing the street right in front of him and figured one must be Mr. Farrow. He moved to get a better look. One of the men stopped in the middle of the street as if he'd heard something. He turned around to look, but Hannibal didn't think he'd seen him. He moved stealthily back behind the tree as the man's head continued to turn away from him.

The man slowly turned back and headed for the gates of the Farrows' residence. Hannibal figured the man must be Mr. Farrow, as he was dressed in an expensive suit and looked well turned out. The other man looked nice but didn't have the tailored look that some men seemed to achieve without trying. Hannibal stood watching as the other man who'd gone to the Farrows' front door, before these two men had arrived, came back down the driveway. That man raised his hat politely to the two men facing him. It was less than a minute before the first man made his way out the gates. The other two men proceeded to the house, used the knocker, and were admitted.

Hannibal pulled some beef jerky out of his satchel and chewed off a piece, thinking about what he'd seen and what he should do. He'd seen no women going in or out, but he'd only been spying on the house for a short while.

After some time Hannibal grew tired of standing and looked around for a place where he could sit and still see what was going on across the wide avenue. He wondered if he should climb a tree and get comfortable somehow, but he'd climbed trees as a boy and knew it was seldom you found one where you could sit comfortably.

He decided to sit partially under a bush on the ground. He no sooner got situated when one of the men came down the long drive from the house. It wasn't the smartly dressed one.

Hannibal was now quite sure that he was correct that the nicely dressed man must be Mr. Farrow, because he didn't come back out.

I need some kind a plan. Maybe I could get into that there house at night or something. I need to find out if Cadence is in there. Reckon I best keep watch for a few more days and see iff'n she comes out. The sun was warm as it filtered through the trees. *Mayhap I shouldn't have eaten that dry jerky. I'm thirsty. I'm awful thirsty...I need a drink.*

Diego rode his horse into town at a gallop. He found Dr. John having a late lunch, but when he heard about Donny, he immediately got up and kissed Sally and the tops of Hannah's and Johnny's heads before leaving the kitchen.

"I'll be home before long," he said to Sally Ann. He went into his office, grabbed his medical bag, and made sure there was some catgut in it. As he checked for it, he had the fleeting thought that it seemed silly to call it catgut when cats were never used—it was sheep intestines that were typically used for suturing. He felt relieved all was in order. With another good-bye to his family, he and Diego climbed on their rides. They didn't speak as they rode to the Rancho at a gallop.

Once they turned into the long lane, they slowed down.

"Did you see how badly Donny cut himself?" Dr. John asked.

"No. Cady, he comed to tell me to geet you. He looking for Matthew, but he only find me. We harvesting the grapes, and Matthew, he be everywhere. Cady, he only tell me Donny cut his feenger really bad on a beelhook."

"On a what?"

"On a beelhook. You know, the knife to cut the grapes."

"Ah," said Dr. John, who had difficulty understanding Diego. *Those things can be rusty and of course dirty. I'd better make sure it's well cleaned*, he thought.

Diego slipped off his horse quickly. "I weel put your horse een the barn, Dr. John."

"Thank you. I appreciate that."

Matthew was in the barn. Behind it was the gigantic bin where grape stomping took place. It would turn into a party where all the women would stomp the grapes to music. They weren't ready for that yet, but the grapes that had been harvested were put into large vats and stored at the back of the barn, where double doors could be opened and the transferring of grapes to the stomping vat was made easier.

Matthew came out of the barn and said, "Welcome, John. Good to see you again. Long time no see!"

"Long time like a few days ago!" Dr. John responded. "Hope Donny isn't cut too badly."

"It's nasty," Matthew said. "He's cut it clear to the bone."

"Did he nick the bone?"

"I don't know. Couldn't see it that well, for all the blood. Hope you can fix him up all right. He's pretty upset with himself."

"Well, I'd better get in there and see for myself. You look pretty busy. Got a lot of workers, I see."

"Yep. Didn't have to go out looking for them this year, either." Matthew turned away toward the dimness of the barn so John would go to the house. He was quite a talker, and Matthew had work to do.

CHAPTER XX

Let us hear the conclusion of the whole matter:
Fear God, and keep his commandments:
for this is the whole duty of man.

ECCLESIASTES 12:13.

DR. JOHN ENTERED THE RANCHO without knocking, knowing he was quite welcome.

"Hello, Dr. John, how ees you?" Conchita asked. "You can feex Donny's feenger. He cut eet very bad."

Donny was sitting at the table with Cady and was glad the doctor had finally arrived. His finger didn't hurt as badly as it had, but he knew as soon as the doctor touched it, he would be in pain again. He simply wanted to get it over with.

Dr. John removed the handkerchief, stiff with blood, and clucked his tongue when he examined it.

"You really cut it, son," he said. "Let's see what we can do."

Conchita had boiled water and stood waiting for directions.

"You have a basin I could use?"

"*Sí*, I geet eet."

Dr. John went over to wash his hands in the sink, washing them two times. He'd read some of Ignaz Semmelweis' exhortations on cleanliness and of Joseph Lister's use of carbolic acid. He'd become a believer in sterilization and was careful to adhere to a strict code of cleanliness, though not all doctors did.

He poured carbolic into the basin Conchita had washed.

"Put your hand in here, Donny," he said. "Never mind," he added when the liquid turned dirty. "Let's wash your hand first. Glad I didn't use all my carbolic. We need to be sure this is very well cleaned out before I stitch it. One good thing is the blood itself helps to clean out the dirt." He led him to the sink and helped to scrub his palm, back of his hand, and other fingers before having him soak it in the carbolic.

"All right, let's get that stitched up," he said. "You cut that really deep. Good thing it's not your forefinger."

He proceeded to stitch up the finger, and Donny stoically endured it.

Once Dr. John was finished, he wrapped it in clean gauze, splitting the end and tying the gauze around Donny's finger.

"There you go. I'll leave some of this gauze. It shouldn't bleed anymore, but"—he turned to Conchita—"I'd like you to change the dressing the day after tomorrow and make sure everything looks good."

"*Sí*, I weel do eet. Did you eat the lunch, Dr. John? Would you like a leetle something to tide you over?"

"Well, I'd like that right fine. I didn't finish my lunch. Thank you, Conchita." He sat down, and for the first time took a good look at Cady. His jaw dropped as he realized that although she was dressed in boys' clothes, she was a girl.

He looked over at Liberty, who'd sat quietly through Donny's ordeal, with a shocked look on his face.

Liberty grinned. "I know," she said. "Quite a shock, isn't it?"

"Why are you dressed as a boy?" he asked Cady.

"My pa is looking for a girl. I saw him in Napa, and Donny saw him another time in Napa. When I ran away, I wore my brother's clothes. He died of the fever. We all thought it best to keep the disguise for the time being, especially with so many people here for harvest."

Liberty added, "Cadence is going to help me once the babies arrive. It will take a big burden off me. Conchita, Lupe, and Luce will all help, of course, but to have Cady will certainly be a boon." She smiled at the younger woman.

Cady said, "Dr. John, please promise you won't tell anyone, not anyone about me. Word has a way of leaking out once tongues begin to wag."

"I promise," he said, "and you're absolutely right. The less said, the better. I won't even tell my wife."

Once he was alone with Susannah, George had thought it could become uncomfortable, but it was no such thing. He was pleasantly surprised.

"Please come with me, George. I'd like you to meet Opal. She's my cook—actually, she's a wonderful chef. You're not shy about going into the kitchen, are you?" She looked George in the eye and added, "I also want you to meet Tess. I know she met you at the door and let you in, but I want you to meet her as a person, not simply a servant."

"I'd like that, and no, I'm not uncomfortable about going to someone's kitchen. Many times investigating includes talking to the hired help. They know and see things that, many times, others miss. Since my wife, Adeline, died, I eat either in the kitchen or in my library, where I can read or do some work at the same time."

"I'm sorry about your wife. I can say with all sincerity that losing a spouse is a traumatic experience. I don't think, even if you're expecting it, that it can be easy. When a body shares their life with another, their joys and heartaches, dreams and disappointments...it's true, as the Bible says, they become as one. It's as if a part of you is gone. I hate it! I wake up during the night, and the breathing I've heard beside me for years is gone. I reach out my hand, and it comes back empty." The blood crept up into her face, and she added, "I'm sorry. I don't usually go around blabbing to anyone my deepest thoughts, except to God, of course. You're easy to talk to, George."

"Thank you for the compliment. It's perfectly all right, madam. I find you easy to talk to also. It's as if we've known each other for a long time, isn't it? I agree with what you said." He was grateful Susannah seemed an intelligent and educated woman. There were so many, these days, who weren't. He added, "Death wasn't part of God's original plan—we were meant to live forever. We are built for relationship, and besides a relationship with God, there is none so intimate nor important as man and wife. I cannot tell you how devastated I was when Adeline died, even though I knew it was coming." He looked closely at Susannah and added, "I know you losing your husband the way you did must have been a terrible shock. I can't imagine it. It's horrible, and I see it so many times in my line of work, but it never is easy. I do know time helps to blunt the pain. I will always cherish the good times and memories I had with Adeline. At first, I just went through the motions of living. I got up every morning and put one foot in front of the other. Everything seemed unreal. Finally, I reached a day where I started living again."

Susannah nodded. "I am still living in the unrealness world—is that a word?" She smiled at him, knowing it was not. "I am putting one foot in front of the other, simply going through the motions of living."

As they entered the kitchen, Opal turned in surprise. It wasn't normal for the missus to be bringing guests into the kitchen.

"Opal, I'd like you to meet Mr. George Baxter. He's a guest and will be staying on here for a couple days or so. George, please meet my friend and cook, Opal Mather. Mostly, we call her Opal. You will enjoy eating the concoctions she can produce at the drop of a hat."

Opal nodded at George. "Pleased to meet you, I'm sure."

George said, "It's my pleasure. I have no doubt it's true what Susannah says about your cooking abilities. I look forward to dinner with anticipation."

He smiled, reeking of charm, and Opal blushed under his smile.

"Where's Tess?" Susannah asked.

"She's upstairs, ma'am. You want me to get her?"

"No thank you. I want George to meet her officially, but please let her know he'll be needing a room. I don't wish to alarm you, Opal, but evidently someone is spying on our house."

Opal gasped and put a hand to her mouth. "Why would anyone spy on the house?"

George replied, "I'm not quite certain, but I hope to get to the bottom of it."

Susannah said to Opal, "George is a detective from San Francisco, who is on vacation. He is a close friend of the Humphries, and he will protect us." She turned back to George. "It's not much of a vacation for you, is it?" "Madam," he replied with a wide smile, "it's the best kind of vacation."

Neither Susannah nor George said anything to Opal about Oscar being murdered or about the poisoning. There was no sense sharing it when it hadn't been substantiated.

"I have no doubt you will solve the mystery while you're here," Susannah said.

The two smiled at each other, Susannah because George seemed to not mind at all staying with her, and he because for the first time in years, a woman interested him apart from work.

Their long perusal of each other was interrupted with the entrance of Tess into the kitchen. She stopped at the sight of George standing there smiling at Susannah, who turned when she heard her come in.

"Tess, I'd like you to meet Mr. George Baxter. George, this is Mrs. Tess Donovan. Her husband is our head gardener."

George took her hand and said, "I'm very happy to meet you, Mrs. Donovan."

"The pleasure is mine, I'm sure," Tess said, a bit puzzled that he'd acknowledge her with more than a nod of the head. She also was surprised to see him in the kitchen.

"Tess, Mr. Baxter is going to be our guest for a few days." She turned to include Opal. "I know how you two love to talk to your friends about the happenings that go on in our house, but, Opal, you and Tess are going to have to keep quiet about Mr. Baxter being a detective until we get a few things straightened out."

"You're a detective?" Tess' eyes widened in surprise.

"Yes, I am, but not here. I'm from San Francisco. I've come to San Raphael to spend my holiday with Mr. and Mrs. Elijah Humphries. Elijah came to my office and told me an interesting story, and here I am."

"Oh, Opal, that reminds me"—Susannah's hand flew to her mouth —"I forgot to tell you that Mr. and Mrs. Humphries, as well as Mr. Baxter, will be here for dinner tonight."

"I certainly don't wish to be a nuisance, but with someone skulking in the bushes, spying on your house, I think it's a good thing I'm staying here," George said.

Tess' eyes grew wide at his comment. "Someone is spying on this house? Whatever for?"

"That, madam, is what I'd like to find out," George said succinctly.

"I feel so sorry for you, Donny. That must hurt like the dickens!" Cadence said.

"Aw, it's not so bad, now," he responded.

The two of them were in the great room, playing Parcheesi.

Matthew had told Donny to take the afternoon off. No more work that day and perhaps the next day too.

Donny wasn't feeling sorry at all. He was eating up the attention Cadence showered on him. She was solicitous, making sure he was comfortable. They'd already played checkers, and after the Parcheesi game, they planned to play rummy.

Cady said, "I'll shuffle and deal the cards for you and me." She smiled, and Donny felt his heart turn over. She seemed totally oblivious of his affection for her. He tried his best to be nonchalant, but if their hands brushed together, his heartbeat quickened. He was amazed at the effect she had on him.

Donny tried to get Cady to talk about her home life, but she clammed up and would say nothing about it.

"I don't want people feeling sorry for me. The way I was raised was miserable. I never knew how wretched it was until I came here. Every day is a new adventure. People care about one another here, and there's no fear that one person will get you if you don't toe the line. I've decided the best way to get people not to feel sorry for me is to say nothing about my pa or anything about the way I was raised. I'd never realized my upbringing wasn't normal. I have been thinking and thinking of my ma and why she would stay with a man who beat his children. I came to the conclusion that she was weak, afraid to be on her own. She told me once when I was about twelve that she had no family, but I knew when she said it she was lying to me. I always wondered why. Maybe her pa beat her, and she thought it was normal. I don't reckon I know. All I do know is I want to live the way we live here. I don't want people feeling sorry and tiptoeing around my feelings. I feel free here, and I love the feeling. Now, stop gaping at me. It's your turn."

Donny threw the dice, but he thought about what Cady had said.

"Cady, not every home is the same as another. My home wasn't like this one at all, and yet it was a happy home. We were poor. Matthew was poor too, at one time. He's worked very hard to get where he is. He loves what he does, but now he's married to Miss Liberty, he doesn't have to work if he doesn't want to. She's richer than anyone I know." He looked around the great room and pointed to the bookshelf.

"You look around and see beautiful things. See those books there? Matthew told me he got them when he was dirt poor. He would set aside a little money every time his neighbor paid him for the work he did. He bought those books one by one. Because of that, he values them. He told me about it because he wanted me to take a little money out of every paycheck for savings. I take ten percent out for the Lord's tithe first, and then ten percent for me. I don't make all that much, but I am careful with what I have. Matthew told me that sometimes when we're handed things easy-like, why, we don't treasure those things nor care for them properly." He looked across at Cadence.

"What's really important to this home and the one I was raised in is that we love and serve God. Things are transitory. They come and go, but a relationship with God through Jesus Christ, his Son, why, it goes on forever. Some people think they're going to heaven because they are a member of a church or rent a pew in a church, and that gets them to heaven. It won't. I don't want to be lying on my deathbed wishing I knew where I was going when I die or be scared to death, no pun intended, because I don't know. I reckon a lot of people just think they'll be put in a hole in the ground and rot there and that's the end of it, but it isn't so, Cady. Believe me—it isn't so."

"How can you know?" Cady spoke a little condescendingly. "How can you sit there and tell me that? No one who's died has come back to tell you that, have they?"

"Why, yes, yes, they have." He looked at her just a little smugly as her eyes widened at his response.

"You're telling me someone died and came back to life to tell everyone what it was like?"

"No, that's not what I'm saying, but Jesus Christ died for us, Cady. He never did a single thing wrong, and yet he was nailed to a cross like a common thief to die for our sins."

"What kind of God would allow His Son to die like that?"

"One who loved us so much He allowed the sins of the world to be heaped on His only Son. Theologians say God turned His back on His Son because He couldn't bear to see the sin heaped on Him. I don't rightly agree with that. That may be one of the reasons, but He looks on our sin every day. I think He turned His back because He couldn't stand to watch His Son suffer the way He did. If He'd have kept watching, He'd have taken Him off the cross, and Jesus wouldn't have accomplished what He had to do. But the awesome part of the whole story is that Jesus didn't stay dead! He rose from the dead and right now is seated at the right hand of God in heaven. A lot of people saw Him after He arose from the dead, and the Good Book tells us this whole story. I'll bet you're able to read the Bible now, aren't you? You can read it for yourself, Cady, but what I'm saying is true. Maybe we could read it together. I do know God has had His hand on you and brought you here to us. You're loved here, Cady, but not even an ounce of the way God loves you."

CHAPTER XXI

Anxiety in the heart of a man weighs it down
But a good word makes it glad.

PROVERBS 12:25

"MY, BUT THESE DISHES ARE BEAUTIFUL," Abigail said. "I think they are the most gorgeous I've ever seen. What are they?" Abigail knew better than to turn a plate over and look at the stamp on the underside, but she had no problem asking.

"Why, thank you!" Susannah replied. "Oscar bought those for me a couple years ago for our anniversary. It's called Moss Rose by Haviland. It's Limoges porcelain."

"Ah, David Haviland. Isn't he the man the White House commissioned to make a dinner service a few years back?"

"Yes, he is. David Haviland was commissioned by President and Mrs. Rutherford B. Hayes. The Hayes' had Theodore Davis, who was an artist for *Harper's Weekly*, design and even create new shapes for the dishes. Haviland then produced them in Limoges, France, where he had opened his company years ago. I thank you, again, Abigail, for the compliment. I enjoy using them. They *are* unusual, aren't they," she said, as a statement. "Oscar told me that they were hand painted, but it's difficult to find dissimilarities, they've been painted so well."

"I'd like to see what Mr. Davis came up with for the pattern for the Hayes'. I knew he designed the pattern but never heard nor read any more about it. Have you?" Abigail asked.

"No, I haven't," Susannah replied.

The dinner was not only delicious, but the crystal and silver sparkled and shone, reflecting the glow from the chandelier. It bespoke of richness, refinement, and gracious living, bringing back memories and images to George's mind of his wife and the enjoyment of entertaining in their home and being invited to many parties and soirées. Being a Cunningham, Adeline had been in great demand at social functions in Boston, and they had gone out several times a week. He hadn't been out much socially since she'd died, declining all invitations, until they stopped arriving. He didn't care to be the odd man out or a replacement partner for some single woman. He hated inane busybody talk. He looked across the table at Susannah, and his heart warmed toward her. Here was a woman of refinement, beauty, and wisdom.

George sat in a comfortable dining chair and looked around. The room was done in palest mint green. All the woodwork was a dark mahogany and together created an affluent elegance that somehow produced a feeling of contentment.

A huge mahogany-framed mirror, ornately carved, reflected and radiated warm prisms of light from the crystal chandelier and cast them around the room. Gilt sconces, lit on either side of the mirror, added to the brilliance. A long, marble-topped sideboard with the same color of mint mixed with cream was gorgeous. George had never seen that color of marble before. The dining chairs were a blend of striped mint, cream, and dark-brown chintz. There were a couple of creamy-colored wingbacks in one corner, with mint and brown pillows on them. George, used to fine things, felt right at home.

He was enjoying the conversation as well as the delectable dinner. Stuffed chicken, roasted to perfection, potatoes and gravy, several salads, a Swiss cheese corn bake, and fluffy rolls were a tongue-tantalizing pleasure. It was difficult to stop eating, because it tasted so good.

Susannah was talking, and George's eyes kept close watch on every expression, every nuance of speech. He knew he was captivated by this woman, and he let the feeling wash over him like a waterfall.

I never thought to love again. Is this love? I can't seem to take my eyes off her even though I feel Abigail's eyes assessing me. Elijah told me she's a matchmaker. It's far too early for Susannah to think of anything other than a friendly relationship. I'm astounded by my feelings for her. I feel protective, and yet I have no right. Abigail is smiling, but then so am I.

After some interesting discussion of religion and politics, with a previous agreement to stay off the subject of Amos Kepler, the four of them finished dinner.

Susannah asked, "Would you care for dessert now, or shall we wait and play whist for a while and then have dessert? What is your pleasure?"

"Oh my," Elijah said, "I don't think I could eat another bite right now. Let's wait, shall we?" He turned to the others inquiringly.

"I've eaten too much, but it tasted so delicious, I couldn't seem to stop," George said, smiling at his hostess. "I vote we wait too."

"I'll echo that," Abigail said. "Let's play cards. Is it couples against each other, or men against women?"

"Let's draw straws, and the longest two will be partners. Excuse me for just a moment." Susannah headed to the kitchen to get two wooden toothpicks. She returned almost immediately with Tess in tow. Breaking short ends off the toothpicks, Susannah handed the four pieces to Tess.

"Here, you mix them up, and we'll let the two men draw first," Susannah said.

Tess smiled, turned her back to the four people waiting to draw, and evened out the tops of the toothpicks. She turned back.

"Elijah, you go first," Susannah said.

Elijah drew out a longer piece of the toothpick.

"Now your turn, George," she said with a smile.

George drew a short end.

"Well, Abigail, it looks as if you will decide who the partners will be. The longer piece and you have your husband. Shorter piece and you have George." Susannah laughed.

"Well, now, let me see. Hmm, I think I'll have…this one," she said as she drew out a longer piece of toothpick. "Elijah, my dear, you'll be my partner." She turned to George and Susannah. "This mightn't be fair. Elijah and I have been partners numerous times, and we know how the other plays."

"Oh pooh, just you wait. George and I will show you a thing or two."

The four went down the hall to a room Susannah called the game room. They sat down at a lovely, small, square inlaid oak table made specifically for playing games. Abigail looked around in appreciation but felt she had gushed enough about the beautiful things she'd seen in the house. Being very good at decorating, Abby liked the tasteful arrangement of books and bibelots in the room, as well as the color choices for the walls and floors. There was a large table with a puzzle started on it, and another table looked as if Susannah must be making a quilt.

Susannah smiled at George across the table. "I do love a good game of whist. Shall we play to five or ten?" She glanced up at a mantel clock and added, "It's still fairly early."

"Let's play to ten," Elijah said. He was amazed at the improvement in Susannah's health. He was quite certain Amos must have been poisoning her.

After finishing a late dessert, the four decided to spend a bit of time in prayer before the Humphries went home. It was a sweet time of fellowship, and they seemed to draw closer as they prayed for each other's needs.

When it was time for the Humphries to leave, Elijah said, "I think, madam, it would be a good thing to keep your gates closed. You have a gatekeeper, do you not?"

Susannah's face wore a surprised look as she responded, "Yes, I do. I hadn't thought of that, but with someone skulking around in the bushes and trees across from those open gates, it would be a good idea to close them, wouldn't it?"

"I'll walk out with you, Elijah, and talk to the man," George said. He stood next to Susannah and had an overwhelming feeling of oneness with her, as if they'd known each other forever instead of less than twelve hours. "What's the gatekeeper's name?" he asked Susannah, looking deeply into her beautiful gray eyes, seeing her cheeks blush becomingly under his perusal.

"Benny—it's Benjamin Barthol, and his wife, Clara, does our laundry." She couldn't seem to tear her eyes away from his.

The spell was broken by Abigail.

"Thank you again for the wonderful time, Susannah," Abby said. "It was a most delightful evening, even if you and George beat us! I can't believe we made book first, and yet you two won." She smiled at George and Susannah, who grinned at each other.

"I thank you, too, Susannah," Elijah said. "I'm gratified you're feeling better. I don't believe you would be if Mr. Kepler were still visiting you."

"I concur, Elijah. Thank you for taking such an interest in my affairs and for bringing George back from San Francisco with you. I can't say I'm sorry he's not spending his nights with you. I'm delighted to have him here. I feel safe having a man in the house, and not just any man either, but one who carries a gun and is a detective!"

Benny had brought up Elijah's carriage and stood holding the reins.

George descended the steps alongside Abby and Elijah.

"Hello, Benny," he said. "My name is George Baxter." He stuck out his hand to shake the gatekeeper's hand. "I am spending a few days with Mrs. Farrow, but we seem to have a bit of a problem. Someone has been spying on the house"—he pointed toward the opened gates—"hiding in those bushes there, across the street from the gates. Could you please close those for her as soon as Mr. Humphries leaves?"

Benny nodded as he shook George's outstretched hand. "Pleased ta meet you, sir. Can't know why a body'd be hiding out spying on the house for, 'less'n someone knows Mrs. Farrow's alone now and they's plannin' ta rob 'er. I'll close them gates and be keepin' a sharp lookout for anyone. You kin be shore of that."

"Thank you, Benny. We also have a couple men who will patrol the perimeter of the property, and I thank you for your diligence. Mrs. Farrow said you were reliable. Can I help you with those gates?"

"You kin thank 'er fer the compliment," Benny said with a grin. "An' no, I don't need no help. I've kept those hinges oiled right well, an' it'll be no problem closin' 'em."

"Good night," Susannah called out to Elijah and Abigail as they started to leave.

"Good night, and thank you again for the lovely evening," Abigail called back.

Elijah clucked his tongue and drove his carriage down the long driveway, glad he'd brought it instead of walking. It was late.

Benny followed the carriage down the drive. He peered across the road before the second gate clanged shut, but it was too dark to see anything.

Early the next morning, Elijah spent quite some time praying for various people and needs. When he finished, he didn't get up right away but lay quietly, thinking about what he must do for the day.

I need to have a meeting with Howard, Stephen, and Jacob, he thought. *I need to be sure none of them talk to Edward or let him see anything more about Oscar and Susannah's will. Enough damage has been done. It will not be pleasant telling my partners there's been a breach of good faith by one of our employees. I need to pray more about how I'm to talk to Edward if George should want it. What a horrible set of circumstances because my clerk did not keep his mouth shut. If Amos Kepler did kill Oscar, Edward will be punished enough for knowing his own mouth wrought a change in his father. Or did it? Lord, I wish that Thee couldst sit and chat with me and tell me the answers to the various questions I have. Was Amos Kepler always bent on having more money than he made? Has he always envied or been greedy and thus committed murder? I suppose I'll have to leave the answers up to Thee. Someday I'm going to have all my questions answered, or perhaps I'll be so enthralled worshipping Thee, I won't care about any of my questions, or perhaps all will become clear in the twinkling of an eye.* Elijah smiled as he carefully swung his legs over the side of the bed, being particularly careful not to pull the covers off Abby. She was sound asleep. He padded into the bathing room to take care of the odious task of shaving his face.

Hannibal Cassidy was in a foul mood. He woke up late. He'd had a difficult time getting to sleep once he got back to his hotel room the night before. He had stayed out there in those bushes and waited and waited once he'd seen the carriage draw up to the front door of the Farrow mansion. He had mosquito bites, which were driving him crazy, and his legs ached from standing so long.

Before lunch he'd seen the one man leave and was pretty sure the same man came back later with his wife. He'd stood there for what seemed like forever before he saw the carriage being taken back to the front door. Then there was a long farewell, but what really stuck in his craw was that once the carriage left, the gates were shut. They had never been closed before that he knew of. They blocked his view of the mansion, and he wondered how he was going to be able to see anything.

Maybe now he'd have to climb a tree. He kicked his boot across the room in anger.

Edward Kepler had spent a very unpleasant night. He'd been sleeping poorly for the past six weeks. He would toss and turn and think about his father, wondering if he should tell Mr. Humphries that he'd spilled the beans about the Farrows' will.

He'd read the entire contents of it, transcribing a copy for Mr. Humphries' records and a copy for the Farrows. He'd not told his father about it for over a month after he'd seen it, but one day, nearly two months ago, he'd blabbed the whole thing to him. Edward remembered back to that day.

His father had awakened that morning in a very bad mood. He'd stomped into the kitchen only to find that their daily, Mrs. McCready, had somehow burned the omelet she was making for him. It stunk, and Edward knew his father wished he could fire her, but she put up with the vagaries of two men, and good help was difficult to find.

"Open the windows, woman!" he'd yelled at her. Edward, who was sitting at the table, jumped. He felt as if his father had scared ten years off of his life.

Simply looking at Edward calmly eating his oatmeal further enraged Amos. He yelled at his son to open the kitchen door and the window and fan the room with the door to blow out the smell.

It seemed to Edward that nothing he did was ever right. His father constantly harped at him. He'd been seriously thinking of moving into a boarding house. It was time he was out on his own anyway.

His mother had run off when he was five. He didn't remember much about her, except a sense of the comfort and refuge she had been. He remembered her love and care for him with nostalgia. A housekeeper had raised him, if he could call it that. His father had fired Mrs. Calann when he was sixteen, never giving him a reason. He'd never gotten close to Mrs. McCready

Edward bore the brunt of his father's displeasure. He constantly felt on edge, never knowing what kind of mood the old man was in. He paid half his income to his father for board and room, but that didn't seem to please him either. Amos continually complained it wasn't enough to even feed Edward, but Edward suspected that wasn't true, however he never contradicted his father. He was continually trying to find ways to gain his father's approval, and that morning he found it.

He'd sat down after swinging the door back and forth for a few minutes. Mrs. McCready quickly made a couple scrambled eggs for his father, and he sat to eat them as Edward told his father the entire contents of the will he'd finished transcribing...Mr. Oscar Farrow's will. It wasn't but a couple weeks later that Oscar Farrow lay dead at the school, and Amos seemed to be the only one around.

Should I tell Mr. Humphries about telling my father about the will? But what if it really was an accident? I don't believe that for a moment, do I? I have to admit I'm afraid of my father, afraid of what he'll do to me if I tell Mr. Humphries the truth. What will Mr. Humphries do to me for breaking the oath of silence about anyone's affairs? Either way, I am in a heap of trouble!

CHAPTER XXII

The LORD is my light and my salvation;
Whom shall I fear?
The LORD is the defense of my life;
Whom shall I dread?

PSALM 27:1

THE DAYS SEEMED TO SPEED BY, and each day, although different, seemed the same. The work was steady, and harvesting the grapes seemed easier this year than last. Because it was so late into the season, Matthew prayed the weather would hold. The days were glorious and not too hot for the workers, most of whom picked at an incredible speed. Everyone seemed to be doing a good job as he went up and down rows, inspecting and making sure things were running smoothly. The oak casks were cleaned and ready for juice. The grapes were plump and juicy, and he felt they were at the perfect ripeness and thanked God for the change from tart to sweet in their taste.

Matthew loved the smell of morning, especially this time of year. He felt strong and invigorated by the fresh, cool air of an early morning. He was grateful that Liberty was feeling well and keeping herself busy. She was, as she said, doing a fall clean. She was washing windows and deep cleaning, and the Rancho was looking sparkling clean inside. He'd heard that some women started cleaning just before their babies were due, and he wondered if that was the case.

He'd told her to take it easy after hitting her head, but she seemed to have recovered just fine.

He came up behind his foreman. "How's everything coming along, Diego?" he asked. "I've been checking out the rows, and the harvest seems to be going well, as far as I can see. What do you think?"

"I am liking the workers thees year, Meester Bannister. They ees working hard, but I am theenking we going to haf the rain soon. I am theenking we need to work tonight…all night."

Matthew pushed his hat back off his forehead as he stared at Diego. "You're sure?"

"*Sí*, Meester Bannister, as sure as I am standing here, eet weel rain."

"I wonder if it'll be a hard rain? We have another couple hard days of picking left." He added, "You and I both know that the grapes can bloat and even burst with rainy weather. At any rate, it certainly affects the taste of the wine. All right, I'll notify the workers, and the ones who are willing to work all night, we'll double their pay for their time. Sure was a good thing to invest in all those poles with lanterns…they'll definitely come in handy tonight. Thanks, Diego, for having a sensitive nose!"

Matthew's brow was furrowed with worry as he started to walk away.

"Eet weel be all right, Meester Bannister. You weel see," Diego called after him. "Eet een God's hands, after all!"

"Yes, you're right, Diego, but we must do what we can. We're far enough into it, I reckon, that it won't hurt to lose some of our crop. I'm thankful the rains we had before harvest didn't seem to hurt anything. In truth, they seem juicier and really tasty. We have a good crop, and I am praying for a good wine."

He turned back, as if he'd just thought of something, and continued to speak, switching the subject completely. "It seems strange to harvest without Kirk here, doesn't it? This is the first time he's not here to oversee the harvest. We don't have to worry about picking the crop he put in, although he'll lose his twenty percent. With the gold they found on McCaully property, he's not likely to quibble over his part of the crop."

"*Sí*, I was theenking the same theeng a bit ago. Eet ees strange, but he one happy *hombre* now he a rancher." Diego grinned widely. "He a real cowboy, that one!"

Matthew grinned back. "Yes, he always did prefer roping a cow to doing anything else. Well, I suppose I'd better get the news out that we're doing a long pick." He strode off toward the Rancho to inform the household first.

Latecomers to breakfast were still sitting at the table when Matthew went to the kitchen. He grinned at Cady.

"Slept in this morning, I see," he said.

"Yes, I was up late last night trying to figure out a few things. I know you're busy now with harvest and all, but sometime I want to show you and Liberty something I need some help with—something I don't understand. I've been thinking and thinking about what I should do, and I finally decided I need to share it with the two of you, but it can wait. I want your full attention when I do show you."

Matthew smiled. "You're right about being busy. Diego said rain is on its way, and we're going to need to pick all night. We still won't get all of it, but we won't go broke either." He turned to Conchita. "I'm glad your husband has a sense about these things."

"What things?" Liberty asked as she came into the kitchen. She looked beautiful to Matthew. She'd just come from having a hot bath, and her copper-colored hair hung down her back in ringlets, still wet.

Matthew walked over and took Liberty's face in both his hands. He kissed her soundly in front of Cady and Conchita. Cady sat openmouthed, staring, not able to look away. Conchita simply grinned.

Matthew pulled back and looked deeply into Liberty's smiling green eyes. "You smell like heaven," he said, "and you asked me before I got distracted, 'What things?' The answer is, Diego told me it's going to rain."

"I could have told you that. My arm started aching like a toothache this morning," Liberty replied as she rubbed her arm.

Cady asked, "Why would your arm ache if it's going to rain?"

"I really don't know, but it has something to do about a change in weather. When my stepfather kidnapped me, my hands were tied together, and he yanked me off a horse. I wasn't able to break my fall, and my arm snapped."

Cady, eyes widened by this revelation, said, "I reckon I'm not the only one who's had a father who's mean."

"Jacques wasn't really my father," Liberty replied, "but I didn't know that until I was twenty-nine."

Matthew said, "You all can enjoy your breakfast and jaw all you want, but I need to go tell my workers th——"

"Anybody home?" The front door banged open, and there was Kirk.

"Well, looky, looky here. Hello there, rancher!" Matthew strode across the kitchen, where Kirk already lounged against the doorjamb, perusing the people in the kitchen. The two men gave each other a bear hug. No one had to tell Cady who Kirk was. The similarity between the two brothers was pronounced, but Cady secretly thought Matthew was the better looking of the two.

"What are you doing here?" Matthew asked.

"Well, I knew you were in the middle of harvest. I decided to bring my crew over and give them a new experience—teach them how to pick grapes." He grinned hugely, and Matthew felt a weight lift from his shoulders. With the McCaully-Bannister cowboys working, they could put in a full day and be close to finishing up tonight.

He slapped Kirk on the back and said, "I cannot begin to tell you how glad I am you came. You are an answer to prayer. The Almighty must have prompted you. Diego thinks rain is on its way, and we just made the decision to pick all night. I came indoors to tell the household. We'll see how it goes, but I can't thank you enough for coming."

"You're welcome. I've never known Diego's nose to be wrong. If he says it'll rain, for sure it'll rain." His glance slid over to Conchita, who stood watching him with a wide smile splitting her brown face.

"Conchita!" He strode over to give her a hug. "How I do miss your *enchiladas* and *sopapillas*! But more than your cooking, *leetle* woman, I miss you." He squeezed her tight.

"I am meesing you too, Meester Kirk. I hear you ees a good rancher, and sometime Diego an' I, we weel come an' veesit your ranch. Where ees your Katie?"

"Coming here was a spur-of-the-moment decision," he said. "Katie didn't come. She and Hannah, who is Ewen's wife, are in the middle of a quilting project, and she couldn't leave right now."

"That's too bad. I always enjoy seeing her," Liberty said as she walked over and gave Kirk a big hug. "But you'll do! Hello, *little* brother. Welcome!" Kirk was even taller than Matthew, but he was younger.

"Looks to me like you're going to be a busy mama pretty soon. I know it's not nice to say, but you're huge!"

"Yes, I am, and I will most likely get bigger. My, but we have so much to tell you. I was thrown off Pookie and knocked unconscious and woke to find out Matthew and I are having twins!" She grinned at her brother-in-law's look of astonishment.

Turning to Cady, she said, "Cady, I'd like you to meet Matthew's brother, Kirk Bannister. Kirk, this is Cady Cassidy, and she is helping out for a while."

Kirk turned his charm in Cady's direction and said, "Pleased to meet you, Mistress Cassidy."

"It's a pleasure to meet you, Mr. Bannister. I've heard much about you. I certainly see the likeness of Matthew in you." She smiled pleasantly. Liberty had been teaching her proper manners, and she felt she'd done an acceptable job of responding. Her eyes slid over to Liberty's, and she saw the slight look of pleasure on her face. Cady beamed with satisfaction.

"Well, I'm going out to see your crew, Kirk. Did you really bring everyone?" Matthew was tickled pink and didn't try to hide it. He'd worked with some of the ranch hands and knew them to be hard workers. They'd make short shrift of the harvest, that was certain.

"Sure did," Kirk replied. "We have a couple new hires you don't know yet, but they seem amenable to working, and that's what we need at the ranch."

The two men went out, and a cheer went up from Kirk's men. All knew Matthew except the two new hires, who looked on curiously.

"Welcome to Rancho Bonito, men!" Matthew took off his hat in respect for the cowboys from McCaully-Bannister's. "It is a godsend you're here! We were planning to work through the night, as it's due to rain tomorrow, according to my foreman, and he's never been wrong about the weather yet!"

He looked over at Kirk and added, "Tie up, and we'll have Donny or someone water the horses and remove saddles. As you know, we don't have enough stalls for all these rides, but we'll get them brushed down and put into the corral. Cady is pretty handy." He lowered his voice so only Kirk could hear. "By the way, I know she's dressed as a female right now, but Cady's a runaway and dresses as a boy when she's outside. Don't let on to anyone she's a girl, all right?"

Kirk grinned. "Now that sounds like a story I'm going to have to wait to hear, but sure. As you know, I met my Katie as a runaway down in San Rafael."

"That's right. You did. I forgot about that. Some of that time is still a bit hazy from me losing my memory and all."

Kirk spoke to his men. "Tie up, boys, and we'll show you all how to pick a cluster of grapes." He grinned and added, "Who knows. Maybe some of you will take to it and forget you're a cowboy."

Sneedy, one of the more outspoken cowboys, spoke up for the group. "Not by a long shot, Boss. We're cowpokes, an' proud of it. We jest don't be a mindin' helping out poor old Conor-turned-Matthew!"

"Well, don't sit there jawing, Sneedy. Let's get to work. At this rate, we just might be up all night. Let's go!"

Kirk had brought fifteen men with him. They climbed off their rides and tied up at the long rail.

Matthew and Kirk each took half the men and demonstrated with the billhook how to cut a cluster of grapes.

"These things are really sharp," Matthew said. "One of my men nearly cut off his finger the other day, and he'd been working with several days experience. Just a warning to be careful."

He and Kirk handed out the knives, and Matthew took the group way out to the area they would be working. He demonstrated again the use of the billhook and showed them the rows they could work on. He was elated to have the extra help and left to tell Diego the newest development. Matthew realized Diego couldn't have seen them ride in, or he would already have been to the Rancho to see Kirk.

He finally found Diego, who'd gone up and down rows, asking the workers to pace themselves if they wanted to work all night, which is why Matthew had trouble tracking him down.

Many of the workers answered in the affirmative to the question Diego posed to them, and he, pleased that most of the grapes would be harvested by morning, hummed to himself as he followed Matthew back to greet Kirk. He suddenly realized his nose twitched, sensing rain on its way.

Elijah walked to work almost every day, which, along with working at the mission when it was being renovated, had trimmed him down. When he and Abby had first purchased the mission, it needed major renovation and repair. He'd hired crews of workers, and he labored for weeks to get everything ready for girls who'd been kidnapped from European ports by white female slavers. It hadn't taken him long to find out he detested manual labor. It had been back-breaking work, but it had started him toward a healthier lifestyle. He now felt better than he had in years.

As he strolled toward his law firm, he ruminated about the evening before. He thought about his matchmaking wife with an inward smile. Abby could scarcely talk of anything else at breakfast. She had enjoyed herself immensely the evening before and kept referring to George being mesmerized by Susannah. Elijah noticed it himself and had been pleased. He'd not known George before his wife had passed away, but he had sensed in his friend a deep devotion to her memory.

He remembered back a couple years before when Abigail had been ill and close to death. He'd been beside himself, knowing there was nothing he could do about her health. He praised God every day for sparing her life. He walked briskly, nodding or speaking a few words to people already out and about.

His step slowed as he approached his office. He was early, but for the first time since he could remember, he dreaded entering. His first matter of business on the docket was to speak to his partners about Edward Kepler's indiscretion.

Saying a quick prayer, he mounted the flagstone steps and pushed open the heavy door. He removed his top hat, and as he did so, was startled to see Edward Kepler busy at work behind the long front counter.

"Good morning, Mr. Humphries. You're earlier than usual, sir," Edward said.

"Good day, Edward. I can say the same to you."

"Y-yes, I came early today, hoping to have a word with you, Mr. Humphries. No one else is about yet. May I please talk with you in your office, sir?" Edward's eyes looked enormous. As Elijah stared at the younger man, surprised by his request, he saw the man's Adam's apple bob up and down several times in quick succession.

"Certainly, come right on down to my office, and we can have a chat." Elijah was seldom thrown off balance, but he was discombobulated by Edward's entreaty, only because he'd thought to have a word with his partners before speaking to Edward. Now he'd have to lay his plans aside. He could clearly see Edward was nervous. As he led the way down the long hall, he whispered a prayer to the Almighty that he would respond to the young man in a godly manner. He had no idea what Edward wished to speak to him about, but a good man was dead because the young man had loose lips. It made Elijah mighty angry at the evil done. He unlocked his office door and ushered Edward Kepler inside.

Elijah's office was neat, his desktop clean of all correspondence and work. Every night, prior to leaving for home, he made sure all was in order in case the good Lord saw fit to take him, or in case an emergency arose and someone else might have to fill in for him and take his clients. He had learned from his father that tidiness in business was necessary to maintain a less stressful environment. He could hear his father's words as if they were newly spoken: *A tidy workplace is evidence of a tidy mind, Elijah.* He couldn't stand clutter, not even *in* his desk. Each drawer was organized and emptied of unnecessary paraphernalia.

His thoughts swung back to the matter at hand.

He gestured Edward to the chair facing his desk, and sat on his own. He leaned back and waited until Edward was ready to talk.

CHAPTER XXIII

*If we confess our sins, He is faithful and just to forgive us our sins
and to cleanse us from all unrighteousness.*

I JOHN 1:9

THE YOUNG CLERK, ALTHOUGH he'd been in Elijah's office countless times, looked around as if it was the first time he'd ever been in it. The walls were done in a light cream color. The bookshelves, pictures, and certificates were framed in a dark mahogany. The chairs for visitors were dark leather, and Elijah's desk chair, a swivel and tilt model, was oak but stained to match his desk. Above Elijah's head, a huge seascape of a frigate running before a storm dominated the wall. The office appeared stark, and yet there was an atmosphere of peace, contentment, and joy that seemed to permeate the very walls.

Elijah, his eyes on Edward's, could see that his clerk was ready.

He cleared his throat and said, "What can I help you with, Edward?" Gazing across his desk at Amos Kepler's son, Elijah's eyes were bland, hiding his thoughts. He perused Edward's face and noticed dark circles under his clerk's eyes, and strain and weariness were stamped on his features. As he stared, he also realized young Edward had lost weight. He was shocked to see a runnel of tears start to pour down the younger man's cheeks.

Edward gulped for air and stared across the desk at his employer. He mumbled, "S-sorry." He grabbed for his handkerchief in his hip pocket, dabbed at his eyes, and blew his nose.

"S-sir, I have to tell you about me being the most wretched of men." He wiped his nose again and continued. "I cannot sleep for the guilt I carry in my breast, sir. I shall confess to you even if it means losing my place of employment here." His speech was rushed, the words tumbling together. "I have committed a heinous crime and need to come clean about it. I can't sleep. I can't eat. I can't even pray. I broke faith with this law firm, sir. I divulged private information about the Farrows' will. I came across it a little over two months ago, and while transcribing, I realized my father stood to come into a windfall should Mr. and Mrs. Farrow die. There was a dreadful morning not long after, and my father was angry at me over a trifling matter. I thought telling him the contents of the will would help to defuse his anger and put him in a better mood." He drew a deep, shuddering breath. "It was only a short time later that Oscar Farrow fell to his death after standing next to my father, with no witnesses to the incident. Truth to tell, Mr. Humphries, I am scared witless of my father. It's taken all of my courage to come to you. If he finds out I've spoken to you about this matter, I don't know what he'll do. I reckon I don't even care at this point. I suppose the honorable thing to do would be to quit working here, but I love what I do, and I'm good at it. I'm sorry, sir. I'm digressing. I believe my father killed Oscar Farrow. He had means and motive. He's been seeing Mrs. Farrow, no doubt in the hopes of courting her at a future time."

Elijah clasped his hands together and rested his chin on them. *But,* he thought as Edward spoke, *he didn't want to marry her. He wanted to kill her.*

"I don't know what else to tell you, sir, except I beg you not to terminate me. I don't know what other employment I could get. If I was to be fired, my father will want to know why. I don't want to lie, but I sure don't want him to find out I've told you what I believe to be true. I will never get over making the mistake of my life. I don't know how to redeem it except to ask my Savior for forgiveness. He's been knocking at my heart for weeks now, telling me I need to confess all this to you. Believe me—I didn't want to. I reckon that was pride. I didn't want to lose the rapport I've enjoyed with you, nor your trust in me. I know trust, once broken, is not easily regained. I finally mustered up enough courage, and here I am. There's nothing else to say, sir, except I'm sorry in the extreme."

While he'd been speaking, he'd leaned forward in his earnest endeavor to communicate with Elijah. Now he sat back and blew his nose again. He looked up to see Elijah smiling at him across the desk, as if he'd never done anything wrong. It jolted Edward, and he wondered at this man he so admired.

Elijah, after a quick prayer for guidance, said, "Edward, the first thing I want to say to you is, I am proud of you."

The young man's mouth dropped open in astonishment. "But, how can you be—"

"Let me finish," Elijah said. "I am proud of you coming to me and confessing the way the Lord convicted your heart to do. I am proud of you because of your obedience to our Lord. Of course I'm not proud of your perfidy. A good man is dead, his wife beside herself with grief, and no one the wiser about your father. Are you sure your father committed the crime of murder?"

Edward swallowed and replied, "I am fairly certain, sir. I cannot prove it, of course, but the evidence and his demeanor point to it."

Elijah simply nodded. He did not divulge to the young man he already knew information pertaining to Amos Kepler's involvement with the Farrows.

"I shall communicate what you have shared with me to my colleagues. Of course, you can be sure they will not share any of this information nor any of your confession with anyone else. We shall quietly take steps to find out the truth of this situation. For the time being, you will continue on here as before. It is not solely up to me to terminate nor retain you. I am thankful you made the righteous choice to confess, and believe me, you will sleep better for it. That being said, I cannot condone what you have done. I am sorely disappointed in your actions, Edward. It grieves me that you would break a trust agreement that you signed before coming here to work. I don't tell my wife anything of import that occurs here if it's something confidential."

Edward breathed a sigh of relief. He knew this was not over, but he was thankful for a reprieve of sorts. His shoulders straightened as the weight of guilt climbed out of his heart. He realized he would never be free of sorrowing for the consequences of his actions resulting in murder. But his sin was not murder—it was the breaking of a vow, a trust that he reckoned would most likely not be regained for a long, long time, if ever. His father, on the other hand, had committed an atrocity, and somehow it needed to be proved.

"Thank you, sir. Thank you so much for not firing me here on the spot. I know I was wrong. I wish I'd never done it. I wish I would stop trying to curry favor from my father. I need to grow up. What I've done by blabbing to my father and the consequences of my actions will never be atoned for." He hung his head.

"I am going to begin looking for ways that will prove his guilt. He keeps a journal, but I've never been allowed to touch it, and I don't know where he hides it."

Elijah didn't think anyone, let alone Amos Kepler, would be foolish enough to journal that he'd murdered someone.

He saw the sorrow etched in Edward's eyes and said, "Let me pray with you. I hear others in the hall, and we need to begin our workday, but I'd like us both to pause and ask the Almighty to have His way in this matter."

The two men stood and bowed their heads as Elijah prayed. "Lord, I thank Thee that Thou art a loving God. I thank Thee for Thy mercy and unrestrained compassion. We ask Thee, Almighty Father, right now, we beseech Thee to pour out Thy wisdom upon this situation. I thank Thee for prompting Edward's heart to come forward and confess what he has done. I thank Thee for his obedience to Thy prompting. Lord, I pray Thy forgiveness, mercy, and compassion upon Edward. I pray too Thou wouldst comfort Mrs. Farrow's heart in this tragic loss. Father, Thou alone knowest her pain, and I pray Thou wouldst ease the heartsickness and grant her strength to bear up under this great sorrow. Lord, we pray also that her daughter might be found. It would be a boon to Mrs. Farrow's heart in this time of sorrow. We thank Thee in advance, knowing that all things are in Thy hands. We give Thee our heartfelt praise for being a father we can depend upon in every situation. Again, we thank Thee. Amen."

Edward raised his head, wiped his eyes, breathed a shuddering breath, and wiped his eyes again.

"Thank you, sir. Thank you. I am grateful to work for a person such as yourself. I could wish you were my father." He turned on his heel and headed out the door, closing it with a light hand.

Elijah sat with a plop back into his desk chair. He felt as if the wind had been knocked out of him. *Now what shall I do, Lord? I suppose the first thing would be to set up a meeting with my colleagues, who must be apprised of the situation. What an amazing turn of events, and I feel sad about Edward. He is suffering mightily. I can understand him trying to get his father to love him. What a horrid man Amos Kepler is. Sometimes, Father, I believe because we feel we should be forgiving or more loving, we forget to abhor sin. Lord, please never allow me to get to the place where I tolerate evil rather than confront it. Help me to abhor it the way I should.*

He exited his office and made his way to Stephen Hancock's office. He was closer to Stephen than the other two lawyers. Stephen was one of the first people he'd met in San Rafael when he'd been looking to buy the mission. Stephen had offered him a place at the office, and after making sure the mission was up and running, Elijah had stepped back into law again.

He tapped lightly on Stephen's door and heard him say, "Enter."

George awakened slowly. He stretched under his coverlet and yawned. It was still quite dark, and he didn't know the time. He rolled over onto his back and sitting up, lit a taper, blinking at the sudden light. Taking his pocket watch off the nightstand, he peered at it. *Three eighteen. Certainly not time to get up.* He snuffed out the taper and leaned back on the thick mattress, pillowing his head with his arms.

I cannot fathom how taken I am with Susannah Farrow. Taken, smitten, enthralled, besotted, enamored, but most of all, enchanted. She is simply enchanting. His thoughts turned into a prayer. *I love her. I never thought to fall in love again, Lord. I thought there'd never be another woman for me after Adeline. I somehow don't feel this besmirches her memory or lessens the love I had for Addy. In truth, it may prove that I can't go forever without companionship, because my experience with Addy was so wonderful. Lord, Thou hast put me into this situation, and I pray with all I have within me that I would honor Thee with my actions. Help me be sensitive to her needs. I think she loved Oscar mightily, and I'm glad for that. But, Lord, the ache of loneliness in me has been dissipated by her presence. I feel more alive than I have in years. I thank Thee for this new lease on life, this feeling of anticipation. I Thank Thee, my Father. Amen.* He rolled over onto his side, thinking about Susannah. *How amazing this gift is that has come to me. I'll have to go slow. She's mourning Oscar, and I certainly know how that feels. Oh Lord, I pray she won't be as I was, closed to any future love and…* He fell asleep before he could think anymore.

Hannibal Cassidy was frustrated. He hadn't made any headway peeping every day, all day, at the Farrows' house. He was glad the weather wasn't hot, but he could smell rain was on its way, and he hated the thought of standing in the rain waiting for a glimpse of Cady. The huge gates were shut during the night, so at least he didn't have to stay late to keep watch. When the gates were closed at night, he knew no more traffic was expected. He did wonder if he was missing something, but a body could only bear so much, and all day watching a house was one of the most tedious things he'd ever done.

He sat on the edge of his bed and counted his money. He couldn't afford to keep paying two bits every night for his room. Without Callie taking in laundry, ironing, and sewing, his source of income was gone. He was going to have to find some kind of work unless he could find Cadence. To him, work was not an option. He dreaded it. He didn't want the drudgery of going to some place of employment every day, doing the same thing over and over again. He knew even though they'd been poor, he'd lived a life of ease, almost like a rich man. Callie had done everything to keep the family going. Now, he wondered why.

With all that beautiful money lying in the bank, why had Callie not gone out on her own or back to the Farrows? Why had she stayed with me? I don't think it was for any feeling of love for me that she stayed. Why did she? His thoughts swung back to his need for money. "I need to get my hands on Cady," he said aloud. "I need that money, and I swear I'm going to get it."

Liberty awoke with a strong gnawing pain in the small of her back. She opened her eyes slowly and heard a soft breeze moving through the trees outside. The window, wide open, intensified the sound of leaves shifting and rustling together.

The pain in her back subsided, and she breathed a sigh of relief. Staring at the ceiling, she wondered why she had awakened so early. She heard gentle breathing beside her and turned her head.

Matthew was still fast asleep. Her heart throbbed in warmth, seeing his tousled head on the pillow beside her. *How I do love him*, she thought.

He'd been up until two in the morning, finishing up the harvest. It'd gone fast with all the workers plus Kirk's crew. He'd come to bed exhausted but elated they'd gotten it all in. Kirk's crew had headed back to Sonoma about one o'clock, and Matthew's people had helped to clean things up, ready for the grape crushing to begin. Liberty lay still, not wanting to wake him up.

I know he said to stop looking back, but Lord, how grateful I am for my life now. I never thought I'd be free of Armand. I opined I would have to live out my days with him. He was so evil and seemed to thrive on chaos and ruination of lives. Every day I lived in dread and fear of him. Thirteen long years of unhappiness.

Father, how grateful I am for Your provision for me. I will never stop praising You for my change in circumstance, not until I breathe my last, and yet I will still praise You for all eternity. Here I am married to a wonderful, loving man who considers my needs before his own. Every day is a blessing and adventure, full of joy and gladness. Lord, I pray—ooohhh! I thought I had a backache, but I don't think that's what this is. Her eyes rounded as she realized it was a labor pain.

Liberty lay quietly, and nothing happened, so she continued to pray. *Father, I praise you this morning. I pray in the name of Jesus that this delivery will be smooth and the babies healthy. Father, I am grateful for this gift you have given Matthew and me. What an awesome thing it is to have children. I know people have them every day, but still, they are a gift, and I pray we always treat them that way. May Your hand be with me today. I know this is a laborious process.* She almost giggled at the word *laborious. I don't think I need to wake Matthew, because I won't be having them anytime soon. He got to bed so late, but I thank you that the harvest is all in. Ooohhh my, oooooh!*

CHAPTER XXIV

Behold, children are a gift of the LORD;
The fruit of the womb is a reward.
Like arrows in the hand of a warrior,
So are children of one's youth.
How blessed is the man whose quiver is full of them.

PSALM 127: 3–5a

LIBERTY SAT UP, HUNCHING OVER. The hair around her face was damp with sweat, and tendrils of curls made ringlets around her forehead.

Matthew groaned with tiredness and rolled over to see his wife's face blanched as white as a sheet. He sat up, his eyes wide open and questioning.

Liberty nodded her head in affirmation. They needed no words.

Matthew said, "I'll get Diego to ride for John." He went to the bathing room and came out wearing his denims. "Are you having another pain?"

"Ooohh, Matthew!" She hugged her extended tummy, as if to relieve the pain.

He ran down the hall to Diego and Conchita's room and knocked loudly on the door.

Conchita answered, dressed and ready for the day. "Eet ees time, noh? I geet Diego. He een the barn already. He weel geet Dr. John."

"He can get John, but I think those babies will be here before he is! Boil some water, and I'll tell Diego."

Conchita ran to the kitchen, where Lupe and Luce had started to make breakfast. "Mees Libertee, she be having the tweens. Boil water, lots of water!" She ran back down the hall and burst into the bedroom. She took one look at Liberty, who was white as a sheet, sweat standing out on her brow.

"*Sí*, eet ees the good time. You wait unteel the harvest ees een. You ees a wonnerful girl, Mees Libbee. You weel be having dose babies soon."

"As if I had anything to do with it!" Liberty gasped. She gritted her teeth and said nothing more, completely absorbed in her pain. After it passed, she nodded her head and gasped, "It came on hard all the sudden. I thought I had a backache, and here—ooooh!" She took a deep breath. "I don't know how to do this!"

"*Sí*, you do…eet comed naturally. You weel do thees and haf the babies soon. I be looking now. I halp *mi* seester an' *mi* couseen haf dere babies." Conchita's accent was getting stronger in her excitement. "You lay down. I muss see how you coming along." She pulled down the blanket to check on Liberty's progress. She said nothing to Liberty, but her eyes widened in surprise. One baby's head was beginning to crown. "You weel haf dose babies soon!"

She rushed to the clothespress in the hall and grabbed another blanket and linens. Holding them in her arms, she ran to the kitchen and said in a hushed voice, "Get Meester Bannister. Hurry! Her first baby, it comed now!" She ran back down the hall.

She helped roll Liberty to her side as Liberty grunted in pain.

"We geet everyting ready, mees. Dose two, dey not waiting. *Sí*, I haf the friend. She haf tree labor pains, an' her baby comed. You weel haf babies soon, Mees Libbee, ver' soon." She talked as she spread the doubled blanket and linen over the bottom half of the bed, rolling Liberty back.

"You can scream eef you want. Eet be all right."

"N-no, I won't scre—ahhhh!" Liberty could think of nothing except the pain consuming her.

Conchita slipped her arm under Liberty's knee and bent her leg up. Going around to the other side of the bed, she did the same with the other leg. "We be ready, mees. I go wash my hands, and we be ready for the first baby." She hurried into the bathing room and scrubbed her hands with soap. She again ran to the kitchen and commanded, "Heat the flannel. The first baby, eet ees coming," she said as she grabbed a clean cloth, wet it, wrung it out, and headed back to the bedroom.

Matthew heard her instructions in amazement as he came in the door. He ran down the hall ahead of Conchita, and taking one look at his wife, he also scrubbed his hands.

Liberty was doing her best not to scream, but the pain was unending. It seemed she had no time to breathe between pains.

Matthew took her hand, gave it a squeeze, and stood to receive his firstborn child. He wished like anything that John Meeks were here to deliver the babies.

As his baby was being born, his eyes misted with tears. He held its head, and Conchita said, "Beeg push, Mees Libbee. You give a beeg push now."

Matthew helped to deliver his firstborn child into the world. "It's a girl, Libby! It's a beautiful, perfect girl!" The infant wailed at the abuse of being born. He laid her on Liberty's tummy, and Conchita expertly cut and tied the cord. Cadence came in with warmed flannel and two buckets of water.

Conchita tested the water with her elbow; it was perfect. She started to clean the baby as a scream rent the air. Liberty's back was arched off the bed.

Matthew, having delivered many animals of their offspring, felt for the second baby's head and realized it was breech—feet first.

He motioned to Conchita, who had wrapped the first baby tightly and handed her to Cadence. She nodded her head in understanding. Breech births were tricky and many times ended up stillborn.

"I wish Dr. John was here," Matthew said softly. He had plenty experience with animals but many times lost an animal to breech birthing.

He reached in, and Liberty shrieked again in anguished pain. He felt the cord wrapped around the baby's head. Finally he could slip it over the baby's head. "Big push, honey. Big, big push!" As she pushed, he pulled the feet of the infant and delivered a boy. No crying, no breathing. He opened the little mouth and reached his finger down the infant's throat, pulling out mucous. Nothing. He gently blew into the baby's mouth, and mucous came out his nose. *Lord, help me,* he cried silently. *Lord, please!* He reached into his son's mouth again, and his finger pulled out a little more mucous, and suddenly, the baby began to cry. It was weak and rattly, but he breathed.

"Praise the Lord God Almighty! We have a son, Libby. We have a beautiful boy!"

Tears of weakness and thanksgiving poured down Liberty's cheeks. She was exhausted and closed her eyes. She bore down again to rid herself of the afterbirth.

"Is he all right?" she asked with closed eyes. She felt shaky and ill with tiredness.

"Yes, a little problem with some phlegm, but we'll take care of it. Rest, sweetheart. You did an awesomely wonderful job. Rest now."

Matthew's eyes were shadowed with worry, but Liberty's eyes were closed, and she couldn't see.

"Thank you, Father," she said in a whisper. She opened her eyes as Conchita cut and tied the cord on the baby boy. "He's beautiful. Oh, Matthew, how blessed we are!" She closed her eyes again.

Conchita bathed him, his cry still weak. Her eyes filled with tears as she handed him to Matthew, but she didn't say anything. Her eyes caught Matthew's, and both looked at the baby in sorrow.

Matthew had held many newborn animals, and his touch was tender on his son. He cradled the newborn upright with his little head resting against Matthew's neck. He rubbed and patted the little guy, praying that the mucous would drain into his tummy and not his lungs.

Conchita and Cadence went to the kitchen, where Conchita made a bottle of boiled water with sugar in it for the baby boy.

"Eet be a girl first, an' a boy," she said to Luce and Lupe. "The boy, he not doin' so good," she added. "He comed feet first. You pray he be all right, okay? I not sure he make eet."

Matthew took his son to the great room and sat to feed him. He too was worried. He'd read an article not too long before, stating that only two out of ten babies lived to the age of two. He hadn't told Liberty about it.

He prayed. *We trust in You, Father, not in statistics. I ask You, in the name of Jesus, to allow this baby to live and not only to exist, but to live mightily for You. May this boy live his entire life in a desire to please You and to bring glory to Your name.*

John finally arrived, shocked to see the babies had already come.

"My goodness," he said. "Liberty didn't waste any time, did she?" His voice held a note of awe. "Usually, the first delivery takes hours and hours and sometimes days."

"Yes, I'm well aware of that," Matthew replied, "but Liberty, or perhaps I should say the good Lord, decided differently. She was in labor little more than an hour." He shifted himself in the chair. "Would you please take a look at this little guy? He was born second and breech... came feet first. I didn't think he'd make it, but once we got some phlegm cleaned out, he started breathing."

John's eyebrows climbed up his forehead, and he sat on the ottoman in front of Matthew and his new baby.

"Let me see," he said. Gently, he took the baby from Matthew and laid him on his lap. He began to check him over, noticing his lips were bluish. He nodded to Matthew and said, "Get my stethoscope, will you?" He took the instrument from Matthew and listened to the newborn's heart and lungs.

"There's fluid in his lungs," he said heavily. "I don't know, Matthew." He looked at his friend, and his eyes misted with tears. "I just don't know."

Matthew, his shoulders drooping, said. "I know, John. It'll be a miracle if he survives." He took the infant, who was struggling to breathe, back into his arms. He sat holding him while John sat facing his best friend, not knowing what to say.

As the baby's breathing became more labored, Matthew said, "I'm going to try something I've done with a newborn calf." Unwrapping the blanket, he laid the tiny baby tummy down onto his lap. Matthew stretched out one of his long legs so the baby's head rested on one thigh, which was much lower than his little chest, which rested on his other thigh. He began rubbing and patting the baby's bare back with his hand formed into a cup.

The cupping pats on the baby's bare back began to loosen the phlegm, and mucous drained out of his nose and mouth. Matthew kept the breathing area clean as it came out.

John was dumbfounded. "Why, I've never seen such a thing! It's working, Matthew. It's working!"

"Praise the Lord!" Matthew exclaimed. "Praise the Almighty for gravity and being able to loosen that stuff up. Thank you, Lord, for answering my prayer. I realize we're not out of the woods yet, but I do praise You just the same." His gaze shifted to John, and he said, "It's difficult to realize the reality of what the apostle Paul said, 'To live is Christ. To die is gain.' We never want to die, or at least very seldom, and to have children die, why, it's unspeakable. We look at death as the end, but it's really the fulfillment of living if you're a believer. Death was never meant to be, and the separation of relationship was not part of the original plan. It's why it hurts so much to lose a loved one." He continued to cup his hand and pat the tiny back, trying to get every bit of mucous out. "I do believe this little guy is going to do mighty things for the Lord."

"What are you and Liberty going to call him?"

"We have several names picked out, but I'm pretty sure we'll go with Matthew Aaron Bannister the Second. We'll most likely call him Aaron or Matty. Liberty would like to call him Matty." He smiled as his little son wailed, his lungs sounding clearer and stronger.

"What about the girl?" John asked.

Matthew lifted the baby off his knees, wrapped him back tightly into the blanket, and put him carefully back onto his shoulder, rubbing his back. After a couple hiccups, he quieted down, snuggling into Matthew's neck.

"We were thinking to call her Faith. We're not one hundred percent sure, but so far, Faith Abigail Bannister seems to get the most votes. Elijah and Abigail have meant so much to us, and especially to Libby. If it wasn't for Elijah, Liberty would most likely still be living in that dark house in Boston. Since meeting Liberty, I've found my faith and trust in Jesus. I am a blessed man, John…a very blessed man."

"Yes, we both are, Matthew. We both are very blessed."

John headed toward the bedroom to check on Liberty. As he strolled down the hall, he remembered when he first met Liberty. He'd been bowled over by her beauty and had wanted to court her. She was the most gorgeous woman he'd ever laid eyes on. He had wanted her for a showpiece. *What a clod I was*, he thought. *I thought to cheat on love. I never meant to fall so hard or so completely, but I sure did. One look at my Sally, and I was a goner. Not only a goner, but hopeless. She would have little to do with me until I became a Christian. Now, I am grateful she had such high standards.*

Liberty was awake and smiled wanly as the doctor made his appearance. Her face was pale but not haggard. She had her baby girl snuggled up next to her. "Meet Faith Abigail Bannister," she said. She lowered her voice and asked, "What about my boy? I know there was a problem. Will he be all right, John?" Her heart skipped a beat as she waited for his reply.

"I couldn't do anything for him," Dr. John said. At the look on her face, he quickly added, "No, no, don't worry! I couldn't do anything, but Matthew did. He saved that little tyke's life. Sorry for my wording. It was not my intention to worry you. Yes, your husband definitely saved his little life, and I believe your baby boy will be fine. I listened to his lungs after Matthew did the most amazing deed, and they are cleared out now and not rattly at all."

He didn't explain how Matthew did it, and Liberty didn't asked, but she drew a huge sigh of relief and said aloud, with no embarrassment, "Thank You, my heavenly Father. I give You the glory for showing Matthew what to do."

"How is your head feeling after that nasty fall?" John asked his patient.

"It feels fine. You're a good doctor, John, and thank you for asking. I haven't had any aftereffects, and my head has healed up quite nicely." Liberty smiled as she added, "And my hair is growing back."

John smiled, focused on baby Faith. He picked her up, but awoke the contented baby, who wailed in protest as he unwrapped her snuggly blanket. He listened to her lungs and checked her over.

"Everything looks good, my dear. She seems to be a healthy little gal. You rest now, and please don't worry yourself about anything. Worry really does affect your milk. Although I know the custom is to be abed for days to weeks on end, I frankly don't agree with that. I have found my patients do much better moving around and getting their body back to normal. My advice is take it easy, but if you want to be up and about, go right ahead. I know Conchita would agree with me. Many women the world over have their babies and continue working in the fields the same day. While I don't recommend that, I do want you up and about within a couple days. No hot salsa and no fresh onions. It taints your milk. Drink plenty of fluids. I need to warn you that it takes a day or so for your milk to come in. When it does, it is quite painful at first. The pain lasts a short time. Meanwhile, nurse your babies even if there's no milk yet. They receive nourishment that's beneficial to them." His smile was benign as he added, "You are a blessed woman, Mrs. Bannister. Yes siree, a blessed woman. Oh, I forgot to mention. Since you have twins, I suggest rotating what side they nurse on. You might keep a record, or you'll forget who goes where." He nearly laughed. "Rest now, and if any problems should arise, don't hesitate to send for me."

"Thank you, John. You've been a blessing to our family." Her eyes teared up with the emotion that welled within her. "Thank you for being such a good friend." She wiped her tears, not knowing why she was crying.

"You'll find yourself quite emotional too. It's normal. Take care now." He left the new mother and headed toward the kitchen.

Dr. John related the whole process to Conchita about Matthew clearing out the baby's lungs. He was still amazed at the procedure. He repeated his directions in detail to Conchita and Matthew, and left the Bannisters' Rancho.

Matthew felt like going back to bed but knew he wouldn't sleep. He rubbed his eyes, which felt as if they had sand in them. Cadence sat at the kitchen table, holding the newborn boy in wonder. Matthew sat next to her after dishing himself up, and Conchita plunked a cup of coffee in front of him.

"You dreenk the coffee first, Meester Bannister," Conchita ordered. "You noh geet much sleep. Today you must be working again to destem the grapes an' geet them ready for crushing. You dreenk lotsa coffee."

"I didn't know women could have their babies that fast," Cadence said. "What a precious little bundle this is. Look! He's got a dimple right there." She nodded toward his cheek, and the other two looked, but it was gone. "I'm happy to help with anything that needs done. Conchita, I don't know a lot, and you'll have to tell me what to do, but I will be glad to do it and feel a bit more useful."

"We would appreciate that," Matthew responded. "I know everyone will be happy to help." He looked toward his housekeeper and added, "Conchita, I put you in charge. You know what is best for those babies and for Liberty. I'll tell Libby she has to mind you."

Conchita snorted. "As eef that weel ever happen!"

CHAPTER XXV

Praise the LORD, for the LORD is good;
Sing praises to His name, for it is lovely.

PSALM 135:3

AMOS KEPLER WAS BESIDE HIMSELF with anger. It was late afternoon when he returned to Susannah Farrow's house, but again Tess wouldn't let him in. Catching a glimpse of George walking across the foyer, his anger boiled over. *George...I remember his name is George...yes! George Baxter. What in heaven's name is he doing here?*

He pushed rudely past Tess and entered the large foyer, to Tess' indignation and George's surprise.

"You can't come barging in here when you're not welcome, Mr. Kepler!" Tess spoke in nearly a hiss. "You get yourself out this door right now, and don't you come back here anymore! You're not wanted here at this time. Perhaps when Mrs. Farrow is finished mourning, but not now, sir. Out!"

"What are you doing here?" Amos ignored the housekeeper as if she'd not spoken to him and asked George, in an insinuating tone of voice, "What kind of mourning is Susannah Farrow doing when she entertains a male guest unchaperoned? It's indecent! It's unconscionable! It's simply not done!"

George had heard enough. He strolled, unhurriedly, across the wide foyer to Amos Kepler and said in a low but commanding voice, "Listen, sir. You get out, and take your sullied mind with you!" He was angry in the extreme and couldn't remember the last time he'd so lost his sense of poise and affable conduct.

Susannah partially descended the stairs but stopped on the landing when she heard Amos Kepler's voice. Her face reddened at his words. She could barely hear George's words, spoken in such a soft but commanding voice. Instead of feeling upset, she felt protected. Kepler couldn't see her, and she didn't wish him to, but she stood where she could hear his response.

"You listen here, sir. I have an understanding with Mrs. Farrow. When her time of mourning is over, we plan to be married."

Tess gasped at his outrageous statement and tried to formulate a reply to such a scandalous remark, but George had no problem articulating a rejoinder.

"Mrs. Farrow is feeling much better now that you are not visiting anymore. I wonder, could that be something we should look into?"

Kepler's eyebrows rose up in surprise, and the hair on the back of his neck prickled in trepidation. He made a sputtering noise and began to back away. His tone was shocked as he responded, "How dare you make such an allegation! Why, perhaps I should have the law onto you!"

"I am the law," George replied. "Now, get out!"

Amos Kepler's face, full of rage, turned to one filled with fear and consternation. He wondered what this man knew and if he was truly a lawman. He turned, and with an ugly look toward Tess, made his escape. He grabbed the knob of the door Tess had been holding open and slammed it shut behind him. Amos needed a plan to get Susannah out of the way. It looked as if marrying her was out of the question.

Susannah finished descending the stairs. "Thank you, George. That should put paid to his visits, don't you think?" She smiled up at George, her face openly admiring.

"I'm sorry, Susannah," George replied. "I didn't mean for him to know I am connected with law enforcement. Frankly, I lost my aplomb. It's not a normal happenstance with me."

Susannah didn't reply. She simply stood there staring up at him.

It made Tess feel as if she were intruding.

The housekeeper asked, "Would you like some tea? I'd be happy to have Opal make some up for the two of you."

Susannah nodded without taking her eyes off George. "Yes, Tess, please have it brought to my sitting room. That is, if you'd like some, George?"

He nodded in the affirmative but did not take his eyes off Susannah's and what he was sure he saw there. He felt mesmerized by her beautiful gray eyes. As Tess left to go to the kitchen, Susannah took George's hand and led him down the hall. He felt a frisson of excitement that tingled his hand as it crawled up his arm and into his heart.

"Please, sit, George," she said. "I need to talk to you. You already know about my daughter, Callie, lost to me for going on eighteen years now. We only had one girl. I've never stopped praying for her. And Oscar, bless his soul...I loved Oscar with a deep, abiding love. It took me a long time, after I was married, to realize I loved him. He was a good man, but we didn't have a romantic love. Oscar..." She dropped her eyes, and for the first time George saw her discomfited.

He started to say something, but Tess tapped lightly on the door and entered, pushing the tea trolley. There were cups and saucers in a beautiful floral pattern. A small matching miniature pitcher held milk. A bowl held cantaloupe cut into bite-sized pieces, and a serving plate contained large cookies and slices of chocolate cake. Napkins, two empty plates and flatware, along with a large floral teapot of hot black tea, completed the service. "Here you are, Mrs. Farrow. You enjoy this little repast, an' I'll be having mine in the kitchen with Opal. Ring the bell if you need anything." She nodded respectfully at George, feeling she had interrupted something, and left the sitting room.

"As I was saying," Susannah said, "I grew to love Oscar. He was a gentle and loving husband. Our marriage was arranged by our parents. I always had a feeling Oscar loved another woman. I suspect out of respect and obedience to his parents, he married me. I don't believe he was ever unfaithful, and he was devoted to making me comfortable. I have never known a romantic attachment. Ours was a marriage of convenience. Our parents wanted to join two wealthy estates. For my entire life I have believed I didn't have a romantic bone in my body." She paused, looked down, and stared at the back of her hands, which lay quietly in her lap. A blush climbed up her neck and suffused her cheeks. She looked up at George with shining eyes. "Never until now," she said in a stilled voice that vibrated with passion.

George was astonished at her frank admission and immediately stood, drawing her hands to his chest as she arose to meet him. "I shouldn't be doing..." He couldn't finish his sentence as she turned her face to his and closed her eyes. "Ah Susannah!" He clasped her to himself and kissed her gently, and then with deepening fervor.

A thrill ran through Susannah as she felt a curling of warmth inside herself as she responded to his kiss. For the first time in her life, she felt romantic passion, and it shook her to the core.

He released her gently and held her back from himself as he stared into her incredible gray eyes.

"Can you believe this has happened to us?" He smiled at her, drawing her close to embrace her.

She rested her head on his shoulder as contentment coursed through her body. "I didn't know it could be like this."

"I didn't think to ever fall in love again," George said. "I love you, Susannah. I believe I fell in love with you the minute I laid eyes on you."

She snuggled closer, and his arms gently tightened. "I know the Almighty has brought us together, George. I love you too, but it's taken me completely unawares. I can seem to think straight for thinking about you. I have never felt this way. I feel as if I'm out of control, and I'm never out of control! What shall we do now? What should be our course of action?"

"Much as I hate the thought, you must go through a period of mourning. If we find we cannot bear it, we can be quietly married and take a trip on the continent and then reside quietly in San Francisco."

"I have a large flat there. Oscar used it whenever he needed to go to the city."

"I have a house in Pacific Heights," George said. "I think you'd love to live there. The view of the bay and Alcatraz is fantastic." He kissed the top of her head as it lay nestled in the curve of his neck. He remembered thinking he needed to go slow, but his Susannah had led the pace. "I do think we need to get you out of here and to a safer place. I don't trust Amos Kepler."

"Neither do I." She thought for a moment. "I've invited Elijah and Abigail to dinner again, and they will soon be here. Perhaps we could use their ideas, as well as our own, to figure out a good plan. I don't trust Amos either. I feel like a new woman since he stopped coming to visit. I believe you are quite right in thinking he was poisoning me. What a despicable man!"

"He is a murderer, and yet he is to be pitied. I have no doubt he murdered Oscar, and to what purpose? For a life of ease riddled with guilt? No, he cannot be a happy man. That type never are. They steal, murder, and destroy because they are controlled by their evil desires. A selfish person is never satisfied. Our job is to pray for such a one as he. You know the verses in Ephesians six where it talks about our struggle being against the spiritual forces of evil in the heavenly realms. Our battle is not against Amos Kepler but against the enemy of our souls, whose grip on Amos is one of pure evil. No, I can assure you—Amos Kepler is not a happy man."

After leaving the steps of Susannah Farrow's house, Amos Kepler walked in high dudgeon, muttering loudly to himself.

There was no one around, and the gates had been left open.

Amos Kepler did not see the man skulking in the bushes.

Apoplectic, he ranted as he walked. "All that work, and where is it getting me? I killed her old man, and now I'm going to have to wait months...months, I tell you! And Callie could be found during that time. I'd be out of everything. I wonder if Callie will ever come back home. I don't think she will or she'd have already shown up here. She'd certainly not want to see me, now would she? No, what I need to do is get rid of Susannah Farrow. I must make a plan." He stomped as he walked, rage evident in every step.

The tirade continued as Amos strode down the road, but Hannibal Cassidy stood up straight in wonder, as the information he'd just heard suddenly made sense.

That man killed Callie's father. This might be just what I need. I haven't seen hide nor hair of Cady, but it sounds as if they're a looking for my Callie. If that's the case, it means Cady isn't even here, else she'd 'ave told 'em Callie's dead. I do believe I can make this information provide me with a needed income.

A large carriage came around the corner as Hannibal came out of the bushes, almost dazed with his new knowledge. He didn't notice the vehicle as he began to stride down the road without further thought other than he couldn't let this man get away. The man hadn't looked back, not one time, and Hannibal was able to follow without suspicion.

Amos recognized the carriage belonging to the Humphries and wondered about their relationship. He muttered to himself, still fuming. "Wonder if that lawyer can change the will? Can he undo the instructions Oscar left? I need to get at Susannah somehow. I need to get her out of the way." He continued to walk, whining to himself all the while. He headed to the law offices, deciding to ask his son, who always worked late, what exactly were the terms of the will.

Hannibal followed at a safe distance, having to hurry to keep up. He plopped down gratefully on the wooden boardwalk across the street to wait for the man who'd entered the office building.

Elijah and Abigail saw the man come out of the bushes, and both stared at him as he hurried down the road after Amos Kepler. They pulled into the drive, and Elijah realized the gates had been left open for them. The gatekeeper came around the manse to take the horses around the back. He helped Abigail down and doffed his hat to Elijah.

"I'll take the horses 'round back, sir," he said. "The stableman has tonight off."

"Thank you. They've already been fed, so no need for anything unless you care to water them," Elijah replied. "We just saw a man come out of the bushes across the road there. He was walking down the road toward town. You might want to keep a lookout in case he decides to come back." Elijah thanked Benny as he took Abby's arm and led her up the steps. The door was opened immediately. The evening was warm, so Abby had left her wrap in the carriage. Tess led them directly to the parlor, where George and Susannah were having some cider.

George strode over to bid them welcome as if the house belonged to him.

Susannah followed at a more sedate pace, still in awe of this thing that had happened to her. Having never experienced romance and the thrill of having the one you love return your love was overwhelming. Always striking in appearance, she fairly glowed as she took Abigail's hand.

One look at Susannah's face, and Abigail smiled inwardly in delight and pleasure. Susannah, unaware the love she had for George emanated from her, greeted her guests with affection.

"Welcome to both of you! I'm so delighted you could join us again. George and I are looking forward to a repeat at beating you at whist." She grinned at Abigail as she took Elijah's hand. "I am grateful for you, Elijah. If you hadn't cared so much about me, I'd never have gotten to meet George. Frankly, I'd probably be on my deathbed. Too, I am grateful for you handling my affairs and taking such good care of me."

"Thank you, madam. It has been a pleasure." He turned to George. "Abby and I witnessed a strange event as we drove up the road in front of this house. As we turned the corner, we saw Amos Kepler marching down the street, but you'll never guess what we witnessed next. We saw the man who's been hiding in the bushes come out and start after Amos."

George's eyebrows climbed up his forehead as he listened. "So our hidden man is now stalking Amos? Remember when we first arrived? I saw the man in the bushes, and Mr. Kepler was coming out of this house. Maybe the hidden man hasn't been after Susannah after all. Perhaps he's been after Mr. Kepler. This is a conundrum, to be sure."

"There's too much happening for my peace of mind," Elijah said. "I think it might be wise to get Susannah out of town for a time. She is in mourning, and none in town would be the wiser. I am thinking we could go up and visit Liberty and Matthew and take Susannah there. She'd be safe. I certainly wish the terms of the will Oscar made up didn't have the stipulations that are in it. It doesn't bode well for Susannah's welfare to keep her within Amos' reach. I might add another fact. Edward confided in me"—he inclined his head in Susannah's direction—"and is quite certain his father murdered Oscar." He glanced at Susannah. "I'm sorry for such disturbing news before dinner." Turning back to George, he added, "Edward is, as you might recall, Amos' son."

"Yes, I do remember. An interesting development, is it not?" George's face was alight with anticipation of solving the mysteries of a good case. "The son tells his father about the terms of the will. Within a few weeks at most, Oscar Farrow has a tragic accident, and only Amos, who stands to come into a great deal of money, is witness to it. Amos Kepler then begins to visit Susannah upward of three times per week, and coinciding with his visits, she goes into a decline, becoming so ill she can barely function. Someone is skulking in the woods across the street, keeping watch on the comings and goings of this house, and has followed Amos Kepler down the street. And now we find, because of the terms of the will, it is of a great necessity to locate Susannah's missing daughter. Not only locate her, but we must move quickly, as we'd obviously like to find her as soon as possible." He grinned at Elijah and added, "Do I have it all down correctly?"

Elijah did not smile back, his big blue eyes serious as he replied. "Yes, yes, you do, George. Yes, you do." As he spoke, there was a tap on the opened doorframe.

Tess entered and announced, "Dinner is served...please come this way."

George took Susannah's hand and placed it on his arm, and Elijah turned and gave Abigail a quick kiss as the others were going out the parlor door. He whispered in her ear.

"Those two aren't the only people in love, my dear. I love you so much it almost hurts!"

"I love you back," she said quickly. She glowed as she took his arm, and they made their way to the dining room.

CHAPTER XXVI

So are the ways of every one that is greedy of gain;
which taketh away the life of the owners thereof.

PROVERBS 1:19

ONCE AGAIN IT WAS A LOVELY EVENING. Conversation flowed during dinner. It was stimulating and ended up with the focus being their proposed trip to Napa. Elijah was nearly as concerned as George about Susannah's welfare.

"Think I'll take an additional week off," George said. "I'll wire Cabot in the morning. He said he'd be in touch with me if there was anything he couldn't handle. I'd like to accompany you to Napa. I would very much enjoy seeing Liberty Alexandra Corlay Bouvier Bannister again."

"Goodness," said Susannah, "that's quite a lengthy name, isn't it?"

Elijah smiled as he replied. "She goes by Liberty Bannister. Her first husband, Armand Bouvier, was also murdered, madam, but her story is quite different from yours. Her first husband was an evil wretch who ruined many lives. He left quite a wealthy estate solely to his partner, Liberty's father, save an undeveloped property in Napa. Liberty's father, Jacques Corlay, found out about the terms of the will and had his son-in-law murdered. As it turned out, Liberty's father was actually a stepfather, not her true father. Corlay came west and kidnapped Liberty, but in the process was killed by a rattlesnake. She has quite a story. I love her as if she were my own daughter. She is due to have a baby anytime now, and it would be a joy to see her again."

George turned to Susannah and asked, "What would you like to do, Susannah? Would you enjoy a trip to Napa, or would you prefer to stay here?"

Susannah was startled by the question. Oscar had never asked her opinion when a decision needed to be made. He, being the man of the house, had maintained the position of making any decision was solely his. If he'd consulted her years ago, Amos Kepler would never have been hired as head of the school. There was something about that man, even then, that caused her to shun away from him.

She glowed with pleasure at George's thoughtfulness. "I believe I would like to meet this woman, Liberty Bannister, if it wouldn't be too much of an imposition. Given the fact that she is ready to have a baby, mightn't we be in the way?"

"If we are, we can stay at her father's house," Elijah replied. "He lives with his mother on the property abutting the Bannister holdings. I'll send a wire tomorrow and let her know we are coming."

"Now that all is settled, shall we play some whist and wait for dessert?" Susannah didn't care to have people worrying about her and was glad to move on with the evening.

Elijah said, "I vote we move to the game room and have dessert later."

"Me too," Abby said.

"Make that three," George added, "or is it four?" He smiled warmly at Susannah, and the blood crept up her neck and into her face.

Her eyes were shining with love for him, and both Elijah and Abby were gladdened to see that George wasn't the only one smitten. Abby took Susannah's arm, and the two women preceded the men down the hall.

As they made their way to the game room, Elijah said in an aside to George, "Wonder what the man in the bushes has to do with Amos?"

"I've been wondering ever since you told me about it," George replied. "Whatever it is, he wouldn't be hiding in the bushes if it was on the up and up."

The evening was a wonderful success, and again Susannah and George beat Elijah and Abby.

"I declare," said Abigail, "it's as if the two of you have the ability to communicate without words. It's not a normal circumstance for Elijah and me to be beaten so soundly, and twice in a row too! We'll have to play up at Matthew and Liberty's and see if it's your deck of cards, Susannah," Abigail jested.

Susannah laughed and replied, "It must be the deck. Why, George and I scarcely know one another, but we are rapidly rectifying that situation." She beamed in George's direction, and he wanted to take her into his arms but restrained himself.

Elijah said, "So we'll plan to leave the day after tomorrow, eight o'clock sharp. Oh, I meant to ask. Susannah, you can ride, can't you?"

"Oh yes, I've ridden since I was three. My father was a great horseman and made sure I had the proper lessons early on."

"I just learned to ride this past year," Abby said. "I never rode anything that didn't have four wheels on it until Elijah said I needed to ride. I have learned to shoot too."

"Have you?" Susannah's gray eyes sparkled with delight. "I'd like to learn. I have a small derringer, but I really don't know how to use it. Oscar said just waving it around at someone would be enough to scare them off. It's not even loaded."

George almost laughed. "A lot of good that would do you. If you carry a gun, madam, you must be able to shoot it. If you simply wave it around someone with evil intent, they will make short shrift of you."

Susannah said, "Why, I haven't heard that term used in ages. Short shrift. Do you know from whence it came?"

George shook his head. "No, I don't."

"I do," said Elijah. "Shakespeare was the first to use it in a different context in *Richard III*, back in the fifteen hundreds, but the word *shrift* means a penance given by a priest in confession. It was used to provide absolution of a sin. During the seventeenth century, criminals were sent to the scaffold immediately after receiving their sentence and had only a 'short shrift' before being hanged. The verb, shrive, is almost unheard of nowadays."

"Goodness, you are a walking encyclopedia!" Susannah exclaimed.

Abigail smiled and added, "He is definitely a word person."

"Back to what George was saying," Elijah said. "It is important to know how to aim and fire a gun. I insisted Abby learn. She scoffed about it at first but came to see the reasoning. Liberty Bannister is a sharpshooter. I think every woman who lives here in the West should be able to know how to use a gun."

The two couples finished planning their trip and who would take what as far as food. After a delightful concoction of chocolate pie for dessert, Elijah and Abigail took their leave.

Amos Kepler entered the law offices to find his son still working. It was suppertime, and everyone else had gone home.

Edward, head bent over some paperwork, looked up in shock to see his father. Amos had never visited the law office before. Dread enter Edward's veins, and his limbs felt leaden with the burden of knowledge he carried in his soul.

"I need to talk to you, young man. Remember that will you were telling me about?"

"What will, Father?" He swallowed, and his Adam's apple bobbled up and down with nervousness.

"You know exactly what will I'm talking about…Oscar Farrow's will." Amos' voice rose in anger, and Edward felt an inward shudder. "What other will would you suppose I'm talking about? You've never shared any information about a will other than Oscar Farrow's."

"I know I told you it, but I didn't tell you about Mr. Farrow coming in about two days after I told you about it. He came in to change his will," Edward said, telling his father a bald-faced lie.

"What!" Amos cried out, his face blanched. "What are you saying?"

"I'm saying Oscar Farrow changed his will. He decided his daughter was never coming back, and he left everything to Mrs. Farrow. If she dies, the estate will go to an orphanage in San Francisco, which is in great need of renovation." Edward didn't even blink as he lied to his father. He couldn't remember the last time he'd lied, but he felt this lie to be one of self-preservation.

Amos strode over to the desk where Edward was standing and grabbed his cravat, lifting his son to his feet. "Are you telling me the will was changed right after we spoke? Why didn't you tell me?" Amos shoved Edward with force, and he stumbled backward onto his chair.

Amos, anger emanating from every pore of his body, strode out the door, slamming it so hard the pictures hanging on the wall wobbled in protest.

Edward, with trembling hands, began to put away his paperwork. He wondered about going home. *Perhaps I should stay at the inn tonight. Truth to tell, I'm scared to death of my father. If he finds out the truth...that I lied about the will being changed...I think he just might kill me.* Edward packed a gun and was a good shot. He pulled his holster out of the drawer and strapped it on. He always wore it except in the office, where it wasn't allowed. If his father came after him, he'd use it if he had to. Still, he shuddered, and his hands wouldn't stop trembling.

Hannibal saw Amos coming out of the office door. He slipped into a store's doorway to watch what the enraged man would do.

Amos was apoplectic. He castigated Edward, talking nonstop, as he stomped down the walk.

"Stupid boy. He's always been stupid. Takes after his mother, that's what! I couldn't stand her ways either. Always mincing around spying on me...always condemning me with those cold blue eyes of hers. I got rid of her and never had a moment's grief over it. Oscar...Oscar was another matter. I've had nightmares about Oscar. Now I find all I've done is for naught. I won't get a penny unless, somehow, I can get Susannah to marry me. And how can I do that when I can't even get near her? I need to make a plan. That George Baxter...wonder if he really is a lawman the way he said. Well, he can't find out anything about me. No one knows the things I've done." Caught up in his own misery, he didn't notice the man following him down the walk, keeping pace with him.

Hannibal Cassidy was finished with waiting around, hiding in bushes, trying to find out some information. He was going after this man to find out what he knew. He slipped out of the recessed doorway and was glad for the inky night. A little blackmail would line his pockets quite nicely. He was nearly broke.

He followed the man past shops with no lights in the windows. It seemed like a ghost town. Most people were home having dinner. Few were out on the street, but the lamplighter had been this way. Although the light was meager, it cast a glow on the outer side of the walk, so Hannibal kept close to the storefronts to avoid being seen. Being short in stature, he had to walk as fast as he could without running. It was difficult not to make noise. Amos was a tall man, and striding angrily down the walk, his long steps ate up the distance. He turned at the corner, and Hannibal slowed his quiet step to make sure the man was continuing to walk and not hiding in the shadows, ready to pounce on him when he turned at the corner.

Hannibal needn't have worried. Amos continued on his way home, totally oblivious to the man following him. He was livid…his anger poured out of him at Susannah, at Tess, at Edward. Caught up in his own emotions, the world didn't exist. He lived in his own world and heard no one following him.

Cadence lay on her bed, looking out at the starry night. It was late, but she could hear sounds emanating from the kitchen. Conchita was still in there getting things ready for the next day. Cady got up, wrapped herself in one of Liberty's robes, and padded on bare feet down the hall to the kitchen.

Conchita looked up in surprise. "You ees steel up?" She made the statement into a question.

"Yes. I can't seem to settle my thoughts and thought I'd come sit awhile and see if I can get sleepy. Why are you still up?"

"For the same theeng. You want a cup of tea?"

"Yes, thank you. I'd like that. Do you have some chamomile? I've heard that makes you sleepy."

"Yes, I geet some for you. I haf the hot water." She poured boiling water into a cup and filled the tea ball with fragrant chamomile leaves. Dropping it into the cup, she set it in front of Cady.

"I steel up so I can halp Mees Liberty. She haf to feed dose babies again soon. That seem to be all she haf time to do. Eet take time to feed one, let alone two. That leetle Matty, he hongry all the time. Mees

Liberty, she so happy. She ees the nicest woman I ever know. When she first comed here, she was not happy, but she glad to geet away from Boston and her evil stepfather. He a bad *hombre*. He murdered Mees Liberty's grandfather when Mees Liberty was newborned. Violet, Mees Liberty's mother, she geeved Liberty's brother to the doctor who deleever the two of them."

Cadence's eyes widened at Conchita's story. "I had no idea. She has had a rough time of it. It's interesting that you can be around someone and not really know them. All you see is that everything seems perfect for them. You have no idea what a story their life has been. I reckon we all have a story to tell, don't we?"

Conchita looked at Cadence sagely. "*Sí, es verdad.* Sorry. I say eet een Engleesh—yes, it is true. We all haf story to tell."

"Conchita, could you teach me Spanish? I think I'd like to learn it."

Conchita, who had been adding flour to the dough she was going to let rise all night, look up in surprised pleasure. "I never haf taught anyone Spaneesh. I be happy to do eet."

"Maybe we could start tomorrow. I think I'd like that. I'm beginning to master reading, and right now I'm in the middle of *The Pilgrim's Progress* by John Bunyan." She yawned. "I think I'm starting to get sleepy now. I enjoy living here. I am never afraid, and everyone is nice to me. I wonder if it's still necessary for me to dress as a boy when I'm outside?"

"I theenk eet steel a good idea. Your father, eef he be in Napa again, he could drop by here and ask about you. I theenk you should still be the boy outside."

"I suppose you're right." Her thoughts switched to another subject, and blood climbed up into her face as she asked, "Do you think I'm too young to get married?"

"You seventeen. That ees not too young. Mees Liberty, she was seexteen. Why you ask? You theenk you sweet on Donny?" Conchita smiled widely and added, "You could do a lot worse than that young man. He a hard worker, heem."

Cadence, eyes shining, said, "I can't seem to stop thinking about him. He's been so kind. At first I felt toward him the same as I did Timmy, but now, oh, Conchita, I think I love him!"

Conchita said, "I theenk he love you too, Cady. Just go slow, and make sure before you make a promise."

Cadence got up and gave Conchita a big hug. "You're so easy to talk to. Thanks for the tea. I think I'll head off to bed now. G'night."

"*Buenas noches*, leetle Cady. You sleep well."

Cadence made her way down the hall and into the bathing room between bedrooms. She looked into the mirror and saw a young woman whose gray eyes had stars in them. "I'm quite sure I love him," she said to herself in a whisper.

She sat on her bed, wondering when she should show the paperwork to Matthew and Liberty. She'd been busy helping Liberty with the babies, and Liberty seemed almost distant. She was so engrossed in taking care of her little babies that Cady didn't feel she should intrude with her own problems just yet. She was a bit afraid that once the papers were read by someone who understood them, things might change for her, and she was quite happy with the way things were right now. She didn't want to leave the Bannisters'. The rest of the world frightened her.

Cady got down on her knees and pulled the red leather satchel out from under the bed. Getting up, she sat on the side of the bed and opened the satchel, simply pondering its contents. Cadence drew out the thick fold of papers. She was beginning to read quite well, but the legalese was beyond her. She read her name, her mother's name, and Timothy's name, but she didn't know what it all meant. She had never even gone through the entire stack of papers. She did notice the date. The papers had been made out a couple days after her seventeenth birthday. Folding them, she put them back into the satchel, but she dumped the jewels and banknotes onto the bed.

She knew there was plenty of money associated with the jewels and banknotes but wondered again why her mother had never used it. Cady thought her pa must have gotten it from the bank the day she ran away. Why had this money never been used to help the family, which was so poor, was a huge question. The only thing she could come up with was that her pa would have taken all of it but that her mother was saving it for her children.

She let the beautiful gems slide through her fingers. They glittered in the lamplight. Finally she put everything back and pushed the satchel against the wall under the bed.

She reached for the pretty, flat jar of cream. Liberty had given her the jar. Her cook from Boston made up a special recipe of skin cream for

Liberty. It was soothing, and the smell was heavenly. Cady rubbed some into her hands and marveled that they were no longer red and chapped. She crawled into the bed, loving the feel of soft sheets. She didn't think she would ever get over the pleasure of sleeping in such comfort. Her nightgown was a soft cotton, and the sheets and pillowcase were white, embroidered with a white pattern across the hems. Cady loved the feeling of luxury.

CHAPTER XXVII

Thou shalt not kill.

EXODUS 20:13

DONNY TOSSED AND TURNED. It wasn't all that hot, but he was. He kept thinking about Cadence. He loved her. There was no getting around it. He thought about her all the time and of the nice things he'd like to do for her. He hadn't seen it yet, but he guessed there was a temper beneath that strawberry-blonde hair of hers. With her coloring he thought she should have a few freckles, but she didn't.

He smiled as he thought about how she'd wrinkled up her nose when she admitted she could cook, but nothing real tasty. She was a quick learner though. She was learning some meals to cook from Conchita. She was practicing reading every day. She showed him a little square of lace she'd made. Liberty was showing her how to tat. She now rode a horse as if she were born to it. Whenever she had some free time, she could be seen talking to a mare called Sunshine. Matthew had bought it for her. She was a beautiful palomino with a sweet disposition.

He rolled to his other side. The moon was shadowed by a few clouds and looked eerie yet beautiful. He stared at it, pillowing his head with one arm. He wondered about Cady not being a Christian. He'd thought she would take that step once she heard about Jesus, but she hadn't.

She'd told him flat out that God hadn't protected her and Timmy from her pa, that He couldn't be all that powerful if He didn't take an interest in what was done to her. He'd tried to explain about free will and that bad things happen to most everybody but that God was there with her. She'd stalked off, not wanting to talk about it anymore.

One thing he knew for certain. There'd be no marrying Cadence unless she was a believer. He'd seen enough of couples having a hard time of it when one partner wasn't a Christian. "Do not be unequally yoked," he whispered to himself. "I know, Lord. I know, but I love her just the same."

Amos entered his house. He was still so angry he could scarcely contain it. "All that planning and work for nothing," he muttered. He lit the main lamp in the living room and strode to the kitchen, where he lit two more. The stove gave off a soft heat that normally felt good when the evenings were cool. This night it felt stuffy. His body was heated up from anger and from walking. He sat at the table, breathing heavily as he tried to collect his thought. *How can I get hold of that money?* He heard a soft click, as if the front door was being closed, and supposed it to be Edward.

"You stupid little runt!" he yelled out. "Not telling me about Oscar changing his will. Why, I ought to—"

He didn't finish his sentence as the shock of seeing a strange man enter his kitchen hit him like a blow. He stood abruptly, alarm and panic spreading throughout his body.

"Who are you? How dare you come in here without knocking! What do you want?"

"Who I am don't matter much," Hannibal answered with a sneer on his face. "What does matter is you killed my wife's father. Now mind you, I won't go around telling 'bout what you done if you pay me a little to keep my mouth shut."

"Your wife's father? What are you talking about? I don't have a clue about whom you are speaking." Amos backed slowly toward the stove, while Hannibal advanced on him.

"I'm talking about my Callie. Callie Farrow Cassidy."

Amos looked at this man in shock. "She married you? Why, you're nothing but a common thief. Callie would never marry the likes of you!"

"But she did, and you murdered her father. Like I said, I won't go around tellin' what I know if you just grease my palm a bit. I'm a bit short on cash and need some help."

"You blackmailing piece of scum. Help you? I'll help you all right!"

Amos reached behind his back and grabbed the iron poker hanging beside the stove.

Hannibal's eyes widened when he saw what Amos was up to. He turned to run, but Amos, the adrenalin pumping furiously, struck Hannibal down, and then he made sure the stranger would never tell a soul what he knew.

He looked wildly around, but he couldn't seem to focus, the blood beating wildly in his brain.

Concentrate Amos! he thought to himself. He suddenly remembered Edward would soon be home. He dragged the late Hannibal Cassidy out the kitchen door and down the back steps. He laid the body next to the rose bushes and hurried back inside, grateful for the dark night.

He ran back outside with a bucket and pumped furiously at the pump, sloshing water over the top as he hastily ran to the back door. He slowed down, realizing he was making a bigger mess. He grabbed some rags from a bottom drawer and started mopping up the kitchen floor. Down on his hands and knees trying to clean up every last spot, he muttered, "I can't believe Callie would ever marry such a man. He was dirty and uncouth. How in the world did he know I killed Oscar? I know there wasn't a soul around when I pushed him over that bannister railing. How did he know?" Amos looked carefully at the walls and chair legs to make sure he hadn't missed anything. He went back outside, threw the rags on the body, rinsed the bucket out, and headed toward the shed to get a shovel.

He dug up two rose bushes, making sure to get below the roots. He began digging as fast as he was able, filling a wheelbarrow with dirt. Sweat ran in runnels down his body as he dug. Finally, when he thought it was deep enough, he drug the body over, rolling it into the grave. He shoveled the dirt out of the wheelbarrow, being careful not to disturb the grass or drop dirt on it. He placed the roses back and placed more earth around them. He dumped the rest of the dirt into the compost pile, beginning to whistle under his breath.

"I did it," he said. "I do believe I buried him right over my dear sweet wife." He chuckled at the thought.

"I think I need to find Callie. Wonder how I could do that?" He took off his shoes on the porch to make sure there was no fresh dirt on them. Breathing a sigh of relief, he went to his bedroom. He was too tired to think of getting something to eat. He felt drained. He moved his nightstand and pushed at one end of the panel in the flooring. Removing it, he reached in and got out his journal. He sat down at a small oak desk in his room to write down all the events of the day. Because of where he kept the diary, he didn't worry about someone ever reading it. He dipped his quill into the ink pot and began to write. A lot had happened this day.

Edward didn't go home after work. He walked slowly toward Three Hawks Inn. It was the only inn having bed and board to be found in San Rafael. The owner, Mr. Stanley, ran his own establishment.

"Good evening, Mr. Kepler," he said. "How can I help you?"

"Good evening, Mr. Stanley. I'd like a room, including dinner and breakfast."

Mr. Stanley's eyes rounded in surprise that Edward would want a room. He knew most everyone in San Rafael and that Edward lived at home with his father. Mr. Stanley didn't care for Edward's father, Amos Kepler, but he kept his lips shut, knowing his business would fail if he poked his nose in where it didn't belong. He was nothing if not discreet.

"Sure thing, Mr. Kepler. I've got a room and will sign you up for dinner and breakfast."

"How's business?" Edward asked out of politeness.

Mr. Stanley, eyes full of curiosity, never asked a question of his own. He was only too happy to let the room to the young man. "Oh, purty slow this time a year. Only have one stranger, an' he's late comin' in ta eat ta night. He's been here nigh unto a week now, but he don't seem ta have any particular business here. Wonder where he is? He's owing me fer a couple nights now."

Edward wasn't paying close attention to what was being said. He wanted to eat and go to bed. He was exhausted, after an emotionally stressful day, but glad he'd confessed everything to Mr. Humphries. He paid for the room and meal and was given a key.

He climbed the stairs and found the room. He had no nightclothes nor anything else, so he locked the door and went down the hall to wash up before going down to eat.

He ordered Salisbury steak and scalloped potatoes. Broccoli came with it, and he enjoyed the meal. He sat there eating slowly with enjoyment and thought out a plan. *I think I should see if I could make a deal with Stanley and just live here. My needs are not great. I mainly live in my room at home too. I don't want the churning stomach anymore. I'm tired of jumping at the sound of Father's voice. Yes, I think this would be a good solution for me. The food is good, and the room will do quite nicely for me.* He sat there calculating his income and the cost of the room. He realized he had plenty for the room and board and some left over, even if he had to pay full price. He was quite sure Stanley would give him a break on the cost, as the innkeeper would have a steady income. He'd actually have more left over than living at home. With that decision made, he felt as if another burden had lifted off his shoulders. He ate the rest of his meal with relish.

Elijah needed to get a few things wrapped up before he would be ready to make a trip for a few days up to Napa. He arrived quite early to work the day after the dinner party. He took his watch out of his fob pocket, and opening it, he laid it on his desk. With no interruptions he got a couple clients shifted to his friend Stephen Hancock and made sure all the paperwork that needed done was accomplished.

Hearing a light tap on his door, he glanced at his watch and saw it was still early. "Come in please," he said.

Edward entered, and Elijah's eyes widened at his disheveled appearance. He was unshaven, clad in the same clothes as the day before. His hair was combed, but not nearly as well-groomed as usual. Edward was normally quite dapper, but today was definitely an exception.

"Good morning, Edward," Elijah said with aplomb.

"Good morning, sir." Edward seemed quite nervous and turned to make sure he'd closed the door all the way.

"I know I look a fright. I didn't go home last night. I stayed at Three Hawks Inn," he said. His eyes looked shadowed. "I worked here until late, and my father came in asking about Oscar's will." His eyes shifted to the floor and stayed there as he admitted his deception. "I lied to him, sir. I told him Mr. Farrow came in a couple days after I blabbed to him, and changed his will, that Mr. Farrow decided his daughter was never coming back and left everything to Mrs. Farrow. I also said if she dies, everything goes to an orphanage in San Francisco. I know it's wrong to lie, but I thought it might take the pressure off Mrs. Farrow, and he might leave her alone."

Finishing his narrative, Edward looked up to see a gleam in Elijah's eyes. He felt a relief, as he had already prayed for forgiveness but felt overwhelming guilt for his actions.

"How did your father receive that information?" Elijah asked.

"He was incensed...nearly foaming at the mouth with rage."

Elijah nodded. "I have no doubt about that." He changed the subject abruptly. "Last night we saw a fellow following your father as we were going to the Farrows' house. Do you have any idea who he was?"

"No, no I don't. As I said, I didn't go home last night. Father was fuming, and I was afraid. But come to think of it, the owner of the inn told me a stranger in town had been staying there for nearly a week and was late to come in for vittles. Said he always came in before a certain time, but he hadn't seen hide nor hair of him. He also said the man seemed to have no business dealings, and he wondered what he was doing here."

"I do thank you for telling me this, Edward. Tell you what. I'm going to give you the day off...with pay. You've been honest and forward with all you know. I just wish you could find that journal you said your father had. It might give us some needed evidence we could use."

"I'd like to find it too. I have a suspicion, one I've had for many years. I won't share it just yet, but I do believe my father has written down every day of his life. He's methodical, and many nights I've seen him reading that journal or one just like the one he's writing in now, as if it were a novel. Yes, I too would like to find it."

"If you do find it, young man, I'd like to see it. I'd be interested to see what your father has done, especially recently. Now, I suggest you go home, since your father is most likely at the school. Get along now and enjoy your day." He smiled, his blue eyes a window to a pure soul.

Edward blinked, looking at the goodness of Elijah, and wished with all his heart he could be like him. "Thank you, Mr. Humphries. Thank you for being a good man." He left swiftly after his comment, embarrassed by exposing his feelings to his boss.

Knowing his father to be at work, he walked home in a leisurely fashion, thinking about all that had transpired. When he arrived, he found Mrs. McCready on her hands and knees in the kitchen.

"I don't know what your father spilled, but there is something red on the floor boards, and it's sticky." She spoke in a complaining sort of voice.

Edward, surprised, moved forward to examine the floor closely. Where the maid had not cleaned, rag marks of someone wiping something up showed across the floor where the sun shone on it through the window. Without letting Mrs. McCready see, he swiped the floor with his forefinger and smelled, but he couldn't place the smell. He licked his finger, and his face blanched, and he felt like retching. It was salty and tasted like blood. In a flash, he was quite sure what had happened.

He went out the back door and over to the rose bed. Sure enough, he could see where the roses had been disturbed, and new dirt stood around two of the bushes.

He went back into the house and asked, "Mrs. McCready, do you know where my father keeps his journal? I've meant to ask you quite some time ago, but I keep forgetting to do so." He'd never spoken so boldly to her before, but the thought that perhaps she knew something spurred him to take courage. He'd always feared his father, but after talking with Mr. Humphries, he felt a strength fill him. He wanted to be an upright man, the same as his boss.

As he spoke, he saw her make a furtive movement, and her eyes turned away from his.

"N-no, I hain't never seed it," she replied as blood suffused her cheeks.

Edward, with a flash of insight, said, "I'm not going to tell my father. In truth, I don't want him to know I know where it is. I simply need to look something up in it."

Mrs. McCready got up slowly to her feet. "You best be a lookin' at it quick-like. You never know when your pa might be a comin' home. He's kept real strange hours in th' last couple o' months. I wisht I could read. I been curious as ta what's in them journals o' his." She led the way to his room at the back of the house. "It's under there." She pointed to the nightstand. "There's a loosen board under there. I sawd 'em git it out one mornin' when he didn't knowd I wuz already here. Tell you what. I'll watch th' walk ta make shore he ain't a comin', an' you can look at th' journal."

She turned and went to the living room as the thought came to her that most likely, she wouldn't be working there anymore. She reckoned once Mr. Kepler found his journal had been looked at, he'd think it was her and fire her. Then she realized he'd never think it was her because he knew she couldn't read or write. He'd know it was Edward. She turned her head and yelled, "You know you'd best clear out of here iff'n you're gonna take that thing. He'll know it weren't me. He knows I cain't read nor write."

CHAPTER XXVIII

A prudent man conceals knowledge,
But the heart of fools proclaims folly.

PROVERBS 12:23

EDWARD REPLIED, "I KNOW HE KNOWS you can't read. He'll know it was me." He pulled out the journal. He reached further back, feeling cloth, and realized it was a bag. He tugged and pulled. It finally moved, and he saw that it was a cotton flour bag with journals in it. Lifting them out, he set the loose one on top, replaced the wood floor panel, and moved the nightstand back into place. He dusted off his pants as he looked around to make sure he'd not moved anything else out of place. He lifted the bag and headed out the door just as Mrs. McCready called out.

"I see him a comin'," she said excitedly. "I see him a comin' this way, an' he's a walkin' right fast."

"I'm finished, Mrs. McCready," Edward said, "but if I were you, I'd pick up that rag off the floor and don't let on you saw anything you needed to clean up in the kitchen. He's done an evil deed, and I'm not quite sure, but he'll get you if he thinks you know anything."

Edward climbed the stairs and went to his room. Dumping the flour sack into a large satchel, he threw it hurriedly under the bed. He changed his mind, scrabbling down on the floor to pull it back out. He opened his window and dropped it. He watched as it landed behind the shrubs on the right side of the house. He closed the window and began to pack his clothes.

He heard his father come in, say something to Mrs. McCready, and start up the steps. He recognized his father's heavy stomping tread on the stairs. As far as Edward knew, his father hadn't been up to the second story in years.

The door was open, and his father filled the middle of the doorway. "I went to the law offices, and your boss, Mr. Humphries, said he gave you the day off. Why is that?" Amos spoke in a sneering tone of voice. He noticed Edward's disheveled appearance. "Why do you look so unkempt? Haven't I told you over and over that your appearance is as important as your character?"

"Yes, Father, you have, except I don't believe it to be true. We have some rough-looking clients at the law office, and yet their character is impeccable."

Amos suddenly realized what his son was doing. "What are you doing...you moving out on me?"

"Yes, I am. I make enough money to live on my own, and I have the feeling you'd be happy to see me out of the house."

"It *is* high time you made it on your own. I'll miss the income you give me, but you cost more than you pay. It'll give me a bit more privacy."

Edward didn't want to give Amos a chance to go down and look into his bedroom. He kept talking to his father.

"I heard through the grapevine that you've been visiting Mrs. Farrow. Talk is that you're sweet on her."

"Where'd you hear that? From Mr. Humphries?"

"No, of course not. Mr. Humphries is an honorable man and doesn't stoop to gossip. No, I heard it from one of the ladies who is a client of one of the other lawyers."

"Who's the lady?" Amos inquired.

"I'm not divulging that information, Father. I am simply saying there is talk going around San Rafael that you're interested in Mrs. Farrow. By the way, I apologize for not updating you about Mr. Farrow's will, but I `ouldn't have said anything in the first place."

Amos' face started to turn red as Edward put the last of his clothes in the satchel.

"Well, that about does it," Edward said with a cursory glance around the small room. It amazed him how little he owned. He tucked a couple favorite books into his satchel and added, "I'll collect the rest of my things later."

Amos stood back as his son descended the stairs. "What's your hurry?"

Edward paused on the stairs and turned to look up at his father. "I'm in no hurry, but on the other hand, I can't see why I should stay around here. I must take after my mother," he said succinctly. "I don't believe we have much in common, Father, except our common blood and last name."

Amos looked stunned at his son's comment but realized he'd thought the same thing many times himself. "Yes, you certainly do take after your mother."

Edward got to the bottom stair and looked up, "Thank you, sir. I take that as a huge compliment. Good bye, Father."

Amos simply nodded his head, but it occurred to him that there seemed to be a finality to the farewell.

Edward went out the front door, and as fast as he could, he ran around to the side of the house, grabbed the flour satchel, and, still stooped, ran back to the walk, just in case his father decided to look out the window when he got to the bottom of the stairs.

Edward walked with long strides down the walk, headed toward work. He'd thought to go back to the inn, book the room, and look through the journals, but as he strode along, he decided he'd be better off to go to the office. What if his father saw his journals were missing? There was safety in numbers. At the office he'd not be alone, but since he had the day off, he could sit at his desk and read the journals without interruption.

Amos looked out the living room window and saw Edward striding down the walk. He felt a moment of bereavement. He was alone and didn't have anyone he could call friend. Oscar had been the closest thing he'd had to a friend, and of course, he was gone. He turned to go into his bedroom but decided he should go back to school. He'd let a lot of things lapse lately. He could read his journal later. He was addicted to his diary and loved reading what he'd done day by day. Perhaps he'd start at the first one and read them all through again.

Shortly after Amos left the house, Mrs. McCready packed up all the little things she owned, which had accumulated in a drawer over the years she'd worked for Mr. Kepler. She looked around to make sure she hadn't left anything, because she certainly wasn't coming back to this house. She strode toward home, trying to decide if she wanted more employment or if she should retire and live on her husband's income. All the sudden, she realized it had been blood she'd mopped up this morning. *Was Amos in some kind of cult and sacrificing animals?* She wondered. *Edward said he was evil.* As she neared home, she felt as if a burden had been lifted off her shoulders. Curious about the journals, she knew she'd never know what was written in them.

Edward Kepler, loaded with the bag of journals and his two satchels, went up the steps of the law offices with alacrity. He was looking forward to finding out exactly what his father had done. He felt no remorse telling Elijah that he believed his father murdered Oscar Farrow. As he entered, he saw his boss at the reception counter.

Elijah, leaning on the top of the reception desk, was talking to one of the clerks. He turned as Edward entered, and his eyes widened in surprise. He started to speak, but Edward gave a quick nod of his head toward the long hall, indicating he wanted to go to Elijah's office.

Elijah turned back to one of the underclerks who was new and said, "You are doing a fine job, young man. Keep up the good work."

Edward nodded to the young man and said, "Good morning." He didn't break his stride as he headed down the hall toward Elijah's office. As soon as Elijah closed the door, Edward said excitedly, "I've got them. I got all of them, I think." He plopped his own satchels on the floor by a chair and swung the heavy flour bag full of journals onto the floor in front of Elijah's desk.

"Here, this is the one he was currently writing in. Look. He's got the dates written on the front of each one. I'm going to look at one of the older ones."

"How'd you get hold of them?" Elijah asked.

"Mrs. McCready, our daily, knew where they were. When I got ᵓe, she was mopping up the floor but didn't know what it was she was cleaning. I realized it was smeared blood. I went out to the garden and saw the earth has been disturbed under a couple rose bushes. I'm quite certain my father killed and buried the man who was following him last night." Edward's voice was even as he spoke, but his hands were shaking.

Elijah said a quick prayer for the man's family—if there was one. He took the journal Edward handed him and went around the desk to sit in his own chair. Leaning forward, he said, "You don't have to sit there on the floor, Edward. Get comfortable, and I'll see if I can rustle up some tea or coffee. Which would you prefer?"

"Tea, sir. I'd love a cup of hot tea, no sugar, but with a little milk. Thank you."

Elijah went back down the hall and asked the underclerk to make each of them a cup of tea. He went back to his office and entered to see Edward crying.

His sympathy deeply aroused, he drew the young man up by the arm and hugged him close as Edward sobbed out his sorrow.

"He killed my mother. My father killed my mother. Somehow, I've always felt something wasn't right about her leaving us. I knew my father didn't love her, but I knew in my heart she'd never leave me with him. If she ran away from him, she'd have taken me with her. He poisoned her slowly with laudanum. It's written right there in the journal."

Same as he was doing to Susannah, Elijah thought.

Edward pulled back and wiped his eyes. "Sorry, sir, for blubbering."

"It's not blubbering. It's called sorrow. It must come as a shock to you. Let me see what he wrote in the journal yesterday, and then I'll go back a couple months to when Oscar died."

The underclerk came in with a tray, which he placed on a small end table, and asked, "Will there be anything else, Mr. Humphries?" He glanced curiously at Edward, who kept his head bowed as if reading.

"No, no, nothing else. Thank you, young man. This is quite sufficient."

The clerk left, closing the door firmly behind him.

Edward poured milk from a little pitcher into his tea and lifted the cup to his lips. He realized how upset he was, because his hand was trembling as he put the cup to his lips. He took the cup into both hands to steady it.

Elijah felt sorry for the young man. He sat down with his tea and started looking at the journal. He read and felt almost sick. It was as if Amos were bragging about what he'd done.

His eyes widened as the information that the man who'd followed Amos home was Callie Farrow's husband. Kepler didn't say where the man had lived or where Callie was now, but he had written the name Cassidy. Elijah felt a wave of disappointment. He wondered if George would be able to track where the man was from.

He read some more of the entry while Edward sipped at his tea. Elijah had difficulty not letting his jaw drop at the information. He flipped back in the journal to the date of Oscar Farrow's death and read the entry. It was exactly as he had supposed. Amos Kepler had pushed Oscar over the railing. *I need to talk to George.*

"Can you please hand me the journal for, let me see, eighteen sixty-seven?"

Edward, his eyes widening, unloaded the heavy bag and found the desired journal. He gave it to Elijah with a question in his eyes.

"Just need to look something up."

"Has he murdered someone else?"

"I don't know. He may have, but that's not what I'm concerned about right now. I have a theory that keeps niggling at me, and I want to see if it's correct. I'll let you know about this later." Elijah began to read excerpts from the journal and then found what he was looking for. His lips thinned with anger as he read the words. Suddenly fed up with the contents, he closed the journal with a snap.

"Edward," he said, "I want you to stay with me—I'm talking close to me. I don't think your life will be worth two cents once your father sees his journals are missing. I don't know how much time we have, but I have a detective friend ensconced at Mrs. Farrow's house. I've thought for some time that your father was involved with Oscar's murder. Now we know for sure." He glanced down at the two journals and pressed his lips together.

"Tonight, you will be a guest at our house, but we need to go to the Farrows' house…right now. I think your father will most likely go home for lunch, and when he does, I'd like my friend to be there waiting for him." He pulled his watch from his fob pocket and looked at the time. "Let's make haste."

They packed up the journals, and Edward carried them as they walked hurriedly to the Farrows' house. Elijah took the brass knocker, giving it a couple good raps. They waited, and the door was opened by George, which took Elijah by surprise.

"Good morning, Inspector," Elijah said as he stepped inside and motioned Edward to do the same.

"I thought you said you had some work to do today before we head north," George said.

"I got most of it finished before my colleagues came to work this morning," Elijah replied. He turned to Edward and said, "Edward, I'd like you to meet George Baxter, chief inspector of the San Francisco Police Department, detective branch. George, this is Edward Kepler, a courageous and astute young man."

Edward flushed under the praise. "Nice to meet you, sir. I am glad to hear someone of your stature is here in San Rafael. I don't feel the local law enforcement would take any action against my father."

George replied, "I am glad to make your acquaintance, Mr. Kepler. Elijah has great appreciation for your work."

"Edward, sir, please just call me Edward. I look around for my father when someone says 'Mr. Kepler.'"

Elijah asked, "May we please go to the parlor or Susannah's sitting room? Edward has unmasked his father's brutal actions. Where is Susannah?"

"She will be right with us," George answered as he led them down the hall.

"So, Edward, what have you found?" George's eyes gleamed with anticipation as he looked upon the young man, and he added, "I am sorry, sir, your father is as he is. I have been praying for him."

Edward's eyes widened as the revelation hit him that he'd never really prayed for his father. He'd always feared him and stayed away from him, but from George's comment, he realized his failure to obey Jesus and pray for the lost. His shoulders slumped as he recognized another huge failure in his life. *I used to feel pretty good about myself, but now...I feel I'm being bombarded by failure.*

George continued to talk. "So many times, we fail to pray for someone because we think they are so evil, they will never change. God's power is stronger and more powerful than anything we can imagine. I was telling Susannah last night that we should pray for

Amos Kepler. He has succumbed to the spiritual forces of evil, and it's our job to fight against that and not the poor, wretched man Amos has become. None of us is above falling. We are cautioned by Scripture to be on our guard and to put on the armor of God as instructed by Paul in the book of Ephesians. If you're feeling like a failure, Edward, for divulging information about the terms of the will to your father, simply and humbly ask the Lord for forgiveness and move on. Don't wallow in your guilt."

Edward's eyes widened again. He felt as if Inspector Baxter could read his soul.

"Please," George continued, "both of you sit down. I'm sure we have much to discuss." The two of them sat on a sofa, and he sat across from them on another sofa.

"I found my father's journals, sir." Edward looked down at the beautiful Aubusson carpet. He was embarrassed to be related to his father. "I'm sorry, sir, but I feel so ashamed. I feel contaminated and brought low by this circumstance. I thank you, too, for your words. I have a tendency to wallow." Tears misted his eyes, but he was able to hold them back.

"We cannot take the actions of another upon our own person," George stated. "We all make our own choices, and most times, those choices don't affect only us—they affect those around us. Nonetheless, you are not responsible for your father's perfidious crimes, whatever they may be, not unless you were privy to them and said nothing, or you took part in them. When you are true to yourself, when you are dedicated to serving God and being true to Him, it's difficult to deceive yourself. Self-deception is a wretched kind of deception. One becomes reprobate, seeing evil as good and good as evil. Each of us must, on a regular basis, examine ourselves and our motives."

CHAPTER XXIX

There are six things which the LORD hates,
Yes, seven which are an abomination to Him:
A heart that devises wicked plans,
Feet that run rapidly to evil.

PROVERBS 6:16, 18

GEORGE LOOKED UP TO SEE SUSANNAH entering the room. The men stood in respect.

"Good morning, Elijah," she said. "I didn't think we'd see you this day."

Before Elijah could reply, Edward, with tears in his eyes, said, "Mrs. Farrow, I am so sorry about your husband. It's my fault, you understand. It's my fault for telling my father about the terms of the will."

"Shush, young man. You know it's not your fault any more than it is mine. You broke trust to tell your father. That is your crime—not murder! No, the responsibility for that lies entirely with your father. It's good to see you again, Edward. It's been quite some time since I've laid eyes on you. Elijah keeps you quite busy, I hear." She sat down, and so did her guests. "I asked Tess to bring us some refreshment, and I'm sorry to have interrupted you, George. You were speaking about deception and being true to oneself?"

"Yes, it's a bit like Shakespeare said, 'To thine own self be true, and it must follow, as the night the day, thou canst not then be false to any man.'"

"Exactly so, sir," Susannah said.

Edward was glad to see Mrs. Farrow in such good spirits. He'd known her since he was young and had heard she was quite ill.

Elijah spoke to George. "Edward and I are here because a murder was committed last night, and we need you to go to Edward's house to arrest his father when he comes home to eat lunch. Edward doesn't trust the police here in San Rafael to arrest Amos, nor do I. He's well-respected, but they don't know what we know. George, please read last night's diary in Amos' journal."

Edward pulled out the correct journal and handed it to George, who opened it to the last entry. He sat there for a minute reading, and his stomach churned at the evilness of Amos Kepler. He started to say something to Edward, but the young man forestalled him with his comment.

"Please, look at this one." Edward picked up the journal, flipped through until he came to the page detailing how his mother died, and handed it to the inspector.

George read the entry, his lips tightening.

"And now, please read the entry in this journal." Without saying the time period out loud, Elijah pointed to the year eighteen sixty-seven, thumbed through until he came to the entry, and handed it to George.

George read the entry, turned back a few months, and slowly read some of the content. His face reddened in anger, and he glanced at Susannah as if she knew what he'd read. Elijah handed him the latest entry again and pointed to a few lines George had not read in his haste to see the murder committed.

He looked at Elijah in shocked amazement and said, "I think later would be a better time to share this. Right now, I need to get myself over to Kepler's house. I have work to do. Elijah, I think you should go immediately to police headquarters and apprise them of the situation. I may need some backup. Edward, you stay here and protect Susannah, just in case he comes here looking for her."

"He won't come after Mrs. Farrow," Edward replied. "I lied to him. I told him Mr. Farrow came back to the office and changed his will to leave everything to Mrs. Farrow, and should she die, it all goes to an orphanage in San Francisco. No, he'll not come after Mrs. Farrow to do her harm. He'll come to court her." Edward's tone was earnest. "He'll kill me if he finds me once he sees his journals are missing. He's never liked me."

Right then, Elijah decided he would begin to mentor and love Edward, letting him know how valued he was by Almighty God. He needed guidance to find normality.

He bear-hugged Edward. "We'll be certain you're safe. You are important to me, Edward. I'm proud of you. You stay here, and we'll let Susannah protect you!" He nodded in Susannah's direction. "Madam, I'll have that tea a bit later. I need to get myself over to police headquarters."

"Here, sir." Edward handed a key to George. "This is the key to the front door. I know most people don't lock their houses, but my father does. Interesting, don't you think?"

George nodded and said, "Thank you. Please rest easy with Susannah." He went over to her, took her hand, his back to the other two men, and mouthed *I love you.*

"Madam, I will return as soon as possible. I'd still like to make the journey tomorrow to Napa. I think we should invite Edward to come with us." George stood holding her hand, thinking quickly. "We don't need to make that journey to Napa now, but I'd like to see Liberty Bannister. The first morning I was here, Elijah suggested we ride up to visit her. I think you'd enjoy it, and it would be good for you to just get away for a bit."

Susannah nodded. "I'd like to go."

Edward looked surprised and pleased by the invitation. "I know I'd enjoy that. Thanks for including me."

As the two men descended the steps, George said, "I need directions, Elijah. I have no idea where Mr. Kepler lives. What a disgusting man. It's amazing the word *evil* isn't written on his forehead!"

"I concur. I was angered when I read that journal. He is definitely a reprobate! How can he stomach living with himself? He's a monster dressed up in civility, but he's not civil."

"He's insane. That's what he is," George said caustically. "Any man who can do the things he's done and gleefully write about it, as if it's to be commended, has to be crazy. He needs to be locked up or hung. Frankly, I prefer hanging."

"I must agree. He'd have been stoned years ago had he lived in Bible times. It's frightening to think a man can take another's life with no compunction—no remorse, no nothing. Amos Kepler is completely amoral."

"Amoral? How about immoral?" George postulated.

"That too. Robert Louis Stevenson wrote about amoral as being without standards, without scruples. To me, Amos seems to think he's a cut above the normal, and therefore our standards of morality do not apply to him."

George nodded. "I certainly agree with that statement." He looked over at his friend as they passed the gates. "I love you, Elijah. You have such a godly way of looking at things, and I appreciate, more than I can say, having you as a friend."

Elijah turned startled eyes upon George, their blueness warming with his statement.

"I love you too, George. Not many men seem to have the courage to say that to another man. Thank you, my friend."

Elijah proceeded to give George directions to the Kepler residence, and the two parted ways.

Things were beginning to settle down into a regular routine around the Bannister household. The grapes had been harvested, crushed, and were now in oaken casks fermenting. It was quite a process, and Matthew thanked the Lord for a bountiful harvest.

Baby Faith and her twin, Matty, were thriving, and the women of the house were beginning to get a bit more sleep. The days seemed to hurry by, each one different yet the same. Liberty's granny, Phoebe, came over every day and sat holding her great grandchildren.

She spoke to Cadence as she rocked Faith, while Cadence held a fast-asleep Matty.

"How blessed I am to have so many great-grandchildren. It was in the early spring of eighty-three when I found out about Liberty. Just a few months after that we found out about her twin. My, how the Lord has blessed me in my old age. I thought never to have grandchildren, let alone great-grandchildren."

"How come you think it was *God's* doing?" Cadence asked, heavy sarcasm in her voice. "I don't think I believe in God. Everything I've ever done, I've done under my own power. I don't even know why I stayed home when my ma was still alive. I'm surprised at myself for not running away earlier. Ma didn't protect me from pa's fists, and I can tell you one thing—neither did God!" Cadence was resentful of a God who would allow bad things to happen.

"Oh, child, you misunderstand. God didn't want those things to happen to you any more than you did. In truth, He wanted you to have perfection. Mankind was created to enjoy perfection, but it was mankind who disobeyed His commands, and now we live in a broken world. We suffer the evilness of mankind, but it certainly is not from God. He could step in and protect us from all evil, but then He would be making us like puppets, controlling us and manipulating us, which goes against His principle of free will. He gave all of us free will, and we get to choose how we live day by day and act toward others. It's not how you live in this physical world that counts so much as how you live within yourself. God doesn't *make* you believe in Him, but I can tell you this—He believes in you. He loves you with a love beyond the scope of your imagination. He guided your steps to us. He has given you a home with wonderful people. Yes, you, young girl, should count your blessings and not look back at the evil done you. Instead look forward to what you can make of your life with the love of God in your heart."

Cadence stared at Liberty's grandmother. She hadn't been around elderly people, not in her entire life, and she respected what Phoebe had to say.

"I'll chew on that for a while," Cady said. "Donny said nearly the same thing to me. I reckon I've never thought of God in terms of love. I've only thought of Him in terms of a mean taskmaster or someone who'll get you, like my pa. My pa doesn't believe in Him at all. My mother did, but it didn't get her out of the drudgery of living with a mean man."

"But she is in a better place now, if she was a believer. Some lives seem to encounter more hardship than others. I don't know why that is, but His grace is sufficient for all our needs. When we trust in Jesus, He gives a greater grace to those who suffer more."

"How can He give greater grace?"

"Well, it's a bit like digging holes in the ground. You can dig a little hole and fill it, and you can dig a deeper hole and fill it. The top is level. It evens itself out, but beneath you can see that one received a lot more to be able to be leveled out on top. That's the way it is with grace. Little sorrows still receive grace, but bigger sorrows need more grace."

"You've given me a lot to think about, Phoebe. Thank you."

Throughout the day, Cady kept thinking about what Phoebe had shared with her. She hugged the information to her heart and decided she would try praying and see what happened.

Liberty woke up from a long nap and was surprised by how well she felt. She was feeling much better now that the twins had settled into a regular routine. Normally if she took a nap longer than ten minutes, she felt worse when she woke up, but not since having the twins.

She lay on her side, thinking how blessed she was. *Lord, I am grateful and thankful for who You are and for always being my constant companion. I thank You that I am not alone. I thank You too for my family. I am grateful beyond measure for the way You have guided my steps and brought me to a place where love and peace abide. I'm thankful, Holy Father, for my husband. I thank You for his goodness and for the peace You have placed in his soul. He doesn't need to go searching for the things of this world to make him content. I praise You for that. Thank You for the bountiful harvest we've had by Your hand. Father, how can I express how blessed I am? I know it in my head, but I also know it in my heart. Thank You for my little babies. How sweet and beautiful they are. I pray we raise them in a manner pleasing to You. And Father, how I do praise You for the heritage I never knew I had. Thank You for a godly father and grandmother. Thank You for relationship and the love we have for one another.* Liberty rolled onto her back and continued to pray.

Father, thank You for Conchita and Diego. May they continue to follow Your ways and be pleasing to You. I'm thankful for all their dedicated help. Lord, I thank You for Donny and his desire to please You. I pray he is careful with his heart. Cadence needs to come to a saving knowledge of You, Father. I am quite sure she views You as one like her earthly father. Open her eyes to see the love and compassion You have for her. Your love is not at all tainted by self-interest but by what is best for us. Grant Cadence a better understanding of You and Your goodness to her. I pray these things in Your precious and holy name. Amen.

Liberty stretched and swung her legs over the side of the bed. She stood and stretched again, feeling strong and capable, but most of all she felt cherished.

She donned her clothes quickly, amazed she was able to get into her black split skirt. It was snug, but already she was trimming down. Her blouses were another matter. Because of breast feeding, she wasn't able to button them up, so she put on one of the maternity tops. She pulled on her long brown boots and buckled on her holster. It felt good to have on her normal attire. She strolled out to the great room, where Cadence and her granny were having a chat.

Liberty stooped over to kiss her granny. "Would you mind watching the babes for a bit longer? I'd like to go for a ride."

"I am totally at your disposal, my dear," Granny said. "I believe your father is coming over for dinner tonight, so I'm here until after that."

Liberty, pleasure marking her face, said, "Thank you." She turned to Cadence and asked, "Would you care to go for a ride with me?"

Cadence asked Phoebe, her tone hopeful, "Do you think you can handle both babies while we're out?"

"Certainly," Phoebe replied. "If I have difficulty, Conchita's here. You girls have a good time. Liberty's long overdue for a good ride. Normally she is out every day for a bit."

"Thanks, Granny. Come on, Cadence. Let's go saddle up our horses."

"I need to change into my male duds and get my hat and holster first," she replied.

Liberty sat for a moment with her granny and then headed to the kitchen.

"Umm, what is that heavenly smell? I declare, you are the best cook in the whole world!" Liberty gave Conchita a big hug and helped herself to a cookie.

"I making thees for you. They tastes good an' good for you, Mees Libby."

"Uhmm, oatmeal, coconut, and raisins. They're delicious." Liberty went to the cooler to pour herself a glass of milk. She sat munching on the cookie. "I'm going riding and wanted you to know. I'm taking Cadence, and we'll probably end up at Papa's, but I'm going to stop at my rock."

Before marrying Matthew, Liberty would ride over to her house. She watched almost daily as it was being built. It was located on the property adjoining the Bannister holdings, and when she married Matthew, she deeded the property to her father.

Many times she would sit fairly close to the house and meditate and pray. One day, she dismounted and prayed on the hill overlooking the small valley where her house was. As she was praying, a hawk dropped a rattlesnake not three feet from her. She couldn't get her gun out fast enough, and the snake struck at her leather boot. She shot it with deadly aim and now called that spot her rock.

Cadence, finally ready, picked up a couple cookies, grinning cheekily at Conchita. "You make the best food in the whole world, Conchita!"

"How you know? You no eat food all over the world. Now, Mees Libby, she can say eet, an' I know eet ees true!" Conchita laughed a full-bellied laugh.

"Well, it's the best food I've eaten in my limited experience." Cadence laughed with Conchita. "I don't think that's as big a compliment though, do you?" She turned to Libby, her mouth full of cookie. "I'm ready whenever you are."

Liberty took her measure and was filled with love for this young girl. She was slim and lovely. Her strawberry-blonde hair was beginning to grow out, and unruly curls covered her head. She wore denims, and her gun was holstered much like Liberty's. Her facial bone structure was beautiful, but looking at her, Liberty thought her eyes were the most startling feature. The gray ringed by darker gray was striking. Liberty knew Donny was in love with Cady, and she said a quick prayer that his heart would not be broken.

"I'm ready." She stood, drank the rest of her milk, and went to the sink to rinse it.

"I do eet. You go. Eet be no time, an' you weel need to feed dose babies again—now go!"

Liberty grinned, kissed Conchita's cheek, and said, "We're going."

CHAPTER XXX

For God sees not as a man sees,
for man looks at the outward appearance,
but the LORD looks at the heart.

I SAMUEL 16:7b

GEORGE BAXTER USED THE KEY. Thinking of Edward's words about locking the door, he thought it was not only interesting but significant as well. He didn't know anyone who locked their doors except businesses. He prowled around to get his bearings. Upstairs were two bedrooms, both devoid of personal items. Descending the stairs, he went to a back bedroom, surprised by how many mirrors were there. *Such vanity*, he thought. It reminded him of the book of Ecclesiastes. When he'd first heard the verse, he'd thought it was Shakespeare, but it wasn't. It was Solomon saying, "Vanity of vanities; all is vanity."

Quickly, he moved the nightstand and poked on one end of the loosened board, gingerly lifting it out. He didn't want any slivers. Feeling inside, as far as his arm could reach, his hand felt cloth—another bag. He pulled it, and the flour sacking snagged on a nail. He tugged, but it was stuck. He reached underneath and lifted, prying it loose. The bag was delicately colored and seemed almost feminine. It was light and looked to contain one journal. He replaced everything, dusted off his knees and frock coat, and carried the bag to the kitchen.

George pulled his watch from his fob pocket and looked at the time. It was nearly eleven thirty. Edward said he would most likely be home by twelve ten. He had a good forty minutes. He sat at the kitchen table and opened the bag.

There was a journal, a lock of reddish-blonde hair tied in a small pink ribbon, and a beautiful tourmaline ring surrounded by diamonds, reminding him of Susannah's eyes. He closed his eyes a second and whispered a prayer for her.

He picked up the journal, and the inscription was not a date but a name. Callie Susannah Farrow. *Susannah's daughter*, he thought. His stomach churned a bit as he opened the journal. "Amos Kepler deserves to hang," he said aloud. "What perfidy. What destruction of a family!" He read the entries, each one detailing his desire for Callie. He courted her in his mind for almost a year. George flipped to the back of the journal.

I knew she loved me, Amos wrote. *She was simply playing the coy game of acting as if she didn't. That day I found her alone at the school, I overcame her pretense of reluctance. She fought me like a tiger, which made my conquest all the more exciting. She was mine and belonged to me. As she lay crying with joy, I clipped a lock of her hair. She was beautiful, and she was mine. I slipped the ring off her sweet finger, which lay still and almost lifeless. I told her she would always be mine. I would love her and be with her until the day I died. Sweet tears slipped down her cheeks. I told her to tell no one about our love. If she did, her parents' lives might be snuffed out.*

There was a lot more about him following her, trying to find her alone again, but he never could.

It was to my shock when she came to me three months later and told me she was expecting a baby. I knew right then she'd played the harlot. I also knew I'd need to get rid of her so no one would know she was a harlot. I struck her cheek and told her to get out. I needed to make a plan, but I was so hurt and felt an incredible loss. I found out later she ran away that day. I tried like the dickens to find her, but I never did.

The journal ranted on, but George had read enough. *Callie feared for her parents' lives if she told them anything. No help from Amos, so she ran away. I need to find her for Susannah, for a restoration of what is left of a family.*

He checked the time. "Amos should be here any time now." He put the journal, lock of hair, and ring back into the bag. He stood and pulled out his gun, checking the chambers in the cylinder. They were full. Hearing a noise at the front door, he slipped behind the kitchen door, waiting to see if it was his backup or Amos. He suddenly realized he'd left the front door unlocked, which would put Amos on his guard. George heard quiet steps across the living room floor. A board creaked, and he heard a soft curse.

Amos, finding the front door unlocked, quietly walked across the floor to the fireplace and reached for his gun hidden behind a picture on the mantel. He sensed something was wrong, but perhaps it was simply his falling out with Edward. All Edward's life, he'd scorned him…he didn't think he'd miss his son. Having an unlocked door was not a normal circumstance. Mrs. McCready had been instructed, in his strictest tone of voice, to keep the door locked at all times.

"Perhaps," he muttered, "Edward has come back, and that's why the door is unlocked. No one else has a key." He breathed a sigh of relief at the thought. Still holding the gun, he headed to the kitchen to get his lunch.

He called out, "Edward! Mrs. McCready!" Entering the kitchen, he started for the back door.

A voice said, "Get your hands up, Kepler, and turn around—very slowly."

Amos, stricken with fear, had his gun hidden in front of himself. He said in a crazed voice, "I'll kill—" He never finished his sentence. He spun around and fired wildly, moving as he pulled the trigger. The bullet zinged past George's ear, and George fired a second later, aiming for Amos' shoulder. George's bullet missed its mark. Amos clutched his chest and crumpled to the floor.

The front door banged open, and the local sheriff and a four-man posse entered at a run. Elijah followed the men into the kitchen, where George knelt over the body of Amos Kepler.

"Hanging would have been my first choice," George said succinctly. "A fast death was too good for him." He looked over at Elijah and nodded to the kitchen table.

Elijah went over as the other men stood around looking at Amos and asking George questions. Elijah quickly took the bag and dropped it into his own satchel. He turned and joined the other men.

Elijah had apprised the sheriff of all that had transpired.

The sheriff went outside and took a look at the rose bed. "Dig it up," he said to the four men who had accompanied him. "How could he live such a double life…more, how could he live with himself?" His tone was full of disgust for a man he'd thought exemplary. "I'm going to want to see those journals. There could be more than a couple people dead by his hand."

George nodded. "Of course. By the way, I'm George Baxter, San Francisco police, detective branch." He held out his hand to the portly sheriff, who looked surprised at George's friendliness.

"I'm a George too." He smiled. "George Headly, San Rafael's sheriff. Looks like you made short shrift of Amos here. I always thought he was such an upright man." He shook his head in amazement of how wrong he'd been. "Reckon we can be thankful God doesn't look at our outer appearance but at our hearts."

"I don't reckon that, sir," George said with a tight smile. "I know that."

Liberty raced across the earth covered with wildflowers, thrilling to the speed and freedom, with Cadence right behind. Liberty pulled up about a half mile from her rock, and Cady followed suit.

The day was fair but cooling compared to the heat they'd had. Liberty looked up at a cobalt sky dotted with fluffy clouds. A slight breeze blew, stirring the flowers to life.

"We're almost to what I call *my rock*," Liberty said. She explained to Cady about the rattlesnake. When she finished her narrative, she said, "I'm glad you're learning to shoot as well as ride. My, but you seem like you were born on a horse. Donny has taught you well. You have a good seat, posture, and keep your heels down."

"That was the hardest part. I kept losing my stirrups," Cady replied with a laugh.

"I can scarcely remember when I learned to ride," Liberty said. "I know our stableman, Chancy, was my teacher, but even though I've been riding all my life, I still enjoy it. I should say, enjoy it immensely. It was a balm to me growing up and now is a thrill."

"I didn't realize you had such a time of it in your first marriage or growing up. Sometimes I feel as if I have had my head buried in the sand, concerning myself with only myself."

As they neared Liberty's rock, the women slowed their horses to a walk, cooling them off from their hard ride.

"Cadence, I know you are a private person, but I'd like to share an insight about you I have. Is that all right?"

Cady nodded but didn't say anything, her eyes fastened on Liberty.

"I know you came from an abusive situation with your father. I did too. I realized, at my last boarding school, that all my perceptions of God were colored by what I saw in my earthly father. The two are poles apart, but I didn't know that."

They arrived at the rock, and both dismounted as Liberty continued to talk.

"Would your father die for you?"

"No, I don't think he even loves me," Cadence replied.

"God's whole nature is love. Everything He does is filtered through His love for us. Many things happened to me growing up, and I hated my father. He was evil. When I became a Christ follower, the hatred slowly dissipated until I felt a kind of pity for him. I don't believe I ever totally overcame my fear of him, but I never let him see it." She turned to the younger woman and took both her hands.

"I am sharing this with you to say, when I accepted Jesus as my personal Savior, all the hurt I had in me began to fade away. I began to bask in God's love for me and realized if I were the only person in the whole world, He would still have died on that cross for me. His love is that great. We cannot begin to comprehend it. You have felt freedom here, but I can tell you there's such a freedom in being a child of God—I cannot even begin to tell you how free I am. And the more I learn about God, the freer I become. I am His child, His object of affection. He loves me with an unending love. You know I love Matthew and he loves me. I could change Matthew's love for me to hate if I turned on him and became evil. God's love is not like that. He loves us even when we're hateful people. He does have justice in His character, so what we sow, we will reap. He is so holy that He cannot allow people to dwell with Him who are sinful. Sin blocks our relationship with Him. The purpose of His love is almost unfathomable, but I do know He wants relationship with us. He created us to have a personal, close relationship with Him. He wants me to talk to Him and to listen to Him and to read His word so I can know Him. Oh, Cady!" Liberty's green eyes filled with tears as she gazed at the younger girl. "He loves you unconditionally. He loves you so much and wants you to love Him and begin to know Him. He is so good, pure, holy, trustworthy, faithful. Oh, Cady, I couldn't live without Him in my life, and I want you to know the same kind of joy I have."

Cady's eyes filled with tears, and she dropped to her knees. "I want that too. I want to feel loved and cherished. I have a lot of love stored up in me that I've never let out. Tell me how to pray, Liberty."

Liberty went to her knees, facing Cadence, and took her hands. "Repeat after me. 'Oh Lord, You know I'm a sinner. I am sorry and repent of all I've done that is contrary to Your will for me. I ask You, right now, to come into my heart. Fill me with Your Holy Spirit. Help me be a child who pleases You, Father. Amen.'"

Cady repeated what Liberty said and asked, "That's it?" She wasn't sure if it "took" with her. "I can't believe something so huge can be so easy."

"It is that easy. The harder part is to follow as He leads. I'll help you with reading your Bible. The Bible is God's Word, and His Word is truth. His Word *is* Him. Becoming a follower isn't a feeling—it's a faith, a belief He will do as He said. As He speaks to your heart, Cady, be sure you are obedient. He will whisper into your mind to keep your attitudes in alignment with His, or He'll speak to your heart to keep your actions pleasing to Him. Oh, Cady, I'm so glad you took this step. You'll come to see all I've said to you is true." She hugged Cady, and the two climbed back on their horses and rode to Liberty's Landing.

It was a glorious morning. Sun filled the sky and gladdened hearts with its cool brilliance. The air felt fresh and clean, and the soft, subtle scent of roses permeated the air.

Abigail and Elijah pulled up in front of Susannah Farrow's mansion. Elijah was riding his horse, and Abigail, who loved to ride, was driving the buggy, for Susannah's convenience. Before they could ascend the steps, Tess opened the door and stood holding it open as

George, loaded with satchels and a small trunk, came out to load up the back of the buggy.

"Good morning!" He grinned as he spoke. "I haven't had the privilege of handling a woman's traveling paraphernalia since my Addie died. Ah, that's not true. I remember helping Sally Ann Brown onto the train. Yes, I'm a good baggage carrier," he stated, smiling as if he couldn't stop.

Abigail stayed below the steps, ready to direct George where to place things. Elijah was ascending the steps as George came down and said in a low voice, "You're also a good shot. One bullet and Kepler's gone. We're frail human beings, are we not?"

"Yes, quite frail," George replied. "It was a moment of kill or be killed. If he'd gotten a second shot off, I might not be loading up a buggy this morning. In a flash, I saw the intent in his eyes, and he knew who I was."

Elijah nodded and spoke earnestly. "It took time for Sheriff Headly to round up a few men. I thank the Lord you're still with us, George." He entered the manse, greeting Susannah, who looked quite fetching in a large pink straw hat and matching traveling dress. She smiled becomingly as Elijah greeted her.

"Good morning, Susannah. I am delighted you are making this trip with us. I sent the telegram yesterday afternoon, so I believe the Bannisters will be expecting us. Where's Edward?"

"Good morning, Elijah. Edward went to the mercantile to buy a little house gift for the Bannisters. I told him to be sure and not buy a bottle of wine." She laughed at her jest and continued to talk. "He'll be back any moment. Thank you for allowing him to spend the night here last night. I know you planned to keep him with you, but I've known him since he was a toddler. Oh, Elijah, I am so excited. After we visit the Bannisters, George is going to begin to look for my Callie. How dreadful for her to suffer at the hands of that monster." She dabbed at her eyes with a beautifully embroidered lace-trimmed handkerchief. "I knew years ago something was amiss about that man, but Oscar had made up his mind, and there was no gainsaying him. I'm going to need another director for the school." She laid her hand on Elijah's arm and pressed it. "Just think, Elijah. I'm a grandmother! If everything went all right for my Callie, I'm a grandmother." She dabbed at her eyes again.

"So, George told you about the contents of the journals?"

"Yes, he did, and quite gently, I might add. It came as a terrible shock."

Edward entered the front door, still being held open by Tess. "Sorry if I've held anyone up." He held up a beautifully wrapped box. "I bought a box of mints, and I'm ready to go. I've already hung my satchel on my horse."

Elijah was not surprised to see Edward dressed in his regular clothes. *There'd be no mourning Amos Kepler by his son,* he thought. He said a quick prayer that Edward would not hold bitterness. *Bitterness can eat up a man's soul, and most times, the person we're bitter toward doesn't even know it. It ends up hurting the one who's bitter.*

He said aloud, "Well, if we're all ready, let's be going. You're sure you can do without a personal maid, Susannah?"

"Pshaw, I can do without a maid, sir!" She glanced over at Tess. "I need my maid," she said, not wanting to hurt Tess' feelings, "but I am quite capable of dressing by myself. I would take Tess with me, but I believe there is already a paucity of rooms. Now I suggest we go before George and Abigail leave without us."

CHAPTER XXXI

But without faith it is impossible to please him:
for he that cometh to God must believe that he is,
and that he is a rewarder of them that diligently seek him.

HEBREWS 11:6

LIBERTY AND CADENCE WERE SITTING in the great room, and Liberty's granny was there too. The women were tatting while the babies, each in a separate bassinet, lay sleeping, their tummies full.

"You are picking this up quickly, child," Phoebe said to Cady. "It took me a long time to get the right snugness. I'd have a tight piece, and the next would be loose, but you are tatting consistently."

It was late afternoon, and the women were awaiting their company.

"My, it will be wonderful to see Elijah and Abigail again." Liberty was excited. "Their telegram said they should arrive late afternoon today. I know George, and I've met Edward Kepler. He is one of Elijah's clerks at the law office. I wonder who Mrs. Farrow is?"

"Mrs. who? Who did you say?" Cady asked in a hushed tone.

"Whom…whom did you say," Liberty corrected.

"Whom did you say?" Cady's fingers had stopped tatting, and she tightened her work into a fist as she stared at Liberty, her eyes widened in astonishment.

Liberty looked up to see the girl's whitened face. "What's wrong, Cady?

"Excuse me. I'll be right back." Cady left the room hurriedly, running down the hall.

Liberty stared at her grandmother and asked, "What was that all about?"

Cadence returned in short order and said, "Look...I found this under my bed the night I ran away. My pa must have brought it home that night and shoved it under the bed." She showed them the beautifully tooled red leather satchel. "I've figured out this must have been in the bank and my father got it when my mother died. I know he didn't know about it before then because there wouldn't have been any money left in it. Ma would say, 'Your pa drinks us poor.'"

Phoebe and Liberty gasped as Cadence carefully poured out the contents of the satchel onto the surface of the coffee table.

"Oh my goodness! Why, I've never seen such jewels, except those my mother had from my grandmother. Oh, aren't they beautiful? Why, you aren't poor, Cady, not by any stretch of the imagination."

"Gorgeous," Phoebe said. "Look at those necklaces! That one is emeralds, and this one is rubies, and matching rings. My goodness, girl. These stones would keep you and a family living in luxury. I wonder why your mother would keep them in the bank and live as poorly as you described."

"I reckon she knew my pa'd sell everything for a song and drink the money, as she would say." Cady's eyes filled with tears. "Why didn't she just leave him?"

"I can answer that one," Liberty said. "I wanted to leave Armand for thirteen years. I married him out of obedience to my parents. God gave me the grace to withstand him, and I felt I had made a commitment to stay. When I think back on it, I don't believe I would make the same choice, but I'll never know, will I? Perhaps your mother was a lot like me. Perhaps her parents married her off to him, and she didn't have a choice in the matter."

"I didn't show this to anyone. I was waiting until harvest was over. I didn't even tell Donny. Donny asked me last night to marry him, and I said yes. He said he couldn't ask me before because I wasn't a believer, but now I am." Her beautiful eyes shone with an inner radiance.

"Best wishes, Cady! Oh, how exciting for you!" Liberty exclaimed. She hugged the younger woman.

"Oh my," Phoebe said, "another wedding in the offing. I offer you my best wishes too, my dear."

Liberty looked back at the coffee table. "What are these papers, Cady?"

"That's what I went to my bedroom to get. I don't understand all the jargon in it, but I read my mother's name, and it says Callie Susannah Farrow, doesn't it? Look right there." She pointed to the names on the document as she scooped all the jewels back into the red leather satchel.

Liberty perused the documents in silence and then said, "These are inheritance papers. This states that you and Timothy are to inherit anything that is due Callie, should she predecease you."

"What does that mean?" Cady asked.

"It means these papers are proof you and Timothy are her legal children and anything that she should inherit from her parents is to go to you if she should die before you are of age."

"Am I of age?"

"You will be in February for sure. I don't exactly know what the age of recognized adulthood is for the state of California. Do you, Granny?"

"No, child, I don't. I reckon soon enough we'll have a lawyer come to visit, and he can tell us what all this means. Wonder if this Mrs. Farrow who is coming is any relation to you, Cady?"

"I have no idea. I know there are many people who have the same last name and are not kinfolk. I wonder how we could tell?"

There was some scuffling noise at the front door, and Elijah opened it and called, "Anybody home?"

Liberty jumped up and hurried to the door. "Welcome, Elijah. Oh, it's so good to see you!"

"Well, what happened to you?" he replied. "You've lost a bit of weight since the last time I saw you!"

Liberty grinned. "Yes, I have, and double." She hugged Abigail, who'd come in after Elijah. She looked up to see George Baxter and smiled over Abby's shoulder at him. Then her beautiful green eyes met and connected with Susannah Farrow's gray ones, and she gasped.

"Oh my goodness!" Liberty whispered.

George was surprised at her comment, but Susannah seeing Liberty's look asked, "Have we met before? I must apologize if we have, because I don't remember."

"No, we haven't met before. I'm Liberty Bannister." She proffered her hand to shake Susannah's. "Please come in. You'll see why I seem so startled." She gestured with her hand, and the guests trooped in.

Phoebe and Cady both stood, looking expectantly as the guests rounded the bookshelf that was a divider from the hall to the great room.

Cadence looked shyly at them until her eyes met Susannah's. She gasped, as did Susannah, whose hand covered her heart in shock. George stood looking at Cadence and knew beyond a shadow of doubt that the girl was closely related to his Susannah. The eyes were identical, and at one time, the hair must have been also. Susannah's was a shade darker now.

Susannah couldn't say anything, as her throat choked with emotion. She stood in front of Cady and held out her arms. Cadence walked into them with a feeling of coming home. She knew this woman was her grandmother. Both women were weeping with joy and sorrow intermingled.

"Oh, my dear girl," Susannah said. "You are a replica of your mother. Is she…is she here?"

"N-no, she passed away the first of September from the fever. So did my little brother, Timothy. I had it, and ma cut my hair short to try to keep me cool, and then she got the fever and died right after Timmy. I don't think she wanted to live anymore," Cady said, and added, "My name's Cadence Jean Cassidy."

"And I'm your grandmother, Susannah Jean Farrow."

"I have a lot of questions for you, Grandmother."

"Well, child, I think I just learned most of the answers last night."

Elijah was amazed at the resemblance between the two women.

Edward was thankful Susannah had family. He knew it would be a long time before he forgave himself for telling his father about the terms of the will.

Elijah said, "I am sorry to be the bearer of bad new, Miss Cassidy, but your father was killed night before last."

"That's not bad news, sir. It's a relief to me." Cady felt the burden lift from her shoulders and was amazed. She hugged Susannah again and pointed to the coffee table. "I was just explaining and asking questions about the contents of the satchel when you arrived. It belonged to my mother."

Susannah walked to the coffee table and picked up the red leather satchel. "I gave this to her to carry her books to school. She loved the color red." Tears stood out in her eyes for all the years and a daughter lost to her over one man's evil, selfish acts.

Abigail, feeling the tension, broke the heavy atmosphere by saying, "Let me see your baby, Liberty."

"No," Liberty said. All heads in the room turned to stare at her, surprised by her answer. Liberty grinned. "Not one baby, Abby—babies. I had twins!"

She pointed to the bassinets sitting in a corner. "Come meet the newest members of our family. This is Matthew Aaron Bannister and his older sister, Faith Abigail Bannister."

Abigail Humphries' eyes filled with tears at the honor done her.

EPILOGUE

Give unto the Lord the glory due unto his name

PSALM 96:8a

DINNER WAS OVER, EVERYONE SATED BY Conchita's delicious meal. They sat around in the great room, lamps casting their glow of warmth and hominess. Talk was quiet, and all felt relaxed and comfortable, having partaken of good food, good conversation, and wonderful fellowship. Noises could be heard from the kitchen as Conchita, along with Luce and Lupe, were making dessert. The smell of fresh coffee and chocolate wafted in the air.

Mathew sat with his arm around Liberty's shoulders. Abigail sat rocking Faith, and Elijah held Matty. Conversation began to flow again, and the room seemed filled with contentment.

Phoebe was still there, with the added addition of Liberty's father, Alexander, who looked young in the soft lighting. His heart warmed at the tenderness shown by Abby and Elijah as they held the twins.

Donny had been included in the evening's celebration, and Susannah could see her granddaughter was smitten with him. Susannah, not to be taken in by a handsome face or flattering words, had taken his measure throughout the meal and was pleased to find she approved. The young man was besotted with Cadence, attentive to her every wish. Now the young couple sat side by side holding hands. An aura of love swirled around them.

Susannah's eyes caught and held George's. *I'm not going to wait. I'm not waiting an entire year before I marry him. I loved Oscar with a quiet love, developing over time, but never with any passion. This has so taken me by surprise. I don't believe I ever thought romantic love was real.* Her eyes continued to hold George's. *I'd marry him tomorrow if I could. Oh Lord, how I love him!* She sat basking in the wonder of fulfillment. Never having had such a love, she was amazed at the feelings that washed over her. *Yes, I am a woman blessed beyond measure.* Her eyes swung to Cady. *Now, to have a granddaughter… Oh Lord, I cannot thank You enough!* Her eyes, full of wonder and contentment, went back to George's face.

George felt her eyes on him and turned to see the look on Susannah's face. He caught his breath as he witnessed the promise in her eyes. His heart sang for joy.

Much of the conversation throughout dinner had been to clarify happenings by Cadence to her grandmother, who several times had to dab at her eyes. Elijah, George, and Edward had filled everyone in on the past week, and some of the information found in the journals.

Elijah, usually quicker on the ball, had a sudden realization and wondered if now was a good time to share it. He decided it was. He shifted Matty slightly.

Clearing his throat, he said, "We've done a lot of talking this evening about the past, but what is of greater import is the future. I'm wondering if you are aware, Cadence, that Edward is your half brother?"

"What? What are you saying to me?" Cady stared at Edward and suddenly realized that what Elijah purported was true. "Oh my! I have a grandmother and a brother!"

Edward looked dumbfounded at the information. "I am! I didn't think of that, but I am! I've always wanted a brother or sister. I hated being an only child." He smiled warmly at Cady.

"I'm thankful we both take after our mothers," Cady said in a low voice. "You know, we're twice brother and sister though. I accepted Jesus as my Savior yesterday, and I understand you're a believer. That makes us double brother and sister." She smiled at everyone in the room. "It's interesting. I prayed a few days ago, after talking to Phoebe, that God would work a miracle in my life. I reckon He answered my prayer and then some!"

Books can be purchased on Amazon
Website: www.maryannkerr.com (signed copy)
Inklings Bookshop, Yakima, WA
Songs of Praise in Yakima, WA
Or by writing me at:
Mary Ann Kerr
10502 Estes Road
Yakima, WA (I charge no tax, sign the book, and the cost of
shipping priority mail is $6.49) (Media rate is ($4.00)

My public e-mail is: hello@maryannkerr.com where you can also
order a book.
You may message me on Facebook page: Mary Ann Kerr
(comments are welcome!)
When readers take the time to write or e-mail me their experience
reading my stories, I sometimes put their comments on my blog if
they don't mind.

Liberty's Inheritance	(sale price. . . . .$14.99)
Liberty's Land	(sale price. . . . .$14.99)
Liberty's Heritage	(sale price. . . . .$14.99)
Caitlin's Fire	(sale price. . . . .$14.99)
Tory's Father	(full price. . . . . $14.99)
Eden's Portion	(full price. . . . . $14.99)
Cady's Legacy	(full price. . . . . $14.99)

Books by Peter A. Kerr (my author son)

Adam Meets Eve (nonfiction)—$10.00 + 5.65 shipping and handling
The Ark of Time (science fiction)—$12.00 + $5.65 shipping and handling

Book by Andrew Kerr (my author son and my cover and design guy)

Ants on Pirate Pond (children's black-and-white chapter book with darling
illustrations)—12.95 + $5.65 shipping and handling

THE WEDDING BARGAIN

PROLOGUE

Let those be ashamed and dishonored who seek my life;
Let those be turned back and humiliated who
devise evil against me.

PSALM 35:4

"QUICK GINGER!" THADDEUS GRABBED his sister's hand. "Under here!" He dragged her down, but Ginger's skirts tangled as she dropped to her knees. Thad pulled hard on her arm as she tried to kick free of her skirts to scoot in.

Ginger raised up on her elbows, covered her ears with her hands, and stared at the scene unfolding before her. She wanted to see but didn't want to hear the deafening noise. The wagon they'd crawled under wasn't theirs, but the children didn't care.

Just a short time before, Thad had started the fire and their mother, who was beginning to make dinner, bade Thaddeus and Ginger to get a couple buckets of water. Thaddeus and Ginger Parker had gone down a narrow trail to the river, buckets swinging happily.

Once at the river, both children had quickly divested themselves of stockings and shoes, wading in the shallow stream. The cool water felt good on their hot, tired feet. It had been a long day but the best one yet.

The wagon-master said they'd come at least twenty-two miles. Some days they only made nine. The children filled their buckets with cool water before putting on their dusty stockings and shoes.

Trudging back through the woods toward the wagons, they heard from a distance the wagon-master, Mr. Turner, yell for everyone to circle the wagons. The two children dropped their water buckets and ran as fast as they could up the trail. It took them several minutes and as they emerged from the woods, they stopped dead in their tracks, seeing the skirmish played out before them.

The group of pioneers were already circling the wagons, having practiced the maneuver several times before entering the plains. Mr. Turner said word was, that attacks from the Shoshone had been frequent that summer. As the two children cleared the woods, the sight before them was one of mayhem—everyone running. This wasn't practice.

Men and women were grabbing for their rifles and handguns. Thad and Ginger had left their rifles in the wagon. The children couldn't tell which wagon was their own quickly enough as arrows began to rain down. Thaddeus dropped to his knees and began pulling at his sister's hand. She seemed frozen in place and he yelled again.

"Hurry! Come on, Ginge!"

Ginger shook off her paralyzing fear and dropped down beside Thad, her skirts jumbled up as he pulled on her arm.

The two crawled under the wagon and watched as men and women alike were shooting their rifles at the oncoming swarm of attackers. A few of the arrows were lit torches, and some of the wagons began to burn. Many attackers jumped over wagon tongues, fighting hand to hand with the men from the wagon train.

The noise was deafening. Ginger screamed when she saw her mother, crouching straight across from them, grab her neck as an arrow struck her. She crumpled to the ground. Ginger started to crawl out, but Thad held her fast, pushing her down with all his might because she was bigger than he.

Thad sobbed, tears running down his cheeks as everything in him yearned to go rescue his mother, but in his heart, he knew she was beyond help. He wasn't about to let go of Ginger and lose her too.

The children watched in terrified fear as a couple other children, within the circle of wagons, were scooped up and carried off by the marauders. One Indian dismounted and grabbed at Ginger's dress. She screamed and scooted closer to Thaddeus. The Indian grabbed at her hair, but she bit his hand. He yelped, dropping to his knees to get a better hold so he could drag her out. Thaddeus had his arm around her waist, trying to keep his sister squeezed up next to his body, but he could feel her slipping toward the Indian. One of the men from the wagon train saw what was happening and fired. The war painted face sprawled in front of the terrified children. Thaddeus squeezed his eyes shut to block out the sight of the man, his face forever frozen in a startled grimace.

As quickly as it had started, it was over. With loud whoops of victory, the band left the wagons mounted bareback on their horses, taking some of the wagon train horses with them.

Thaddeus waited until he was sure their attackers were gone before he let go of Ginger, who went running across to where their mother lay. The girl made no sound as she dropped to her knees, pulling her mother into her arms. Clasped tightly in her arms, Ginger rocked her mother back and forth as tears streamed down, making rivulets on her dirty face. Thaddeus walked with slow measured steps over to his sister, watching as she held their mother. Two months before, the children had lost their father to cholera, the disease raging through the ten wagons traveling together to California. Thaddeus dropped to his knees and wrapped his arms around them, stretching as far as he could reach. His heart felt as if it would burst from sorrow.

Turning his head away from the shocked horror on his sister's face. Thaddeus whispered, "She's gone, isn't she, Ginger? Our mama has gone to be with Pa."

Ginger looked away from him. She held her lips tightly shut, set in a straight line as tears poured from eyes full of anguish. She made no reply.